# THE APEX BOOK OF
# WORLD SF

# THE APEX BOOK OF
# WORLD SF

## 4

### EDITED BY
# MAHVESH MURAD

**Series editor**
**Lavie Tidhar**

An Apex Publications Book
Lexington, Kentucky

The Apex Book of World SF: Volume 4
ISBN: 978-1-937009-33-5
Edited by Mahvesh Murad and Lavie Tidhar
Cover Art © 2015 by Sarah Anne Langton
First Edition, August 2015

Published by Apex Publications, LLC
PO Box 24323
Lexington, KY 40524

www.apexbookcompany.com

# CONTENTS

# Introduction

## Lavie Tidhar

WHEN WE SET out to publish the first volume of *The Apex Book of World SF*, the idea of a series of such anthologies was only a dream—an impossible one, it seemed then. Yet somehow, the idea resonated. People took up the book, and before I knew it I was editing a second, and then a third volume.

The World SF anthologies have become a library, a map charting the contemporary scene of truly international, speculative fiction. So much has changed in the years since I began editing the first volume, so many more stories are now published, so many authors are making their mark, and it is wonderful to see. The books even crop up, increasingly, on various academic curriculums, and I am told have inspired other people to translate, publish, and edit works that may not have otherwise appeared.

It has been wonderful to be a part of this for so long, with the books as well as the accompanying web site, the World SF Blog, which ran for four years, and with the World SF Travel Fund, which is ongoing. I am grateful to our wonderful publisher, Jason Sizemore, without whom none of this would have been possible, and to all the authors, translators, editors, and friends throughout the years who have helped make these books a reality.

It was obvious to me, however, that after three books, a new set of eyes was needed, that a new voice should be heard.

Mahvesh Murad is that new voice. A fiercely intelligent and dedicated reader, reviewer, and broadcaster from Pakistan, this is her first anthology—but far from being her last. I couldn't be happier that she stepped in to breathe new life to this, Volume 4, and I am delighted with her choices.

I have stayed on as Series Editor, offering, beside continuity, my support in the background—handling paperwork, forwarding reading material, providing contact, offering advice if any was needed—but this book belongs entirely to Mahvesh.

I hope you enjoy it as much as I did.

—Lavie Tidhar, 2015

# Introduction

## Mahvesh Murad

DIVERSITY IS A tricky word. We talk about it all the time. We talk about the need for diverse voices and diverse books but I've always wondered what that really means. Diverse for whom? Not for me, surely? I've lived in Karachi my entire life—stories from Asia are not diverse to me; they're my childhood. Diversity is a problematic term for me, because it often seems to indicate that the inclusion of who or what the West sees as the exotic Other into Western mainstream literature is enough to make a difference. But it isn't. And it won't be until there is a shift of the entire status quo. So while there are stories in this book about aliens and spaceships, stories about strange beings, politics, family and love, stories about magic and power, there are, most importantly, stories *with* the magic and the power to change the way you see speculative fiction.

But let me make this claim: this is not a book of diverse stories. This is a book of really great stories from all over the world, by writers who bring a new perspective that doesn't fit in with the mainstream western status quo. These are writers who don't care what the mainstream thinks or wants, can understand or digest. These are writers who write with a ferocity and a truth that represents their cultural heritage, their lives and our world.

This is a book that comes as close to representing the world I know and live in, the world I am excited by, frustrated by, the world I marvel at every single day. Diversity isn't something I need to find—it isn't something you need to find either. It's always been around you. Embrace it. Let it in. It has a story to tell you. The world is always bigger and better than we know.

I'm so grateful for the opportunity to edit this volume, and so immensely grateful to each of the writers who let us publish their stories. This book belongs to each of you, to the world you are a part of and the worlds you create. These are your voices, your visions, your futures. Thank you for sharing them with us.

Changing the status quo, shifting the centre away from the West and forcing it wider to encompass more is never going to be easy, but that doesn't mean we don't try. To paraphrase the Urdu poet Allama Iqbal: don't be frightened of these furious violent winds—they blow only to make you fly higher.

—Mahvesh Murad, Karachi, 2015

# The Vaporization Enthalpy of a Peculiar Pakistani Family

## Usman T. Malik

*Usman T. Malik is a Pakistani writer currently living in Florida. His work has appeared in Tor.com, Nightmare, Strange Horizons, and elsewhere. The following story won the 2014 Bram Stoker Award and was nominated for a Nebula Award.*

### 1

THE SOLID PHASE of Matter is a state wherein a substance is particulately bound. To transform a solid into liquid, the intermolecular forces need to be overcome, which may be achieved by adding energy. The energy necessary to break such bonds is, ironically, called the *heat of fusion.*

On a Friday after jumah prayers, under the sturdy old oak in their yard, they came together as a family for the last time. Her brother gave in and wept as Tara watched, eyes prickling with a warmth that wouldn't disperse no matter how much she knuckled them, or blinked.

"Monsters," Sohail said, his voice raspy. He wiped his mouth with the back of his hand and looked at the sky, a vast whiteness cobblestoned with heat. The plowed wheat fields beyond the steppe on which their house perched were baked and khaki and shivered a little under Tara's feet. An earthquake or a passing vehicle on the highway? Perhaps it was just foreknowledge that made her dizzy. She pulled at her lower lip and said nothing.

"Monsters," Sohail said again. "Oh God, Apee. Murderers."

She reached out and touched his shoulders. "I'm sorry." She thought he would pull back. When he didn't, she let her fingers fall and linger on the flame-shaped scar on his arm. *So it begins*, she thought. How many times has this happened before? Pushing and prodding us repeatedly until the night swallows us whole. She thought of that until her heart constricted with dread. "Don't do it," she said. "Don't go."

Sohail lifted his shoulders and drew his head back, watching her wonderingly as if seeing her for the first time.

"I know I ask too much," she said. "I know the customs of honor, but for the love of God let it go. One death needn't become a lodestone for others. One horror needn't—"

But he wasn't listening, she could tell. They would not hear nor see once the blood was upon them, didn't the Scriptures say so? Sohail heard, but didn't listen. His conjoined eyebrows, like dark hands held, twitched. "Her name meant 'a rose'," he said and smiled. It was beautiful, that smile, heartbreaking, frightening. "Under the mango trees by Chacha Barkat's farm Gulminay told me that, as I kissed her hand. Whispered it in my ear, her finger circling my temple. *A rose blooming in the rain.* Did you know that?"

Tara didn't. The sorrow of his confession filled her now as did the certainty of his leaving. "Yes," she lied, looking him in the eyes. God, his eyes looked awful: webbed with red, with thin tendrils of steam rising from them. "A rose God gave us and took away because He loved her so."

"Wasn't God," Sohail said and rubbed his fingers together. The sound was insectile. "Monsters." He turned his back to her and was able to speak rapidly, "I'm leaving tomorrow morning. I'm going to the mountains. I will take some bread and dried meat. I will stay there until I'm shown a sign, and once I am," his back arched, then straightened. He had lost weight; his shoulder blades poked through the khaddar shirt like trowels, "I will arise and go to their homes. I will go to them as God's wrath. I will—"

She cut him off, her heart pumping fear through her body like poison. "What if you go to them and die? What if you go to them like a steer to the slaughter? And Ma and I—what if months later we sit here and watch a dusty vehicle climb the hill, bouncing a sack of meat in the back seat that was once you? What if…"

But she couldn't go on giving name to her terrors. Instead, she said, "If you go, know that we as we are now will be gone forever."

He shuddered. "*We* were gone when *she* was gone. We were shattered with her bones." The wind picked up, a whipping, chador-lifting sultry gust that made Tara's flesh prickle. Sohail began to walk down the steppes, each with its own crop: tobacco, corn, rice stalks wavering in knee-high water; and as she watched his lean farmer body move away, it seemed to her as if his back was not drenched in sweat, but acid. That his flesh glistened not from moisture, but blood. All at once their world was just too much, or not enough—Tara couldn't decide which—and the weight of that unseen future weighed her down until she couldn't breathe. "My brother," she said and began to cry. "You're my little brother."

Sohail continued walking his careful, dead man's walk until his head was a wobbling black pumpkin rising from the last steppe. She watched him disappear in the undulations of her motherland, helpless to stop the fatal fracturing of her world, wondering if he would stop or doubt or look back.

Sohail never looked back.

Ma died three months later.

The village menfolk told her the death prayer was brief and moving. Tara couldn't attend because she was a woman.

They helped her bury Ma's sorrow-filled body, and the rotund mullah clucked and murmured over the fresh mound. The women embraced her and crooned and urged her to vent.

"Weep, our daughter," they cried, "for the childrens' tears of love are like manna for the departed."

Tara tried to weep and felt guilty when she couldn't. Ma had been sick and in pain for a long time and her hastened death was a mercy, but you couldn't say that out loud. Besides, the women had said *children*, and Sohail wasn't there. Not at the funeral, nor during the days after. Tara dared not wonder where he was, nor imagine his beautiful face gleaming in the dark atop a stony mountain, persevering in his vigil.

"What will you do now?" they asked, gathering around her with sharp, interested eyes. She knew what they really meant. A young widow with no family was a stranger amidst her clan. At best an oddity; at her worst a seductress. Tara was surprised to discover their concern didn't frighten her. The perfect loneliness of it, the inadvertent exclusion—they were just more beads in the tautening string of her life.

"I'm thinking of going to the City," she told them. "Ma has a cousin there. Perhaps he can help me with bread and board, while I look for work."

She paused, startled by a clear memory: Sohail and Gulminay by the Kunhar River, fishing for trout. Gulminay's sequined hijab dappling the stream with emerald as she reached down into the water with long, pale fingers. Sohail grinning his stupid lover's grin as his small hands encircled her waist, and Tara watched them both from the shade of the eucalyptus, fond and jealous. By then Tara's husband was long gone and she could forgive herself the occasional resentment.

She forced the memory away. "Yes, I think I might go to the City for a while." She laughed. The sound rang hollow and strange in the emptiness of her tin-and-timber house. "Who knows? I might even go back to school. I used to enjoy reading once." She smiled at these women with their hateful, sympathetic eyes that watched her cautiously as they would a rabid animal. She nodded, talking mostly to herself. "Yes, that would be good. Hashim would've wanted that."

They drew back from her, from her late husband's mention. *Why not?* she thought. Everything she touched fell apart; everyone around her died or went missing. There was no judgment here, just dreadful awe. She could allow them that, she thought.

## 2

The Liquid Phase of Matter is a restless volume that, by dint of the vast spaces between its molecules, fills any container it is poured in and takes its shape. Liquids tend to have higher energy than solids, and while the particles retain inter-particle forces they have enough energy to move relative to each other.

The structure therefore becomes mobile and malleable.

In the City, Tara turned feral in her pursuit of learning. This had been long coming and it didn't surprise her. At thirteen, she had been withdrawn from school; she needed not homework but a husband, she was told. At sixteen, she was wedded to Hashim. He was blown to smithereens on her twenty-first birthday. A suicide attack on his unit's northern check post.

"I want to go to school," she told Wasif Khan, her mother's cousin. They were sitting in his six-by-eight yard, peeling fresh oranges he had confiscated from an illegal food vendor. Wasif was a Police hawaldar on the rough side of sixty. He often said confiscation was his first love and contraband second. But he grinned when he said it, which made it easier for her to like him.

Now Wasif tossed a half-gnawed chicken bone to his spotted mongrel and said, "I don't know if you want to do that."

"I do."

"You need a husband, not—"

"I don't care. I need to go back to school."

"Why?" He dropped an orange rind in the basket at his feet, gestured with a large liver-spotted hand. "The City doesn't care if you can read. Besides, I need someone to help me around the house. I'm old and ugly and useless, but I have this tolerable place and no children. You're my cousin's daughter. You can stay here forever if you like."

In a different time she might have mistaken his generosity for loneliness, but now she understood it for what it was. Such was the way of age: it melted prejudice or hardened it. "I want to learn about the world," she said. "I want to see if there are others like me. If there have been others before me."

He was confused. "Like you how?"

She rubbed an orange peel between her fingers, pressing the fibrous texture of it in the creases of her flesh, considering how much to tell him. Her mother had trusted him. Yet Ma hardly had their gift and even if she did, Tara doubted she would have been open about it. Ma had been wary of giving too much of herself away—a trait she passed on to both her children. Among other things.

So now Tara said, "Others who *need* to learn more about themselves. I spent my entire childhood being just a bride and look where that got me. I am left with nothing. No children, no husband, no family." Wasif Khan looked hurt. She smiled kindly. "You know what I mean, Uncle. I love you, but I need to love me, too."

Wasif Khan tilted his head back and pinched a slice of orange above his mouth. Squeezed it until his tongue and remaining teeth gleamed with the juice. He closed his eyes, sighed, and nodded. "I don't know if I approve, but I think I understand." He lifted his hand and tousled his own hair thoughtfully. "It's a different time. Others my age who don't realize it don't fare well. The traditional rules don't apply anymore, you know. Sometimes, I think that is wonderful. Other times, it feels like the whole damn world is conspiring against you."

She rose, picking up her mess and his. "Thank you for letting me stay here."

"It's either you or every hookah-sucking asshole in this neighborhood for company." He grinned and shrugged his shoulders. "My apologies. I've been living alone too long and my tongue is spoilt."

She laughed loudly; and thought of a blazing cliff somewhere from which dangled two browned, peeling, inflamed legs, swinging back and forth like pendulums.

She read everything she could get her hands on. At first, her alphabet was broken and awkward, as was her rusty brain, but she did it anyway. It took her two years, but eventually she qualified for F.A. examinations, and passed on her first try.

"I don't know how you did it," Wasif Khan said to her, his face beaming at the neighborhood children as he handed out specially prepared sweetmeat to eager hands, "but I'm proud of you."

She wasn't, but she didn't say it. Instead, once the children left, she went to the mirror and gazed at her reflection, flexing her arm this way and that, making the flame-shaped scar bulge. *We all drink the blood of yesterday*, she thought.

The next day she enrolled at Punjab University's B.Sc program.

In Biology class, they learned about plants and animals. Flora and fauna they called them. Things constructed piece by piece from the basic units of life—cells. These cells in turn were made from tiny building blocks called atoms, which themselves were bonded by the very things that repelled their core: electrons.

In Physics class, she learned what electrons were. Little flickering ghosts that vanished and reappeared as they pleased. Her flesh was empty, she discovered, or most of it. So were human bones and solid buildings and the incessantly agitated world. All that immense loneliness and darkness with only a hint that we existed. The idea awed her. Did we exist only as a possibility?

In Wasif Khan's yard was a tall mulberry tree with saw-like leaves. On her way to school she touched them; they were spiny and jagged. She hadn't eaten mulberries before. She picked a basketful, nipped her wrist with her teeth, and let her blood roast a few. She watched them curl and smoke from the heat of her genes, inhaled the sweet steam of their juice as they turned into mystical symbols.

Mama would have been proud.

She ate them with salt and pepper and was offended when Wasif Khan wouldn't touch the remaining.

He said they gave him reflux.

## 3

The Gaseous Phase of Matter is one in which particles have enough kinetic energy to make the effect of intermolecular forces negligible. A gas, therefore, will occupy the entire container in which it is confined.

Liquid may be converted to gas by heating at constant pressure to a certain temperature.

This temperature is called the *boiling point*.

*The worst flooding the province has seen in forty years* was the one thing all radio broadcasters agreed on.

Wasif Khan hadn't confiscated a television yet, but if he had, Tara was sure, it would show the same cataclysmic damage to life and property. At one point, someone said, an area the size of England was submerged in raging floodwater.

Wasif's neighborhood in the northern, hillier part of town escaped the worst of the devastation, but Tara and Wasif witnessed it daily when they went for rescue work: upchucked power pylons and splintered oak trees smashing through the marketplace stalls; murderous tin sheets and iron rods slicing through inundated alleys; bloated dead cows and sheep eddying in shoulder-high water with terrified children clinging to them. It pawed at the towering steel-and-concrete structures, this restless liquid death that had come to the city; it ripped out their underpinnings and annihilated everything in its path.

Tara survived these days of heartbreak and horror by helping to set up a small tent city on the sports fields of her university. She volunteered to establish a nursery for displaced children and went with rescue teams to scour the ruins for usable supplies and corpses.

As she pulled out the dead and living from beneath the wreckage, as she tossed plastic-wrapped food and dry clothing to the dull-eyed homeless, she thought of how bright and hot and dry the spines of her brother's mountains must be. It had been four years since she saw him, but her dreams were filled with his absence. Did he sit parched and caved in, like a deliberate Buddha? Or was he dead and pecked on by ravens and falcons?

She shuddered at the thought and grabbed another packet of cooked rice and dry beans for the benighted survivors.

The first warning came on the last night of Ramadan. *Chand raat.*

Tara was eating bread and lentils with her foundling children in the nursery when it happened. A bone-deep trembling that ran through the grass, flattening its blades, evaporating the evening dew trembling on them. Seconds later, a distant boom followed: a hollow rumbling that hurt Tara's ears and made her feel nauseated. (Later, she would learn that the blast had torn through the marble-walled shrine of Data Sahib, wrenching its iron fence from its moorings, sending jagged pieces of metal and scorched human limbs spinning across the walled part of the City.)

Her children sat up, confused and scared. She soothed them. Once a replacement was found, she went to talk to the tent city administrator.

"I've seen this before," she told him once he confirmed it was a suicide blast. "My husband and sister-in-law both died in similar situations." That wasn't entirely true for Gulminay, but close enough. "Usually one such attack is followed by another when rescue attempts are made. My husband used to call them 'double tap' attacks." She paused, thinking of his kind, dearly loved face for the first time in months. "He understood the psychology behind them well."

The administrator, a chubby short man with filthy cheeks, scratched his chin. "How come?"

"He was a Frontier Corps soldier. He tackled many such situations before he died."

"Condolences, *bibi*." The administrator's face crinkled with sympathy. "But what does that have to do with us?"

"At some point, these terrorists will use the double tap as a decoy and come after civilian structures."

"Thank you for the warning. I'll send out word to form a volunteer perimeter patrol." He scrutinized her, taking in her hijab, the bruised elbows, and grimy fingernails from days of work. "God bless you for the lives you've saved already. For the labor you've done."

He handed her a packet of boiled corn and alphabet books. She nodded absently, charred bodies and boiled human blood swirling up from the shrine vivid inside her head, thanked him, and left.

The emergency broadcast thirty minutes later confirmed her fear: a second blast at Data Sahib obliterated a fire engine, killed a jeep full of eager policemen, and vaporized twenty-five rescuers. Five of these were female medical students. Their shattered glass bangles were melted and their headscarves burned down to unrecognizable gunk by the time the EMS came, they later said.

Tara wept when she heard. In her heart was a steaming shadow that whispered nasty things. It impaled her with its familiarity, and a dreadful suspicion grew in her that the beast was rage and wore a face she knew well.

## 4

When matter is heated to high temperatures, such as in a flame, electrons begin to leave the atoms. At very high temperatures, essentially all electrons are assumed to be dissociated, resulting in a unique state wherein positively charged nuclei swim in a raging 'sea' of free electrons.

This state is called the Plasma Phase of Matter and exists in lightning, electric sparks, neon lights, and the sun.

In a rash of terror attacks, the City quickly fell apart: the Tower of Pakistan, Lahore Fort, Iqbal's Memorial, Shalimar Gardens, Anarkali's Tomb, and the thirteen gates of the Walled City. They exploded and fell in burning tatters, survived only by a quivering bloodhaze through which peeked the haunted eyes of their immortal ghosts.

*This is death, this is love, this is the comeuppance of the two, as the world according to you will finally come to an end.* So snarled the beast in Tara's head each night. The tragedy of the floodwaters was not over yet, and now this.

Tara survived this new world through her books and her children. The two seemed to have become one: pages filled with unfathomable loss. White space itching to be written, reshaped, or incinerated. Sometimes, she would bite her lips and let the trickle of blood stain her callused fingers. Would touch them to water-spoilt paper and watch it catch fire and flutter madly in the air, aflame like a phoenix. An impossible glamor created by tribulation. So when the city burned and her tears burned, Tara reminded herself of the beautiful emptiness of it all and forced herself to smile.

Until one morning she awoke and discovered that, in the cover of the night, a suicide teenager had hit her tent city's perimeter patrol.

After the others had left, she stood over her friends' graves in the twilight.

Kites and vultures unzipped the darkness above in circles, lost specks in this ghostly desolation. She remembered how cold it was when they lowered Gulminay's remains in the ground. How the drone attack had torn her limbs clean off so that, along with a head shriveled by heat, a glistening, misshapen, idiot torso remained. She remembered Ma, too, and how she was killed by her son's love. The first of many murders.

"I know you," she whispered to the Beast resident in her soul. "I know you," and all the time she scribbled on her flesh with a glass shard she found buried in a patrolman's eye. Her wrist glowed with her heat and that of her ancestors. She watched her blood bubble and surge skyward. To join the plasma of the world and drift its soft, vaporous way across the darkened City, and she wondered again if she was still capable of loving them both.

The administrator promised her he would take care of her children. He gave her food and a bundle of longshirts and shalwars. He asked her where she was going and why, and she knew he was afraid for her.

"I will be all right," she told him. "I know someone who lives up there."

"I don't understand why you must go. It's dangerous," he said, his flesh red under the hollows of his eyes. He wiped his cheeks, which were wet. "I wish you didn't have to. But I suppose you will. I see that in your face. I saw that when you first came here."

She laughed. The sound of her own laughter saddened her. "The world will change," she said. "It always does. We are all empty, but this changing is what saves us. That is why I must go."

He nodded. She smiled. They touched hands briefly; she stepped forward and hugged him, her headscarf tickling his nostrils, making him sneeze. She giggled and told him how much she loved him and the others. He looked pleased and she saw how much kindness and gentleness lived inside his skin, how his blood would never boil with undesired heat.

She lifted his finger, kissed it, wondering at how solid his vacant flesh felt against her lips.

Then she turned and left him, leaving the water and fire and the crackling, hissing earth of the City behind.

Such was how Tara Khan left for the mountains.

The journey took a week. The roads were barren, the landscape abraded by floodwater and flensed by intermittent fires. Shocked trees, stripped of fruit, stood rigid and receding as Tara's bus rolled by, their gnarled limbs pointing accusatorially at the heavens.

Wrapped in her chador, headscarf, and khaddar shalwar kameez, Tara folded into the rugged barrenness with its rugged people. They were not unkind; even in the midst of this madness, they held onto their deeply honored tradition of hospitality, allowing Tara to scout for hints of the Beast's presence. The northerners chattered constantly and were horrified by the atrocities blooming from within them, and because she, too, spoke Pashto they treated her like one of them.

Tara kept her ears open. Rumors, whispers, beckonings by skeletal fingers. Someone said there was a man in Abbottabad who was the puppeteer. Another shook his head and said that was a deliberate shadow show, a gaudy interplay of light and dark put up by the real perpetrators. That the Supreme Conspirator was swallowed by earth soaked with the blood of thousands and lived only as an extension of this irredeemable evil.

Tara listened and tried to read between their words. Slowly, the hints in the midnight alleys, the leprous grins, the desperate, clutching fingers, incinerated trees, and smoldering human and animal skulls—they began to come together and form a map.

Tara followed it into the heart of the mountains.

## 5

When the elementary particle boson is cooled to temperatures near absolute zero, a dilute 'gas' is created. Under such conditions, a large number of bosons occupy the lowest quantum state and an unusual thing happens: quantum effects become visible on a macroscopic scale. This effect is called the macroscopic quantum phenomena and the 'Bose-Einstein condensate' is inferred to be a new state of matter. The presence of one such particle, the Higgs-Boson, was tentatively confirmed on March 14th, 2013 in the most complex experimental facility built in human history.

This particle is sometimes called the *God Particle*.

When she found him, he had changed his name.

There is a story told around campfires since the beginning of time: Millennia ago a stone fell from the infinite bosom of space and plunked onto a statistically impossible planet. The stone was round, smaller than a pebble of hard goat shit, and carried a word inscribed on it.

It has been passed down generations of Pahari clans that that word is the *Ism-e-Azam*, the Most High Name of God.

Every sect in the history of our world has written about it. Egyptians, Mayans, Jewish, Christian, and Muslim mystics. Some have described it as the primal point from which existence began, and that the Universal Essence lives in this *nuktah*.

The closest approximation to the First Word, some say, is one that originated in Mesopotamia, the land between the two rivers. The Sumerians called it *Annunaki*.

He of Godly Blood.

Tara thought of this oral tradition and sat down at the mouth of the demolished cave. She knew he lived inside the cave, for every living and nonliving thing near it reeked of his heat. Twisted boulders stretched granite hands toward its mouth like pilgrims at the Kaaba. The heat of the stars they both carried in their genes, in the sputtering, whisking emptiness of their cells, had leeched out and warped the mountains and the path leading up to it.

Tara sat cross-legged in the lotus position her mother taught them both when they were young. She took a sharp rock and ran it across her palm. Crimson droplets appeared and evaporated, leaving a metallic tang in the air. She sat and inhaled that smell and thought of the home that once was. She thought of her mother, and her husband; of Gulminay and Sohail; of the floods (Did he have something to do with that, too? Did his rage liquefy snow-topped mountains and drown an entire country?); of suicide bombers, and the University patrol; and of countless human eyes that flicked each moment toward an unforgiving sky where something merciful may or may not live; and her eyes began to burn and Tara Khan began to cry.

"Come out," she said between her sobs. "Come out, Beast. Come out, Rage. Come out, Death of the Two Worlds and all that lives in between. Come out, Monster. Come out, Fear," and all the while she rubbed her eyes and let the salt of her tears crumble between her fingertips. Sadly she looked at the white crystals, flattened them, and screamed, "Come out, ANNUNAKI."

And in a belch of shrieking air and a blast of heat, her brother came to her.

They faced each other.

His skin was gone. His eyes melted, his nose bridge collapsed; the bones underneath were simmering white seas that rolled and twinkled across the constantly melting and rearranging meat of him. His limbs were pseudopodic, his movement that of a softly turning planet drifting across the possibility that is being.

Now he floated toward her on a gliding plane of his skin. His potent heat, a shifting locus of time-space with infinite energy roiling inside it, touched her, making her recoil. When he breathed, she saw everything that once was; and knew what she knew.

"Salam," she said. "Peace be upon you, brother."

The *nuktah* that was him twitched. His fried vocal cords were not capable of producing words anymore.

"I used to think," she continued, licking her dry lips, watching the infinitesimal shifting of matter and emptiness inside him, "that love was all that mattered. That the bonds that pull us all together are of timeless love. But it is not true. It has never been true, has it?"

He shimmered and said nothing.

"I still believe, though. In existing. In *ex nihilo nihil fit*. If nothing comes from nothing, we cannot return to it. Ergo life has a reason and needs to be." She paused, remembering a day when her brother plucked a sunflower from a lush meadow and slipped it into Gulminay's hair. "Gulminay-jaan once was and still is. Perhaps inside you and me." Tara wiped her tears and smiled. "Even if most of us is nothing."

The heat-thing her brother was slipped forward a notch. Tara rose to her feet and began walking toward it. The blood in her vasculature seethed and raged.

"Even if death breaks some bonds and forms others. Even if the world flinches, implodes, and becomes a grain of sand."

Annunaki watched her through eyes like black holes and gently swirled.

"Even if we have killed and shall kill. Even if the source is nothing if not grief. Even if sorrow is the distillate of our life."

She reached out and gripped his melting amebic limb. He shrank, but didn't let go as the maddened heat of her essence surged forth to meet his.

"Even if we never come to much. Even if the sea of our consciousness breaks against quantum impossibilities."

She pressed his now-arm, her fingers elongating, stretching, turning, fusing; her flame-scar rippling and coiling to probe for his like a proboscis.

Sohail tried to smile. In his smile were heat-deaths of countless worlds, supernova bursts, and the chrysalis sheen of a freshly hatched larva. She thought he might have whispered sorry. That in another time and universe there were not countless intemperate blood-children of his spreading across the earth's face like vitriolic tides rising to obliterate the planet. That all this wasn't really happening for one misdirected missile, for one careless press of a button somewhere by a soldier eating junk food and licking his fingers. But it was. Tara had glimpsed it in his *nuktah* when she touched him.

"Even if," she whispered as his being engulfed hers and the thermonuclear reaction of matter and antimatter fusion sparked and began to eradicate them both, "our puny existence, the conclusion of an agitated, conscious universe, is insignificant, remember…remember, brother, that mercy will go on. Kindness will go on."

*Let there be gentleness,* she thought. *Let there be equilibrium, if all we are and will be can survive in some form. Let there be grace and goodness and a hint of something to come, no matter how uncertain.*

*Let there be* possibility, she thought, as they flickered annihilatively and were immolated in some fool's idea of love.

§

*For the 145 innocents of the 12/16 Peshawar terrorist attack and countless known & unknown before.*

# Setting Up Home

## Sabrina Huang

### Translated by Jeremy Tiang

*Taiwanese author Sabrina Huang has published several short story collections under the pseudonym Jiu Jiu. Her work has won many Taiwanese short story competitions, including the China Times Literary Award and the United Daily Literary Award.*

THE ANTIQUE ROSEWOOD day-bed, sturdy in the Ming Dynasty style, sat casually at his front door as if it belonged there, as if waiting for some monk to reveal an oracle or incantation that would allow it to move. Its carved legs were slender, its filigreed back elegant, and on the couch surface was a piece of scarlet paper, his name black-inked on it.

He'd heard that during the heady boom years of the eighties, Taipei residents regularly threw out sofas and dining room sets after just a few months of use. University students and impoverished office workers could furnish their squalid apartments entirely by scavenging from rubbish dumps. But in this day and age, who'd be willing to be the kind of fool who sends a gift with no expectation of a return? He almost didn't dare to smile, frightened his joy would send away the windfall. Instead, he hastily pulled it inside the flat.

This was wonderful. The empty living room had previously looked as gloomy and neglected as he himself. With this new item, the place seemed to develop a personality, acquire some kind of background. Now it looked more like somewhere a proper person might live. He looked at it from several angles, and his belly filled with happiness.

Coming home the next day, he opened the door to find the new sofa still present. He sat down delightedly, setting his takeaway dinner down on the wide armrest while flicking on the television. Hmm, had this little table been there the day before? But at that moment the commercials ended and the theme tune to his show began, whisking away his apprehension.

On the third day, the ceiling spouted two red glass lanterns, one to either side of the day-bed, like twin drops of bloodshot tears from eyes too brimful of emotion to blink. Was this strange? Of course something felt wrong, but then it wasn't like the originally empty space had seemed right. As he reclined, red light pouring down on him, he allowed himself shyly to think about women.

Day four brought a trunk of tiger-striped camphorwood, which he used as a coffee table. On day five a long table with turned-in legs arrived—a television stand. The next day, the partition between living and dining rooms was transformed into an openwork screen carved with arabesques, and all this began to seem normal to him. On the seventh day—when, it is worth noting, even the Lord felt the need to rest—he woke first thing to find the entire apartment had been fitted with wooden floorboards. He didn't notice during daylight hours, but as night fell, elegantly languorous words appeared on these boards, written in gilt: the heart sutra. "…no eyes no ears no nose no tongue no body, no sensing colour or sound or scent…"

In the days after that, more things appeared: a four-poster bed here, a green silk canopy there, as well as all kinds of ornaments he didn't even know the names of. Led by that day-bed, they arrived in a constant stream. He sat amongst them, straining to keep track of his new possessions, beginning to wonder if these gifts from nowhere might eventually crush him to death.

But he needn't have worried. On the forty-ninth day, it came to a halt. He searched through the whole apartment three times, inside and out, and found nothing new except a thin sheet of notepaper on his pillow.

"Dear son, I've calculated that you'd be about the right age to set up home. I've burnt everything I thought you'd need. And there's a girl, too. She used to be your mother's home nurse, she's gentle and meticulous, she'll take good care of you. Please apologise to her on my behalf, tell her uncle that was too anxious at the time. I should have chloroformed her before setting her on fire—it must have hurt, being burnt alive. Tell her Uncle Chen couldn't stand the thought of her becoming someone else's daughter-in-law. You must be good to her. Love, Dad."

He understood now. The pile of ashes now appearing by the sofa was slowly assembling itself into a pair of legs, a delicate pair of clasped hands resting on them. And what was forming above them, right in front of his eyes, was probably a waist, curved and shapely.

Very, very carefully, afraid of startling her, he sat down beside her half-body, and gently, gently stroked her thigh. The initial sensation was gritty, like his voice, "What's your name? ...Oh, right, your head hasn't formed yet. But anyway, let me welcome you. Welcome to our home."

# The Gift of Touch

## Chinelo Onwualu

*Chinelo Onwualu is a writer, editor, and journalist living in Abuja, Nigeria. She is a graduate of the 2014 Clarion West Writers Workshop, which she attended as the recipient of the Octavia E. Butler Scholarship. Her writing has appeared in the* Kalahari Review, Saraba Magazine, Mothership: Tales of Afrofuturism and Beyond, *and elsewhere.*

B RUNO STRODE ACROSS the causeway, scanning the three land skimmers hanging from their docking harnesses with a critical eye. His footsteps echoed through the cavernous space of the docking bay. The diagnostic reader he held showed the surface vehicles were fuelled and in perfect mechanical condition. They were decades out of date, lacking the smooth, sleek designs of newer models, but they worked—and that was all that mattered.

Bringing passengers on board always set him on edge; they had a tendency to poke about in places they didn't belong. But running a haulage freighter doesn't pay much when there isn't much to haul. Now that the technology for instant matter transportation had improved movement between the five planets of the star system, work was becoming rarer. Bruno needed the money and he had to know that his ship, *The Lady's Gift*, was in perfect shape.

He keyed an all-clear code for the docking bay into his reader and sent the message to the main computer. Slipping the flat pad into his tool harness, he headed for engineering. Ronk, the ship's mechanic, met him at the entrance to the engine room. At almost seven feet of solid muscle, with skin a glossy brown so dark that it seemed to drink in light, Ronk was an intimidating presence. Bruno had no doubt the engineer could snap him in half. Luckily, Ronk was a pacifist.

"How's she looking?" Bruno asked, though he needn't have bothered. The burly engineer was scowling, which made Bruno smile. Ronk had grown up on a religious colony whose people believed that life was a burden and death was its only release. They frowned on anything meant to keep one comfortable.

"We'll live," Ronk snapped. Bruno watched him lumber back into the dark recesses of the engine room, wondering, as usual, how a man so big could move so delicately.

Bruno continued toward the bridge. Passing through the mess hall, he saw his twin sister, Marley, sitting at the dining table. Her chestnut brown skin was a shade lighter than his and she liked to dye her black hair a vibrant orange, otherwise everyone said she was a female version of him. Which was unfortunate, because the square jaw and broad physique that gave him his rugged good looks made her look homely.

Marley had taken up half of the dining table with an assortment of metal parts. Knowing her, it was some machine she was reassembling. He watched her work for a time.

"What's this?" Bruno picked up an unidentifiable bit of metal.

"This, fearless leader,"—he hated when she called him that— "is a V-26 Skyhammer with 10-volt action, 15-meg rounds and a zoom scope that could see Neptune—if it still existed."

"Try that again, this time in a language I can understand."

"It's a very big gun."

Bruno nodded and dropped the piece he'd picked up. He should have known. She had an intuitive grasp of machinery that she focused exclusively on armoury, making her the ship's default security officer.

"I'm trying to fix the balance, though. Thing's so top-heavy, you'd need to prop it over a barrel to shoot it straight."

"And what's wrong with the collection of very big guns you already have?"

"Nothing, but you never know when you might need a back-up. This baby could pop a hole in a military freighter—with the right modifications."

"Marley, we're a trawler not the Sixteenth Battalion. Why would we possibly need this?"

"You never know."

Bruno sighed. Sometimes it was like talking to a very small child.

"Just put that thing back together and stow it. I don't want any sign of it when the passengers board, got it?

"Aye, aye, fearless leader." Marley grinned and snapped him a salute.

"And stop calling me that!"

He continued toward the bridge. There, he found Horns, his navigator, frowning over a display console. She was small-boned, at full height she barely cleared his chest, with a round child-like face that dimpled when she smiled. It was rumoured that she was part Scion, the ancient race that had developed most of the technology that underpinned their world, but Bruno doubted it. The Scions had disappeared centuries ago. Still, given her porcelain pale skin, silver blonde hair, and almond-shaped grey eyes, it was clear that someone somewhere in her genealogy had fooled around.

"Did you look at this clearance ticket before you filled the passenger register?" asked Horns. Before a ship could take on passengers clearance tickets were required from the Imperial Command certifying that none of the guests had outstanding warrants or, worse, unpaid bills.

"Yeah, they checked out. Why? What's wrong with it?"

"Nothing's wrong with it exactly," she said. "But take a look at the seal." Bruno leaned over her shoulder to stare at the screen. Her hair smelled like lemons. "Notice the extra cross over there? That's a top-level Imperial symbol. Only government brass use those."

"All we've got on the register are a widow and her kids."

"I know. Why would anyone that high up in the Imperial Command sign off for a farmer travelling on a broken-down freighter?"

Bruno didn't like this. He and Marley had grown up on a smuggling scow in the rough waters of Moonlight Bay on Old Antegon, and it had been a long time since he had been on the wrong side of the law. They had worked hard to get off-planet and he wasn't eager to go back.

"Scrub them through the system again. If anything looks even remotely funny, flag 'em."

"Should I drop their booking, too?"

"Heck no! We need the money too badly for that. No, I'll have Marley keep her big gun handy. Anyone tries to start something on my ship, it won't be pleasant."

As soon as they walked onto the ship, Bruno knew they were trouble. They were dressed as farmers, but he knew none of them had ever seen a farm. The older woman was too straight. She moved like someone who was used to giving orders—shoulders thrown back and a steady, penetrating gaze. The young man was a soldier. Barefoot, dressed in a threadbare shirt and trousers two sizes too small, he carried nothing more dangerous than a cloth bag, but Bruno had seen too much of war to be fooled. The girl was something else entirely.

She could not have been older than fifteen. Her coal-black skin was so smooth it was luminous. She was bald as an egg with delicate features and a grace that made her seem as if she was gliding. She kept her gaze down for the most part, but for a moment, when she glanced up, Bruno saw that her eyes were as golden as the heart of a flame.

The woman called herself Ana. She introduced the young man and the girl as her children, Drake and Bella. She handed over their identification cards and Bruno checked them one last time. They were clean. Just like her clearance papers. But they had the same high-level seal he had seen on the manifest. Bruno hesitated over the cards, debating whether he needed this kind of trouble. There would be other passengers, surely. Then his eye fell on her payment receipt. The amount she'd paid was more than double what he had charged.

"Is there a problem, captain?" Ana asked softly.

"Not at all, ma'am," Bruno said. "Welcome aboard."

Usually, all the crew—except Ronk—would come out to the entrance of the docking bay to welcome new guests, but by the time they reached the loading bay only Marley had arrived. Bruno let out a relieved breath to see that strapped to her back was her big gun. He caught the young man's face when he saw Marley. His eyes had narrowed at the sight of the gun, but he had quickly smoothed his features into a careful blankness. Bruno resolved to watch him carefully.

"My, that *is* a big gun," Ana said after Bruno had made the introductions. She spoke as if she was talking to a slow-witted child. Luckily, Bruno's twin had no ear for sarcasm.

"Yeah, I call her Jane."

"That's a lovely name."

"Thanks! Hey, follow me, I'll show you where you'll be staying." Marley looked over at Bruno and mouthed: *I like her.* Bruno sighed inwardly. His sister was such a poor judge of character sometimes. As they headed into the heart of the ship, the intercom in his ear cackled to life.

"I need to talk to you." Horns' voice sounded strained.

"Can it wait?" Bruno wanted to keep an eye on his guests and he was in no mood to deal with any more strangeness.

"No, Bruno. It really can't." Horns only ever called him by his name when she was being serious. Otherwise it was 'Boss'.

When he got to the bridge he found Horns pacing. Her pale hands were fluttering like live things. He had never seen his hard-as-nails navigator so agitated.

"I didn't know, Bruno. I mean, I suspected something was shady, but I had no idea," she said.

"Horns, calm down. What are you talking about?"

"You've got to get them off the ship."

"Our passengers? Are you crazy? They've already paid—and you should see how much. We can finally fix our hyperdrive, maybe even get one that was made in the last decade."

"Bruno, you don't understand." She took a deep breath to calm herself before she continued. "They're *Mehen.*"

Bruno's smile froze on his face. The Mehen di Gaya were the highest class of priests in the Amethyst Order, the religious institution that controlled the Empire. There were rumours that the Mehen even operated a shadow arm of elite warrior monks who could make whole families disappear overnight.

"How can you be sure?" Bruno asked.

"Because I used to be one of them."

"You're Mehen? You never told me that."

"It's who I *was*, not who I am now," she said, waving her hand dismissively. "Besides, you never asked." She gave him a sad look.

"That's not fair, you could have said something if you wanted to. It's not like you talk about your past all the time. I mean, I don't even know your real name."

"Well, there never seemed a good enough time. It was always one crisis or another with you." She turned toward the control banks and stared out the giant windows. "It still is."

Bruno thought he heard a hint of tears in her voice. "What do you want me to say, Horns? I run haulage; if it's not someone trying to ship stolen goods off-planet, it's not having the right papers, or stowaways, or…there'll always be something."

"I know, but sometimes it's like you don't have space in your life for anything beyond this ship."

They had had this conversation a thousand times. He fought the urge to touch her, to wrap her in his arms and feel the way her body curved into his. He longed for the familiarity of her smell and her skin. He had never been good with words, but his touch could make her promises. Yet they had been down that path before. Only heartbreak lay that way.

"Doesn't matter anyway," she said, cutting into his thoughts. "We have bigger problems. I think the girl is in danger."

"What do you mean?"

"Most people don't know this, but the Order started out as the tenders of the fire pits in the old temples, back when people would burn sacrifices in the sacred flames. In those days, the priests would pick a child—a special child who no one was allowed to touch—and when this child reached a certain age, it was sacrificed, burned in the Holy Fires. When I was a novice, they told me the Order stopped the practice hundreds of years ago." She turned. "But I don't think they have. I think they just took it off-planet."

"So you think they're going to kill that girl?"

"It's worse than that. I ran that symbol through the system and I found records going back nearly fifty years. Every fourteen years or so, this symbol would show up in the passenger manifests of a small M-class vessel—like ours—going to the moon of Osiris. The thing is, all the ships would go in…but none of them ever came back out."

A cold feeling settled at the base of Bruno's spine. "Are you sure?"

Horns nodded. "They didn't even bother to hide the records."

They were silent for a minute or two. "Well, no one's killing anyone on my ship," said Bruno. "It'll raise the insurance premiums."

"What are you going to do?"

"I'll figure out something, don't worry."

"I'm not worried," she said, and reached out to touch his cheek. He had forgotten how calloused her fingers were from gripping the navigation console. He closed his eyes and turned to brush his lips against them, but she withdrew her hand too quickly. Her touch lingered for long afterward as if he had been burned.

"I just don't see what the big deal is," Marley said.

"It's your eternal soul," growled Ronk.

"I know," she said quickly. "I just don't see why it matters. I mean, if I were an ant or a dog or a chimpanzee, nobody would care what my soul was up to. But just because I'm a person, suddenly my soul is important? I don't get it."

They had gathered at the dining table, all except the girl; Ana said she was ill and would be eating in her cabin. Tonight's dinner was a special treat, Ana and Drake had brought meat-dried strips of *real meat*. Between that and the greens and tomatoes—Horns grew them in a small hydroponic garden on the ship's abandoned leisure deck—it was almost a true meal. Almost.

Bruno had tried to ignore the increasingly heated conversation between Marley and Ronk, but in spite of himself, he found he was listening with growing interest. Besides, this was the most he'd heard Ronk say in one sitting in all the time he had known him.

"But we are better than animals or insects," Ronk snapped. "We are made in the image of the Creator himself."

"See, that's the thing, how do you know that? How do you know what the Creator looks like? No one's seen him. It's like we looked around and thought, 'Hey no one else looks like us, we must be special.' But what if we're not?"

"We *are* special. We have reason and compassion," Ronk said in a low voice. His voice seemed calm, but Bruno noticed the engineer was gripping his knife tightly, as if to keep his fist from shaking. "It does not matter that no one has seen the Creator's face. We have seen the works of his hands. You have never seen the wind, yet you feel its power. Do you doubt *its* existence?"

"Oh, come on, I'm not arguing about whether the Creator exists. I can't prove that and neither can you. What I'm saying is you can't know anything about what the Creator is thinking or what he wants just by looking at the universe. Just like you can't look at my fork and guess what I had for lunch."

"We do not need to guess. The Creator has told us what he wants of us through the words of his Prophet." Ronk's voice broke slightly at the mention of the Prophet. "Those who heed his words, follow in the path of truth."

"Oh! And that's another thing, how do you know the Prophesies are right? I mean, we're talking about a book collected from a bunch of other books, like, five thousand years ago. It's been translated and retranslated so many times that I'm pretty sure stuff's been lost. How do you know that what you're reading is even what was written in the first place? And why choose this book over any other ancient book? All you have is your belief. I'm sorry, man, that's just not enough for me."

Suddenly, Ronk stood up, knocking his chair over and juddering the table. He stared at Marley for a moment, his face unreadable. Then, without another word, he stalked off. Bruno watched him go, bemused.

"Oh no! Did I say something wrong?" Marley was immediately distraught and turned to each person at the table. "I didn't mean to offend him; I was just making a point."

"I'm sure he's okay." Bruno took the opportunity to look over at Ana at the opposite end of the table. "What about you? Do you think everything the Prophesies say are the 'unvarnished' words of the Creator?"

The older woman wiped her mouth deliberately before she spoke.

"Oh, I never discuss religion," she said. "Especially not over dumplings." She gestured at the young man beside her who produced an insulated food flask filled with dumplings—whose pork might possibly have even come from actual pigs. Amazingly, they were still hot. Bruno's mouth watered at the sight of them. Now, it was a real meal.

"He hates me," said Marley.

"He doesn't hate you," said Bruno.

"Yes, he does. I insulted his religion." She fingered the strap of the large gun she carried on her back. Bruno had asked her to keep it on her at all times.

"It's a big religion; it can take a little criticism," Bruno said, distractedly. He had not seen the girl since she arrived on the ship the day before. Their destination on the small moon formerly known as Ganymede—before it was terraformed for human habitation and renamed Osiris—was only two days away. He had to draw the girl out and get her away from her captors before then. Once they landed, they'd be in hands of the Mehen and there was no telling what would happen to them after that. A plan had started forming in his head. It was vague and dangerous, but it just might work.

They rounded a corner and Marley almost collided with Ronk as he emerged from the engine room. She ducked her head, unsure of what to do. They hadn't seen each other since the disastrous dinner the night before. The big engineer frowned and looked at his hands. He started to speak, but Marley spoke first.

"I'm sorry if I said anything blasphemous last night," she said. "It's just... I never think about that stuff—I mean, religion and all that—and you know me, sometimes when I open my mouth I don't know what comes out."

Ronk's frown deepened and he took a deep breath before speaking. "I am not insulted," he said. He spoke in his characteristic short, clipped sentences. Apparently, only religion brought out his loquacious side, Bruno observed wryly. "What you said last night made me think. I have never truly thought about my faith. When I left the colony, I wanted the freedom to do as I pleased. Now, you have given me the freedom to think as I please. For that, I thank you."

Marley blinked at him, owl-eyed. Ronk nodded curtly and retreated back into the gloom of the engine room. She stared after him for a moment, and then broke into a smile that made her beautiful.

"Did you hear that?" She turned to Bruno, beaming. "He thanked me. I think I'm going to die of happiness."

"We all have to die of something," Bruno said dryly. He continued on to the cargo hold, Marley skipped after him like a little girl. In the depths of the hold, he began moving boxes and crates.

"He said I freed his mind, can you believe that?" Marley chattered as she helped him move the detritus of past adventures. She stopped. "Hey, if we get married, will I have to convert?"

Bruno's cry cut her short. "Found it!"

"Wait, that's—"

"Yes, it is."

"You still have that? You can't be serious, Bruno. You use that and we'll be flagged for sure. Captain Moran warned us."

"We'll be fine. There's a lot more going on in this ship than some illegal smuggling."

"I hope you know what you're doing, fearless leader."

"Me too," said Bruno under his breath as he headed back to the bridge. "And stop calling me that!"

The young man called Drake was sitting alone in the small lounge in the cabin bay. It was less a lounge than two armchairs and a tiny table in the middle of a rounded cul-de-sac just off from the mess hall. From there one could see all the doors of every cabin in the bay. It was the perfect place to keep watch—if that was one's intention. He was examining his hands as if they belonged to someone else and looked up as Bruno stepped in.

For all his size, he was much younger than Bruno had initially thought. No more than fifteen, if that. "Drake, right? How's your sister?" he asked. "We haven't seen her since you all came aboard."

"She...she prefers to be alone."

"Oh? Is she sick?" Bruno moved toward the door, but the boy—for that was what he was, really—stood up to block his way.

"No! I mean, well, she's just resting."

Bruno nodded sceptically. He had expected a hardboiled veteran and had come prepared for a fight. This was not going as he had planned. He studied Drake a moment. "Is this your first time off-world?"

He nodded.

"How old are you?"

The boy blinked in confusion. It was clear he wasn't often asked personal questions. "Sixteen," he answered slowly, as if afraid of getting it wrong.

"That's a good age. You know, Marley and I were about that old when we first went off-planet, too."

"Yeah?" The boy was impressed, and Bruno could see he struggled not to show it. "How did you leave?" He asked too casually.

"We stowed away on a trade ship not much bigger than this one." Bruno chuckled at the memory. The captain had been so angry he threatened to put them both in an airlock and flush them out to space. Instead, he had put the two orphans to work, caring for them like a father for three years. It was tough, but they had been lucky. They could have been sold to slavers.

"What about your parents?" Drake asked.

"Never had any." That wasn't exactly true. Bruno and Marley had never known their father, but their mother had been a dockside runner on Moonlight Bay. She'd sold charms and trinkets to sailors and spacers when the work was good and sold other things when it wasn't. One day, when the twins were ten, she'd told them she had found work on a smuggler's scow. She had Bruno and Marley wait for her on the deck of the ship while she went to see a man about some money he owed her. She never returned.

"But we survived, Marley and me. We had each other. It's important for family to stick together, isn't it?"

The boy shifted his weight at that, his eyes darting quickly to the door of their cabin. "That's important," he agreed reluctantly.

"Then tell me the truth, what's wrong with your sister? What's she got?"

"What? No, she's not sick."

"Look, she's been holed up in there since we've been space borne. You're the only one who ever goes in there, so whatever she's got, you can't catch it. If it's the shakes, we've got ways to deal with it—"

"No, you don't understand, it's not like that, she's fine."

"Then let me see for myself." Bruno made to shoulder past, but Drake remained firmly in his path.

"You can't go in there!" There was a note of desperation in his voice and a look on his face almost like fear. Otherwise, the rest of him was steel.

"You don't tell me where I can and cannot go on my ship." Bruno's voice was dangerously low. "Do you understand?"

"Is everything all right, Captain?" It was Ana.

"I want to see your daughter."

"Has she done something wrong?" The crackle of the overhead speakers interrupted his response.

"Boss, we've got company." Horn's voice was steady, but Bruno could hear the note of fear in it. "Big Brother is here." He cursed softly. It was too soon.

"I thought you said you didn't have any brothers," Drake said accusingly. The boy seemed hurt. He was so young, Bruno realised—younger than Bruno had ever been, even at that age.

"It's a literary reference, child, from a classic of Old Earth," Ana said. There was amusement in her eyes. "I didn't know you could read, Captain."

"You'd be surprised what I can do." And with that, Bruno stalked off to the bridge.

Captain Alistair Moran was a grizzled veteran of half a hundred battles and you could see every one of them on his body. He wore smoked glasses to hide the cybernetic implants that had replaced his eyes and one of his hands was robotic, though it was impossible to tell which because he wore black gloves all the time. He was a small man, bald—whether by choice or from another accident, no one could say—with a clean-shaven face crisscrossed with scars from laser blades, and a jaw that seemed permanently clenched. He stood rod straight in his grey Army Ranger uniform, black boots polished to a high shine. Bruno suspected that if anyone cared to measure, they would find that Moran stood at a precise 90 degree angle from the floor.

His ship, the *S.S. Gilgamesh* had overtaken *The Lady's Gift* easily and locked onto them with traction hooks. Twenty of his men had forced their airlock open and stormed the ship through an airtight bridge connecting the vessels. They rounded up the crew in the main hanger bay. Horns and Ronk both had looks of controlled fear, but Marley looked ready to beat someone's head in. They had confiscated her gun and her lip was bleeding, but otherwise she seemed unharmed. Bruno noted that they had not found his guests yet, but knew it was only a matter of time.

"Bruno Tertian." Moran's voice was hard as a leather whip. "What did I tell you about trawling contraband through my sky?"

Bruno chose his words carefully. He was in very dangerous territory; Moran did not like wrong answers. "We don't want trouble, we're just on a routine run to Osiris."

"Oh? And if I search this ship I won't find anything...

untoward?"

"We don't—"

But before he could finish, Moran's hand flashed out and pain bloomed across Bruno's face. Bruno fell to one knee in agony, blood pouring from his nose. He heard someone gasp—Marley or Horns, he could not tell whom. Moran had broken his nose with a casual flick of his wrist.

"Don't lie to me, Tertian," he said quietly. "You know how much I hate being lied to." He turned to his lieutenant, a big, pale-skinned man with a shock of red hair. "Search the ship."

It could not have been more than a few minutes, but it seemed like an eternity. Soon the big man returned carrying a sealed metal chest. It was very heavy, Bruno knew, but the lieutenant carried it with ease. Behind him, Ana and Drake followed. There was no sign of the girl. Ana showed no trace of fear; in fact, she had a small smile on her face. It grew larger when she saw Bruno on his knees trying to stanch the blood from his broken nose.

"I hope there is no problem Captain…" She hesitated to get his name and the captain supplied it. "Captain Moran," she finished.

"No problem, ma'am. Did you know this ship was carrying contraband goods?" He nodded to the sealed chest. "A serious violation of the law."

"I had no idea, captain. We are just humble farmers on our way to a homestead on Osiris."

"Of course, ma'am. But we're going to have to take you in for questioning. Just to be sure, you understand."

"Oh, I don't think there'll be any need for that. If you just confiscate the contraband, you can let us go on our way."

"That won't be possible ma'am."

"I'm sure your command will understand," Ana said, and produced an ID disk that Bruno had never seen before. It was a dull metal grey with no holographs on it except for a strange symbol in one corner. She flashed it at the captain, smiling broadly.

"I'm sorry, ma'am, but rules are rules."

Ana's smile died. "Who are you?" she demanded, but the truth had begun to dawn on her. "Where are your badges? What command do you belong to?"

Moran smiled thinly. He still wore his Ranger uniform and still flew his military-class schooner. He made sure all his men wore their uniforms and that they carried standard-issue ranger rifles, but it was all a ruse. Alistair Moran hadn't been an employee of the empire for a very long time.

He turned to Bruno. "I've warned you, Tertian. Don't let me catch you in my sky again. Next time, it won't be your nose I'll break." He nodded to his lieutenant. The big man tucked the chest under one arm and grabbed Ana with the other. She squealed in pain as he twisted her arm, marching her off toward the airlock.

Bruno almost felt sorry for her. "What are you going to do with her?" he asked.

"Whatever I want," Moran smirked. "The Red Priests are the reason I had to leave the army. They owe me."

"What about the boy?"

Moran examined Drake closely. The boy was expressionless, but the old pirate seemed to see something in his face.

"He's yours. Not my type anyway." With that, he marched off. His soldiers filed silently after him. They still retained their military discipline, Bruno noted.

He sighed with relief as the last of them walked through the airlock, sealing it shut behind him. He heard the metallic *thonk* as the traction hooks disengaged. Horns rushed to his side, helping him to his feet. The pain in his nose was now a dull throbbing. It was no longer bleeding, but he knew he had to tend to it soon.

"Everyone all right?" Bruno asked his crew.

"A bit roughed up, but fine," said Horns. Marley gave him a thumbs up, grinning. A bruise was forming on her jaw, he saw. Ronk noticed it, too. He touched it gingerly; she winced in pain but did not turn away.

"Good, let's get out of here." Horns nodded. Reluctantly, she let him go and headed to the bridge. Ronk headed to the engine room while Marley went down to the hold to check to see how much of their supplies Moran had taken.

It was just him and the boy left. Drake looked lost and scared, but there was a determined cast in his jaw. He would be fine, Bruno knew.

"I'm sorry about your mother," Bruno said.

"She was not my mother." Drake's voice was hard.

"What happened to your sister? How come Moran didn't find her?"

Just as Drake opened his mouth to answer, the ship was rocked by a violent blast that sent them both stumbling. High above them, the skimmers swayed dangerously in their harnesses.

Horn's voice crackled over the intercom. "Bruno, they're firing on us!" she cried.

"Get us out of here!"

"I can't," she said. "I can get the shields up, but nothing else is responding—"

Ronk's voice cut in.

"Captain, they disabled the engine systems. They destroyed every control bank down here."

Bruno cursed under his breath. He knew it had been too easy. "Can you fix it?"

"It will be difficult, but I think so. Otherwise, we will all die." Ronk almost sounded pleased.

"Do it," he snapped. Haulage freighters were not usually equipped with weaponry, but then again, most haulage freighters didn't have Marley. "Sis? Tell me they left something behind."

"Never fear, fearless leader." Marley's voice was light. Chaos was her element. "They took our food, our meds, and all our spares—they even took Martha—but Jane and the rest of the family are still here."

Another blast rocked the ship, but they held onto the walls for support and kept their feet.

"Can you handle a gun?" Bruno asked. Drake nodded. "Good, follow me."

Bruno had never liked the bio-suits—they smelled like old bananas and they made him feel claustrophobic, though he would never admit that to anyone—but they were their last hope. Bruno and Drake met Marley in the ship's lowest cargo hold. Marley hadn't been exaggerating about her collection, Bruno realised. Over the years, she had collected and modified dozens of high-calibre weapons, making them lighter, more accurate, and above all, more powerful. She picked out the two largest. The gun she'd been modifying was big, but it was hardly the largest in her arsenal. That honour went to the one she gave Bruno; it was the size of a small cannon.

"I call her Bertha," Marley said, grinning.

There were more hideaways, pockets, and vents on the ship than Bruno could count. It had been modified and refitted dozens of times and every time they wrenched out and replaced an old system with something smaller, faster, and more efficient, those old spaces would be closed off or converted to storage. One of these retrofitted spaces was the series of tanks from when the ship still used liquid fuel. They were massive carbon-fibre drums with two outlets: one at the top to allow for manual checks, and the other at the bottom where intake nozzles fitted. Located on the ship's underbelly, they were the perfect place to slip out unnoticed.

The tanks normally held the ship's extra water, but right now one of them was nearly empty. They climbed down into it and, amid an increasing barrage from Moran's ship, put on their bio-suits. The three of them slipped out of the ship through the intake valve. Marley immediately headed for the starboard side, while Bruno and Drake headed for the port side, the tiny air jets on their suits propelling them through the zero gravity of space. Bruno tried not to look out at the vast blackness beyond the ship; it always made him dizzy.

Soon, he could spy Moran's ship just over the bow. *The Lady's Gift* was facing the *S.S. Gilgamesh* directly and her front shields were taking most of the blasts. They were holding, but Bruno could see sparks form every time they took another hit. They would not last much longer. Bruno manoeuvred the large gun off his back. He snapped on the suit's magnetic boots and they held him fast to the hull. A few feet away, still near the underside of the ship, Drake did the same. Bruno knew that on the other side, Marley was doing it, too.

"Ready?" Bruno called to the others through the suit's intercom.

"Aye, aye, fearless leader," sang Marley.

"Ready, sir," came Drake's voice. The boy had taken on a military precision that Bruno knew could have only come from long years of training—likely since childhood.

"Horns, on my signal, lower the shields. One…two…now!"

In a flash of light, Marley fired her gun. Moran had not been expecting return fire and hadn't bothered to raise his shields. A spot of fire bloomed on the other ship's hull and was quickly quenched by the vacuum of space. Marley was right; Jane really could pop a hole in a military freighter. Then, Bruno and Drake fired their guns. Their aim was true. Both rounds hit the same spot on the ship that Marley's had. Suddenly, all the lights on the *S. S. Gilgamesh* went out.

Bruno smiled grimly, snapped off the boots, and jetted toward the nearest airlock.

"Captain, I have made some adjustments," Ronk's voice crackled over the intercom. "We cannot go very fast or very far, but we can fly."

"Then let's get out of here."

The girl Bella was waiting for them when they returned. It was the first time Bruno had seen her since she arrived on the ship. Standing in the light, Bruno could see that her skin was darker than he'd first thought. She was coal-black—like something burned to a crisp—and she had no eyebrows. She was dressed in the same clothes she had worn when she boarded. But it was as if she was a different girl. Gone were the hunched shoulders and downcast eyes that had made her seem like some small, hunted, haunted thing. She stood straight, her red-gold eyes boring into him.

"The red woman, is she gone? Truly?" Her voice was low, almost masculine, and smooth as silk slipping through the fingers.

Bruno nodded.

A look of sadness passed over her face. "She was broken inside," she said quietly. "I could have fixed her, but she would not let me."

As Bruno took off the bio-suit's helmet, it brushed his broken nose, sending a lance of pain searing across his face. In all the excitement, he had completely forgotten about it. He let out an involuntary grunt.

Bella moved like silent lightening. Suddenly, she was in front of him, reaching out to touch him, ignoring Drake's shout. It was as if time slowed down for Bruno. He was aware of Drake's voice, of movement behind him, but somehow it did not matter. As her hand crept closer to his face, his skin began to prickle and his hair stood on end, as if he was too close to a high-voltage wire.

Her touch was electric. A searing light burned through him— as it passed he could feel the cartilage in his nose crunch back into place, the old laser blade wound on his shoulder melt away, the pitted scars on his hands from his childhood as a dockworker knit back up, the first beginnings of arthritis in his knees loosen—and then it was gone.

Bruno sagged to the ground; he would have fallen over had Marley not caught him in time. The girl stepped back, cradling her hand against her chest. Then she smiled and broke into a laugh. It was the most beautiful sound Bruno had ever heard.

A few weeks later, as Bruno made his way up to the leisure deck, he passed Marley and Ronk sitting at the mess hall dining table. She was sitting on his lap.

"I did not leave the table in anger," Ronk was saying. "I just needed to think. So I went down to the cooling vents in the engine room."

"Oh yeah, I think better when it's noisy, too. I like to go up to the main air turbine shaft. I have to be careful 'cause I could get sucked in if I stand too close."

Ronk laughed at that; it was deep and rich like soil. It was still strange to hear him do so, but Ronk was a man transformed. In some ways they all were.

"So, I've been meaning to ask you, what does 'Ronk' mean?"

"It's short for Aderonke. It's Yoruba…"

Bruno continued on.

Bella and Drake were in the cabin bay lounge talking heatedly in low tones.

"Captain!" Bella called out when she saw him and bounded down the short hallway to meet him. Dressed in a mix of Marley and Horn's hand-me-downs, she almost looked like a normal teenager. "I have the most wonderful news." She spoke like someone who had learned to speak out of a book—an old, old book.

"Yeah? What is it?"

"Have you ever heard of the Acolytes of Oshun?"

"Aren't they the priests who run a high-class prostitution scam?"

"No, no! They are honoured servants of the Goddess of Love," she said, her face animated by excitement. "They are priests and priestesses who dedicate their bodies to service; they spend years learning the intricate arts of pleasure, which they use to help bring devotees closer to the divine. Their main temple is on Mars."

"That's nice, but what's that got to do with anything?"

"I want to join them!" she burst out and clapped her hands to her mouth as if she'd spoken without thinking. "Please, please, please may I join them?"

"I don't know Bel, you sure that's what you want?"

"Captain, I've spent my whole life craving the touch of others," she said. "The life of an Acolyte would be paradise for me."

"What about your…abilities?" She shrugged and stuffed her hands in her pockets.

"I can only fix those who want to be fixed." She glanced at Drake who folded his arms and turned away. Bruno noted Drake's tense shoulders and obstinate scowl and resolved to talk to him later. The boy had been trained as a warrior-priest, though the warrior part had stuck long after the priest part had fled. He had spent his life keeping Bella safe from accidental contact. Would he be able to handle her new role? Bruno hoped so. The Amethyst Order was most likely still looking for them and she would need his protection.

It would be a few weeks before they wrapped up their current job and at least a week before they reached Mars. He had some time yet.

"If that's what makes you happy, Bel. Let's talk about this later, huh?"

She beamed and nodded.

Horns was waiting for him among the greenery of the hydroponic garden, tending a plant in the far corner of the room.

"You said you had some information for me," Bruno said, greeting her with a kiss.

"I've finally found Drake and Bella's files with the Order." She pointed at a reader on a nearby counter. Bruno thumbed through the different screens.

"Not a whole lot here," he said.

"I know, its deep cover stuff. Most of it is Drake and Ana, really, all I managed to get on Bella is her name."

"Nefertiti? Huh. What kind of name is that?"

"Well, once you become *Mehen*, you're given a 'true' name, something more spiritual."

"What was your true name?"

"I don't remember."

"Come on, Horns, if you don't want to talk about it…" She laid a gentle hand on his arm.

"Honestly, Bruno, I don't remember. I paid a guy in Qom six hundred credits to have that memory erased."

"Why?"

"I didn't want to be reminded of my former self. I was an Enforcer—like Drake. I did some pretty awful stuff."

"Did you torture people?" Bruno had been tortured once. A job had gone wrong and he'd ended up owing money to the wrong people. It had been the most hellish few hours of his life. He had often wondered about the blank-faced man, who had methodically pulled out his fingernails, who he was in the life outside that room.

"Torture doesn't work." Horns had gone curiously blank, as if something in her had closed off her true self. Bruno knew he was looking at the Enforcer she had once been.

"I'd disagree."

"Physical torture, I mean. The threat of pain will only get you so far. Once you start inflicting it, people will say anything to make the hurting stop, and it'll usually be lies. If you really want to find out the truth, you threaten what they love. And it doesn't always mean going after their families. You could go after their ideals or their sense of security. If they know anything, they'll tell you. If they don't, they'll be more than eager to help you find it."

There was a silence between them.

"You were good, weren't you?"

"I was the best."

"So why erase the one memory?"

"It was all I could afford. And by the time I got enough money for more treatments, I realised that I didn't want to forget my past. My memories make me who I am. Without knowing how bad it was then, I can't appreciate how good I have it now."

"You're amazing, you know that?" Bruno said, and Horns smiled. He watched the blankness dissolve into relief and Bruno realised just how much she had risked in telling him about her past. He was filled with tenderness for her. The force of it hit him like a blow to the gut.

"I love you," she sighed and slipped into his arms.

Bruno smiled and wrapped her in his arms. He began to kiss her, slowly and softly. His touch could make her promises, and this time, he was sure he could keep them.

# The Language of Knives

## Haralambi Markov

*Young Bulgarian writer Haralambi Markov is a recent Clarion graduate, and has stories published in* Electric Velocipede, Tor.com, *and elsewhere.*

A LONG, SILENT day awaits you and your daughter as you prepare to cut your husband's body. You remove organs from flesh, flesh from bones, bones from tendons—all ingredients for the cake you're making, the heavy price of admission for an afterlife you pay your gods; a proper send-off for the greatest of all warriors to walk the lands.

The Baking Chamber feels small with two people inside, even though you've spent a month with your daughter as part of her apprenticeship. You feel irritated at having to share this moment, but this is a big day for your daughter. You steal a glance at her. See how imposing she looks in her ramie garments the color of a blood moon, how well the leather apron made from changeling hide sits on her.

You work in silence, as the ritual demands, and your breath hisses as you both twist off the aquamarine top of the purification vat. Your husband floats to the top of the thick translucent waters, peaceful and tender. You hold your breath, aching to lean over and kiss him one more time—but that is forbidden. His body is now sacred, and you are not. You've seen him sleep, his powerful chest rising and falling, his breath a harbinger of summer storms. The purification bath makes it easy to pull him up and slide him onto the table, where the budding dawn seeping from the skylight above illuminates his transmogrification, his ascent. His skin has taken a rich pomegranate hue. His hair is a stark mountaintop white.

You raise your head to study your daughter's reaction at seeing her father since his wake. You study her face, suspicious of any muscle that might twitch and break the fine mask made of fermented butcher broom berries and dried water mint grown in marshes where men have drowned. It's a paste worn out of respect and a protection from those you serve. You scrutinize her eyes for tears, her hair and eyebrows waxed slick for any sign of dishevelment.

The purity of the body matters most. A single tear can sour the offering. A single hair can spoil the soul being presented to the gods...what a refined palate they have. But your daughter wears a stone face. Her eyes are opaque; her body is poised as if this is the easiest thing in the world to do. The ceramic knife you've shaped and baked yourself sits like a natural extension of her arm.

You remember what it took you to bake your own mother into a cake. No matter how many times you performed the ritual under her guidance, nothing prepared you for the moment when you saw her body on the table. Perhaps you can teach your daughter to love your art. Perhaps she belongs by your side as a Cake Maker, even though you pride yourself on not needing any help. Perhaps she hasn't agreed to this apprenticeship only out of grief. Perhaps, perhaps...

Your heart prickles at seeing her this accomplished, after a single lunar cycle. A part of you, a part you take no pride in, wants her to struggle through her examination, struggle to the point where her eyes beg you to help her. You would like to forgive her for her incapability, the way you did back when she was a child. You want her to need you—the way she needed your husband for so many years.

No. Treat him like any other. *Let your skill guide you.* You take your knife and shave the hair on your husband's left arm with the softest touch.

You remove every single hair on his body to use for kindling for the fire you will build to dry his bones, separating a small handful of the longest hairs for the decoration, then incise the tip of his little finger to separate skin from muscle.

Your daughter mirrors your movements. She, too, is fluent in the language of knives.

The palms and feet are the hardest to skin, as if the body fights to stay intact and keep its grip on this realm. You struggle at first but then work the knife without effort. As you lift the softly stretching tissue, you see the countless scars that punctuated his life—the numerous cuts that crisscross his hands and shoulders, from when he challenged the sword dancers in Aeno; the coin-shaped scars where arrowheads pierced his chest during their voyage through the Sea of Spires in the misty North; the burn marks across his left hip from the leg hairs of the fire titan, Hragurie. You have collected your own scars on your journeys through the forgotten places of this world, and those scars ache now, the pain kindled by your loss.

After you place your husband's skin in a special aventurine bowl, you take to the muscle—that glorious muscle you've seen shift and contract in great swings of his dancing axe while you sing your curses and charms alongside him in battle. Even the exposed redness of him is rich with memories, and you do everything in your power not to choke as you strip him of his strength. This was the same strength your daughter prized above all else and sought for herself many years ago, after your spells and teachings grew insufficient for her. This was the same strength she accused you of lacking when you chose your mother's calling, retired your staff from battle, and chose to live preparing the dead for their passing.

*Weak.* The word still tastes bitter with her accusation. *How can you leave him? How can you leave us? You're a selfish little man.*

You watch her as you work until there is nothing left but bones stripped clean, all the organs in their respective jars and bowls. Does she regret the words now, as she works by your side? Has she seen your burden yet? Has she understood your choice? Will she be the one to handle your body once you pass away?

You try to guess the answer from her face, but you find no solace and no answer. Not when you extract the fat from your husband's skin, not when you mince his flesh and muscle, not when you puree his organs and cut his intestines into tiny strips you leave to dry. Your daughter excels in this preparatory work—her blade is swift, precise, and gentle.

How can she not? After all, she is a gift from the gods. A gift given to two lovers who thought they could never have a child on their own. A miracle. The completion you sought after in your youth; a honey-tinged bliss that filled you with warmth. But as

41

with all good things, your bliss waxed and waned as you realized: all children have favorites.

You learned how miracles can hurt.

You align his bones on the metal tray that goes into the hungry oven. You hold his skull in your hands and rub the sides where his ears once were. You look deep into the sockets where once eyes of dark brown would stare back into you.

His clavicle passes your fingers. You remember the kisses you planted on his shoulder, when it used to be flesh. You position his ribcage, and you can still hear his heartbeat—a rumble in his chest the first time you lay together after barely surviving an onslaught of skin-walkers, a celebration of life. You remember that heart racing, as it did in your years as young men, when vitality kept you both up until dawn. You remember it beating quietly in his later years, when you were content and your bodies fit perfectly together—the alchemy of flesh you have now lost.

You deposit every shared memory in his bones, and then load the tray in the oven and slam shut the metal door.

Behind you, your daughter stands like a shadow, perfect in her apprentice robes. Not a single crease disfigures the contours of her pants and jacket. Not a single stain mars her apron.

She stares at you. She judges you.

She is perfection.

You wish you could leave her and crawl in the oven with your husband.

Flesh, blood, and gristle do not make a cake easily, yet the Cake Maker has to wield these basic ingredients. Any misstep leads to failure, so you watch closely during your daughter's examination, but she completes each task with effortless grace.

She crushes your husband's bones to flour with conviction.

Your daughter mixes the dough of blood, fat, and bone flour, and you assist her. You hear your knuckles and fingers pop as you knead the hard dough, but hers move without a sound—fast and agile as they shape the round cakes.

Your daughter works over the flesh and organs until all you can see is a pale scarlet cream with the faint scent of iron, while you crush the honey crystals that will allow for the spirit to be digested by the gods. You wonder if she is doing this to prove how superior she is to you—to demonstrate how easy it is to lock yourself into a bakery with the dead. You wonder how to explain that you never burnt as brightly as your husband that you don't need to chase legends and charge into battle.

You wonder how to tell her that she is your greatest adventure, that you gave her most of the magic you had left.

Layer by layer, your husband is transformed into a cake. Not a single bit of him is lost. You pull away the skin on top and connect the pieces with threads from his hair. The sun turns the rich shade of lavender and calendula.

You cover the translucent skin with the dried blood drops you extracted before you placed the body in the purification vat and glazed it with the plasma. Now all that remains is to tell your husband's story, in the language every Cake Maker knows—the language you've now taught your daughter.

You wonder whether she will blame you for the death of your husband in writing, the way she did when you told her of his death.

*Your stillness killed him. You had to force him to stay, to give up his axe. Now he's dead in his sleep. Is this what you wanted? Have him all to yourself? You couldn't let him die out on the road.*

Oh, how she screamed that day—her voice as unforgiving as thunder. Her screaming still reverberates through you. You're afraid of what she's going to tell the gods.

You both write. You cut and bend the dried strips of intestines into runes and you gently push them so they sink into the glazed skin and hold.

You write his early story. His childhood, his early feats, the mythology of your love. How you got your daughter. She tells the other half of your husband's myth—how he trained her in every single weapon known to man, how they journeyed the world over to honor the gods.

Her work doesn't mention you at all.

You rest your fingers, throbbing with pain from your manipulations. You have completed the last of your husband's tale. You have written in the language of meat and bones and satisfied the gods' hunger. You hope they will nod with approval as their tongues roll around the cooked flesh and swallow your sentences and your tether to life.

Your daughter swims into focus as she takes her position across the table, your husband between you, and joins you for the spell. He remains the barrier you can't overcome even in death. As you begin to speak, you're startled to hear her voice rise with yours. You mutter the incantation and her lips are your reflection, but while you caress the words, coaxing their magic into being, she cuts them into existence, so the veil you will around the cake spills like silk on your end and crusts on hers. The two halves shimmer in blue feylight, entwine into each other, and the deed is done.

You have said your farewell, better than you did when you first saw him dead. Some dam inside you breaks. Exhaustion wipes away your strength and you feel your age, first in the trembling in your hands, then in the creaking in your knees as you turn your back and measure your steps so you don't disturb the air—a retreat as slow as young winter frost.

Outside the Bakery, your breath catches. Your scream is a living thing that squirms inside your throat and digs into the hidden recesses of your lungs. Your tears wash the dry mask from your cheeks.

Your daughter takes your hand, gently, with the unspoken understanding only shared loss births and you search for her gaze. You search for the flat, dull realization that weighs down the soul. You search for yourself in her eyes, but all you see is your husband—his flame now a wildfire that has swallowed every part of you. She looks at you as a person who has lost the only life she had ever known, pained and furious, and you pat her hand and kiss her forehead, her skin stinging against your lips. When confusion pulls her face together, her features lined with fissures in her protective mask, you shake your head.

"The gods praise your skill and technique. They praise your steady hand and precision, but they have no use of your hands in the Bakery." The words roll out with difficulty—a thorn vine you lacerate your whole being with as you force yourself to reject your daughter. Yes, she can follow your path, but what good would that do?

"You honor me greatly." Anger tinges her response, but fights in these holy places, father only misfortune, so her voice is low and even. You are relieved to hear sincerity in her fury, desire in her voice to dedicate herself to your calling.

You want to keep her here, where she won't leave. Your tongue itches with every lie you can bind her with, spells you've learned from gods that are not your own, hollow her out and hold onto her, even if such acts could end your life. You reconsider and instead hold on to her earnest reaction. You have grown to an age where even intent will suffice.

"It's not an honor to answer your child's yearning." You maintain respectability, keep with the tradition, but still you lean in with all the weight of death tied to you like stones and you whisper. "I have told the story of your father in blood and gristle as I have with many others. As I will continue to tell every story as best as I can, until I myself end in the hands of a Cake Maker. But you can continue writing your father's story outside the temple where your knife strokes have a meaning.

"Run. Run toward the mountains and rivers, sword in your hand and bow on your back. Run toward life. That is where you will find your father."

Now it is she who is crying. You embrace her, the memory of doing so in her childhood alive inside your bones and she hugs you back as a babe, full of needing and vulnerable. But she is no longer a child—the muscles underneath her robes roll with the might of a river—so you usher her out to a life you have long since traded away.

Her steps still echo in the room outside the Baking Chamber as you reapply the coating to your face from the tiny, crystal jars. You see yourself: a grey, tired man who touched death more times than he ever touched his husband.

Your last task is to bring the cake to where the Mouth awaits, its vines and branches shaking, aglow with iridescence. There, the gods will entwine their appendages around your offering, suck it in, close, and digest. Relief overcomes you and you sigh.

Yes, it's been a long day since you and your daughter cut your husband's body open. You reenter the Baking Chamber and push the cake onto the cart.

# In Her Head, In Her Eyes

## Yukimi Ogawa

*Yukimi Ogawa lives in a small town in Tokyo, where she writes in English but never speaks the language. Her work has appeared in* Strange Horizons, The Book Smugglers, *and elsewhere.*

TRILLS OF SILVER, trills of blue. She wanted to watch on. She wanted to remember them, wanted to make them her own. But soon, too soon, she was pulled up, back into the air, where she had to fight for breath, fight to be on her feet.

She hit the hard workshop floor, heavy head first. Though her head was protected, she cried out anyway. Slowly, she raised herself up and tried to glare at them, all of them standing around the stale pot of unused indigo dye in which they had just tried to drown her. Most of them kept laughing at her, but a few seemed to sense her unseen glare, and backed off warily.

Then, a voice from the entrance to the workshop. "What is going on in here?"

The bullies scattered instantly at the voice's calm authority. Everyone knew who commanded that voice, just as everyone knew he was the only person who would dare stand up for the strange new servant. Drenched in old dye, the servant girl shifted and dipped her heavy head, and busied herself squeezing her sleeves. Slowly the owner of the voice walked in, frowning. "Hase. I told you to come or call for me when in trouble. Are you all right?"

Hase bowed as low as she could, unbalanced with the substantial weight atop her head. "Yes. I appreciate our young master's concern."

The young man—the third noble son of the family of artisan dyers—knelt before her. "Hase," he said. "You must tell them they'll be in trouble if they do anything to you. Use my name. Who were they?" He was the only person in the entire house who called her by her real name and not Pot Head.

"Again, I appreciate my master's concern," Hase said, "but in truth, I am fine. And here, my robe—now it's dyed in indigo and looks pretty!"

Still kneeling, the young man grinned. "You smiled. At last!"

Hase hurriedly composed herself and looked down. Suddenly she was aware of how her robe was clinging to her skin, how the blue-black pungent water was running down her dark hair, down her torso, how quickly the warm dye was starting to cool off. "Young master, this is not a place for a noble. I must tidy myself up now."

"Yes. Be sure to keep yourself warm."

Hase bowed again, watching the young man leave before standing and rushing abruptly to the servants' quarters in search of solitude and warmth.

No one knew why Hase wore a pot on her head. No one in the noble house, in the region, had even seen the materials from which the pot was made. *It must be some sort of iron*, people would whisper marveling at the reflective surface shining brightly as a mirror in the space where her eyes should be. No one had ever seen Hase's eyes, or anything behind the pot's smooth countenance—only her nose and mouth were visible below its cold protective edge.

Since her arrival at the house, of course many had tried to rip the pot from her head, but to no avail. The pot, so closely fitted to Hase's skull, would not, could not, come off. Yet others tried to crack it open to reveal the girl beneath, but no tool could do it any damage. Eventually, they all gave up.

The only thing anyone knew about Hase for certain was that she came from The Island—a fabled place, far away from their shores. Even nobles, such as the ones who owned this fine home, were not rich enough to travel to The Island. How pot-covered Hase ended up here, people could only speculate.

Beyond the metallic pot concealing her head, Hase appeared perfectly plain, which only added to the mystery surrounding her. The people of Hase's island were rumored to be great beauties, with skin and hair and eyes of all colors: hues of flowers and jewels, of stars and sunsets. Some, it was rumored, even bore patterns on their skin—not tattooed or painted on, but opalescent designs born from the womb. It was common knowledge that everyone from the Island was beautiful, inspiring poetry and art, stories and dreams.

One only had to look at Hase. She had ordinary skin just like everyone else, without a single shocking color or pattern to be seen. Her hair was thick, beautiful, and dark as a crow's wing, but perfectly ordinary. So no one in the household, neither noble nor servant, believed her claim as to her birthplace—no one, that is, save the family's third son.

A few nights after her arrival at the house, Sai visited Hase's makeshift cot inside the storehouse. At first she shied away, thinking he had come to take advantage of her. But he waved his hand dismissively and sat down by the door, leaving it fully open. There was no light inside, for no fire was allowed in the storehouse; only moonlight illuminated the room, spilling through the door and reflecting off her potted head.

Sai gestured toward the moon. "Look at how beautiful the moon is here, without all the lights of the house. Don't be greedy and keep it all to yourself!"

Slowly, Hase closed the distance to the door where he was, her thin blanket wrapped tightly around her body. She peered at him cautiously, the starry night reflecting in the cool metal of her gaze. "We have a pond the color of moonlight," she said quietly.

"On your island? Where they say everyone is beautiful?"

"There is no such place where everyone is beautiful. People always try to find the flaws and imperfections in all things. On my island, there are other plain things. As plain as Hase appears here." She bowed her spherical heavy head and clutched her blanket tighter around her.

"And the pot…"

"It has nothing to do with Hase's island, master." Hase gave her heavy head a little shake.

The young man nodded. He looked as though he had more things he wanted to ask, but said no more and looked on at the moon.

Unlike the younger servants, the adults didn't quite bully Hase, though no one seemed to like her much. They knew a certain amount of money had been exchanged for her service, enough of a sum to make them believe that she must be from the Island and that she genuinely must want to work under the dye masters. Still, among any of the servants, any kindness toward Hase remained to be seen. For when Hase, dripping with old indigo dye and shivering, finally made her way to the servants' quarters to ask for towels, she found little sympathy. The elder dye master, Hase's superior, simply wrinkled her nose and dropped the towels at Hase's feet. "For once, just have a bath. I can't let you serve at the meeting tonight in that state, and we can't spare a hand."

"What meeting?"

"You don't notice anything, do you?" The woman sighed. "The eldest and the middle brothers' wives and other relatives are coming to visit."

Hase tilted her heavy head to one side in question. "What about the third brother's wife?"

"You know he doesn't have a wife yet." The dye master snorted. "If he did, we'd all have stopped him before he went into that storehouse your first night to have you."

Hase stared blankly at the dye master, smooth impassive metal reflecting the older woman's sneer, until the dye master shooed her away.

Hase didn't have much time to enjoy the bath. Soon the relatives started to arrive, and she was herded along with the other servants, bustling tea and refreshments to the family. All the relatives openly stared at Hase and the smooth pot covering her head, mouths agape at her strangeness. *Pot Head*, they whispered behind her back, quickly picking up the servants' name for her. The wives of the first and second brothers took great delight in her peculiar appearance, laughing at her gleaming helmet of metal. The elder wife quickly tired of the game and Hase's calm, and exclaimed, "Why, I hate her face!"

"But she doesn't have a face!" The younger wife laughed even harder than before.

"I hate that she doesn't. We are laughing at her and she should be angry, or embarrassed at the very least! Look at her, with her stupid mouth, her tiny nose." The elder wife gestured rudely at Hase, trying to engage the servant. "The only parts of her face you can see, and she has no reaction."

Hase bowed as gracefully as she could in the style of her fellow servants, the movement awkward in many ways. The angle of her neck and back were tilted just wrong, the speed with which she retreated to the more comfortable, upright position to alleviate the weight of her head a little too fast. The jerky movements only fueled the younger wife's amusement, her laughter renewed with malicious glee.

"Oh, Pot Head, heavy-head, just try not to get in our way!" The younger wife pushed Hase by the pot on her head, cackling harder still when Hase fell to the wooden floor with a dull thud, potted-head first.

Slowly, slowly, Hase dragged herself up onto her feet, as she heard the two wives walk away, laughing and laughing.

Both wives and their husbands were young and relatively newlywed, and the two women measured themselves against each other in every regard. They compared their wedding gifts and the favor of their new parents-in-law; they compared their best robes, their skills in music and poetry. Every day and every night, the wives would compare their positions, while their men drank sake, the women tea, and a steady barrage of refreshments flew from the kitchens into their mouths.

All the while, Hase lurked in the background, her domed, impassive head missing not a single detail. From the hallways and the corners of each room, Hase stole glimpses of the fine embroidery of the women's robes, fascinated by the expensive, exquisite artifacts that shimmered in the wives' hands.

One day, the elder wife caught Hase staring at her robe and sneered, her venomous glare focused on Hase's reflective helmet. Hase shivered, transfixed by the wife's disdain, unable to look or move away.

"Here." Sai handed her a bundle. "Of all the gifts the women brought, these were the only things my relatives weren't much keen on. I'm sure you can have it."

Hase opened the bundle and found two spindles of fine gold and silver threads. She turned the spools in her hands, feeling the fine filigree of each thread, and sighed. "These must be expensive enough that someone may like to save them for later use. Is it certain that Hase can have it?"

"We are dye masters here, not for embroidery or even weaving." Sai smiled at Hase encouragingly. "But you like patterns, I've heard? That's why you've come all the way here, isn't it?"

"Yes." She nodded, a slow, languid inclination of her heavy, masked head. "On my island, we need more colors, more patterns. Patterns, especially, to be reflected on the beloved children of the Island. I must study."

"You mean you can decide what colors and patterns your babies will bear?" Sai leaned forward eagerly.

"No, sir. We create new patterns, we discover more colors, but our goddess alone can decide. We all wish to please our goddess."

Sai frowned, confused. Hase almost smiled at that.

After a moment of silence, she said quietly, "These look as though they represent the young wives themselves. They are so different and yet, they go so well with each other."

Sai, leaning in closer to hear her better, laughed. "Are you being sarcastic?"

"No, sir! They are lovely, those two."

She had said this a little louder, but still, the third son did not lean back. She knew what that meant. And though everything was awkward with her heavy pot, the hard wooden ground, the thin futon, this time Hase smiled. The pot weighed her down, pinned her to the floor, as if Sai's eyes intent on her covered face weren't enough to affix her there already.

When she was alone again, Hase pulled the spindles Sai had given her out from the folds of her sleeves. She placed them on the ground beside her futon, then changed her mind and put them on the pillow and carefully laid her heavy head beside them. The two colors filled her reflected sight, shimmering and twining in cruel beauty, fueling rather than smothering her desire.

The next day, Hase walked dreamily through the dyed cloths fluttering in the wind, being dried. Some bore glue for patterns to be washed away later, and some still had strings marking the fabric for simpler patterns. A few plain cloths with no patters at all fluttered alongside these elaborate designs, forming a small sea of color and texture upon which Hase and her metal potted head were afloat. Her heavy head swiveled in wonder, slowly, taking in all of the colors and styles. She had to memorize all these patterns, for the dye masters would never teach her how to make them. The blues. The whites. Everything in between. But just then she heard a voice, interrupting her quiet study. "You seem to have had a very good time last night."

Startled, Hase spun around, searching for the source of the voice though she already knew its owner. She walked on in between the waves of cloths, currents and bubbles, seaweeds of patterns, toward the voice. At the end of the last row, she found her.

Hase bowed as well as she could, and asked: "Was that statement aimed at me, mistress?"

*Trills of blue, a line of silver.* For a moment, the older of the two wives—the one Hase called in her mind Silver—looked away from her. "Why did you come here? What is it you want from us?"

"I come to learn about dyeing…"

"Oh, do you? So seducing our brother-in-law was part of your plan?"

Hase shook her head; that was all she could do.

"With a face like yours it must be really easy to lie, isn't it? Are you even really from that Island everybody's talking about? Does it even exist? Did you think looking ordinary would make us feel you're one of us, or did you think we'd be too easy to deceive, so you didn't bother mocking those colors and patterns of the Island's people?" The elder wife's anger and spite burned in her eyes.

Involuntarily, Hase raised her hand through Silver's tirade, resting it gently over a nearby cloth and marveling at its fine knots and textures. She tried to imagine the pattern the knots might make eventually, and failed. "My patterns, I guess, are in my head."

Silver frowned. "In your head? What are you talking about?"

Hase stroked the cloth again, trying to coax the pattern into life. "Yes. I'm the head pattern designer of my clan, as I have told the great mistress here." She recalled Sai's mother in her finest robes, her eyes cold as she assessed Hase and her claims. "I have to extract the patterns from my head, and to do that, I need to know more ways to express the patterns, of course!" Hase's voice rose in pitch, in eagerness and fervor. Her potted head glittered in the sunlight. "But, but the people in this region, especially the dye masters, wouldn't allow the dye or dyeing methods out of the region. We—my aunts, and other guardians and I, of course, of course—had to promise I wouldn't take any—*any!*—indigo out of this place when we arranged my apprenticeship here! But nobody can prevent me from taking these blues and whites and everything else with me inside my head! And…what is the matter?"

Silver had backed away from Hase, the hate in her eyes faded into wariness and fear at Hase's rambling outburst.

At Silver's discomfort, Hase immediately reverted to her usual quiet demeanor. "Forgive me, I shouldn't have kept our young mistress standing here, listening to Hase's useless babblings! Did I answer the question well enough?"

Silver shook her head. "I…no. Not at all. Now, there are only more questions than before."

"Forgive me, mistress. Please, pardon my rudeness!"

"Don't." Silver raised a hand toward Hase, who had just taken one step closer to her. "Come no closer. And don't you dare look at me like that."

"Like what, mistress?"

But Silver just waved her hand and walked away in a flutter of silk, leaving Hase standing amid the sea of patterned cloth, her face as smooth and impassive as ever.

Sai's words were always gentle. Hase felt as though she could fall asleep listening to him.

"Is it true," the young man asked, waking her up from her reverie, "that on the Island, some people change their colors as they grow old? I heard that from one of the relatives; they'd heard that somewhere along the trip here."

Hase inclined her potted head. "Some do, yes. I know a person whose eyes changed from light green to viridian, yellow, and eventually brown, like leaves. They crumbled in the end, and the person went blind."

"Oh. I'm sorry to hear that."

"That person knew what was going to happen and worked hard to prepare for it. It's not that bad, when things are predictable like that."

After a while he sighed. "I cannot imagine the life of your people."

"There is no need, sir."

"But I want to. I want to know more about you."

Hase turned from Sai and remained silent, playing with the twines of silver and gold spindles he had given her.

In her eyes she wove her patterns of gold and silver. With occasional blue that punctuated the new design, it shaped hearts and veins.

But then, just before she could wholly grasp the new pattern, her heavy head was yanked back as another pair of hands held onto her shoulders. Her shoulders ached under the hands' vice-like grip, pain blossoming in sharp edges and radiating from her chest. And yet, despite the ache, Hase felt the most bitter edge of frustration at losing the pattern she had been imagining, weaving in her eyes.

Below her, Hase could see a large basin of water as the pair of hands holding her shoulders yanked backwards further and the other hands pulling at the pot on her head went the other direction. She coughed, and heard a young servant's voice: "Mistress, if we go any further she might be sick, or even, she might die. I wouldn't be able to explain to our masters what happened, if asked."

"Simple, tell them you punished her because she had stolen the gold and silver threads." Silver's calm voice. "If she dies, it's an accident."

She'd have preferred drowning in the dye pot, especially now with the new indigo being brewed, the bubbles from fermentation slowly blooming like a nebula over the dark liquid. But that would spoil the new dye. Through the pain she imagined the dye's warmth, the smell, explosion of stars as the liquid rushed into her head. Hase shivered.

Behind her, the younger of the wives burst out laughing, her voice full of gold dust. "Then let me do it! I want to choke her with my own hands!"

Silver glowered at Gold. "Are you stupid? We cannot do it ourselves. We are going to say that the servant did it to impress us, of his own will. Be careful not to get your robe wet or touch anything that could prove we were here."

At that, the servant boy's hands loosened a little from Hase's shoulders. Hase whimpered as she heard Gold make a frustrated noise.

"Anyway." Silver came around to where Hase could see her, and crouched down to flash the two spindles of thread. "These are confiscated. You don't need them, anyway, do you? Because the patterns are all in your head, like you said."

"No! Please, I need them! They are my inspiration!"

Silver smiled her cold, cold smile. Hase tried to reach out for the spindles, but the servant boy pulled her back. She heard Gold laughing again, saw Silver tuck the spindles into her sleeve.

Hase could feel her aunts' frustration. She wasn't making enough progress. Seeing the color of indigo change in impossible gradation, learning simple knots that revealed unexpected patterns weren't enough yet for her to create new, satisfying designs. She needed inspiration, and it seemed as though the people here were determined to snatch away that inspiration just when she thought she had found it.

Until one night, at the far end of the house, where she found the three young nobles.

She watched as they tangled and disentangled, making new patterns for her every second. The unreliable screen of organdy, which they must have chosen so that they *would* be seen, provided her with even more inspirations, as it swayed and added a sheen to their passion. Patterns, patterns, patterns.

"What is it that we don't have and the pot girl does?" Silver's cool voice carried through the night as she gracefully moved to ride the man.

"The pot hides her face and lets me see my own lovely self on it," Sai said breezily. Gold sighed with pleasure behind them.

"And also," he said, pushing up a little to grab at Silver's buttocks, "she is from an island full of treasures. Why not make her a slave of mine, let her serve as a liaison between us and the Island?"

"Did you say 'us'?" Gold crawled up from behind Sai and kissed him upside down.

"Besides." Sai lay fully down again and reached out to touch Gold now. "She looks ordinary, I mean, apart from that pot, but who knows what her children will look like? I know her aunts have the colors, because she just told me, because she trusts me, so why not her children?"

"So then you can sell them?"

"Or we could give them to the high generals or perhaps even the Emperor!"

The three all laughed. Then Silver said, while Gold's laughing voice was still trilling in the air: "How did you make her trust you? She doesn't have a face, it's hard to tell what she thinks. Even if you're good at putting up with your own face staring back at you."

"Oh, that was easy. Just being kind to her is more than enough. Treat her as a woman, as no one else does around here, and she's yours."

Gold laughed. Sai chuckled. Silver grinned and licked her lips as she cast her glance upward. "Really? If that's true, you must be a very, very undemanding person, aren't you, Pot Head?"

Sai followed Silver's eyes. Hase, previously hidden in the dimness of the corridor behind the screen, stepped into the light and moaned softly, her sigh swaying the cotton organdy in front of her. Sai bolted upright, pushing Silver off him. "Hase!"

Silver let out a laugh, a trilling of cold, cruel bells. "Oh, Sai, didn't you know she uses this path to get to that stupid cot of hers in the storehouse? You should have paid more attention! If you intended to fool her long enough so that she would take you to that stupid Island, that is!"

Sai looked embarrassed, seemed to be searching for the right words. But soon he gave up, knowing there were no right words to save face with Hase. He looked at her mouth, her smooth, potted head and spoke. "Yes, I was using you, but you had to know this. Why else would I, a man with a rank, place special favor upon an odd girl like you if it weren't to use you?"

None of the three could read Hase's face, of course, with that mirrored helmet of hers. But they could see her shaking. Silver and Gold looked pleased. Sai still looked a little embarrassed, a little uncertain, despite his declaration.

"So why don't we make a child here?" Gold said.

Taking that as an invitation, Hase stepped over the threshold, pushing the organdy out of the way. "But why? Why are you so interested in me?" she asked.

Sai frowned. "No, I told you, I'm more interested in your…"

But Hase wasn't listening to him. She crouched down, not to face him, but to face Silver beside him. "You are like a cold fire that seeks to burn me out."

Silver's grin became wider. "Of course, I hate you, your pot, your behavior, your strangeness—"

"Am I? Am I strange enough? Everybody says I'm plain, with

my ordinary hair, my ordinary skin, my plain colors. Everybody's disappointed!"

"What?"

She turned to Sai. "And to you, yes, I don't mind having your genes. We always need more variations."

"We…what?"

Hase moved on her hands and knees, scampering toward Gold. "Oh, I love the way you laugh. Like gold dust exploding and filling the space. Laugh! Laugh, laugh, laugh at me!"

By then, even Gold was frowning with discomfort, and the silence drew out between the four.

"You are disgusting," Silver spat, breaking the quiet.

"Yes!" Hase turned around to her. "Yes, I'm disgusting! I love being bullied! I love being punished! Bully me! Punish me! You like it too, don't you!"

The three young people slowly backed away from Hase. She swiveled her heavy smooth head back and forth between Silver and Gold—Sai was no use now for her, not paying enough attention to her and therefore, misunderstanding her. Of course, in retrospect, all the questions he had asked her were about the Island, not Hase herself. Gold was nicely cruel, but she was more like a small child, always looking for a new toy. She'd probably tire of Hase sooner or later. So she looked at Silver, whose hateful stare almost choked Hase, like a flood of warm indigo dye.

Trills of silver, quiver of gold.

"Aunts," Hase whispered, grinning impossibly wide, resembling a huge-headed, one-eye monster. "I finally found what I needed. My offering to our goddess!"

Silver backed further away on her hands and buttocks, eyes shining with fear. Her terror made a sharp pang run through Hase, a shiver that wove new patterns, a shiver that pierced colorful stitches over her bright darkness, her white-out canvas.

Silver winced at her own reflection on the mirror of Hase's helmet; what she didn't, couldn't know was that it was a mirror both outside and inside alike. The inner mirror was always connected to the server, where her aunts received and observed every pattern Hase formed. The outer mirror projected and transferred information of the outside world onto Hase's brain, in the place of her long-crumbled eyes. Pains and hurts, both physical and psychological, inspired her more than anything; they had known that much through years of observation. That was why her aunts had sent her to this strangely feudal place—as much for the pain as for the rare colors and dyes that weren't allowed to be exported.

"I'm the head designer of the clan, you see," Hase said, smiling her eyeless, reflective smile. "We need more patterns, colors, and shapes to satisfy our goddess. Favor of our goddess means wealth, and wealth means we will be able to afford a more expensive, lighter-smaller-better helmet for me. But if you prefer me in this heavy old thing, if you'd bully me more in this thing, I want to keep wearing it forever!"

Hase's breath came in quick pants of arousal and excitement, while Silver's breathing turned ragged with terror. Hase could hear Gold making strange noises, like choking, like gagging, like she was about to vomit. No noise, no move could be heard from Sai. *Has he fainted?* Hase queried halfheartedly. *Useless youngest boy.*

"What do you want?" Silver choked out.

Hase shifted into a *seiza* position. "I want you inside my helmet." She thought for a split second, and then, waved her hands in excited denial. "Not you, but the copy of your mental map, so that you'd keep on inspiring me." She stopped her hands and placed them on her chest, and crooned, "Yes, those eyes. I want your eyes, spiteful, hateful, always on me. Don't worry, it won't hurt you!"

"I don't understand." Silver backed away further, frantically looking for an exit. "If I let you do that, you will leave us alone?"

Hase's cheeks and lips were enough to tell Silver that the pot headed girl was disappointed. "I thought you wanted to keep me around, to hate me, to laugh at me. But yes, if you let me have your copy, I'd simply go home with it. And I'll send you treasures with the patterns you inspired, if you'd like that."

Quietly, slowly, as to not startle Hase into excitement again, Silver shifted to sit cross-legged. "Do send them, then. You are going to be rich, right? Why not us, too?" Silver's eyes turned calculating, momentarily forgetting her fear.

Hase grinned wide again. Behind them Gold started to sob. "Sister, no! What if she's lying about not hurting you?"

"I am *not!*" Hase whipped her large head back, wobbling slightly, making Gold jump. "It's just like…drawing a picture of her! Surely you've been drawn a portrait before? A beautiful person like you? Did it hurt you, ever?"

"N-no, but…"

"I'm all right," Silver said. "She looks much more interested in being hurt, rather than hurting people, anyway."

Hase nodded eagerly.

Silver said, "All the beautiful things sent from her are mine, then."

Hase slowly lifted the helmet, the mirror in front of her eyes.

Gold couldn't see what her sister-in-law saw, but she saw Silver's incomprehension as she took in whatever lay beyond the girl's helmet, and began to scream. Silver screamed on, and on, until she lost all her breath, until her throat started to bleed.

Until her sanity was lost.

Apathy seized Sai after Pot Head disappeared, people concluded. As for the two young wives, no one could determine what caused their sad turn of situation. The older one kept her eyes open unseeing, her lips slightly parted but always unspeaking—and when she saw something beautiful, anything remotely beautiful, she'd start to scream anew. The family decided to keep her in a white-walled room with plain white doors, where she was always dressed in coarse linen robes without design, color, or pattern. The younger wife fared a little better than her sister-in-law, but not by much. She wouldn't leave Silver's side, sometimes crying loudly like a small girl, sometimes giggling hysterically, especially when anyone ever tried to detach her from her sister. But she took care of Silver and of herself without problem, so people decided to keep her in the white room, too.

People laughed at Sai and despised him for his laziness. They treated the women as if they didn't exist, and the first and the second brothers of the house remarried. The white room became a small fish bone stuck in the household's throat; it hurts and you want to get rid of it, but it might hurt even worse if you try to force it out.

There are things people don't forget. Things like the way the people of the house mistreated the strange woman from the Island with her heavy, potted head. Things like how, eventually, the hired woman disappeared, and all those close to her were driven to madness. No one wanted to go near the family after that.

Slowly, the once prosperous house decayed.

It happened on a crisp autumn day, the clouds high, the air thin, the cold enfolding the quiet, decaying house. It arrived, alone, bearing nothing. It walked through the people who gazed, who gaped. Without searching or asking or even hesitating, it walked into the house, toward the white room. And it opened the white doors.

It was a child.

Its hair was indigo, its eyes the color of young leaves. Its face—every surface of its skin—bore intricate patterns, woven with silver, gold, and every shade of indigo. It was a thing of beauty framed in the whiteness of the room.

No one had to ask; the two women recognized it as soon as they saw it. It was Hase's creation.

"I have come, to be yours," the child said.

The women started to scream.

# The Farm

## Elana Gomel

*Elana Gomel lives in Tel Aviv and is the author of six academic books and multiple fantasy stories that have appeared in* New Horizons, People of the Book, *and elsewhere. Her fantasy novel,* A Tale of Three Cities, *was published in 2013.*

WHEN HE SAW the cherry blossoms, he reached for his gun.

The wind threw a handful of pink petals into his face. He rubbed them away but they stuck to his kinky hair. His leather jacket was so worn that some patches became fuzzy and these, too, accumulated pink ornaments. It looked as if his red-star badge was spawning.

The farm lay below him, in the hollow between the hills. Everything about it was tidy: the whitewashed main house with the tiled roof, the sturdy barns, and the clean-swept yard, empty in the predawn light. Beyond it, the fields were shadowy with a heavy harvest. And the cherry trees cradling the hollow, the treacherous trees with their unseasonable blossoms.

His horse shied and trembled, and he struggled to keep it calm. He was not good with animals. The milky smell of cattle wafting from the barn doors made him want to puke. He was a town boy, wary and contemptuous of the countryside. It was in cities that the new world would be born. But now he had learned the hard lesson of hunger: if the battle for food is lost, all the other battles don't count. The Eaters had taught him the value of the land.

His stomach rumbled. He thought of tightening his belt but there was no time to drill an additional hole, even though his khaki trousers threatened to slide down his skinny hips.

An indistinct figure separated itself from the shadows at the main house's porch and ran up the dandelion-fringed path toward him. He waited, trying to calm the horse, to calm himself, and failing at both.

The figure was small and slight, nimbly scurrying up the slope.

His finger caressed the trigger of his Mauser.

It looked like a girl.

He fired.

The heavy bullet slummed into the girl and made her stumble backwards, almost lifting her off the path. The second shot spun her like a dreidel. And then she flopped down and was still, a rivulet of blood snaking away from the crumpled heap of embroidered clothes and tangled braids.

Yakov cursed himself in the coarse words he had learned from his peasant comrades-in-arms and tried to use frequently. His fear got the better of him. He did not come here to shoot Eaters: they bred faster than bullets could fly. He came for victory.

The horse neighed and pranced, foam dropping from its nostrils. It was not a trained cavalry steed—most of those had been eaten. It was a scraggy yearling, unused to the sight of blood.

Blood?

Yakov's frown deepened as he looked down at the prostrate body. The girl's embroidered shirt was stained the colour of his badge. This was unexpected. In his previous encounters with the Enemy he had seen all kinds of unclean ichor, but never this bright, honest red.

He dismounted and the horse bolted. It did not matter; whether successful or not, he would not need it to retreat. Retreat was not an option.

He bent over the girl, who seemed to challenge him with her glazed eyes and slackened features. The shot had gone through her heart, killing her instantly, which was not supposed to happen. And yet here she was, dead. He had seen enough corpses on various battlefields to be an expert on mortality. But these had been *human* corpses...

Could he have made a mistake? He had heard rumours about a new strategy whereby the Enemy tried stealth and sabotage, seducing those who could not stand the hunger away from their communities with promises of bread. Of course, one would need to be half-witted to succumb to the blandishments of the Eaters, but Yakov had no illusions about the intelligence of his cadres.

Small but buxom, she lay on her back, spread-eagled like a starfish: in addition to her flung-out arms, her ribbon-tied braids also fanned out on both sides of her body. They were very long, probably falling down to her knees when she stood up. Peasants went into raptures over these ropes of hair that unmarried girls wound around their heads and decorated with paper flowers. Yakov found them repellent, redolent of lice and sweat. He kept his tastes to himself, vaguely ashamed of his fastidiousness. On the other hand, the fact that he did not share their appetites made shooting rapists, looters, and drinkers so much easier.

Not that it mattered nowadays. Hunger tended to obviate other needs

Her face was in keeping with her folk-song image: a rosebud mouth, silky black eyebrows under the sallow forehead, brown-nut eyes, now staring emptily at her killer.

She looked entirely human.

So he had killed a peasant girl. She was probably a collaborator, a servant of the Enemy. And yet it made him uneasy. He tried hard to avoid killing women and children unless it was absolutely necessary.

On the other hand, this mistake may have ultimately been to his advantage. He wanted to penetrate as far as possible into the nest before the commencement of his mission. Killing an Eater would bring the entire colony out in force. Killing a human probably would not.

He cast a wary glance at the farm. There was no movement there.

He sighed and looked at the girl again. If she had been from a poor family, she might have deserved life, after all.

"Forgive me, comrade," he said and started down the slope.

Something looped around his ankle and yanked him off his feet. He was thrown onto the dusty path and dragged back, kicking and flailing, toward the dead girl.

He expected her to stand up like the Vourdalak of old-wives' tales, but the body was as lifeless as before. The only part of her that was alive was her hair.

The braids slithered and coiled in the grass like the tentacles of a squid. One caught his ankle in a noose and was contracting, squeezing it in a vice until he felt the bone crack. Another stood up, a hairy serpent, and lashed him across the face with the force of a Cossack's whip. He tasted blood from his broken lip.

He reached for his Mauser but the vertical braid snatched it from his hand and tossed it into the bushes. He was dragged almost on top of the girl whose flaccid inertness contrasted horribly with the frantic activity of her braids that danced and swished through the air, coming down upon him like a cat-o'-nine-tails, pummelling and blinding. He tried to catch one of them, but it was like trying to hold onto greased lightning. Dripping with rancid hair-oil, they slipped through his fingers.

The second braid managed to wind itself around his throat and started squeezing. His vision dimmed with blue spots. The other braid crawled up his body, pinning him down.

'Shma...' something mysteriously whispered in his head, an echo of the discarded past.

With a superhuman effort he managed to loosen the coils around his body and release one arm. Instead of tugging futilely at the hairy noose, he reached down to his worn belt and pulled out his knife. He stabbed the braid but the knife went harmlessly through the plaited strands of hair. The pressure on his windpipe increased until he was about to pass out.

He stabbed again, desperately, and this time the sharp edge of the knife caught the soiled white ribbon that held the braid together and ripped through it. And the pressure relaxed.

Coughing and sputtering, Yakov shook off the loosening coils and jumped to his feet. One braid puddled in the grass, a puffy mass of hair; the other still twitched and flailed. He raised his knife and slashed through the second ribbon. It was gristly and tough, not like fabric at all.

The dead body shuddered and came undone.

First the hands broke away and skittered daintily on their fingertips into the undergrowth. Legs humped away like giant inchworms. The pale belly-beast hissed at him from its hairy mouth, its single eye blinking furiously, but hopped into the bushes when he raised his knife again. The head, its human features disappearing into undifferentiated, swelling flesh, rolled and bounced down the slope like a ball. The only things left were the empty blood-stained clothes and the braids that had fallen apart into hunks of lifeless honey-blonde hair, probably the remnant of some Eater meal.

Massaging his bruised throat, Yakov considered his options. One glance toward the farm showed it as peaceful and deserted as before.

A trap?

But how could they entrap a prey that *wanted* to be trapped?

He took a long, deep breath and walked down the path toward the farm compound.

*The smell of chicken bones in the pot, his mother, pale and scrawny and hugely pregnant, scurrying around to finish cooking before Shabbat... The sounds of a harsh jargon, forgotten but not forgiven, overlaid with the wailing of his baby brother...*

He was eight when he was taken by the authorities to the military school, a community tax in the shape of a frightened child. He was sixteen when the war made him a soldier instead of a sacrifice. He was nineteen when the Revolution washed away the stain of his origin. He was twenty-five when the Eaters came. A handful of red-coloured dates that defined his life.

Strangely, though, he was not thinking of the night when he first confronted the Enemy, an unheard-of menace that he, the only survivor, stumbled through the night to report to the incredulous headquarters. They did not believe him; he was almost executed for fear-mongering. The firing squad was only halted when other reports started pouring in. But he was the first, and it put him under a special obligation to the Revolution. He had been a passive witness to the beginning of the assault; he would be an active agent in trying to bring about its end.

But his perverse memory refused to focus on the struggle and instead brought up a mélange of counter-revolutionary dross.

*A woman lying in the congealing pool of blood, her belly slashed open by a bayonet...*

He had seen the aftermath of a pogrom in his shtetl. He did not look too closely at the faces of the dead. But there was little chance he would recognise anybody. By this time he had lost touch with his family. He believed they had moved away but did not know where. He did not care. He had never forgiven them for handing him over. The fact that they had no choice only enhanced his contempt for their cowardice.

*Fat moustachioed faces paling in fear when his squadron rode into town, their crude* muzhik *voices falling silent as he commanded that the perpetrators be brought to justice...*

There were no Jews in the eyes of the Revolution. There were only comrades and enemies.

And now there were also Eaters.

He stood in the middle of the courtyard, listening. The farm was eerily silent. Had they eaten the livestock already? This would be terrible: the nascent commune he was organizing in the nearby village depended on the spoils of this operation for its survival. The winter was coming and the grain and meat requisitions had to be filled. They would be, but unless he found stores here, there would be few people alive in the spring to keep the commune going and to send more food to the hungry city.

Finally he heard the moo of a cow coming from the barn and breathed a sigh of relief.

Still, there was no sign of life in the house. Its door was ajar, opening into the darkness of the hallway like a parted mouth.

Slowly, he inched toward the door. There was a strange smell wafting from the hallway: a thin, sour reek that reminded him of the moonshine his peasants were brewing out of rotten straw and composted leaves. He would have to shoot Ivan to stop this shocking waste of resources.

He sidled through the doorway. The interior was very dim as the carved shutters in the main room were closed, admitting only a scatter of dusty rays. He glimpsed the shining ranks of icons in the corner and the white cloth on the table.

There was a loaf of bread in the middle of the cloth.

His mouth flooded with saliva, and he was distantly surprised that there was enough moisture left in his wasted body. The sour reek had disappeared, overpowered by the yeasty aroma of freshly baked bread, as unmistakable and enticing as the scent of a woman. He moved toward the table, tugged on the leash of hunger. He could almost see the thick crust with its pale freckles of flour and taste the brown tang of the rye...

He stopped. He had not come here to eat.

He came to be eaten.

Yakov lifted his hand to his mouth and bit deeply, drawing blood. The pain and the salty burn on his tongue centred him. He turned away from the table and walked out of the living room, back into the hallway where other rooms of the house waited behind closed doors. The short distance he traversed from the table to the hallway felt like the longest walk of his life.

*Abe gezunt!*

His mother's reedy voice, shrilling this incomprehensible phrase every time a new disaster fell upon the shtetl with the inevitability of bad weather. He had forgotten what it meant, had forgotten the language of his infancy altogether, deliberately expunged it from his memory. But sometimes falling asleep in the cold mud of the trenches, he would hear it again: as annoying and compelling as the buzz of a mosquito.

The military campaigns were also receding into the past. The civil war, with its familiar enemies, appeared in retrospect to have been a mere light rehearsal for the war with the Eaters. What were those haughty landlords, perfidious capitalists, and rapacious kulaks compared to the nauseating evil of the Enemy? Mere humans, easily comprehended and handily killed. It afforded him grim amusement to think about all the propaganda clichés he had once come up with to motivate his troops. The opposition were bloodsuckers, cannibals, shape-shifters, beasts in men's clothing. Strange how these inflated metaphors were sober truths when applied to the Eaters!

*Abe gezunt!*

He shook his head, trying to get rid of the almost-audible voice. He had to focus on the task at hand. And the task was becoming more puzzling by the minute.

The farm was empty. He had searched the main house. It must have belonged to a kulak, a prosperous peasant whose fate had been sealed long before the Eaters appeared. Whether serving as their meal was preferable to starving in exile was something Yakov did not speculate upon.

The new masters had not made many changes in the house and this was puzzling, too. Previously, in clearing out Eater nests, Yakov and his soldiers had encountered living nightmares: granaries filled with bloody gnawed heads, children's limbs on chopping blocks, rats the size of a sheep dog. But this house was unnaturally clean— cleaner than most poor peasants' hovels, truth be told—and silent. The beds were made with fresh linen, there was water in a wash- bucket, and the wooden floors were scrubbed. The large stove was empty and cold: in the human lands, the winter was coming, but here the summer was lingering still. It was not only the blooming cherries and yellow dandelions that defied human seasons: Yakov was beginning to sweat in the still, warm air of the hollow. He did not think to take off his leather jacket, however. It was the uniform of the Revolution, and he would not part with it until his service to the Revolution was done. Then he would be dead and he did not care how he was buried.

He then went out to the barns and stood, gawking, as the sleek, well-fed cows mooed in their stalls and clacking chickens scrabbled in the yard. The animals were clearly being taken care of, so the farm could not be abandoned. But perhaps the creature he had killed had in fact been its only inhabitant. This seemed impossible, considering the giant swarms that had attacked them in previous battles. But the more he thought about it, the more the idea appeared plausible.

The Eaters were natural entities. He had ruthlessly squashed the superstitious talk among his soldiers, some of whom, still infected with the religious bacillus, whispered tall tales of demons and fiends. In fact, he had to execute one particularly devout muzhik who was a corrupting influence both on his comrades and on the commune members. Yakov, immune to the peasants' religion and oblivious of his own, had no doubt that the Eaters had come from another planet rather than from hell. He had read Alexander Bogdanov's magnificent *Red Star*, in which the Revolution reached Mars, and was moved to tears; so much so that he procured a novel by a pro- gressive Englishman in which Martians came to Earth. He had been disappointed by the Englishman's war-mongering but in retrospect he had to concede that the writer had a point. The aliens came and they were neither socialist nor peaceful.

Inspired by the novels, he had started a surreptitious study of the Enemy. That was not encouraged by headquarters, who tended to remain silent about the exact nature of the Enemy or resort to recycled propaganda clichés. But the food situation being what it was, anything that could conceivably increase procurements had to be attempted. Ultimately, his supreme task was to keep the requisitions going and—of secondary importance—keep his commune alive. And knowing the true nature of the Eaters was instrumental to both ends.

He had come to the conclusion that their many different forms were not independent creatures but something like the parts of a single body capable of acting at a distance from the central core.

But perhaps not all Eaters were parts of a single organism. Perhaps separate swarms of them constituted individual entities, much like his unit sometimes felt like an extension of his own body. If that was true, such entities had to reproduce, to bear young, as was in the nature of life everywhere. The pseudo-girl he had killed was a colony of parts. He shuddered remembering her tentacle braids, her skittering hands, and her rolling head. But she was much more closely integrated than any Eater he had seen. Didn't it follow that she was an immature version of a swarm, growing in the seclusion and plenty of the farm until she was big enough to disassemble into her component monsters and send them off to pillage and devastate the neighbouring communes? If so, the sleek appearance of the farm animals and the cared-for condition of the farm were no mystery.

He went back to the main house and sat at the table. His injuries were beginning to smart. He felt tired and strangely disappointed that his sacrifice was not needed. He had steeled himself for the mission for over a month, seeing that the commune was about to fail, telling himself that he could not allow his life's work to have been in vain. He would have much preferred to stay in the city rather than mingle again with the peasants…

…*who had killed his family?*

He had no family any more and needed none. His cadres were his children. If he had to die for them, for the Revolution, so be it.

But now, it seemed, he did not need to die at all. He could walk back to the commune—a longish walk since his horse was gone—convene the committee, order them to organise a search party that would take over this farm and move the animals into the communal barns

*...hope they won't slaughter them to fill their bellies...*

Collect whatever grain was there to fill the procurement quota for the city and hope that something was left over for the winter.

It reminded him how hungry he was. Surely there was no harm in eating a little now. He lifted the loaf from the table and twisted it to break off a chunk.

"Don't," said the loaf.

He dropped it, jumping to his feet. The loaf ended on the floor with the round side up. The crack he had made in the crust formed a long misshapen mouth that lengthened as it spoke.

"You..." he whispered stupidly.

He looked around. In the deepening dusk the room was filled with shadows that moved and whispered to each other. He wondered how blind he had been to think that the farm was empty.

The haloed saints on the icons leaned forward, staring at him intently. The pots on the shelves smacked their glazed lips. The white curtain flowed down to the floor in a waterfall of putrefying flesh. The ceiling joists blinked with a multitude of rivet eyes. A post rippled as it adjusted its stance.

The Eaters looked at him and he looked back.

"Go ahead!" he cried, his voice shriller than he intended. "Eat me! Bloodsuckers! Parasites! I am not afraid of you!"

And indeed he was not.

It had been a gradual realisation: from the paralysing fear that gripped even the most seasoned fighters as they confronted the alien menace; to the survivor's guilt that his soldiers died all around him and he remained unscathed; to the growing conviction.

Eaters would not touch him. He was immune.

He did not know whether there were others like him and he did not care. He was only a spark in the cleansing flame of the Revolution and it was his duty to burn whatever thorns came his way. He had been sent to this starving, dim-witted countryside, to make the best of the coarse muzhiks who were under his command, and he would do so. When he had realised that the commune was failing, that the procurement quotas were not going to be filled, he knew he had to do something drastic. If the requisitions were not met, he was a dead man walking in any case.

If, for whatever reason, the Eaters were afraid of him, he would turn it to his advantage. He remembered that in the progressive Englishman's novel, the aliens succumbed to earthly microbes. Perhaps he was a carrier of some hitherto unknown disease that would infect and destroy the invaders. And if they refused the bait, if they ran away from him, well, then he would requisition the farm and carry on his Revolution-given task.

But this was not as he expected it to happen.

The entire farm was swarming with Eaters, perhaps the entire farm *was* Eaters, and they did not run away from him. The pseudo-girl had attacked him: the first time he was the target of alien aggression. He was not untouchable, after all.

But they were not attacking now. He felt himself to be in the crossfire of innumerable eyes but nothing moved.

"Why me?" he asked finally.

It was the post that answered, sprouting a notched mouth.

"You were the first. You gave us form."

He shook his head.

"I don't understand."

"We are the enemies you wanted."

He remembered the night of their coming.

*A fire blazing in the night, a smell of blood and unwashed feet. His own voice, hoarse but full of conviction:*

*"Kulaks, rich peasants are your enemies, enemies of the people… Bloodsuckers, shape-shifters, cannibals. They devour your land, your crops, your family…"*

*The fire in the dark, the fire of belief in his rag-tag soldiers' eyes. And then a mocking peasant voice:*

*"Dirty Yid!"*

*His hand on the Mauser. Refusing to draw, forcing himself to remember that it is not their fault: they are just ignorant, backward muzhiks. They are not the enemy.*

*A cry in the night. Heads turning, hands grasping their worn rifles.*

*A line of otherworldly shapes shambling toward the encampment, their distortions not the fault of the dancing shadows.*

*A creature whose head is a giant clenched fist, the fingers parting to reveal a fang-studded maw.*

*An impossibly obese waddling sack of flesh, two slobbering nostrils gaping at the centre of his belly, his arms wickedly sharp sickles.*

*A crafty insect-like monster, half haughty man, half praying mantis,*

*clicking the serrated blades of his upper limbs.*
The Eaters.

"Me?" he whispered incredulously.

"Your hatred. We needed a shape to feed. You gave us one."

"Why me?"

"You were the first."

Did they come in an artillery shell fired from a distant planet as in the Englishman's novel? Did they stumble upon his encampment as he was giving his nightly political talk to his dispirited troops? Did they zoom in on the bright beacon of his pure hatred, his uncompromising devotion?

And had they been leaving him alone out of some alien gratitude? Or was it because they still needed the energy of his belief?

But now they were turning against him, beginning to attack… Was his faith in the Revolution waning? No, it couldn't be!

"There are others," said an icon. "Haters like you, believers like you."

"You don't need me anymore."

"There are others," said the loaf of bread. "We will feed."

And as they advanced toward him, he saw, beyond the ranks of household objects, a human-shaped Eater enter the room and stand on the threshold. The new enemy, the new monster.

He gazed on his own face as long as he had eyes, which was not very long.

# The Last Hours of the Final Days

## Bernardo Fernández (Bef)

### Translated by the author

*Mexican author Bef has published three science fiction novels, as well as a series of crime novels. He has also published graphic novels. His short fiction has been published in* Mexico City Noir, Three Messages, *and* Warning: Contemporary Mexican Short Stories, *and he is a winner of Spain's Ingnotus Prize.*

OUR BIKE RAN out of gasoline as soon as we crossed the intersection of Reforma and Bucareli. The bike coughed to death. Just like that. Cursing, Wok tried to start it again; he kicked it furiously, refusing to accept that the ride was over.

"What's so funny, bitch?" he asked, half angry, half amused. "Stupid Aída!" I'm always laughing.

We left the bike beside Sebastián's Caballito. The huge sculpture used to be a brilliant yellow monument; now it's a rusty wreck blocking Reforma, as are most of the other statues that we've been playing dodge'em with since we found the bike.

Silently, Wok climbed the sculpture's carcass. From the top, he scanned the horizon in search of a vehicle we could steal. Or at least milk some gasoline from.

"Nada," he mumbled from his watchtower.

We could hear a few distant explosions.

"Let's walk, baby," he said, as soon as he got down.

Our skateboards hung from straps on our backpacks. Inside the packs we had everything we had left from before the collapse. It was not much, and it wasn't heavy, but we were going to miss that bike.

We still had a couple hours of light left, and we looked for a building that wasn't too badly damaged. The best ones were already occupied, but finally we found a hotel that seemed safe.

Inside, it was a disaster. The rugs and wallpaper were ripped up, but I couldn't tell if it was from looters or just aimless vandals. As usual, none of the intruders had even bothered to go up to the second floor. Lazy bums. Wok and I kept quiet, in case there was someone else inside, but as it turned out, the building was empty.

On the upper floors, the guest rooms were untouched.

"Weird," said Wok.

We chose a room that overlooked Reforma Avenue. It was already night. Everything was dark: you couldn't even see the bonfires that sometimes flickered in the buildings.

We felt very lonely.

I discovered that the shower had hot running water. Without hesitating, I undressed and took a shower. It had been a long time since I had had such a luxury. Wok joined me shortly after, but not before blocking the door. I was rubbing his tattooed back while he played with my nipple piercings. We thought we might run out of water, but didn't. It was still flowing when he ejaculated between my soapy hands.

"I don't get it," he said, while we were using the towels we found. "Everything here is so...fine."

I laughed. "You're being paranoid, you silly boy. Just enjoy it."

"It's just not normal. If I had been here from the beginning, I would never leave. I'd defend it."

"Maybe they got tired of waiting for the big one."

Wok didn't reply. We stared into the darkness beyond our window, looking out over Reforma Avenue. We fell asleep shortly after.

I was woken by Wok's weeping. He twisted among the sheets, the first clean ones we've slept on in weeks. His dreams were unpleasant, as usual. Finally he rose screaming. He was soaked in his sweat.

"Easy. Everything's okay," I said.

"It's...the nightmare. The fucking nightmare."

"Thought so."

He hugged me tightly, mumbling something I couldn't understand.

"What?"

"The big one. It's coming. I can feel it."

I laughed.

"Not funny, Aída. It's the fucking end. The world is over."

I laughed again. I said, "It's been over for months now. And nothing happens. There's no reason for anything to happen right now."

The Nightmare was a collective dream that haunted little children when it all began. They said they could feel the pain of millions dying. Later it was dreamed by more people: teenagers, elders. Soon it became one more of the signals of doom. I never dreamt it. I don't remember my dreams.

I hugged Wok, and held him in my arms. Soon, he fell back to sleep.

We were woken by the thundering march of a procession northbound on Reforma. I guessed they were headed for the hill of Tepeyac: after the news broke about the meteorite, the Basilica of the Virgin of Guadalupe became the obligatory destination for the thousands of desperate religious sects that had emerged.

Careful not to be seen, we watched them through the window as they marched by. There were thousands, all of them suffering from the long journey on foot. I felt sorry for them. Wok stared at them in silence.

At the front of the procession, their prophet was sitting on a throne that was carried by four men, addressing the people through a loudspeaker he had salvaged from the trash. I recognized him at once: he was Rodrigo D'Alba, a former TV host. He now wore a tunic and had grown out his hair and beard, but there was no doubt it was him.

"Another one who has resolved his life," said Wok, softly. Many celebrities, actors, and singers had created sects like this.

When the last of the caravan had disappeared, Wok rose to say:

"Well, let's go find something to eat."

We discovered that the hotel had a very well-stocked kitchen, which just made Wok more paranoid ("Everything here is too good, too damn good, fuck it," he repeated like a mantra). Me, I just got hungry. In the end, he cooked some shrimp egg foo-yung. Wok's half-Chinese, and he's a fine cook if he has the right ingredients.

We ate in silence; he was afraid that the smell of food would attract some punk. We were starving. When we were done, we left the place to retrieve the bike. Whatever was left of it.

It was really quiet outside; you couldn't hear any more explosions. Everyone thought that the abandoned city would become a bloody battlefield. But the reality was worse. Nowadays, it seemed that everybody was successfully avoiding everyone else.

The bike was gone. Some scavengers must have picked it up during the night. It was nice while it lasted.

Wok raised his eyes to the sky. High above, the meteorite looked like a brilliant dot, just the size of a pixel. Nobody would ever imagine that it was going to destroy our planet.

"Do you think that the big one is going to be a lot longer?"

"Don't know. We should be dead by now."

"How can you tell?"

I unzipped my backpack to show him my quartz clock. I had it from before the world collapsed. Thanks to it, I hadn't lost the notion of time, as almost everyone else had. With a little luck, the batteries would last till the impact. Maybe a little longer.

"It should have happened already," I told him. "Something went wrong. We've been living on borrowed time for two weeks now."

Wok didn't reply. We left the spot.

We came upon a man at the bus stop on Reforma Avenue. He wore a suit and seemed to be unarmed, but you never know. Wok palmed his switchblade, and I took out my nunchucks. We got closer.

"Hi, there," greeted Wok.

"Good afternoon," replied the guy. He was an old man.

His clothes were worn but clean. His shirt was perfectly ironed and his tie neatly knotted.

"Waiting for someone?" I asked, just to break the silence.

"No, miss. It seems that my bus has been delayed."

Wok laughed. For the very first time in a long time, the situation didn't strike me as funny.

"Are you nuts? There hasn't been a bus by here in months. It's not going to happen."

The man looked at my boyfriend with total seriousness.

"Young man, that's no excuse."

"No excuse?…For what?" I asked.

"Not to go to work, of course."

We were silent. The man looked at us as if *we* were the loonies.

"Sir, the world is coming to an end…"

"Look, young man, this is a country of institutions. If my bus doesn't come along in five minutes, I'm walking to my office, as usual. Period. We are not going to let things like this defeat us. We, the Mexican people, are bigger than any misfortune. We survived the earthquake in 1985.

I didn't know what to say. The smile had faded from Wok's face.

All we could do was to wait there with the man.

Five minutes, waiting for a bus that would never come.

"Well, I can't wait any longer. I'll walk. Pleased to meet you."

Puzzled, we watched him walk away, until he almost disappeared among the rubble on his way to the Centro. For a second it seemed to us that he disappeared into thin air, just like a ghost. Anyway, we've seen weirder things all these months.

Without a word, we started to walk north, away from the Centro.

In the sky, the meteorite had grown. Now it seemed bigger than the sun.

We decided to skate. We tried not to do it very often, to save the wheels, but we lost our bike, and it didn't seem like we'd find anything similar. It made sense to skate.

Silence was almost deafening. We skated for a long time without talking. Only sound we heard seemed to be that of our boards. As we skated, the ruined buildings and heaps of rubble seemed to repeat, over and over, like the background in an old Scooby-Doo cartoon.

After a long time we reached the woods of Chapultepec Park, or what was left of them—just a few hollow logs. We passed by one of the few statues still standing. It was covered with graffiti.

"Wait a minute," said Wok. We stopped.

"A national hero," I said.

"Not this one. He was a presidential candidate, but he got shot."

"Isn't that good enough?"

"Guess so. No better president than a dead one. He was the best of this country."

We laughed. Wok took his last can of spray paint out of his backpack. He shook it up and wrote on the pedestal THIS COULD BE HEAVEN OR THIS COULD BE HELL.

"Why that?" I asked.

"Just felt like it," he replied.

We kept walking.

"Funny thing," I said after a while.

"What?"

"The future always seems better when it doesn't happen. Like that guy, who got a statue for something he never got to be."

"Any future is better than ours. And yes, it will happen."

He meant the meteorite.

"Of course not. Wouldn't you rather grow up, go bald, and turn into an old fart telling the kids the music of your time was better?"

"I'd never do that!"

"Sure you would. Everyone does. Take my parents, for instance. They were punk rockers. Look at how they ended up: desperate, joining Vicente Vargas's quest for the promised land of Aztlán. Vargas wasn't even a rocker, he sang ranchero"

Wok said nothing.

"Don't just live through your own destruction. Enjoy it!" I turned back to continue skating. Wok stayed there for a minute, thinking. Then he caught up with me.

"Bitch. You're always right."

Life's not as cruel as Wok says. Can't be. It isn't a raw onion, and it isn't a bowl of cherries. It's bittersweet, like love.

Sweet as loving, bitter as pain.

But sometimes there are surprises. Right there, just around the corner, waiting to leap out at you, saying "Hey there! At last, here's a surprise for you. A *nice* one."

That's what finding the car was like. An electric car, one of those luxury supercompacts, waiting for us right next to the Oil Workers Monument, as if we'd rented it over the phone. A silver Matsui. This year's.

Of course, at first Wok thought it was a trap. He wouldn't even go up to it. We hung back a long time, waiting for something to happen, something awful.

Nothing happened.

Tired of waiting, I sneaked into the car.

"Aída!" he yelled, frightened.

I don't know what fear is anymore. What I've seen has worn out that word. When the world collapses, there's no place left for fear.

There were dried bloodstains inside the car. There had been a fight, and the Matsui's driver had lost. Maybe he was some rich guy who had hidden in a bunker in his Las Lomas mansion.

Maybe he ran out of water or food. Maybe, one night, he tried to get out of the city. Bad idea. A hungry pack of cannibals must have blocked his way, folks who weren't interested in cars. It's a shame about the guy, but I'm sure he fed a few nomad kids.

When he saw it was not a trap, Wok came over and got into the car. He started the engine.

"They left the lights on. Battery must be almost gone."

"It sure beats skating," I said while kissing his cheek.

We got out of there. I've never ridden in a luxury car before.

We had fun for a few minutes, dodging debris on the freeway, but then the battery died, just as we reached the northern suburbs. Wok got it started again without stopping, but as soon as we reached the Satélite Towers, not far from there, the engine shut down for good.

We left the car right there where it stopped. We got out, holding hands and laughing like children, and got away from there fast.

The scavengers would thank us.

We spent the rest of the afternoon the way we spent the rest of every afternoon since everything went to hell: looking for something we were not going to find, since we didn't know what it was.

We really wanted to skate in the ruins of the Plaza Satélite mall. It's so huge. The floor was smooth, and there were no nomads camping in the Liverpool store anymore. We decided to spend the night in its furniture department, even though I would have preferred the previous night's hotel.

"There's no going back," said Wok. "For us there are no yesterdays or ways back."

I felt an unexplainable sorrow. I couldn't find any more reasons to laugh. My happiness dried as my eyes watered, but I decided to drown my sadness with the very last laugh I had. With my last reserves of happiness.

We were still skating when it got dark. Without warning, I felt an icy chill shoot down my spine. I stopped short.

"What's the matter?" asked Wok, frightened.

"I can feel it," I said. He could feel the anguish in my voice.

"What is it? What do you feel?"

There it was, clear and loud, no doubt left: the chill was slowly crawling up to my neck.

"Aída! What are you feeling? You're scaring me!"

I turned to him. A tear came down my cheek. I thought I had forgotten how to cry.

"I feel…the pain of millions of people about to die."

The first shock came in the middle of the night. We ran out into the parking lot, barely in time to grab our stuff. The mall collapsed among screeching metal and crumbling concrete.

I've never seen an elephant die, but I guess it must be something similar.

A hard wind was blowing. It blew away the dust in just a few minutes.

We stood, uneasy, in the empty parking lot. There seemed to be no one around for kilometers. We could hear only the wind's howl, as it tried to drown the silence. Without a word, we lay down on the floor.

"Did your parents know each other in 1985, when the earthquake hit?" asked Wok.

"Course not," I replied. "You already know that."

"Uh."

"Mom was seven in 1985. Dad was thirteen," I added, in the dark.

Wok replied with a groan.

"I'm scared," he whispered in my ear.

It seemed as if the ground was slowly sinking.

"So this is the end of the world," I said with a sigh.

A glowing rock crossed the sky. It was a fireball the size of an orange, and it fell to earth several kilometers away.

"It's better to burn out than to fade away," he whispered.

"That's a quote from an old movie."

"Thought it was a song. Dad mumbled it every Sunday, drinking beer in front of the TV."

"My parents used to say it, too. Where are they now?"

"Praying, for sure," said Wok.

We laughed.

"I have a surprise for you," I said. I groped for it in my backpack. It was hard to find without a lamp, but finally I got it and gave it to him.

"Some shades?"

"They're Ray-Bans," I said, putting on mine. "You always wanted a pair. I found them in that first Sanborn's store we slept at."

"You've been carrying them around since then?"

"I knew we'd need them. Don't forget that I wanted to be an astronomer. I was already accepted into college—in physics."

There was a new quake.

"I dropped out of school," he was suddenly gloomy.

"It doesn't matter. You're only nineteen."

"Not a day older," he replied, as the sky lit up again. He looked gorgeous in the shades. He kissed me.

"I love you." I managed to whisper it, then the roar of the earthquake drowned me out.


Our bike ran out of gasoline as soon as we crossed the intersection of Reforma and Bucareli. The bike coughed to death. Just like that. Cursing, Wok tried to start it again; he kicked it furiously, refusing to accept that the ride was over.

"What's so funny, bitch?" he asked, half angry, half amused.

"Stupid Aída!" I'm always laughing.

But suddenly, I stopped. It was so unexpected that Wok stared at me in surprise. "Hey, what's the matter?"

"I…it's just…"

"What?"

"The end of the world doesn't seem funny anymore."

We stood there, beside the yellow wreck of El Caballito. Only sound we could hear was the wind blowing the debris.

"Come on, baby," he said, hugging me, "It's been your laughter that keeps me going on."

In silence, we walked down Reforma Avenue.

"So…this is the end of it all," said Wok to break the silence.

I started laughing again.

"You see? That's my babe," said Wok.

"Been there, done that," I said.

He held my hand. We kept walking.

In the distance, an old man seemed to be waiting for a bus.

# The Boy Who Cast No Shadow

## Thomas Olde Heuvelt

### Translated by Laura Vroomen

*Dutch novelist Thomas Olde Heuvelt is the author of five novels and many short stories that have been published in English, Dutch, and Chinese, among other languages. He has won the Paul Harland Prize three times and was nominated for both the Hugo and the World Fantasy Award. Olde Heuvelt's horror novel* HEX *will be published in the UK and US/Canada in 2016, with a TV series currently in development based on the book. The following story was nominated for a Hugo Award for Best Novelette in 2013.*

MY NAME IS Look. You've probably heard about me in the papers or on TV. I'm the boy without a shadow. You can shine spotlights at me all you like, but it won't do you any good. Physicists say I'm an evolutionary miracle. The Americans said I was a secret weapon, by the Russians that is, because they figured Al-Qaeda would be too dumb. Christians say I'm divine. Mom calls me an angel, but of the earthly variety. But I'm not. I'm just Look. I wish I knew what that meant.

It's something to do with my genes, they say, but they don't know what. Molecular structures and the effects of light, blah-blah-blah. I don't give a shit, 'cause they can't fix it anyway. You won't find a shadow under my chin, armpits, or ribs, no matter how you illuminate me. They say it makes me look two-dimensional. I don't know what I look like because I have no reflection. My left hip bears a scar in the shape of a question mark. I got it when the midwife dropped me as she held me up in front of the mirror. Mom told me that only a floating umbilical cord was visible and that the midwife screamed, fleeing the room. The photos of the delivery showed a lot of *aaaw* and *coochie-coochie* but no baby. The only images ever captured of me are Mom's sonograms. They use sound, not light.

'You should be proud of your genes,' Mom and Dad always say. They're the founders of the Progressive Parish, a local political party that worships being different. Get-together: 'We just adopted a little Filipino.' 'No kidding! Our son is gay.' 'Really? Well, ours has no shadow.' Three-nil, nobody beats that. Mom does yoga and is Zen, and Dad would rather cook for the homeless than for us. Like a lot of bleeding hearts, their charity ends at home.

Until I was seven, they managed to keep me under wraps. But you don't have to be Einstein to figure it was bound to come out. One day two men in dark sunglasses snatched me from the classroom, bundled me into an armored car, and stuck a needle into my arm. When I woke up I found myself at an army base in the United States, where a team of scientists and agents spent four months examining me. The first three weeks I claimed I was from Mars and that my goal was complete world domination, then they got extremely rude and started threatening me. I lost it when I woke up one morning to find that they had sliced a piece of skin from my butt to grow a culture. I told them to go fuck themselves, but that same week I was told I was of no use to them and got reunited with my parents. To compensate for our inconvenience we were offered a feature in *National Geographic*. First my parents flipped and considered legal action, but when they discovered that the men who had kidnapped me were in fact *above* the law and that the following media hype was a goldmine for the Progressive Parish's coffers, they soon came round.

And me? I became a celebrity, thanks a bunch. On Oprah they wouldn't let me wear make-up 'cause they figured a floating, painted mask with no eyes or mouth would look too freaky on TV. Practical upshot: a completely invisible boy, which meant that everybody who wasn't actually in the studio just saw clothes moving and me picking up objects and standing behind an infrared machine to prove my existence. When Oprah asked how the scientists had treated me, I responded: 'I think the government has no right to experiment with my ass.' That cost them three million in hush money, and still the accusations of sexual abuse came pouring in. Suckers.

One-all, you'd think. Not by a long shot. In the years that followed, our front yard was overrun by camera crews eager to catch a glimpse of me. Which is technically impossible. Twelve circuses and twenty-three freak shows, including Ripley's, offered astronomic amounts to exhibit me. I've been called a Saint 268 times and have 29,000,000 hits on *Google*, as many as Brad Pitt. Cool, Mom and Dad, being different. Until it's you who's different. Everybody knows who I am. Everybody, except me.

Splinter once said your dreams make you who you are. But I don't dream. Loads of people say this, but I really don't dream. To tell the truth, I don't even know what dreams are. The countless EEGs that I've had show that my brain performs absolutely zilch activity during REM sleep. They never found a link with my condition, but duh. I suppose that's why I have no friends, no feelings, and no imagination. I lack a goal. I lack depth. Like I care.

I guess my only wish is to find my reflection. If I have no idea what my face looks like, how will I ever know who I am? And you know how saints and celebrities go. They get pinned on a cross, and while they watch the life seeping out people piss on their shadows.

The arrival of Splinter Rozenberg changed everything.

I was fourteen by then and living a relatively quiet life. The hype had died down, as hypes do. We had moved a couple of times within our shit-hole town, and in exchange for a statement that I had *not* been abused during my stay in the US, two men in dark sunglasses were stationed in front of our house for a year, removing pilgrims and other freaks from our front yard.

Obviously all this had an effect on my school rep. I've got no friends, and because I'm tall I have a lot of nerve where others don't. They avoid me, which is exactly how I like it. Sometimes I beat up someone, not because I like it, but I'm helping an image along. And come on, it's not all that obvious, unless I'm in front of the mirror. I wear long sleeves. Only my face is a dead give-away. With the sun on my right, I look luminous on the left. Mom tried to hide the effect with make-up, but then I look like a drag-queen, so I don't think so.

Even Jord Hendriks lets me off the hook, confining to trash

talk. On a good day I'm 'See-Thru'. On a bad day, it's 'Zero' or just 'Freak'. He says without a reflection I don't actually exist, except that my fuck-face hasn't figured that out yet.

He exaggerates if you ask me. If I'm supposed to believe the stories, I'm no oil painting, but it's not as bad as all that. Lots of artists, including my grandpa, have made impressions of what I look like. None of the drawings look alike, and none of them really suit me. The charcoal drawing on the cover of *People* I can't take seriously for starters, because it creates the illusion of shadow. Some show a boy with a broad, roughly hewn face. Mom says Grandpa's is the best likeness. But Grandpa also did a portrait of Mom that sort of makes her look like a man instead of a woman—so much for Mom's opinion.

Too bad that Jord Hendriks is such an incredible dick. The other kids are afraid of him. I think he's hot. I mean, just look at that body in the locker room before P.E., holy fuck!

Of course that's about the last thing you'd say to him if you know what's good for you. One disorder is more than enough, trust me. Mom and Dad would love it, and that's exactly why I won't tell them. They'd drag me to lunatic parades and conferences on tolerance by the Progressive Parish, and then the whole media circus would start all over again, so no. The Internet is no good either. It's easy to click *Yes, I am 18 or over*, but chat-rooms kick me out 'cause I'm supposedly too scared to show myself on webcam.

Oh, well. The thought of Jord Hendriks putting his mouth to better use and my right hand offer plenty of release for a healthy boy like me, exclamation mark smiley face.

Splinter was new in class, so I was old news. Thanks in part to his mom, Mrs. Rozenberg, who had made the unforgivable mistake of accompanying him to school the first day to explain all about his condition. I remember them standing there side by side, Mrs. Rozenberg like she was lecturing some rugrats and Splinter staring glassy-eyed into the room. Splinter always stared at things glassy-eyed. That's because his eyes were made of glass. As was the rest of his body. It's one of those funny little accidents you get in certain gene pools. Polished, he was a perfect mirror. He had some flexibility and was able to move his limbs, but slo-mo, like Neil Armstrong on the moon. Facial expressions were a different story.

Mrs. Rosenberg, all flesh and blood, told us to think of him as a china cabinet, which wasn't all that far from the truth. He wasn't allowed to play games during recess or P.E. A well-aimed football would surely kill him. Jack-assing was out of the question. When we heard an old bag like her say that, we screamed with laughter. Mrs. Rozenberg was delighted, thinking she was cool. Splinter knew he was doomed.

From day one Jord Hendriks and his friends put him under siege. Paperclips, coins, biro springs, and ballpoint pens were fired at him in a game of finding out which part of the body to aim for to get the opening notes of *Man in the Mirror*. 'You're a dick, okay?' Splinter said when the teacher had left the classroom. 'Will you please stop now? It's dangerous what you're doing.'

Whoops, that only made things worse. Splinter knew how fragile he was, and that paperclips and coins would probably cause no permanent damage. But accidents will happen and when Jord launched a biro that scratched his neck, he grassed on him.

Big whoops. Suspensions aren't forever. After some third-year kid acting on Jord's instructions concocted a story to lure the shop teacher out of the classroom, Jord took Splinter under his arm and put him on the workbench. Splinter screamed. Not with pain—he didn't have nerves—but to catch a teacher's attention. He didn't put up a struggle, because he knew that any wrong move would break him in two.

'I've always wanted to be a glassblower, shitbag,' Jord said, as he ignited the Bunsen burner. 'Mirror, mirror on the wall, who in the land will have the crookedest dick of 'em all?'

Three or four boys formed a cordon around them to keep the softies away. The rest of the class smirked or pretended not to notice. Me? I was glad it wasn't me lying there.

Jord stopped at Splinter's left pinky. He heated the tip and squeezed it with a pair of pliers, so Splinter would never need another spoon to stir his tea. Then one of Jord's mates sounded the alarm about Splinter having a welding accident and all that. Anyone who blabbed, we were told, would suffer the same fate, glass or no glass.

I was convinced that Jord wouldn't get away with this. But he did. Feel free to dismiss it as schoolyard law. We give each other hell and we cover each other's backs—a matter of self-preservation. Bubbles of deceit and lies will burst sooner or later. But that's too easy. Time has taught me that we live in a world full of Jord Hendrikses, a world that thrives on the destruction of its rare wonders and where people live under a blanket of smog, the stench of sameness.

Why did I feel attracted to Splinter?

He was the only person in my life who understood me. He was looking for a glimmer of happiness, which no-one was prepared to give him. And let's face it, how could he ever discover himself when all he saw in his skin was the outside world reflected?

'Dad says I should look for happiness within,' Splinter once said to me, during one of the many afternoons in his room. 'But then I'll never find it, unless I smash myself to pieces. A glass cousin of mine threw himself off the roof to see if it was true, but the chimney sweep didn't find anything of importance among the shards. So what am I supposed to do?'

'Well, you gotta break some eggs to make an omelette.' I grinned, but the joke failed to disguise the sadness in my voice.

Splinter felt attracted to me because I was the only one who actually saw *him* when I looked at him and not myself. One time Mrs. Rozenberg rushed in, right before she was due at a reception. She placed Splinter in front of her, squinted into his face, tousled her hair until she was happy, and ran out again. People always looked ugly at Splinter, 'cause people happen to find themselves ugly in the mirror. Splinter took that personally. With me, it wasn't there. If I looked ugly at him, he knew that I was in a rotten mood. If I laughed at him, he knew my laugh was meant for him.

During Splinter's first few months at school—between summer and Christmas—I hadn't exchanged more than five words with him; no more than with any other of my classmates to be precise. If I had to take a leak during recess, I would go to the Boys room in the old part of the school to avoid any smart-ass remarks or frightened freshman. Around here, there were only echoes in the hallway. To get there you had to cross the foyer by the assistant principal's office, where just before Christmas he had put up an enormous tree.

That day a voice made me jump: 'Err…could you give me a hand?' I looked around, didn't see a thing.

'Up here.'

Then I saw. It was Splinter. They'd stripped him to his boxers, sprayed him with red paint, and put him up in the tree amongst the other balls.

'Holy fuck,' I said. 'What happened to you?'

'Jord Hendriks,' he shrugged. Who else? 'Worst thing is that the assistant principal has already walked by three times without noticing me.'

I'd never really took much interest in Splinter, had always thought of him as a bit of a goofball. Now, semi-naked, I got my first proper look at him. His chest rose and fell smoothly with each breath. I'd never realized that he *could* breathe. I noticed the silver garland tied around his neck like a noose that would have strangled any other kid.

'Hey, aren't you the boy that has no shadow?' Splinter asked with that peculiar, crystal voice of his.

Lying, with all those Christmas lights, seemed pointless. 'Yup, hullo.'

'Cool! I saw that item on the Discovery Channel about you. I thought that theory about light-transmitting cells was totally awesome.'

I didn't say a word.

'You're famous, man. I mean, everybody's talking about you. You wanna come over to my place sometime? My dad's got an ultraviolet lamp. We could do experiments.'

So I did have feelings: I pitied him, for his naiveté. Splinter just stared at me with those sparkling eyes and said: 'Shit. You're even more of a fuckup than me.'

I looked at him dangling up in that tree and held my tongue.

'Look, I need to take a leak,' I said.

'Would you...would you mind helping me down?'

For a split second I hesitated, then grabbed a chair and pushed it toward the tree.

'Careful,' Splinter said, as I clambered up on the chair and pine-needles stuck in my arms. 'Drop me and I'm dead.'

He wrapped his arms around my neck. Although I should have been prepared, it still gave me goosebumps. The touch of something so far out, so alien, filled me with both revulsion and curiosity. He was unnaturally cold and didn't weigh a thing. I didn't even dare grab hold of him, scared he would crack. Splinter was sensitive about my reservations and said: 'That's it, I've got you. You can release me now.'

So I did, and even now I come back to that moment, how casually he trusted me with his life, and without all the psycho-babble I put it down to the fact that he had no choice. But in these few seconds it took me to lift him from the tree and put him on the ground a tremor went through his glass body that made me so acutely aware of the fragility of life that it rattled me big-time. That's when I understood just how precarious the things are that you take for granted. As soon as his feet touched the ground I got my hands off him as if I'd burned myself on a hot stove.

'Wow, thanks man,' he said and pulled the tinsel from his neck. 'If I'd still been up there after the bell, they'd have serenaded me with Christmas carols. You've spared me the humiliation.'

'Don't mention it,' I muttered, ill at ease. On a whim I added: 'Good luck.'

I was halfway down the corridor when I heard his xylophone footsteps coming after me. I turned around and saw Splinter, barefoot and with a bundle of clothes in his arms.

'I just wanted to say if there's anything I can do for you…I owe you one.'

'That's okay.' I pushed open the swing doors to the Boys room. Just in time I realized that I'd almost let them slam into his face. So I waited and held the doors for him. I did it grudgingly. The guy got under my skin. He'd touched a nerve with those glass fingers of his, which had upset the normal state of affairs. I didn't like it when the normal state of affairs got upset.

'Could you turn on the tap for me?' he asked with a twinkle. 'I can't put out any pressure with my hands.'

I did as he asked. Splinter began to wipe the red paint off his face with tissues. It sounded like rubbing your wet finger across a window. While I was washing my hands he looked curiously at the absence of my reflection in the mirror. I reckon he didn't know whether to comment. Finally he took the plunge and asked: 'How do you fix your hair?'

After a moment's hesitation I answered. 'My mother. And if you tell anyone I'll smash you with a baseball bat. There's a reason I keep it short. Normally I wear a beanie. But fucking rules in this school…'

'I hear you,' he said. 'Wanna hear something? My arms aren't flexible enough to reach everywhere. I'm fourteen for fuck's sake and my mom's still washing me.'

'Even your...'

He shrugged, looking embarrassed.

We stared at each other sheepishly and then burst out laughing. Right then we'd become friends. At our age you thought the depths of your own hell are the darkest; Splinter proved it could be worse. A little self-reflection ain't a bad thing. Splinter was all reflection. Seeing him wash his face in front of the mirror made my head spin. A mirror in a mirror in a mirror, an optical illusion of infinity. That's friendship. You give and you take, even if you have nothing to give.

We spent our time talking and watching TV in our rooms or fishing on the canal. In many ways Splinter and I were completely different. He had ideas, he had interests, he had dreams— everything I had not. His greatest interest was the sea and his greatest dream was to become a captain in the navy. That's how I got to know Splinter: unworldly, naïve, full of ideas and fantasies.

Sad thing was that we both knew his dreams would never come true. I often wondered how he could remain in such a positive attitude with his condition. Death was just a door away for a nine-pound boy made of mirrored glass. He was born a victim. 'And that was a Caesarean,' he told me. 'Imagine the bloodbath if there'd been contractions. I would have exploded in my mom's birth canal.'

He often speculated about his death, no matter how much it brought me down. 'It's a miracle that I've even made it this far,' he said. 'I mean, my cousin tripped on the doorstep when he was eleven and fell to pieces, and another was caught by the wind when she was four and splattered against a tree. I'm the longest-living mirror boy in the family. The chances of me graduating are slim to none.'

'No surprise, with your choice of friends,' I said. 'I heard that Jord's planning to dump you in the bottle bank.'

He gave me the glass finger and I pretended to whack him; you know how these things go.

Mr. and Mrs. Rozenberg were overly protective. They wouldn't allow Splinter to do anything besides reading and fishing. His mom made him go about in hand-knitted clothes: triple jumpers, beanies, scarves, mittens, anything soft. His dad insisted on taking him to school every morning, even after a sleepover at my place. It really bummed him out.

'It's okay, Dad, we can walk. The way Mom's wrapped me up I'd survive the Niagara Falls.'

But Mr. Rozenberg wouldn't budge. 'Far too dangerous,' he said. 'Especially with that road by the tennis courts. You know what happened to Uncle Henk.'

'I'm not allowed to do anything,' Splinter said when the car pulled up outside school, his shoulders hanging. 'And he's right, I *can't* do anything. A little arm wrestling will crush me. I'll never be able to join the navy.'

Jack-assing was out of the question, quoting Ms Rozenberg. I thought she spoiled the fun. I mean, Splinter wanted so much. Why deny such a one the rare moments that make life worth living?

So when I'd spent the afternoon racing along a country lane in a go-kart borrowed off our neighbors (they were on holiday and technically speaking hadn't given me permission, but not refused it either) and he timidly asked if he could have a go, I couldn't refuse. I ran home to fetch rope and cushions. I tied his hands to the wheel, his legs to the frame and his torso to the seat, so that he couldn't blow it and tumble out. Everywhere his body touched the kart I stuffed cushions.

Splinter stepped on it and off he went. His body jerked about like a dummy. For an instant I was afraid I'd made the biggest mistake of my life, that he'd be catapulted out of the kart and shatter into a million crystals. But it held. His screaming laughter rang out above the throbbing petrol engine and over the fields.

It was a moment I'll never forget. Splinter was ecstatic, and you know what? I got tears in my eyes. Call me a sissy, I don't give a fuck. For the first time in my life I felt something other than indifference going through my veins. It felt like I'd done something that mattered. I might not know what I looked like, but I'd given somebody a spark of happiness. Whenever I think back on Splinter, this is how I see him: tied up in his kart and covered in cushions, his face illuminated by a watery spring sun reflecting off the visor of his helmet. He was one of a kind, trust me. He even had it in him to blow up the sun.

Finally, he got back, and I was applauding like a madman. 'Wow, Schumacher! You were fucking faster than the speed of light, you freak!'

When I yanked the helmet off his head he threw me a dazed smile. 'That was by far the sickest thing I've ever done.'

'You did it!'

'Yeah, only it didn't go all right,' he said calmly.

'What's that, man, you—'

'Seriously. Have a look at my neck, something's not quite right.'

Suddenly I got scared. I did as he asked. Initially everything seemed fine; then I saw. Just above his collarbone and the neck of his T-shirt. A tiny star.

'Fuck.'

'It was a pebble, I think. I heard it bounce off.' He frowned and turned his head from left to right as if he'd pulled a muscle. Then we heard a crack. His eyes widened and my heart sank. The star had gotten bigger and small veins had appeared in the glass.

'Freeze,' I said as I began to untie the ropes with trembling hands. I choked back panic, cursing myself. What was I thinking? I should never have let him have a go on that thing. But Splinter disagreed and took my hand, forcing me to look him in the eyes. He wouldn't have missed it for the world, he said, and would be eternally grateful, no matter what.

I rushed him to the ER. The attending doctor didn't know glass, so after a phone call he summoned us to his car. I thought he was taking us to the Amphia hospital. Instead we pulled up in front of Auto Glass.

'Sweet Jesus on a stick,' the mechanic said at the sight of Splinter. 'We've had someone come in with a glass mannequin before, but they were turned away.'

The operation was done in no time, although I was shitting bricks as I watched the mechanic's rough hands seal the star-shaped crack. He polished Splinter's neck with something that sounded like a dentist's drill. The man did a first rate job: it didn't leave a trace. When the mechanic broached the issue of money, Splinter explained that he wasn't entitled to any healthcare insurance and that his parents would kill him if they found out what happened.

The mechanic shrugged and said: 'Oh, bloody hell.' In fact I believe he was genuinely touched. 'You spend your whole life waiting for a chance to resuscitate someone and save a life. And then you come along.'

'Don't even think about a heart massage,' Splinter said.

That evening we ate at my place. 'The two of you are having a little too much fun for my taste,' Mom said as she was serving dinner. Splinter and I looked at each other and bit our lips. He'd promised to carve me up if I told anyone where he'd been repaired; that indignity was just *too* great. We'd been plagued by erratic laughter all afternoon. My parents were cool with it, just glad that I wasn't a complete sociopath.

'Say, Splinter,' Dad said, 'what do you want to be when you grow up?'

'A mirror,' I said before Splinter had a chance to open his mouth.

'Look!' Mom said. 'You don't joke about that. You ought to know.'

'Oh, but he's right you know,' Splinter said innocently. 'Sounds cool to me, hanging in a department store, nicely framed. Any other job and I'll break anyway.'

I sang: 'Auto Glass repair, Auto Glass replace…'

We roared with laughter. Mom shook her head and said: 'Hopeless. Sometimes I just don't get the two of you.'

No, she didn't get the two of us. The reason is simple, and that's something that parents just don't understand. When Jord Hendriks & Co take the piss out of you, it's a drag. When the world treats you like a sickness, it's embarrassing. But when your parents treat you like you're made of glass, it leaves permanent damage. Splinter and I needed each other. We needed to take the piss out of each other, to have a good laugh at ourselves. If you weren't laughing, you'd be crying.

That spring Splinter got miserable. I don't know if the go-kart incident had anything to do with it or whether it was just puberty. The sudden change caught me off-guard. He'd always been upbeat. Overnight, his eyes glazed over. Sometimes I worried that he might follow in the footsteps of that cousin of his, the one who'd gone to look for happiness within.

'What's the point of it all?' he said, as we were lying by the canal; me with my hands locked behind my head, my elbows up in the air; he with his arms half-stretched alongside his body as he couldn't bend them any further. I knew what Splinter meant: everything. The murmuring water, the dragonflies, the brilliant sunshine. He meant life.

We'd played Ghost Ship for a while; me the ghost, he the ship. It was a game we'd sometimes do. Splinter would undress and lie down in the canal. In the reflecting water he was virtually invisible. I would stand beside an old fisherman who'd nodded off and stare into space. Splinter would then tug at the bait to wake him. First he would see his reflection in the water, then me, then *not* me in the water. He thought he was seeing a ghost. Next thing I would point like a zombie at the canal, as Splinter rose from the water and hauled himself ashore, groaning *The Grudge*-style.

The fishermen would always run off screaming. It's *the* way to get hold of rods or bait.

'My grandpa took me to the sea once,' Splinter said. 'My parents went nuts when they found out. I never stayed at grandpa's again. But you know, I had the time of my life. That's what they didn't get. We stayed until after sunset to see the sun sink into the sea. Did you know that the sun actually sinks into the sea? I'd kill to see that again.'

'Then I know where you ought to go,' I said. 'Mom and Dad sometimes rent this cottage in Portugal. There's no place where the sun sinks into the sea like over there.'

Splinter didn't say a thing; didn't have to. We were both thinking the same. He'd never get to see that sun and that sea. Sure, there was danger in any wobbly cobblestone, smashed tennis ball, or sweeping branch. But what about his parents? If you ask me, they were the biggest threat of all. The uneasy atmosphere was so strong you could taste it. You could hear the awkward silences. Mr. and Mrs. Rozenberg were blind to their son's dreams. In their efforts to protect him, they neglected his happiness. I understood they were afraid to say good-bye, but fearing his death they forgot to let him live.

That's when I got the idea.

'You wanna chase that sun?'

He sat up and looked at me. 'To…Portugal, you mean?'

I grinned. 'You and me, buddy.'

'My parents…'

'Fuck your parents. Wanna see that sun or what?'

'As in…running away?'

'Nah, we'll be back.'

His eyes began to shine. 'Can we go out to sea if we do?'

'Whatever you like, man. It's your party!'

Splinter laughed. 'Fuck. Let's do it.'

More was said, but that was the gist of it. I drew the plan: 'Tomorrow. Go to school, but skip class and wait behind the bike shed so your parents won't know you're gone until late afternoon. It will give us a head-start. Leave your books home and take some clothes. I'll take care of the rest.'

He held out his hand. I squeezed it and his knuckles clinked. The only thing that made my smile waver was the touch of his maimed teaspoon finger.


Jord Hendriks entered the Boys room just before the first period bell. The door to the rear cubicle was outside the range of the mirror where he began fixing his hair, and he didn't notice that it was ajar. I had taken off my t-shirt so my reflection wouldn't betray me and tiptoed up to him until I was close enough to smell his shampoo. Jord was bleating some rap crap, with no rhythm or melody, ruffling his hair. Without a moment's hesitation I grabbed his left pinky and planted my other hand firmly on his hip—just for fun.

Jord actually squealed; it was almost comical. He jerked and knocked the pot of gel to the floor. 'Jesus!'

He turned round, red as a brick. I'd scared the shit out of the poor kid. His eyes fell on my half-naked body and he said: 'What the fuck are you doing, faggot?'

'Looks crystal clear to me,' I said. 'Holding up a mirror.' And with that I neatly broke his pinky. The crack sounded satisfying, but no more satisfying than the touch of his body against my skin had been.


We boarded the train in Roosendaal and changed in Antwerp for the high-speed Thalys to Paris. Flying was no option, because then we could be traced. Out on the streets, we had nothing to fear. I was world-famous, but nobody knew what I looked like. Folks like Splinter were rare, but hey, looks don't kill. We paid for the train tickets with the Progressive Parish's credit card, which I'd swiped from Dad's wallet. I also withdrew the maximum amount with his debit card, before he found out and had everything blocked.

As soon as we crossed the border Splinter's reservations vanished. He gazed out the windows for hours with a running commentary on everything he saw: grain silos, different colored number plates, how the cows looked different in France. We played cards for fifty euro notes.

At the Gare du Nord we ate slices of pizza and considered what was up next. Splinter said he wanted to go all the way. He wanted adventure. He dumped his woollen jumper in the trash and swapped it for a t-shirt from a kiosk that read: *Live Dangerously*.

It was late when we hitched a ride. A scrawny Frenchman with dark glasses and an express delivery van stopped for us. Through the open window he said: 'Where to, boys? You name it and I'll take you.'

'How about Spain?'

He promised to take us to the border. Cities gave way to sloping fields. I wondered if my parents had found the note on my pillow. *Don't worry, I'll be back*. When you tell your parents 'don't worry' it's a sure sign that they will, but luckily mine were fairly level-headed. No doubt Splinter's parents would have warned the police the minute he hadn't come home from school anyway, and my parents can put two and two together.

For the first time it dawned on me that I hadn't just done it for Splinter. Running away, I mean. It was an adventure, but it was also something bigger than that. Splinter was looking for the sea. I was looking for myself.

When I woke up we were north of Bordeaux, and it was dark.

We spent the night by the side of a gravel path, not far from the motorway. Wild blueberries grew along the shoulder. Splinter was exhausted and fell asleep in the truck; the delivery man and I sat outside watching shadows drift across the farmland. He talked about his job, about his wife and kids, and then said that he wanted to blow me for his pains. I let him do it. I leaned on my elbows, my head thrown back. I watched the world upside-down and in this position I listened to the crickets until I came. It wasn't how I'd always imagined it would be. It meant more. It meant nothing.

When he sat up I told him that it was my turn. First he didn't get my drift, and when he did, he protested. But my fingers had already found his belt buckle and soon my lips pressed against the warmth within.

'Er...hang on...what you're doing now can get me in big trouble.'

I looked at him like he was nuts and said: 'What *you* were doing earlier can get you in big trouble, too.'

The delivery man groaned and grunted and tugged at my hair when he came, which hurt. His sperm tasted like tears and made me sad, but I still swallowed. And all this time the driver never mentioned the fact that the moonlight fell right through me. Perhaps he hadn't even noticed.

His hands trembled as he smoked a cigarette and let me have a drag, too. It was disgusting. Then he gathered up his stuff, pulled a drowsy Splinter out of the truck, and sped off. We had to walk all the way back to the motorway.

Three days later we reached our destination in Portugal. The second night we'd spent in a haystack and the third outdoors near a gas station. The truck driver had warned us about scorpions, but we didn't see any.

Our destination was called Espelho de Agua, because legend has it that the sun and the sea are at their most beautiful there. At least one person knew the legend, and that was me. At least one person knew it was true. Espelho de Agua is on the west coast of the Algarve, and it smells of almond blossoms, eucalyptus, and thyme, a heady scent that fills the air and reminded me of the times I'd been there with my parents. It's a shame Splinter had no sense of smell. It adds so much.

We bought figs and freshly baked *bolinhas* at the market and wandered the village streets for a while. An old glassblower who was smoking in front of his shop fell to his knees and cried at the sight of Splinter. I smiled. That's what the reunion of Geppetto and Pinocchio must have been like. When the man touched his glass face and arms Splinter glittered with pride. The glassblower spoke just as much English as we did Portuguese, that is, not a word, but he insisted on showing us round his workshop. It was so jam-packed with all manner of glass objects that I felt like a stilt-walker in a room full of air bubbles.

Geppetto found it hard to let go and watched us till we got to the end of the street. He had caught a glimpse of a miracle. Tomorrow he'd think that it had all been a dream.

You didn't see the sea until the very end.

The narrow path wound through a sweltering pine forest, and then all of a sudden it was there, calm and infallible and bright green, until it blurred and merged with the horizon. At first Splinter smiled, so delighted that I thought his face would split in two. Then his smile faded, leaving only awe. I saw the sun's glare on the water reflected in his face.

'It's bigger,' he said, as simple as that. 'Bigger.'

We found a spot on the orange cliffs, far from the children playing football and sunbathing tourists. I fashioned our clothes and backpacks into a little bed on the barren soil. Then I stripped naked and lay down. After a moment's hesitation Splinter followed my lead. Not because of the heat or to get a tan, but because he could. Given the chance to be free, you take it. Splinter was here now, shrugging off the last constraints of home.

I tan quickly. Whichever way I lie, the front and back always tan simultaneously.

'I read somewhere there are birds flying more than 6,000 miles non-stop across the Pacific,' Splinter said, staring at the horizon. 'From Alaska all the way down to the warm islands at the equator. They don't take time to rest, eat, or drink. They just fly on, for nine days. They know exactly where they're going. I bet I could do the same. In a rowing boat, I mean, if I hit the right current. No one can go without food as long as me. Besides, I know the way. I know all about the sea.'

'Yeah, and half-way there you'll be swallowed by a blue whale,' I said without opening my eyes.

'I always wondered why Geppetto was looking for Pinocchio at sea, when the whale gobbled him up,' Splinter said. 'It doesn't make sense. The movie never explains.'

'Send a complaint to Disney. Oh, and apply for a role in the sequel while you're at it.'

Somewhere, a seagull cried.

Splinter rose on one elbow and said: 'That glassblower was the first person in the world who ever thought I was beautiful.'

'That's because he was senile.'

'Fuck off. Seriously. I've never kissed anyone, you know. How can a girl ever like me?'

'Try a glassblower,' I joked.

But Splinter was serious. 'Look at me. Nobody finds me attractive. And I can't blame them.'

I glanced over his body and shrugged. His body was all right, nothing special. There was only one problem. It was made of glass.

'Surely there must be some glass girls?'

'Have you seen any? Besides, I'm not hot for glass. I fancy skin.'

A grin appeared on my face. 'You know, I've always wondered. Can you...?' I simulated jerking off with my hand.

'Oh sure,' Splinter said promptly. 'I'm made of glass, but I'm anatomically correct. Good thing I can't exert much pressure, so there's no need to worry about squeezing something.'

I roared with laughter and rolled onto my stomach. Something stirred; fucking puberty. I thought about asking what he squirted, cum or molten glass. I didn't—some things are better left to the imagination.

Early evening a breeze picked up, drying the sweat on my body. That was nice. We played blackjack waiting for the sun to set. Splinter kicked my ass. I had just dealt a new hand when a gust of wind picked up the cards and blew them off the cliffs. Without a word, we watched hearts, diamonds, clubs, and spades flutter to the west. The low sun transformed the ocean into a bright, orange mirror.

'You see that?' Splinter whispered. 'That's where we're sailing tomorrow. I want to touch the sun as it sinks into the sea.'

I could have said something, but didn't need to. There, where the playing cards were drifting away, was Splinter's heart. You could see the magic lure of the sea reflected on his body. I think in that moment I somehow knew that I wouldn't be taking Splinter back home. Perhaps I'd known it all along. But then why did I keep thinking: *what about me?*

'See how it mirrors? That's where I belong. There everything is just like me. There I won't have to worry about what I can and can't do.'

'Surely it's not that bad,' I suggested, but I knew better.

'Everybody looks at me like I'm some kind of freak,' Splinter said. 'I'll never have a girlfriend. It's too dangerous. I don't even know what it feels like to be touched. A simple hug is too much, even for my parents. All they do is look at me. They never touch, afraid of breaking something.'

I didn't say a word, wished he hadn't told me that.

'I dream about it a lot, you know. I mean, about what it's like to undress a girl. To have my arms around her and feel her skin against mine.'

'But I thought you didn't feel anything, technically speaking?'

'I may not have nerves, but I do have feelings,' Splinter said. He went quiet. 'Maybe…no. Maybe I just want to know what it's like to be incredibly close to someone.'

Then I did something that I had never thought of before. I did it on the spur of the moment, and maybe I wouldn't have done it if I *had* given it some thought, but it was all I could do right then. I turned toward him and wrapped my arm around his waist. I pulled him toward me. He gasped but didn't stop me when I rolled over on my back and carefully lifted him on top. The gap between our bodies closed. Splinter's eyes widened, orange crystals in the setting sun. I don't know if I'll ever be able to evoke the sensation of that glass body against mine. What struck me most was how infinitely fragile it felt.

My hands were on his back.

Splinter's fingers were on my shoulders.

He was incredibly close.

'I didn't realize…'

'If you tell anyone, I'll smash you to pieces.'

He grinned and said: 'Faggot.'

I saw the ground where we lay reflected in his face, not me. But when I breathed out his lips misted up, proof of my existence.

While behind us the miracle of Espelho de Agua unfolded, he kissed me. Splinter was the second person to discover the legend was true. The legend of the sun and the sea. Our tongues found each other while my hands caressed his gleaming back, and when our teeth touched it sounded as the tinkling of a wine glass. Splinter cried, warm tears of molten glass that rolled down my cheeks. After they solidified I plucked them off. I still have them, cones of mirrored glass. I'm glad they're tears of happiness, not of sorrow. I keep them as mementoes.

And so the sun sank into the sea.

I can't remember exactly how it happened. What I do recall is that we were both excited and that I felt his heart beat like mad in his chest. It pounded like a pestle in a glass mortar. Perhaps it pounded so hard that it split his back—I like to pretend it did. But I think I just held him too tight. My only consolation is that I can say in all honesty that I killed him with love, not anything else.

We just lay there, staring at each other in shock while the crack faded in our ears. It had sounded like a football smashing into safety glass: it didn't shatter, but formed a spider's web. A dent. I felt his back. It began on his shoulder blades and ran along the muscles of his spine all the way down to the small of his back.

'Oops,' Splinter said.

I carefully slid him off me. When I set eyes on the damage, my gut tightened into a knot.

'No,' I said. 'Fuck, no, no, no!'

I guess I panicked. I put my fingers on his back, withdrew them, ran my hands through my hair. Worst thing was that the spider's web *moved*, up and down to the rhythm of his breathing. I could see the chunks of glass chafing together.

'How bad is it?' Splinter asked calmly. How could he be so calm? I jumped to my feet, told him to stay where he was, not to move, that I would go and get the glassblower, that I would be back in a flash. The more I said, the less sense I made.

Splinter grabbed my wrist. 'There's no point.'

I was stunned. 'What the fuck, there's no point?' But I knew and tears welled up.

'There's nothing I don't know about glass, Look. If the damage is any bigger than a large coin, replacement is the only option. And replacement is no option for me.'

'Of course it is, he could blow another layer on top of it, fuck if I know!'

I said more, a lot more, but what I said was blubbered out by my sobbing. Splinter tried to get up. A square of glass, less than half an inch across, fell in. We both heard it clink as it bounced off glass organs and slid down the hollow of his leg. There was no doubt about it. Splinter was damaged beyond repair and any movement would make it worse. He would break in two. Maybe he had twenty-four hours to live. Maybe less.

'It was bound to happen, Look,' he said. 'You think I don't know that? It's not your fault. It could have happened anytime.'

But that's not how it felt, not to me; it was my fault and tears poured down my cheeks. Splinter draped his glass arms around me and held me in a clumsy embrace while I burrowed my face in his neck.

'It's okay,' he comforted. 'I found out it doesn't matter when you die. What matters is that you live before you do.'

'I'm so sorry,' I whispered, inconsolable. 'What do you want me to do?'

'I want you to stay here with me tonight. I'd just like to be incredibly close for a bit longer.'

So we lay down and I held him in my arms as the last light faded in the west. I cried continuously, repeating over how sorry I was. Splinter said I wasn't to blame, that for the first time in his life he'd been genuinely happy. My eyes got all swollen and sticky and sore. In the end I guess I cried myself to sleep, a restless sleep, full of dreams I couldn't remember. Did I say dreams? Yeah. I dreamt. Sometime in the middle of the night I woke up because Splinter was blowing his cooling breath on my eyelids. I think he sensed I was having nightmares.

When I woke up again it was getting light.

I jumped up. Splinter was gone. I looked around, called out his name, got no response. His things were still there, though. I scanned the beach below and was alarmed to see the tide coming in. Maybe I was afraid that he'd jumped, that somewhere down there I'd discover a heap of shards, but I didn't see anything. I called his name again and then I heard him.

He staggered out of the forest, pulling a battered wooden cart covered with a ragged old blanket. I was shocked to see the state he was in. His skin had lost its lustre, was no longer reflective. He was worn out. No, dying.

'I did it,' he croaked. 'If I walk very stiffly, hardly anything breaks off, and the glassblower put some bandages on my back. Now I'll hold a bit longer.'

But when he took another step I heard the splinters rattling in the hollows of his feet. I rushed to his aid and took the cart from him. When I lifted the blanket, I saw it held a glass fishing boat, just big enough to fit it. I looked at Splinter.

'I'm finished, Look. I get sicker all the time. I wanna see if I can pull it off. I've got all day to row to the horizon. I wanna see if I can touch the sun when it sinks into the sea tonight.'

We looked at each other for a long time. I kept trying to say something, don't know what, but my voice had given out. Finally I managed to utter a single word. It was the only time I've ever begged someone.

'Please,' I said.

'But I'm the one to say please,' Splinter smiled. 'I need you. To push me off.'

What went through my mind as I pulled him in the cart, over that narrow path winding down to the beach? About a million voices in my head were telling me to turn around, yelling that it wasn't fair and why was this happening to me? But I buried it all inside, deep down where nobody could ever reach.

The sun wasn't up yet and save for a lone jogger, it was quiet on the beach. Splinter showed me a video camera wrapped up in the blanket. 'Give that to my parents. It has a message. For you, too.'

Next I put him in the glass fishing boat and pulled him across the tide line. I was up to my waist in the water. The sea was smooth here, slick and oily, like a mirror. The boat was very well crafted, the work of an artist. Geppetto had even fitted it with glass oars.

I held him in my arms for a long time. Then I let go, I let him go. He took the oars and started rowing, slowly and concentrated, careful not to break his back. He looked back once. The first few rays of sunshine cast a faint glow on his body, and his lips formed a single word. That word was *thanks*.

I waded back to the beach and watched him disappear, saw him grow smaller, a glittering speck on a glittering ocean. Like this, I stared for hours. The beach filled with day-trippers. People squabbled over trivialities, children cried over nothing. I felt drained. Eventually I clambered back up the cliffs. When I reached our stuff, I thought I caught a few more glimpses of the boat, but it was probably just a trick of light. Still, I didn't leave.

I wanted to see if he'd pull it off.

I wanted to see if he could touch the sun.

I was detained at Faro Airport. Not because they recognized me from some description, but because the X-rays at security fell right through me. Descriptions don't come any better than that. They questioned me in a small holding cell. I wobbled in my chair, couldn't find a comfortable position. I was pissed off because I missed my flight, which had cost me four hundred euros last-minute. The Portuguese official was pissed off because he had a lousy job. After he'd been in contact with the Dutch police, he asked me if I knew anything about Splinter Rozenberg's disappearance. I tried not to cry and kept my mouth shut, said I wouldn't say a word until I'd spoken to his parents. At that he got all worked up and banged both fists on the table.

'Talk to me, you glass-eyed monkey!' he yelled in broken English.

I flew off the handle: 'You don't know shit about glass.'

'Did he die?'

'No,' I said. 'He lived.'

They must have searched my luggage, but they didn't find the tape or the glass cones. I'd wrapped them in something soft and hid them in a dark place; you guess where. And so I was escorted back to the Netherlands and reunited with my parents.

A lot more happened, none of which is really relevant. What is relevant is that watching Splinter's video message made Mr. and Mrs. Rozenberg realize that his dream had come true. Splinter told them not to be sad for him. I saw very little of it. Tears blurred my vision when I heard his voice. I thought about how I'd sat there on the beach that long afternoon, plagued by doubts whether I'd done the right thing to let him go. Whether I should have joined him. But I also remembered how the sun had finally set, the ocean a brilliant mirror of orange light. Then I'd known. You make your final journey alone.

Afterwards Mr. and Mrs. Rozenberg came to me and asked: 'Did he do it? Was he happy, in the end?'

'Yes,' I said. 'He touched the sun.'

I wish there was more, that I could give you a happier ending. But there isn't one. Who am I? My name is Look.

Somewhere in Portugal, scanning the waves with his binoculars each night, there's an old glassblower. And every so often, I believe, he espies a blue whale.

# First, Bite
# Just a Finger

## Johann Thorsson

*Johann Thorsson is a native of Iceland who spent his youth in Israel and Croatia. He writes regular features about books for Bookriot.com and his short stories have been published in both English and Icelandic.*

JULIA TRIED IT for the first time in a party uptown, a party she only went to because her friend, *that* friend, the one who knows all the cool people, convinced her to come. Which is how, at the unwinding of the party with the buzz wearing off and after the first stifled yawn, someone suggested everyone try this thing he had heard of.

He, the handsome guy with the receding hairline, started them off by biting the front of his right pinky clean off. Julia laughed nervously at the neat party trick and wondered where the blood was coming from, since surely he didn't just *actually* bite off part of his finger.

"Not *that* again, Toussaint," someone said, and Julia realized that in addition to the bright eyes and the receding hairline, the handsome guy who was sucking blood from the end of his right pinky was missing the tip of his *left* one as well. Toussaint's eyes rolled back into his head, and he let out a deep long sigh and bent his knees a little.

Monday and then suddenly it was Tuesday and she was calling her mother and then felt bad about herself, about a stagnant career and no baby to post photos of on the internet. Wednesday and she had lunch with *that* friend and they talk about Toussaint and that trick with the finger and how apparently it was a thing now.

The new drug. As her friend stuck her fork into the steak she had ordered Julia noticed that her left ring finger was a stub.

That evening she stood naked in front of the wall-to-ceiling mirror that totally tied the apartment together and she thought about the weight she recently gained and what the chances were of getting married at thirty-nine and then she was biting down on her pinky, biting hard and it hurt and the bone grated against her teeth but suddenly with a *snap!* it was off.

She rolled it around on her tongue and felt a single heartbeat of pain in her finger but then her mind flushed with ecstasy and she was standing on her toes, arching her back and there was a tingle *there* and she sucked the blood and was reminded of something and the tingle went on and she had to finish herself, by herself.

It was the best she felt in years, physically and emotionally, and all it cost was the little front part of a finger she didn't even really use. She got looks at work, glances at a bandaged little finger, but they were sympathetic and she liked it and didn't explain. The day went by a little brighter than the others and once she got home she undressed and did it again.

Julia called in sick to work. She had decided to never do it again, that it was madness, but she felt dizzy and afraid of the shadows. By Sunday Julia was pacing around her apartment, jumping at the phone as it rang but not answering. She needed to eat but all she wanted was her own flesh and in the end she gave in, but clever: she took a knife to her smallest toe (couldn't reach it with her teeth) and cut it off with a quick slice and then in it went.

Euphoria.

She could quit if she wanted to and she did, and went until Thursday evening, when the rest of the toes of the left foot, all of them, were severed and chewed and rolled around in the mouth and *oh!* the taste and the surge of pleasure rushing through her, seeking out all nerve endings and setting them alight with joy and a numb pain that followed but was quickly forgotten.

She could quit if she wanted to, really.

Her friend, *that* friend, came over and drew the curtains back and let in a little sunlight and air.

"Julia," she said. "What the hell are you doing to yourself?"

"Nothing," Julia said. "I can quit if I want. And anyway this is your fault, you took me to that party."

"Julia," she said, an unexpected actual sense of caring in her voice. "That was just a stupid boy doing a stupid thing."

Julia shouted at her and she left, and then she felt sorry for herself.

She ate her left foot, then her leg up to the knee, and spent a glorious weekend basking in the joy it brought. She didn't need it to walk; she *floated* through the apartment, and the phone was ringing somewhere in the background but there were just so many new avenues of joy to travel that she didn't care. Her friends cared, and her family, but Julia told them to leave her alone, she was fine. Besides, she could quit anytime she wanted.

She ate her back, bit by bit but it all went down and she put on a cape to cover what was missing. A superhero now, our Julia.

Julia stood in front of a mirror and instead of seeing all the parts of herself that were missing all she saw was what was left but she stopped for a while and she tried normal food but it was bland and didn't sit well in her bowels. She went back to work, on crutches, wearing a cape but they looked at her and she heard what they said behind her (not) back. She got in a fight with her boss and went back home. They didn't understand, no one understood.

She could quit if she wanted to but she didn't want to, not really, and then her legs were.

She smiled by herself in the darkness. But she could quit anytime she wanted.

Just one. More. Bite.

# The Eleven Holy Numbers of the Mechanical Soul

## Natalia Theodoridou

*Natalia Theodoridou is a media and cultural studies scholar from Greece, who has lived in the US, the UK, and Indonesia for several years. Her fiction has appeared in* Clarkesworld, Interfictions, *and other places. She has received a Rhysling nomination for her poetry.*

*a=38. This is the first holy number.*

STAND STILL. STILL. In the water. Barely breathing, spear in hand. One with the hand.

A light brush against my right calf. The cold and glistening touch of human skin that is not human. Yet, it's something. Now strike. Strike.

Theo had been standing in the sea for hours—his bright green jacket tied high around his waist, the water up to his crotch. Daylight was running out. The fish was just under the point of his spear when he caught a glimpse of a beast walking toward him. Animalis Primus. The water was already lapping at its first knees.

He struck, skewering the middle of the fish through and through. It was large and cumbersome—enough for a couple of days. It fought as he pulled it out of the water. He looked at it, its smooth skin, its pink, human-like flesh. These fish were the closest thing to a human being he'd seen since he crashed on Oceanus.

Theo's vision blurred for a moment, and he almost lost his balance. The fish kept fighting, flapping against the spear.

It gasped for air.

He drove his knife through its head and started wading ashore.

Animalis Primus was taking slow, persistent steps into the water. Its stomach bottles were already starting to fill up, its feet were tangled in seaweed. Soon, it would drown.

Theo put the fish in the net on his back and sheathed his spear to free both his hands. He would need all of his strength to get the beast back on the beach. Its hollow skeleton was light when dry, but wet, and with the sea swelling at dusk—it could take them both down.

When he got close enough, Theo placed his hands against the hips of the advancing beast to stop its motion, then grabbed it firmly by its horizontal spine to start pushing it in the other direction. The beast moved, reluctantly at first, then faster as its second knees emerged from the water and met less resistance. Finally its feet gained traction against the sand, and soon Theo was lying on his back, panting, the fish on one side, the beast on the other, dripping on the beach and motionless. But he was losing the light. In a few moments, it would be night and he would have to find his way back in the dark.

He struggled to his feet and stood next to the beast.

"What were you doing, mate?" he asked it. "You would have drowned if I hadn't caught you, you know that?"

He knelt by the beast's stomach and examined the bottles. They were meant to store pressurized air—now they were full of water. Theo shook his head. "We need to empty all these, dry them. It will take some time." He looked for the tubing that was supposed to steer the animal in the opposite direction when it came in contact with water. It was nowhere to be found.

"All right," he said. "We'll get you fixed soon. Now let's go home for the night, ja?"

He threw the net and fish over his shoulder and started pushing Animalis Primus toward the fuselage.

*b=41,5. This is the second holy number.*

Every night, remember to count all the things that do not belong here. So you don't forget. Come on, I'll help you.

Humans don't belong here. Remember how you couldn't even eat the fish at first, because they reminded you too much of people, with their sleek skin, their soft, scaleless flesh? Not any more, though, ja? I told you, you would get over it. In time.

Animals don't belong here, except the ones we make.

Insects.

Birds.

Trees. Never knew I could miss trees so much.

*Remember how the fish gasped for air? Like I would. Like I am.*

It will be light again in a few hours. Get some sleep, friend. Get some sleep.

The wind was strong in the morning. Theo emerged from the fuselage and tied his long grey hair with an elastic band. It was a good thing he'd tethered Animalis Primus to the craft the night before.

He rubbed his palms together over the dying fire. There was a new sore on the back of his right hand. He would have to clean it with some saltwater later. But there were more important things to do first.

He walked over to the compartment of the craft that he used as a storage room and pulled free some white tubing to replace the damaged beast's water detector. He had to work fast. The days on Oceanus waited for no man.

About six hours later, the bottles in Animalis Primus were empty and dry, a new binary step counter and water detector installed. All he had to do now was test it.

Theo pushed the beast toward the water, its crab-like feet drawing helixes in the wet sand. He let the beast walk to the sea on its own. As soon as the detector touched the surf, Animalis Primus changed direction and walked away from the water.

Theo clapped. "There you go, mate!" he shouted. "There you go!"

The beast continued to walk, all clank and mechanical grace. As it passed by Theo, it stopped, as if hesitating.

Then, the wind blew, and the beast walked away.

Dusk again, and the winds grew stronger. Nine hours of day, nine hours of night. Life passed quickly on Oceanus.

Theo was sitting by the fire just outside the fuselage. He dined on the rest of the fish, wrapped in seaweed. Seaweed was good for him, good source of vitamin C, invaluable after what was left of the craft's supplies ran out a long time ago. He hated the taste, though.

He looked at the beasts, silhouetted against the night sky and the endless shore:

Animalis Acutus, walking sideways with its long nose pointed at the wind,

Animalis Agrestis, the wild, moving faster than all of them combined,

Animalis Caecus, the blind, named irrationally one night, in a bout of despair,

Animalis Echinatus, the spiny one, the tallest,

Animalis Elegans, the most beautiful yet, its long white wings undulating in the wind with a slight, silky whoosh,

and Animalis Primus, now about eight years old, by a clumsy calculation. The oldest one still alive.

Eight years was not bad. Eight years of living here were long enough to live.

*c=39,3. This is the third holy number.*

Now listen, these beasts, they are simple Jansen mechanisms with a five-bar linkage at their core. Mechanical linkages are what brought about the Industrial Revolution, ja? I remember reading about them in my Archaic Mechanics studies.

See, these animals are all legs, made of those electrical tubes we use to hide wires in. Each leg consists of a pair of kite-like constructions that are linked via a hip and a simple crank. Each kite is made up of a pentagon and a triangle, the apex of which is the beast's foot. The movement is created by the relative lengths of the struts. That's why the holy numbers are so important. They are what allow the beasts to walk. To live.

Each beast needs at least three pairs of legs to stand by itself, each leg with its very own rotary motion. All the hips and cranks are connected via a central rod. That's the beast's spine.

And then, of course, there are the wings. The wind moves the wings, and the beasts walk on their own.

They have wings, but don't fool yourself into thinking they can fly, ja?

Wings are not all it takes to fly.

In the morning, Theo was so weak he could barely use the desalination pump to get a drink of water and wash his face. He munched on seaweed, filling up on nutrients, trying to ignore the taste. After all these years, he had still not gotten used to that taste. Like eating rot right off of the ocean bed.

The beasts were herding by the nearest sand dune today, mostly immobilized by the low wind. The sun shone overhead, grinding down Theo's bones, the vast stretches of sand and kelp around him. The beach. His beach.

He had walked as far from the sea as he could, the first months on Oceanus. All he had found was another shore on the other side of this swath of land. All there was here was this beach. All there was, this ocean.

He poured some saltwater on the new wounds on his knees. The pain radiated upwards, like a wave taking over his body.

The winds suddenly grew stronger. There was the distant roar of thunder.

Theo let himself be filled by the sound of the sand shifting under the force of the wind, by the sound of the rising waves, by this ocean that was everything. The ocean filled him up, and the whole world fell away, and then Theo fell away and dissolved, and life was dismantled, and only the numbers were left.

*a=38 b=41,5 c=39,3 d=40,1 e=55,8 f=39,4 g=36,7 h=65,7 i=49 j=50 k=61,9 a=38 b=41,5 c=39,3 d=40,1 e=55,8 f=39,4 g=36,7 h=65,7 i=49 j=50 k=61,9 a=38 b=41,5 c=39,3 d=40,1 e=55,8 f=39,4 g=36,7 h=65,7 i=49 j=50 k=61,9 a=38 b=41,5 c=39,3 d=40,1 e=55,8 f=39,4 g=36,7 h=65,7 i=49 j=50 k=61,9 a=38 b=41,5 c=39,3 d=40,1 e=55,8 f=39,4 g=36,7 h=65,7 i=49 j=50 k=61,9 a=38 b=41,5 c=39,3 d=40,1 e=55,8 f=39,4 g=36,7 h=65,7 i=49 j=50 k=61,9 a=38 b=41,5 c=39,3 d=40,1 e=55,8...*

At night, like every night, Theo sent messages to the stars. Sometimes he used the broken transmitter from the craft; others, he talked to them directly, face to face.

"Stars," he said, "are you lonely? Are you there, stars?"

*d=40,1. This is the fourth holy number.*

You know, at first I thought this was a young planet. I thought that there was so little here because life was only just beginning. I could still study it, make all this worthwhile. But then, after a while, it became clear. The scarcity of life forms. The powdery sand, the absence of seashells, the traces of radiation, the shortage of fish. The fish, the improbable fish. It's obvious, isn't it? We are closer to an end than we are to a beginning. This ecosystem has died. We, here; well. We are just the aftermath.

Stars, are you there?

Day again, and a walk behind the craft to where his companions were buried. Theo untangled the kelp that had been caught on the three steel rods marking their graves, rearranged his red scarf around Tessa's rod. Not red any more—bleached and worn thin from the wind and the sun and the rain.

"It was all for nothing, you know," he said. "There is nothing to learn here. This place could never be a home for us."

He heard a beast approaching steadily, its cranks turning, its feet landing rhythmically on the sand. It was Animalis Primus. A few more steps and it would tread all over the graves. Theo felt blood rush to his head. He started waving his hands, trying to shoo the beast, even though he knew better. The beast did not know graves. All it knew was water and not-water.

"Go away!" he screamed. "What do you want, you stupid piece of trash?" He ran toward the beast and pushed it away, trying to make it move in the opposite direction. He kicked loose one of its knees. Immediately, the beast stopped moving.

Theo knelt by the beast and hid his face in his palms. "I'm sorry," he whispered. "I'm so sorry."

A slight breeze later, the beast started to limp away from the graves, toward the rest of its herd.

Theo climbed to his feet and took a last look at his companions' graves.

"We died for nothing," he said, and walked away.

At night, Theo made his fire away from the craft. He lay down, with his back resting on a bed of dried kelp, and took in the night, the darkness, the clear sky.

He imagined birds flying overhead.

*Remember birds?*

ʃ

*e=55,8. This is the fifth holy number.*

A few years ago the sea spit out the carcass of a bird. I think it was a bird. I pulled it out of the water, all bones and feathers and loose skin. I looked at it and looked at it, but I couldn't understand it. Where had it come from? Was it a sign of some sort? Perhaps I was supposed to read it in some way? I pulled it apart using my hands, looked for the fleshy crank that used to animate it. I found nothing. I left it there on the sand. The next morning it was gone.

*Did you imagine it?*

Perhaps I imagined it. Or maybe this planet is full of carcasses, they just haven't found me yet.

*How do you know it was a bird?*

*Have you ever seen birds?*

*Are you sure?*


Theo's emaciated body ached as he pulled himself up from the cold sand. He shouldn't sleep outside, he knew that much.

*How much of this sand is made of bone?*

Had the winds come during the night, he could have been buried under a dune in a matter of minutes. Animalis Elegans was swinging its wings in the soft breeze, walking past him, when a brilliant flash of light bloomed in the sky. A comet. It happened, sometimes.

*Are you there?* he thought.

*Are you lonely?*


*f=39,4. This is the sixth holy number.*

*Animalis* (Latin): that which has breath. From *anima* (Latin): breath. Also spirit, soul.

Breath is the wind that moves you; what does it matter if it fills your lungs of flesh or bottles? I have lungs of flesh, I have a stomach. What is a soul made of?

Do you have a soul? Do I?

The breath gives me voice. The fish is mute, the comet breathless; I haven't heard any voice but my own in so long.

Are you there? Are you lonely?

When I was a little boy I saw a comet in the sky and thought: Wings are not enough to fly, but if you catch a comet with a bug net, well… Well, that might just do the trick.

Breath gives life. To live: the way I keep my face on, my voice in, my soul from spilling out.

Night already. Look, there is a light in the black above. It is a comet; see its long tail? Like a rose blooming in the sky.

If we catch it, maybe we can fly.

Tomorrow I think I'll walk into the sea, swim as far as I can.

*And then what?*

Then, nothing. I let go.

Instead of walking into the sea, in the morning Theo started building a new animal. He put up a tent just outside the fuselage, using some leftover tarpaulin and steel rods from the craft. He gathered all his materials inside: tubes, wire, bottles, cable ties, remains of beasts that had drowned in the past, or ones which had been created with some fundamental flaw that never allowed them to live in the first place. Theo worked quickly but carefully, pausing every now and then to steady his trembling hands, to blink the blurriness away. New sores appeared on his chest, but he ignored them.

This one would live. Perhaps it would even fly.

The rest of the beasts gathered outside the makeshift tent, as if to witness the birth of their kin.

*g=36,7. This is the seventh holy number.*

Come here, friend. Sit. Get some rest. I can see your knees trembling, your hip ready to give, your feet digging into the mud. Soon you will die if you stay this way.

I see you have a spine, friend.

I, too, have a spine.

Theo was out fishing when the clouds started to gather and the sea turned black. Storms were not rare on Oceanus, but this one looked angrier than usual. He shouldered his fishing gear and started treading water toward the shore. He passed Animalis Elegans, its wings undulating faster and faster, and Animalis Caecus, which seemed to pause to look at him through its mechanical blindness, its nose pointed at the sky.

Theo made sure the half-finished beast was resting as securely as possible under the tarpaulin, and withdrew into the fuselage for what was to come.

*h=65,7. This is the eighth holy number.*

Once, a long long time ago, there was a prophet on old Earth who asked: when we have cut down all the trees and scraped the galaxy clean of stars, what will be left to shelter us from the terrible, empty skies?

Theo watched from his safe spot behind the fuselage's porthole as the beasts hammered their tails to the ground to defend their skeletons against the rising winds. Soon, everything outside was a blur of sand and rain. The craft was being battered from all sides; by the time the storm subsided, it would be half-buried in sand and kelp. And there was nothing to do but watch as the wind dislodged the rod that marked Tessa's grave and the red scarf was blown away, soon nowhere to be seen. It disappeared into the sea as if it had never existed at all, as if it had only been a memory of a childish story from long-ago and far-away. There was nothing to do as the wind uprooted the tarpaulin tent and blew the new animal to pieces; nothing to do as Animalis Elegans was torn from the ground and dragged to the water, its silken wings crushed under the waves.

Theo walked over to the trapdoor, cracked it open to let in some air. The night, heavy and humid, stuck to his skin.

*i=49. This is the ninth holy number.*

The night is heavy and humid like the dreams I used to have as a boy. In my dream, I see I'm walking into the sea, only it's not the sea any more, it's tall grass, taller than any grass I've ever seen in any ecosystem, taller than me, taller than the beasts. I swim in the grass, and it grows even taller; it reaches my head and keeps growing toward the sky, or maybe it's me getting smaller and smaller until all I can see is grass above and around me. I fall back, and the grass catches me, and it's the sky catching me like I always knew it would.

The storm lasted two Oceanus days and two Oceanus nights. When the clouds parted and the winds moved deeper into the ocean, Theo finally emerged from the fuselage. Half the beach had turned into a mire. Animalis Elegans was nowhere in sight. Animalis Primus limped in the distance. The beach was strewn with parts; only three of the beasts had survived the storm.

"No point in mourning, ja?" Theo muttered and got to work.

He gathered as many of the materials as had landed in the area around the craft, dismantled the remains of the new animal that would never be named.

He had laid everything on the tarpaulin to dry, when a glimpse of white caught his eye. He turned toward the expanse of sea that blended into mire and squinted. At first he thought it was foam, but no; it was one of Elegans's wings, a precious piece of white silk poking out of a murky-looking patch in the ground.

He knew better than to go retrieve it, but he went anyway.

*j=50. This is the tenth holy number.*

Listen, listen. It's okay. Don't fret. Take it in. The desolation, take it all in. Decomposition is a vital part of any ecosystem. It releases nutrients that can be reused, returns to the atmosphere what was only borrowed before. Without it, dead matter would accumulate and the world would be fragmented and dead, a wasteland of drowned parts and things with no knees, no spine, no wings.

Theo had his hands on the precious fabric, knee-deep in the muck, when he realized he was sinking, inch by inch, every time he moved. He tried to pull himself back out, but the next moment the sand was up to his thighs. He tried to kick his way out, to drag himself up, but his knees buckled, his muscles burned, and he sank deeper and deeper with every breath he took.

*This is it, then*, he thought. *Here we are, friend. Here we are.*

He let out a breath, and it was almost like letting go.

*k=61,9. This is the last holy number.*

So here we are, friend: I, *Homo Necans*, the Man who Dies; you, ever a corpse. Beautiful, exquisite corpse. I lay my hands on you, caress your inanimate flawlessness. I dip my palms into you, what you once were. And then, there it is, so close and tangible I can almost reach it.

Here I am.

In your soul up to my knees.

The sand around Theo was drying in the sun. It was up to his navel now. Wouldn't be long. The wind hissed against the kelp and sand, lulling him. His eyes closed and he dozed off, still holding on to the wing.

He was woken by the rattling sound of Animalis Primus limping toward him.

The beast approached, its feet distributing its weight so as to barely touch the unsteady sand.

"I made you fine, didn't I?" Theo mused. "Just fine."

Primus came to a halt next to Theo and waited.

He looked up at the beast, squinting at the sun behind it. "What are you doing, old friend?" he asked.

The beast stood, as if waiting for him to reach out, to hold on.

Theo pulled a hand out of the sand and reached for the beast's first knees. He was afraid he might tip the animal over, take them both down, but as soon as he got a firm grasp on its skeleton, Primus started walking against the wind, pulling Theo out of the sand.

He let go once he was safely away from the marsh. He collapsed on the powdery sand, trying to catch his breath, reel it back in, keep it from running out. Animalis Primus did not stop.

"Wait," Theo whispered as he pulled himself half-way up from the ground, thousands of miniscule grains sticking to his damp cheek. The beast marched onwards, unresponsive. "Wait!" Theo shouted, with all the breath he had left. He almost passed out.

The wind changed direction. Theo rested his head back on the sand, spent, and watched as Animalis Primus walked away—all clank and mechanics and the vestige of something like breath.

# Djinns Live
# by the Sea

## Saad Z. Hossain

*Saad Z Hossain lives in Dhaka, Bangladesh. His debut novel,* Escape from Baghdad! *was published in the US in 2015.*

THE DJINN WHO sat beside me was incorporeal at first. He was smoke, a ghost, a faint etching of diamond molecules only visible to me. He had been haunting me. I thought I was mad. I got x-rayed and cat scanned, persecuted by doctors and psychiatrists. Pretty soon there was talk of long term therapy, of setting up a trust fund, of taking all my wealth and making a new wing at the hospital.

Lawyers started disputing my signature, crack pot mullahs lurked in street corners with their hands out, urging me to grow a beard, to wash my head with holy water, to pray, pray, pray. They offered me magic black string loaded with Koranic verse, potent stuff worth lacs of taka, protection against devils unseen. Unknown creditors started popping up with forged documents, claiming I owed them vast sums. At this point I stopped. I faked my own recovery.

That day, 12th of July, 2014, I got out of bed, showered, shaved, dressed in my suit, ate breakfast, drank tea, found and kissed my wife and kids—who had moved to other parts of the house in fear, greeted the cowering servants, in effect did everything like a normal human being, ignoring the antics of the past eight months. I issued a five line letter to all concerned parties: lawyers, doctors, mullahs, madrasas, old friends, parents, relatives, and the many business partners scattered throughout town.

§

"Dear Friends, Family, and Concerned Ones,

I have been grievously ill for the past 8 months. I was suffering from a rare malady which is hard to explain, but has a specific scientific cause and remedy. By the grace of God and all your prayers, the medicine has worked! I am cured. All the tests show a full remission of adverse conditions. I feel excellent, and am resuming my duties as a husband, a father, and an industrialist. I thank you all for your support, and apologize for any difficulties you have faced during this trial.

Yours, etc…"

"In reality I know that many of you are dismayed to hear of my recovery, and are now frightened that you'll have to return all of the money you've stolen, or answer for all of the liberties you've taken."

I wanted to add this postscript, but obviously did not, as that would have been taken as a sign of further eccentricity. At this moment, I needed to avoid any sign of eccentricity. It's remarkable how quickly society can decide to dump you into a sanitarium when they decide it's in their favor.

They all buzzed around me for a few days; Welcome back! Knew you could do it! Missed you! What medicine? Congratulations! Which doctor cured you? How much did it cost? Can I keep the company car I appropriated? What medicine? Fortunately, by this point I had so many doctors, no one alive could navigate the malaria infested swamp which was my medical plan. I had been ripped off by so many different kinds of quacks, that no one could actually discover whose treatment had worked.

It took me a few days to organize my affairs. I wrote down a schedule and followed it rigidly. Sit, smile, talk, pray, eat, pray, TV, sleep. They started to leave me alone after that. My wife and kids lost their strained, frightened looks, they returned to the family room, took up their various activities around me, made jokes and laughed, poked fun at me, hesitantly at first, and then naturally. The ability of the human mind to adapt to peculiar situations is astounding. The words nervous breakdown, insanity, early onset Alzheimer's, began to fade.

After a week I prepared myself to tackle the real problem. Throughout this period, the djinn had waited patiently, winking in and out of the light. My first gambit was based on the theory that he wasn't haunting me; there was nothing haunting about him, no air of menace. His wild gesticulations had not been the threat of magic—they had, in fact been the gestures of a man trying to communicate.

By this time, I had lost my initial fear for the thing. In fact, given my ordeal with humans hell bent on curing me, I had come to take comfort in the relatively undemanding presence of the djinn. Thus, I took a chance and sat down across from him with a bunch of kids' picture books, and pointed.

He got the idea right away. He wanted to touch the books, to flip through them. He started to solidify, oozing into reality like glue hardening on a stick. I locked the door, my heart racing, terrified once again. He was rather calmer. He sat politely across my desk, being patient, exuding a sense of harmony.

He looked like a slightly elongated man. Everything was off about him, problems of scale, and subtle, worrisome differences, like his enormous nail beds, or the tiny ears. I took a mirror and showed him, pointing out the problems, guessing that he might have a way of altering himself. He did, in fact, and was most cordial in taking care of it. After several hours, he looked like a very dapper man, and I dressed him in my spare suit, and we stared at the mirror together, subtly alike.

"Apple," I said, pointing to a picture. "A for apple."

The learning flew by. The djinn was hideously intelligent. After three days he was proficient enough to communicate in English, with the aid of pictures. He was a marvelous artist, could render a likeness with only a few lines. Conversation was now possible, through signs, words, and quick sketches.

He told me that he was old, hideously old according to our timeline. He had been gone for a long time, absent from human affairs. Men had spoken Sanskrit when he had last been in these parts. He expressed his amazement at the development, the roads, buildings, and cars.

"The languages are similar," he said with a smile, when I spoke Bangla to him. "Your people are the descendants of those I knew in the old kingdom."

He had powers. He could materialize and dematerialize at will, back to some dark dimension. He extruded some kind of field, could affect objects in his sphere. He was a djinn, a mythical creature. Yet his bewilderment was real, his unease with the jostle of the crowd, a palpable discomfort with the future.

He took to cigarettes and whiskey with elan; soon he was as human as me, a chameleon. His English became good enough for proper conversation. He confessed that he had known human languages before, or what passed for them when he had last been among the living. Memories were coming back to him, proficiencies fallen either through disuse or some injury. I imagined some tragedy in his past, some accident or illness which must have laid him low, sent him into hibernation.

He spoke of the places he had been, the nature of the darkness outside. It was frightening. His very presence filled me with unease, opening a window into something awful and unreachable. It took me some time to realize that I held the same dread for him, that he was just as unmoored. We were opposites in anxiety. To me he was the great emptiness of other dimensions. To him, I was the claustrophobic press of present day, of humanity ruling the world and crowding out every other living thing, of six billion people breathing in and out, of living and dying and using up every scrap of land until no empty space was left.

My time with him was limited, because I still had to follow the schedule. Any deviation was a risk. They were still watching, waiting for cracks to develop. Once people write you off, it's very difficult for them to revise their opinions.

Ludicrously, my first instinct was to ask for wishes.

"You know, three wishes," I said.

His look of bemusement was comical.

"My people think that djinns grant wishes."

"Well," he said. After some consideration, "What would you want?"

"I don't know," I said. "Money, I guess. I would have said money, before I actually met you."

"You are already quite rich," he said.

"Yes, but men can never have enough money," I said. "Forget the money. I really don't give a shit anymore. I mean, I don't care if I leave anything behind. How about immortality? Is that something you can grant?"

"I think that's a power reserved for God."

"You believe in God? I thought perhaps you all had found a better answer."

"I could lengthen your life, perhaps. By aligning the defects in your body," the djinn said. "And we are no closer to God than you."

"I'm not that keen on living forever anyways," I said, after some self-examination. "Right now, I despise everyone around me."

"Well, they thought you were crazy."

"Yes, imagine dealing with that forever and ever," I said. "No thanks."

"That's one of the reasons I went into hibernation," the djinn said. "I wish I hadn't. I've missed some remarkable times. The problem is that it all goes so slowly, when you're awake for it."

"I know what I want," I said. "If I had wishes, that is."

"Three wishes you'd get, you said," the djinn said.

"I just need one. And it's a wish you can grant, actually, if you were of a mind to."

"You realize that I have no actual wish granting powers," the djinn said. "It's all physics, what I can do…"

"I want to know secrets."

"It's supposed to be palaces, gold, and wenches," the djinn said.

"I have those things already, to some degree," I said. "At this point in my life, they're useless. I want to know something amazing. Some piece of secret knowledge. I want to know how the universe really works."

"I'm quite sure I do not know how the universe works," the djinn said with distressing promptness. "I am not even sure I know how this little corner of the world we live in works. For example, what exactly is electricity? I must say I'm completely baffled."

"Look, I know all of that stuff," I said, frustrated. "That's just science. I can get you a book. Or use the internet."

"That's another thing I don't understand," the djinn said, shaking his head.

I was forced to smile. I still wasn't too comfortable with computers, although I appreciated how utterly useful they were. I guess my generation had just missed out on it. We were still stuck in the land of two fingered typing.

"It seems like I'm the one granting *you* wishes," I said. I was cross. He was being deliberately obtuse. "Let's start with basic things. What is your name, for example?"

"I prefer not to say."

"Aha!" I said. "It is common in many mythologies, that knowing the true name of someone or something gives us power over them. You fear to give me your name. Is this the basis of your power?"

"Nothing so romantic, I'm afraid," the djinn said. "It is merely that my name is associated with certain painful memories. I am an exile of sorts, in fact."

"Oh."

"I wish for a new name, a fresh start. You must pick one. Something modern, something suited to today's world."

"This is ludicrous," I said. "It's very stressful picking a name. I cannot do it. A name must reflect everything about you, your background, your family, your religion."

"Well think about it," he said. "You are the only person I know. My only friend, if you like. In return, I will think about a great secret I can share with you."

"Alright," I said, secretly flattered that he would call me friend.

For the next week, I did not see him. I went back to work, started checking budgets, projections, and sales reports. In my absence things had started to slip. Money was disappearing, people were slacking, it was as if something vital had gone from the machinery, and I realized that it was me, it was my will that had been propping this whole thing up. Even now, as I saw the numbers swimming around, I couldn't muster up any interest. Something had dissipated. It is normal to go through life with a vague dissatisfaction. The childhood promise of magic, *answers*, slowly gives way to a methodical plodding of problems encountered, problems solved, assets accumulated, debts paid. You wake up one day surrounded by expensive things, with the discomforting conclusion that you haven't learnt anything, really, haven't really plumbed the depths.

The djinn, by his very tenuous existence, had reduced everything. *Here* was the other, if not the answer, at least hope. I had intimated my desire for secrets. In truth the idea of secrets had overwhelmed my thoughts. I did not crave women, or money, or power. I wanted to know secrets. I wanted to know how things worked.

As the days passed I feared that he was gone. When he returned, I was relieved. I was relieved that I hadn't imagined it. How can an insane person tell the outside from the inside? The only logical thing to do is see it through; to continue as if everything is real. I often arrived at this conclusion when I doubted myself.

"I have been thinking," the djinn said, ensconced in my office. "That our collaboration requires me to be more forthcoming. I am aware, that aside from irrefutable proof of my existence, I have not given you much else."

"Yes," I said. "Yes. I have so many questions."

"This is not deliberate. Somewhat like you, I am damaged. My identity, my memories, are fractured," the djinn said. "I cannot give you answers, because I myself do not have many of them. However, I will give you my name, meaningless as it is. I am called Jivar the broken. I was imprisoned, then exiled by my people."

"What was your crime?" I asked, fascinated now.

"I refuted some long held truths among my people, about our own creation, our place in the world. My people believe, like man, that we were made by God. Except in our creed, we were the chosen race, bequeathed the worlds of light as well as darkness, as evinced by our physical superiority. Were we not alone bequeathed a universe of our own, one of pure holy energy?"

"A not unreasonable belief," I conceded.

"My great crime? I suggested that like all life, we were mere accidents; that we ourselves had no idea about the dimension we inhabited, or this physical world, that we were all as lost as each other, humans and djinns, adrift in time."

"Jivar," I said. "Jivar the broken." I rolled it around my tongue, relishing the thrill. It seemed like a grand title. Here was a creature of myth, conversing with me. "This name sounds greater than anything I could give you."

"I was thinking on your request," Jivar said. "There are old places here, places which were old when I was young. Many have been swept under the sea, but some still exist. There is a place near here, in the region you call Narshingdi. It is the remnant of an ancient city. Or rather, the upper layer of a city that once existed. I travelled there the past week."

"There's an excavation there, in Wari-bateshwar," I said. I remembered the articles some years ago. "They found an old city."

"Once, before the world was ice, there was a great kingdom of djinn here, when we were less scattered. Afterwards, men rebuilt it in the same name, the ancient civilization of Gangaridai. We must have private access to that site. Take me there, and I will show you a secret."

"That will not be hard," I said. "As I recall, the archaeology team was out of funds. Give me three days."

I started making phone calls. The site was controlled by a local university, an impoverished archaeology department which could barely staff the site year around. A friend of a friend was a tenured professor there, and before long I had an appointment with the chief archaeologist. The man was earnest, and held forth on the many wonders of Gangaridai, and the relative penury of our efforts compared to international digs. I offered to fund him for the next three years, and it was sad to see the way his eyes lit up with desperate hope.

"I will need two days with my team there," I said. "For promotional reasons. They will find a way to get this money from the marketing budget."

He agreed, of course. He would have agreed to give me his firstborn. The next call was to the UP chairman, a political thug who visited his area twice a year to throw lavish banquets for the 'poor'. His 'nephew', another embryonic politician, actually ran the area with an iron fist, serving as chief drug dealer, pimp, toll collector, bureaucrat, police, and magistrate. He was actually a capable boy by all accounts and would probably become home minister one day. Normally I would have spent time on chit chat, but I just didn't care anymore. I didn't care to save money, and I certainly didn't care about his dignity. I stated my request baldly, followed by a number. It was sufficient. The Chairman came to my office the next day, took his cash, and called his nephew in front of me, as well as the police station in his area for good measure. In his mind I was now a man Who Did Not Waste Time. The entire political cadre and police force in the area was now at my disposal.

"This had better be worth it," I said to Jivar, when all was readied. If my directors knew how much I had spent, they would have bundled me back to the sanitarium. Luckily, I alone knew all the gopher holes in this company, how money flowed around and around, and whereas I had always been the policeman, now I was the thief. It was strangely liberating.

"It will be," he said with a smile. "Just remember, some things you cannot unsee."

We took two Pajeros out of town, giant SUV's with their windows blackened, one for me and the djinn, the other full of armed bodyguards. I normally didn't go for this kind of thing, but I wanted privacy, and the guards were necessary to make sure no one saw too much of Jivar. We got to the site, and after half an hour of formal greetings and tea ceremonies, I lost my patience and kicked everyone out. Luckily, my advanced years allowed some rudeness.

Jivar waved away my guards. I protested. I was an old man, I would need help.

"I will help you," the djinn said. "Do you not trust me?"

I wasn't sure I did, but at this point, I didn't really care.

We went to the dig, it seemed to be mainly a series of waist high walls and mounds, not very impressive. I had envisioned something like the pyramids. I tried to hide my disappointment. What could the djinn show me in all this mud and dirt? We wound our way through, he seemed to know what he was doing. At a certain point, where the ground was undisturbed, he paced and measured.

"It's here. There is a tunnel, a kind of staircase going underground."

"How do we get to it? I'm too old to dig," I said. It was hot, and I was getting tired, irritable.

Jivar moved me aside. "I will use my power. There is a mechanism still alive, which will open the way."

He put both hands on the ground and pushed. Whatever strain he was under was not physical, but it told all the same, for the air darkened around him, the leaves rustled, and I felt a terrible vertigo. The ground shook, there was a kind of grating noise, and suddenly a great calamity of dust covered us, and we fell down, as if in an elevator in free fall. I shouted in fear, but Jivar held me close, and his wiry strength was a comfort. I could see nothing, a great roaring made my ears drum, and I was about to pass out when it all stopped.

We were in complete darkness, but the ground was still at least, and it was blessedly cool, almost clammy. Jivar flicked his fingers, and an orb of light, like a meager sun, came to live behind his shoulder. We were in a kidney shaped chamber, the walls and roof set with roughly hewn rocks, devoid of adornment, yet clearly manmade. I did not know how deep underground we were, but my ears felt strange, and it was completely, eerily soundless.

Jivar ushered me to a hole in the ground, crude stairs made of blocks seemingly hacked into the body of a sloping tunnel. I felt claustrophobic dread at having to enter that coffin shaped hole, but Jivar led the way, and I followed quickly lest I lose his light. We kept going down, and everything was damp, clammy, the air fetid with some rotting smell. An hour rolled by on that terrible descent, and then two, and I began to rest frequently, leaning on the djinn, my breath coming in great shallow bursts; I was no longer enamored of this secret, I was now contemplating whether I would ever see daylight again.

Jivar urged me on, half dragging me the last twenty minutes, until we at last came to an abrupt end. One second we were in that closed tunnel, and the next I was almost plunging into the abyss, my foot clawing through open air until Jivar pulled me back. The djinn made a motion and the light above his shoulder became luminous, like a bright star. We were on an interminable ledge that bordered an inky blackness, and as the light slowly penetrated, I could see the edge sloping down, faced with stone, smooth and horrible in proportion, and far across a similar sloping shore, a distance and scale of masonry which beggared the imagination.

"It is an inverted pyramid," Jivar said, sending the light out to hover high in the air, illuminating the structure further. "We must go down."

We walked along the lip of the precipice, and I followed the sloping sides with my eye, trying to fathom at which far away depth lay the apex of the triangle. After some time we reached a break in the ledge, and there were steps going down, long shallow ones, the stone edges rounded from great use. How many men had gone up and down building this thing? How long ago? As we descended, dank and unpleasant smells filled the air. Soon the light showed disturbing things underfoot; I tripped on a femur, and it crumbled to dust, and then my foot kicked a ribcage, sending it skittering. There were skulls, heavy browed, eyes pinched together with elongated craniums, things not quite human, bones with subtle wrongness about them that even my untrained eye recoiled from.

Jivar noticed my disquiet. Indeed, we were now walking entirely through bone, for the steps and surrounding slope were covered by a latticework of the dead, a gently settled creeper bearing fruits of grinning heads, the flesh and skin long gone, all stacked in delicate balance, so that our mere passage was enough to send out mini avalanches in our vanguard. There were thousands of dead, hundreds of thousands!

"The workers," Jivar said. "They sealed them in of course, to hide the secret."

"Were these men?" I asked, in a hushed tone.

"Not quite," Jivar said. "It was long ago. We called them Grass people. They had longer skulls, and their eyes were different. They were shorter, and wider than men, but very similar otherwise. They were very skilled with their hands, and thus prized workers."

"Grass people. So many dead here."

"It was a great sacrifice. The Grass people ceased to exist afterwards. This is the entirety of their population, I believe."

I stared with loathing at Jivar, overcome by the matter of fact tone covering such an enormous, hideous crime.

"It was much before my time," Jivar said, noticing. He was adept now at reading my expressions, he missed nothing. "Things were different between djinn and men then. Indeed, there *was* no human civilization, not as you know it now."

"What is the point of this?" I asked. "This is like a giant cup filled with the dead. An entire species extinct. For what? Some kind of temple? Some monument to a pharaoh?"

"It is a machine," Jivar said. He smiled. "Do you think I would waste your wish in such a paltry way? This is one of the great secrets of the djinn."

I no longer wanted it, but there was nothing to do but carry on. We ploughed through, soon covered in the shattered dust of these mournful people. I reflected on their name, on what misfortune had caused a people of green and sunlight to be trapped and killed so far below the earth. What possible machinery could be worth this? Still we descended, Jivar carrying me on his back, and after countless hours the bones changed. They were much larger now, heavy with knee joints and great thick rib cages. I thought of the American football players on TV, the bones of those men would be like this.

"Another people gone, these were the Neanderthals, that famed race of extinct cousins," Jivar said. "Too many were brought to work here, too many died. What was left above was not enough to survive. They were enormously strong, and smart, much smarter than your own great ancestors."

"How many species were destroyed for this?" I asked, aghast.

"At least one more," Jivar said. "A more advanced race, truly civilized, capable of the finer work of the machinery itself. They were small in number, however, perhaps bound for extinction regardless. They called themselves the Dedra."

Finally, when even riding on the djinns' back was unbearable agony, we reached a landing and a bridge, which extended across toward the other side. The far shore was so distant that I could not see the opposite landing. Here lay the bones of the Dedra, thin, graceful figures. We began to cross, and just walking across level ground again was a relief. By this time I had already given up hope of ever seeing the surface again. I did not think I could make the return journey up, even with the help of the djinn. It occurred to me that Jivar had never intended for me to outlive the unveiling of his secret. I did not care too much. This brought renewed vigor to my limbs, a surge of adrenaline and pumping blood, and I urged Jivar not to slow down. I would see this dread machine before the end.

The bridge was slender, beautiful, made of a translucent black material, arcing across with no visible supports, a marvel of engineering. We crossed to the midway point, and there was a chamber and a door. The room looked slight in proportion to the pyramid, but as we approached the portal, I measured it by eye, and estimated that it was at least 10 stories tall, a graceful tower with air slits in various points, but no further ingress. Jivar laid his hands on the door and it opened with a hum. The room stretched down below us, with a winding staircase going down, moving through gigantic gears made of dull beaten gold, the teeth slowly moving, each notch as big as a man's leg, a king's ransom hung on each giant wheel. We were inside a god's clocktower, a cathedral of arcane purpose, a titan's church organ of wound springs, pendulums, bearings, and rotating gears, everything moving in soundless splendor.

"What is this?" I asked in awe.

"One of the last great works of the djinn," Jivar said. "The Lords of Gangaridai had grand ambitions. Come, a few more steps only."

The stairs wound down into a featureless chamber, a gash of darkness, and as I stumbled down I passed through some kind of membrane, a flash of ice so brief that it barely flickered on my nerves. Disoriented, exhausted, I knelt on the rough stone floor. Jivar was ahead of me, but the light was gone, and the night seemed to swim against me, waves of a physical ocean. There was a window, a strange, distant window, and as my eyes misfired against the oppressive darkness, I walked toward it, hands in front of me like a blind man.

There was water outside, or something like it, something velvet and black, which glimmered in places as if reflecting something luminous held out of reach. Far, far away, there was a moon, a pearl suspended in the void, and as my eyes focused, I saw a fairy tale city trapped inside, minarets and domes, and bells ringing.

"You see the city?" Jivar asked.

I nodded dumbly.

"The Lords of Gangaridai didn't like the way things were panning out. They didn't like the idea of time running out for them," Jivar said. "More specifically, they didn't like this idea of entropy—their perfect city, doomed to dissolution. So they moved it. They moved it outside of time."

"That is the city of Gangaridai?"

"The First City, yes, the first city of djinn," Jivar said. "A place of grandeur and beauty, now faded from memory."

"And this black sea?"

"It is the world of the djinn, the place we exist when we are not flesh," Jivar said. "The machine holds open this window, a last tenuous path. The Lords intend to return, you see, when times are more favorable for them."

I staggered toward the window and a cold wind scoured me, drilling me with holes. The suicide's temptation to step through was overwhelming. I felt hands on my back, a gentle push from behind, and I was tumbling on, flesh shredding into that acid substance, not quite water, not quite cold, an intense, blazing pain until there was nothing left, just the hard kernel of my mind. I looked back through a grey, eyeless gaze and saw the window and the chamber were already far away. Jivar stood on the other side, dressed in my clothes, waving, and I thought that perhaps he *had* been haunting me after all. The tide pulled me, and I lost interest. I turned and began to swim for the city.

# How My Father Became a God

## Dilman Dila

*Dilman Dila is a writer and filmmaker from Uganda, whose work has won the BBC Radio Playwriting Competition, the Commonwealth Short Story Prize, Short Story Day Africa prize, the Million Writers Awards, and the Jalada Prize for Literature. His movie* The Felistas Fable *was nominated for Best First Feature at AMAA 2014, and won four major awards at the Uganda Film Festival 2014.*

M Y FATHER WAS a god, though he looked like any other old man. He had a thick white beard and a bald head with tufts of hair above his ears. He had no wrinkles. His ribs showed. His gait was slow, shuffling. He always wore large, green earrings, a rainbow-coloured necklace, and a black goatskin loincloth. He looked ordinary, but I knew he was a god. This was confirmed the day he showed me the egg-shaped thing. The object stood on two, bird-like legs that were taller than he was, and it had a pair of wings that was so large my father must have skinned twenty cows to make them. I wondered where he got the hide, for he had no wealth to buy cattle.

"It's buffalo skin," he said.

"You don't hunt," I said.

"I paid a hunter."

I frowned, but was too courteous to ask how he had paid the hunter. He was so poor he could not afford to buy a chicken.

"I sold him a trap," he said.

It had to have been a unique trap for this hunter to pay with twenty buffalo hides. I did not press him about it. The egg-shaped object enthralled me.

"Can it fly?" I said.

"Not yet. But one day, it will take you into the sky to become the bride of the sun."

I giggled. "Is it a new type of bird?"

He smiled. "No. I call it a bruka. Do you remember Bruka?"

I nodded. Bruka was an eagle. A boy had tricked it with a chicken, and it had come to the ground. Then he had jumped on its back and rode it through the skies. Yet this egg-shaped thing had no life. How would it fly?

"Will you put the spirit of a bird in it?" I said.

"No. I am still making its—" He paused. "I don't know what to call that thing." He pointed at a box-shaped object fixed between the wings. "For now, let's just call it a heart. It will make the bruka fly, but it needs special sap for it to work. I haven't yet found that sap."

We were behind a hut that looked like a fallen tree trunk. He called it the ot'cwe, the house of creation. My family had banished him from the homestead, so he lived alone in this hut. The walls did not have the beautiful red-and-white designs Maa had painted on our home. The walls here were cracked and full of drawings of the things Baa tried to create. The grass-thatched roof had holes that leaked when the rains came. I wished I was old enough to help him with repairs so he would not sleep in a place worse than a kraal. When the rains became too heavy, my mother allowed him to sneak into her bed. I could hear them giggling all night. She had to be careful or else my uncles would beat her up. They once thrashed her when they discovered she had prepared a dish of goat meat for him. They insisted he should eat only their leftovers, which they dumped in a calabash at the edge of the compound. He never ate that garbage. Maa secretly sent me with food for him.

"Lapoya!" Okec, my eldest brother, shouted from a distance, interrupting us.

He had come to the ot'cwe. A bush still hid me from his view. Baa gave me a look of surprise. They forbade anyone to visit him. They wanted him to live in isolation like a leper, hidden away from the eyes of the public, because they thought he was a lapoya, a mad man, and a shame to the family. Whenever I visited him, I made sure no one saw me. Why was Okec here? Had I made a mistake? Had he seen me?

"Hide," Baa said.

He lifted me onto a window. I jumped into the hut and hid in a giant pot. They thought Baa was a lapoya because he tried to make magical things that did not work, like this pot that would make water during droughts. Nothing he made worked, but I had faith in him. In the great stories, Lacwic, the creator, kept trying to make humans. Each time he failed, he instead created an animal or a bird, so we have all these different species. Eventually, he succeeded.

Baa was a god. He had to experiment until he came up with the thing he was supposed to create. He had spent all his life on this pursuit. Everybody laughed at him, but he did not stop. He could not stop.

"What do you want?" I heard him say.

"I have a husband for Akidi," Okec said.

When I heard my name, my flesh turned as hard and cold as a hailstone. Baa had ten sons. I was the only daughter, the youngest child from his third wife. Since he was a poor man, his sons had no cattle to pay dowry for brides. Because he had no mature daughters, there was no hope of wealth coming into the family anytime soon. His sons could not get married.

"She's still a child," Baa said. "She's too young to have breasts or to know that women bleed."

"Okot has offered a thousand head of cattle," Okec said.

A thousand? Only the Rwot's daughter could command such a rich dowry, not me. If it were true, then all my brothers would have enough cattle to marry.

"She's still a child," Baa said.

"That's why she's valuable," Okec said. "Okot lost his manhood. The ajwaka says he needs a wife as young as Akidi to regain it. That's why he's offering all this cattle. You can't refuse."

"If you mention it again," Baa said, "I'll cut off your head."

"You are cursed," Okec said. "Your madness has wasted our wealth. We now can't get married. This is our best chance. Don't say no."

My father was not listening anymore. I knew, for I heard him entering the ot'cwe. He sat on a stool beside my hiding place.

"We don't need your permission," Okec shouted. He remained outside. They feared to enter the ot'cwe, which they believed was infested with demons. "You are a lunatic, so your brothers will give the permission."

He stomped away.

I climbed out of the pot. Baa's face had wrinkled. I hugged him. His tears fell on my cheeks.

"I'll go to the forest." His voice crackled like dry leaves. "I'll find the obibi tree. Its sap will make the bruka fly. We'll go to the clouds, just you, me, and your mother. We'll start a new home up there."

I held him tighter. My fingernails dug into his flesh in anger. I was still a child, but I knew obibi was a myth, a monster that lived only in fairy tales. Before I could berate him for giving up, love drums started to beat. The musicians were already in our homestead, which was a short distance from my father's hut. My brother had come to ask for Baa's permission only as a formality. He had conspired with my uncles, and they had already organised the amito nywom feast. In the ceremony, boys gathered at the bride's homestead and danced larakaraka, and she chose the best dancer for a husband. Rarely did the bride choose a man only because of his dancing talent or good looks. Often, she would know her choice long before the function. In some instances, like this one, her family would force her to pick a boy they preferred.

"Akidi!" I heard my mother shout. "Run, my daughter! Run and hide!"

Baa charged out of the hut with a vunduk, a lightning weapon he had created. Shaped like a gourd, it was a ball with a long pipe attached to it. I followed him out, praying to Lacwic to make the vunduk work.

Maa ran through the bushes with three of my brothers chasing her. It reminded me of a hunt I once saw, where a group of boys chased a hare with bows and arrows. They did not catch it. My brothers, however, were faster than Maa. They overtook her, pushed her aside, and came for me. Baa pointed the vunduk at them and pulled a string that dangled from its ball. The weapon made a low sound, like a harp's string when strummed, but it did not produce lightning to strike my brothers. They kept running toward us. Baa pulled the string, again and again. My brothers started laughing at him.

"Run!" Maa was shouting. "Run, Akidi! Run!"

I ran. Unlike the hare, I could not outrun my brothers, but I could hide. I saw a hole in an anthill. Someone had dug it up recently in search of a queen. I ducked into the hole and into a tunnel big enough for me to crawl on my hands and knees. I went in deep, where my brothers would not be able to get me. I snuggled in the darkness, trying not to cry. I felt safe until the mouth of the burrow darkened with someone peeping in.

"She's inside," Okec said. "Make a fire. We'll smoke her out."

"You'll kill her!" Maa cried. "Don't use fire! You'll kill her!"

The burrow went deep under the ground. It became so dark that I could not see. I groped, but as long as I could feel open space ahead, I did not stop moving. The voices became faint, until I could not hear them anymore. I feared a giant snake would swallow me or a hundred rats would attack me. Still, I did not stop. Such a fate was better than marrying Okot.

When the smoke flowed into the tunnel, I was so far away it did not bother me. The burrow widened, becoming big enough for me to stand. I ran, stumbling over the uneven, soggy ground. I ran for such a long time I feared the tunnel had no end, and that I would get lost in an underground maze. Still, I refused to cry. I went round a bend and saw a light. A draught of fresh air tickled me into laughter. The tunnel narrowed again. I went down on my knees and crawled out.

At once I wished I had remained inside.

I was at the Leper's Swamp. No one ever went there, not even powerful shamans. It was about the size of four large homesteads and deep enough to swallow a man. In the middle stood a black rock, shaped like the mortar we used to pound groundnuts into flour. The rock was larger than three huts put together, two times taller than the trees, and it had a surface as smooth as a polished pot. Every full moon, blood dripped out of it to colour the water. They called it Leper's Rock. Spirits lived there.

I ran away from the haunted water, to find a place to hide, but then I heard hunting dogs. They had picked up my scent and were coming after me. Wherever I hid, they would find me, though not in the water—they would lose my scent if I went there.

But there were spirits in the water.

The dogs came nearer. Their barking pricked my eardrums. My brothers were urging them to get me, and my mother screamed, "Run! Akidi! Run!"

I saw my face in the water. I resembled my father. He was a god. Surely, spirits would not hurt the daughter of a god. The barking grew louder, angrier, and I had no choice. I closed my eyes, said a prayer to the creator, and slipped into the swamp. The cold water stung my skin. Goosebumps sprouted all over my arms. I waited for something else to happen, for fire to consume my body, for spirits to strike me dead. Nothing happened. I swam fast through papyrus reeds. Frogs and fish swam with me. I took it as a sign that Lacwic had answered my prayers. The spirits would not harm me. I reached the middle, where I climbed onto the rock. Still, the spirits did not do anything to me.

Long ago, a thirsty leper had found a group of girls at a well. He had asked for a calabash to drink water, and the girls had laughed at him. One, however, had given him her calabash. After he had quenched his thirst, he told her to stay away from the dance that night. She had heeded the warning. The other girls did not. During the fiesta, this rock had fallen from the sky and buried all the dancers. The well from which the leper had drunk dried up, and a swamp grew around this rock. It was not just another fairy tale. The blood that seeped out every full moon proved it to be true. Red stripes stained the rock's surface.

I sat still in the reeds. The dogs whined on the banks. They had lost my scent. My brothers were shouting, my mother was wailing. Their voices came as if from another world. I longed to hear my father.

"Did she enter the water?" Okec said.

"She wouldn't dare," someone responded.

"Useless dogs!" I recognised Okot's voice. "Useless!"

A dog yelped in pain. Maybe Okot had kicked it.

I could not stand my mother wailing as though I were dead. I put my fingers in my ears, but that did not shut her out. I walked around the rock. The tall papyrus hid me from their view. On the other side, their voices were faint. I saw a cave and went in. The mouth was low, but inside it was bigger than a hut and I could no longer hear Maa or my brothers. I felt safe, and cried myself to sleep.

A dripping from further inside the cave awoke me. Something glowed on the floor and filled the room with a weak, reddish light. I was not afraid. Baa was a god, so this spirit would not harm me. I crept to the light, which came from a pool of thick blood. Above the pool, on the cave roof, hung a sculpture that resembled a cow's breast with three nipples. Somebody, or something, had carved it up there. Blood dripped out of the nipples.

Was it really blood? It looked to be thicker than porridge. When I touched it, the liquid stung me like a thorn and left a glowing stain on my fingertip. Blood could not do that, but sap could. Maybe it's what Baa needed to make the bruka fly and take us to a paradise in the heavens.

I ran out of the cave. The sun had sunk low into the horizon, giving the world a red tint. I had been asleep for far longer than I had thought. I could not hear my mother, my brothers, or the dogs. I crossed the swamp and crept through the bushes. By the time I reached the ot'cwe, darkness had fallen. A small fire flickered under the tree in front of the hut. My parents sat beside it like prisoners, their backs to me. Baa still had the vunduk, and held it as though it was a real weapon. Okec, Okot, and an ajwaka in a costume of bird feathers, stood around them. I climbed up a tree, silent as a cat, and curled up in the branches to hide.

"She's our sister," Okec was saying. "We can't harm her, but every girl has to get married. Why delay her happiness when a wealthy suitor is interested?"

"There are other girls in the village," Maa said.

"We are the poorest," Okec said. "We don't even own chickens."

"Work for your wealth if you want to marry," Baa said.

"You squandered our wealth," Okec said through his teeth. "You must make amends by giving us Akidi. Where is she?"

"Even if I knew," Baa said, "I wouldn't tell you."

"I won't stop looking for her," Okot said. "I'll marry her, whether you like it or not."

He walked away. The ajwaka said something to my parents in such a low voice that I did not catch it, then followed Okot. My brother jeered, hissed insults, and went away, too. After a while, my parents begun to roast maize. They worked in silence. I stayed in the tree for a long time, watching them, until I felt it safe to climb down. They did not notice me until I had crept right up to them.

"Baa," I whispered. "I found it."

They turned to me. Their faces were bruised from a beating.

"Akidi," Maa cried.

They hugged me tightly.

"The sap." I wrung myself out of their grasp. "It's in the Leper's Rock." I showed Baa the stain, which still glowed on my finger.

"The Leper's Rock?" Baa's eyes turned white in terror. "You were there?"

"Oh, my daughter." Maa's tears shone in the lights of the fire.

"Nothing happened to me," I said.

That night, I dreamt that my father's bruka took me to the stars, where I became a princess in a world whose sky was red like blood. My finger with the sap stain glowed while I was awake to give this world day. When I awoke, the stain had peeled skin off my finger, leaving a scar that I still have to this day.

My parents had sat up through the night, Maa armed with a machete, Baa with the vunduk, ready to defend me, but my brothers had not attacked.

"We shall hide in the Leper's Rock," Baa said.

They must have reached that decision while I slept. Maybe Baa also knew that, being a god, the spirits would not harm him or his wife. We set off before dawn. Baa took some of his creations, and I carried his tools and other materials in a sack. I wanted him to take the bruka, but it was too big and heavy. Maa packed a basket of food that she had secretly taken from the gardens during the night. At the swamp, Baa built a papyrus raft. We rowed to the other side just as light broke.

We hesitated at the cave, where a strong red glow spilled out. Was it spirits?

Maa took several steps away, her face tight with fear. "Let's wait a little," she said. "It's still dark."

Baa grinned at her, then crawled into the cave. I wanted to follow him, but Maa grabbed my arms and made me stay with her. We sat on a boulder and waited. Baa took such a long time I feared the red light had eaten him. The sun rose. The red light weakened until it went out completely. Still, Baa had not returned.

"Baa!" I called, alarmed.

He crawled out, smiling, and brushed dirt off his knees and palms.

"There are no spirits," he said. "The light came from the sap. It seeps out of the rock and people think it is blood. It shines at night and goes out at sunrise. I'll call it the leper's blood."

I looked at the scar on my finger and thought of the red world in my dream. Had the Leper's Rock fallen from there? I did not tell my parents about the dream.

We settled in the cave, in a spot as far from the breast as possible, though it had stopped bleeding. By the time it started again, just before sunset, the pool had dried up.

Baa went to work at once. He made gloves that enabled him to touch the sap without it pricking him. I prayed that the leper's blood did not turn out to be useless. I wanted it to make the bruka work so we could escape from my brothers, but this made me think of the world in my dream. The blood red sky suspended over a land without vegetation or soil, without living things as I knew it, but full of black, mortar-shaped rocks. I suddenly did not want to go to that world.

Maybe Baa could create something else, like the cooking stone that used the power of the sun rather than firewood. I hated collecting firewood. I had to walk with other unmarried girls far from the village. The snakes did not scare us, nor did the monkeys or elephants. These were merely animals.

We did not fear obibi, for we knew they were mythical, but we dreaded the warabu. These were evil spirits in the shape of humans, with albino skin and black hair that was long and straight like a lion's mane. They kidnapped people and put them in black ropes of a strange material, which was harder than rock, and took them across the great desert to work as slaves in the land of the dead.

If Baa made a stove that cooked without firewood, he would become wealthy, for every homestead would want to own such a stove. With such wealth, my brothers would not force me to get married.

Baa did not want to make the stove. It would take a long time to bring him wealth. But if he had a super weapon, no one would dare touch me, so he concentrated on the vunduk. He worked fervently for the next three days. On the fourth, as he tried to make the vunduk shoot fireballs, he accidentally created something that worked. He moulded clay into an orange shape the size of my fist, mixed it with leper's blood, and put it out in the sun to absorb heat, but the ball was harmless. Instead of fire, it gave off the sunlight it had absorbed. The longer Baa left it in the sun, the brighter it shone.

Baa groaned in disappointment, though the ball could be a valuable source of light in every household. Back then we relied on kitchen fires and the moon for lighting. He called it the sunball.

"It's a step forward," I told him. "You made a ball that can trap the light of the sun. Don't give up. Now make one that can trap its heat."

That night we went to the mainland for firewood and food. We dug up wild roots and collected fruits. We stole hares from traps. As we returned to the swamp, we thought we heard someone following us. We hoped it was only our imagination, but the next day we heard shouting from across the swamp. People were singing and chanting. I could make out Okec's voice, and that of Okot, but the ajwaka's voice rang clear above that of everyone else as he led them through a ritual.

"He is preparing to enter the home of spirits," Baa said.

Spies had seen us during the night and now Okot and my brothers knew where we were hiding. They could not attack us at once, for they still believed there were spirits on the Leper's Rock.

We crept back into the cave. My parents did not know what to do. In a short while the ajwaka would finish the ritual and the men would row rafts to attack us. My brothers would then force me to marry that old devil.

"I know what to do," I said.

Before they could stop me, I put seven sunballs in a goatskin bag to mask their light, then I crept out of the cave. The ajwaka had finished the ritual. The papyrus hid them from my view but I could hear oars as the men rowed in silence. I could smell their fear. I took a deep breath and went underwater, where I released the balls, one at a time. They sank to the bottom, right in the path of the rafts, and sent seven red beams jetting out of the papyrus. I silently crept out of the water.

"Demons!" the ajwaka screamed. "Go back! Go back!"

I clamped my hands on my mouth to stifle laughter. Their oars splashed frantically as they scrambled back to the other bank. Then I heard running. I finally laughed aloud. Even today, I laugh every time I picture men running from lights.

"They'll come back," Baa said. "Okot has enough wealth to hire Olal."

Olal was a famous sorcerer. Some claimed he was a god who lived among mortals. They said he could raise the dead, and that he once caused the sun to stand still because he did not want to travel after dark. If Olal came, red lights would not frighten him. Baa had two days to make the vunduk work, because it would take messengers a day to reach Olal and another to return with him.

Baa did not sleep for those two days. On the third day, when he pulled the string on his vunduk, it spat out a ball of flame as big as my head. The fireball fell in the swamp and, rather than frizzle out in the water, it rolled about as though it was a rat looking for an escape hole. The papyrus it touched dried up and burst into flame. By the time it lost its energy, half the swamp was on fire.

"People will stop calling you a madman," Maa said, watching the flames.

"You are a god." I said it aloud for the first time, and Baa laughed at me. His laughter sounded as though he was singing in a strange language. It reassured me of his divinity. Normal people did not have such beautiful, musical laughs.

"If I'm a god, then what are you?" he said, and laughed harder, but it turned into a coughing fit.

"Do you use magic?" I said.

"No," he said.

"Then how did you make this thing to trap the heat of the sun?"

He laughed and coughed. "How did the first woman learn how to cook?" he said. "How did the first farmer know how to plant? How did the first butcher know how to skin goats?"

I thought about that. Maybe in the future, making fire-spitting weapons would be an everyday activity. But knowing how to put the fire of the sun in clay was not the same thing as knowing how to skin a goat. If he did not use magic, then he had special powers of his own, and that was proof that he was a god.

The fire died, leaving a black waste on the water, and revealing to us a turtle-man on the other side. He had a long, green beard that dangled over his chest, and hair that stood on his head like green flames. For a moment, I feared the fire had destroyed the home of a spirit, and now this spirit stood on the other side of the swamp, glaring at us. Surely that turtle's shell, that green beard and green hair could not belong to an ordinary man.

"Olal." Baa's voice was hoarse, as though with thirst. Other people stood in the far distance behind Olal, hiding in the bushes and behind trees. I could only guess they were my brothers and Okot.

"Burn them!" Maa said.

Baa pulled the string of the vunduk. His hands trembled. He could not release it. Setting the swamp ablaze had been easy, but taking a life was something even gods hesitated to do.

"Are you Ojoka the madman?" Olal shouted at Baa.

"I'm not a madman," Baa shouted back.

"Did you burn the swamp?" Olal said.

"Yes," Baa said. "And I'll burn you, too if you don't leave us alone."

"Do you know me?"

"Yes. You are Olal."

"So you should know better than to threaten me. I can kill you even if you are in the protection of spirits. But if you hand over the girl, we can settle—"

He did not finish speaking, because Baa released the string and a fireball flew over the water. Olal gaped at it for several heartbeats, then he stepped away shortly before it landed right where he had been standing. The fireball danced on the ground, drying up the wet green grass and setting it all ablaze.

Olal waved a bull's tail at the fire. Maybe he was casting spells to put it out, but the ball of flame seemed to grow in intensity, and it sped faster from here to there, and the bush came alive with terror. Grasshoppers jumped away, frogs ducked into the water, rats scampered from their holes, and birds flapped away in panic. Okot and my brothers fled. Even Olal, seeing he could not fight the fire, dropped his wand and took flight.

Well, that is how Baa earned his place among the gods. Okot dropped all his plans of marrying me. He gave Baa three hundred head of cattle in apology, and he lived the rest of his life with the torment of a lost manhood. Baa became famous and wealthy from his creations. His other two wives and his sons begged on their knees for mercy. He forgave them. I do not have to tell you all this, but if you are good children, I'll tell you of all my escapades in his house, especially my adventures in the bruka. I can tell you a story every night until you grow as old as I am. Just pray that the jok grants me a long life to tell it all.

# Black Tea

## Samuel Marolla

### Translated by Andrew Tanzi

*Samuel Marolla lives in Milan, Italy and writes both fiction and comics. He is also the co-founder of Acheron Books, publishing Italian speculative fiction in English translations.*

▼

*The principal lodger of Jean Valjean's day was dead and had been replaced by another exactly like her. I know not what philosopher has said: "Old women are never lacking".*
*—Les Miserables, Victor Hugo*

▲

T HE MAN WALKED through the shadows, over crimson carpets, past the mesmerizing patterns plastered on the walls. The air was sultry with no windows or other apertures, just a never-ending progression of forking, dead-end hallways, scattered with dust-laden mirrors, stairs leading nowhere, vaulted arches groaning under concrete masses. The wallpaper concealed other doors leading to cubbyholes and more empty rooms. Dark shelves held up old trinkets thick with dust. The plank ceiling was moldy. Sunlight had been foreign to this place for years.

He looked down at himself, touching his clothes that clung to him like a second skin. He was wearing an Elite Maintenance waistcoat suit, a white T-shirt, baggy dark-blue cotton pants, and work boots. He couldn't remember his own name but he had a nagging feeling in his mind—a glimmer of consciousness dimmed by that still air in those dull, vacant hallways. Who was he? Where was he? And why?

He rummaged through his pockets and found a folded, squared notepad sheet with the Elite Maintenance heading at the top. Right in the middle, large capital words ground onto the sheet with a red marker:

*DON'T TRUST THE OLD LADY!*
*SHE WANTS TO* **KILL YOU***!*

The man stood there staring at the words, his hands damp and trembling. What-the-*fuck* was going on here? An electric fever flamed up in his temples as he considered everything over again. He was some sort of special-maintenance technician. He and his team had been sent to do a job but then everything became a haze, names and faces dissolved into a greyish light, a shroud of sleep and forgetfulness.

What the hell was this place?

He walked on trying to understand and remember. A house—a large, empty house—with nobody living in it, its halls full of carpets and old drop-lamps exuding a hazy, murky, pestilent light; the walls plastered with old, damp, rotting paper with baroque patterns, dirty blue on a beige background, etched with alien, narcotic patterns, and in the air there was this stale, closed, sick smell. Hall after hall but no windows, *no way out*.

Countless twists and hallways later, he came to a wooden door with a colored glass panel. He could just see a vague shape beyond that opaque glass. A presence.

Nicola. His name was Nicola. Yes, Nicola was his name, and he worked for the waterworks. They were meant to do some maintenance along the Martesana waterway along the cycling path close to a Rom encampment, where a few isolated houses had sprouted up like weird mushrooms amidst neglected, yet luxurious greenery invaded by Milan's July mosquitoes. There were four of them—that much he could remember. The rest had been swallowed up in a vortex of unreality.

He opened the door and on the other side he found a room, a small room thickly furnished with antiques: dark wooden wardrobes and highboys, a different kind of wallpaper even more morbid and hypnotic with its labyrinthine twists and turns, and a round table covered with a white lace cloth. From the ceiling hung a drop-lamp larger than the others. Once again, no doors or windows on the outside, no way out.

Sitting at the table, facing the door Nicola had come through, was an old lady knitting away with needle and thimble, both held masterfully in her tiny wrinkled hands. Her deftness was mechanical and nerve-wrecking as she sat there bent over her ball of pretty emerald yarn. She ignored him—in fact, she didn't seem to notice him. She hunched over, working intently, her white hair done up in a fine bun, her body small and frail and dressed in a brown woolen robe.

Nicola took a few steps forward and swallowed—his throat was burning up. "Excuse me, Madam…"

The old lady looked up. Her feeble, perspiring face glistened like a wax mask. Her eager blue eyes had thick dark bags underneath. The skin on her cheekbones fell in heavy arches like the skin on the face of certain lurchers. She had an earthy olive complexion. Her familiar, unctuous expression was reminiscent of a cherished old aunty you hadn't met in ages.

"Poor dear, are you lost?" she asked with a buttery voice as she paused her knitting. She smiled sweetly.

"I…I don't think I feel too good, and…"

"Have a seat then—have a seat! You're tired and perspiring… I'll be right back." she said as she got up slowly, moving aside her wooden chair, laying on the table the unfinished sweater with her needle and thimble.

Almost overcome by some hypnotic command, Nicola drew up the chair (but he didn't remember seeing it when he came into the room) and sat down. He leaned against the table, exhausted, his arms crossed, his head resting on them. Just a few seconds.

Just *(don't trust the old lady)*

a few seconds' rest.

He was so tired.

Details were coming back to him now but in flashes—grey flashes. The Rom encampment to the right, a sudden Polaroid in his memory. The still, dark green waters of the Martesana to the left. Tall vegetation all around and in the background the chimneys of old factories, and a large, dark-grey mushroom-shaped tower—perhaps an old water tank. He and three other men, each wearing an Elite Maintenance vest, were walking through the high bushes, complaining about the heat, the thorns, the mosquitoes. Five o'clock on a scorching and murky August afternoon. A Polaroid of a dilapidated house, hardly visible on the horizon, behind a field of unharvested rotten corn. A piercing whistle ripped through the ice-blue sky.

Nicola opened his eyes and looked up. The old lady, smiling, had walked up to a stove with a kettle boiling on it. The plastic whistle (*it sounds like a cock, not just any old bird, listen carefully, you waning wanker, you human waste, you bottom feeder, it's a cock, Jesus*) was emitting that obtuse hiss. Nicola realized that when he entered the room there was no stove, no kettle boiling. But there they were now, yes, and tea was ready.

"I've made you some nice strong black tea—it'll perk you up!" The old lady's shadow sprawled out contortedly.

"But where are we? I can't…I can't really remember, and…"

The old lady laughed, shrugging slowly. She turned sideways to look at him. "Don't bother yourself about it. It's the heat, this terrible heat—it's scrambling your brains. You're in my home—Villa Bartoli."

"We're from Elite Maintenance," said Nicola slowly, more to himself than to his host. "We were just meant to fix the main… well, something."

"Of course, my dear," said the old lady as she brought a black enamel tray with a teapot, two teacups, and a plate of cookies to the table. "You went to the greenhouse—that's where the pipes are but it's even hotter there—I did tell you to take a break. This house is very large and (*may Hell regurgitate you, you bastard sodomite*) old; my husband Alfonso designed it—he was an eccentric architect, may God bless him, and it's quite easy to get lost amidst."

"*What?*" said Nicola, bringing a hand to his forehead. He felt feverish—that fiery fever from before that cooked his senses.

"I said if you wanted to try one of these butter cookies—I made them myself in my wood oven," she said, handing him a cookie.

Nicola took it and started to chew. The taste multiplied a thousandfold. A sweet, toffee-like taste; the dough was chewy and melted in his mouth.

But there was that sheet of paper in his pocket—the sheet with those words on it. He was starting to remember now and his throat burned so much it hurt.

"Drink up, have some tea—it's black tea and it will make you feel better," said the old lady, as if she had read his mind. She got back to her knitting, smiling all the time, and lifted her long metal needle, studying its tip.

Nicola seized the china cup. His hands were shaking. The old lady stood again and walked up holding her long knitting needle. "Drink up, drink up."

Nicola took a deep breath and brought the cup to his lips. The hot steam filled his nose—an intense, sweet fragrance of blossoms.

Polaroid: the four of them walking up to the porch of that very house—a house that seemed to have been abandoned for years, its windows barred shut, the grass unkempt, the sun choking everything in a metal vice. In the terse heat, a dog barked from far away, a suffused, rhythmic bark, as if he were in the midst of a dream. Around them a desert of rotten, dark yellow wheat. The world seemed to end there.

Nicola's lips touched the cup and he sipped the tea. It was delicious. He'd never tasted anything as good. The old lady stroked her knitting needle. "Do you feel better now?" she inquired.

Nicola put the cup back down on the table. "I'm such a fool, Madam. The heat just got went to my head. I must've wandered about looking for the bathroom and then sss ss sss…"

His throat snapped shut like a trap. Fiery fangs gouged at his carotid and vomit burst up his throat, a morbid mix of stomach acid and blood, a purplish slop erupting from his nose and mouth as he shot up and staggered back. Tears welled in his eyes. He gasped and flapped his hands blindly, grasping at the lace table-cloth, pulling it and upsetting everything—the teapot, the cups, and the cookies. Twitching convulsively, he saw the old lady smile and come toward him, her arms spread open, as if to embrace him. Her face was sick greasepaint, a hybrid accumulation of maliciousness and distorted craving, her torso tapering sickly into a toothless mouth that clicked and clicked like castanets.

Nicola backed toward the door and it opened behind him. He collapsed in the hallway and a gust of rancid stench covered the taste of blood and vomit in his mouth; it was the old lady *croaking* and clawing at his vest. Nicola was quick enough to wriggle his arm free and get out of the room, and he slammed the door shut. The old lady was imprisoned again in her room, and the door remained shut.

Nicola crawled along the carpet and felt a second stomach spasm more violent than the first. The tea was tainted. He knew he was done for—he realized it with the last flickers of consciousness leaving him. There were the others. The other guys on the team. He had to resist for them. He had to resist a few more seconds.

He took his sheet of paper from his pocket and unfolded it, staining it with his blood. He took his pen from his coat pocket— the pen with "Elite Maintenance" etched onto it—and, as he lay in a heap on the crimson carpet winding through the endless maze of hallways defaced by dead ends, dusty mirrors, stairs to nowhere, that abandoned and endless house that corrupted reality, its architectural entrails rent by inhuman pangs, he wrote something, and as he wrote, behind him, beyond the ground glass of the white wood door, a shadow moved, a small diaphanous shadow.

There were two left. Lying in the greenhouse, wearing their Elite Maintenance overalls, in opposite corners, every now and then they glanced at each other but didn't have the nerve to utter a word. They had clearly heard the choked sobs and wheezes of Nicola. He hadn't made it. And now there were two left.

The short one knew his name was Marco. That much he could remember. They had come here with a task and, from the papers strewn on the floor, he could see it had something to do with the pipe works. Of course—the greenhouse. The human rampart in this nightmarish hell. The stop-over, the last refuge. Things here worked more or less normally—time and space were not the demented distortions of some obscure power reigning over the abandoned mansion. Here, everything was *still* and there was no smell of mold—two important factors. But the third... well, the third was that the *old lady* couldn't get in here.

That wasn't all. The normality of this niche—a four-by-six-meter patio some grotesque sense of humor had dubbed a "greenhouse"—a vertical concrete duct, scorching under the perpendicular sun up there, and ornate with creepers like huge macrophages chewing on their grey guest, this normality was represented also by the regular functioning of the memory. Marco *remembered*. In gusts, with wrenched thoughts like a rag drenched in black scum, but something was there, for God's sake. Something was there. But out there, outside the greenhouse, passing through one of the two wooden doors, you went back into the *house*, into that perverse, multiform maze of halls and dead ends and secret rooms and barred doors and impossibly high windows, closed off by rusty steel lattices, and that—that was the old lady's realm.

He could remember the cycle path filling up with cyclists when they came in, along the road, beyond the weeds. That was the last vision in Marco's mind. The cyclists with their glitzy outfits and their reptilian helmets, catching sight of them as they arrived on the house's porch. Then it all became confused—a phosphoric fog possessed his mind. Dark, heavy hallways, with scarlet carpets, arabesqued wallpaper with dizzying patterns, small windows like portholes, closed off by intertwining lattices, and the old lady coming to the door to welcome them in—the old lady. Smiling, genial, petite. She led them to those roomless hallways and there something changed, something inside them broke. The four men looked at each other dumfounded, astounded, unable to recognize each other, or even recall what they were doing there. The only reason they hadn't questioned anything had been the old lady's calm, persuasive voice—a chirping voice that calmed them, cajoled them, but concealed under its warm modulation an age-old secret, an invisible mask, beneath that nice-old-lady voice Marco could distinctly remember a different plane of reality, a deviated din, a miasma of raucous, underground voices.

She had led them into a room—the only one that seemed to make any sense, with a hint of normality (*but the bodies of dead children hide and crawl behind that arabesqued wallpaper, you polymorph bastard, the bodies of dead children are* oozing *out of that wallpaper*), she'd had them sit around her knitting table, she had served them cookies, buttery greasy cookies (*guess what they're made of, you sick dog, think beyond the* wallpaper), she had made some black tea and, while they looked at each other, without saying a word, like freshly reanimated corpses, like overdosed opium junkies, their eyes languid, glimmering, begging for mutual help but unable to do anything but mechanically reach out for a cookie, bring it to their mouths, chew on a morsel, swallow slowly, and then start begging again; well, the old lady came back to them, she approached Mastorna, the foreman, and emptied on his head the entire content of the teapot—a liter of boiling black jasmine tea.

In the greenhouse, Marco crawled on the floor of the dusty patio, covered with tiny dried-out leaves from that morbid and ever-present creeper, and he remembered what happened after, in flashes of memory. Mastorna didn't even manage to scream. He just sat there, with the boiling water eating away at his bald head, with a sound of sizzling oil; it dripped down his ears and on his face and his look was one of petrified devastation, cookie-crumbs still in his mouth, and at that point they had all stood like weird puppets, trying to overcome the oblivion that surrounded them (like that *shitty* creeper, but in their souls), each of them moved by their own feeble instinct of survival, they had walked out the door, the first, Nicola, the second was Lotfi, the Egyptian guy, and he was the third. Marco had turned around before leaving the room and saw its true form.

It wasn't a little living room with antique furniture—none of that. It was a cube with impossible corners, with a *multitude* of impossible corners, it was like the inside of a wooden prism, its furniture writhing like living creatures as they bent and twisted following those skewed slants, and the old lady was the same as always but she was also something else, something that didn't show itself, hiding within the folds of reality, slithering between those folds as quick as a scolopendra, barely more than a wild smirk and that look in her eye, and Marco knew that Mastorna was the old lady's meal, and he knew he'd end up in pieces behind the room's wallpaper, he'd end up like…

"Marco," mumbled Lotfi as he pushed himself up on his elbows. With a superhuman effort the Egyptian guy tried to get up; he got on all fours, then to his feet, clutching at the creepers and tearing them away. "She got Nicola."

"Yes," said Marco, and it was quite an effort. He tried to get up, too. This place dragged you into an abyss of delirium. They had to fight back. They had to resist.

"Which of us is next?" he asked the Egyptian.

Lotfi turned his back to him. Then he took out a crumpled pack of cigarettes from his coat pocket. He drew out two cigarettes. He broke one. Then he clenched them, with the filter poking out. The two filters looked the same. He turned around and held out his fist.

Marco walked up to Lotfi and pinched one of the filters. He pulled. It was the long cigarette. Lotfi slit his eyes and a wicked gleam flashed through them. It was the gleam that strikes men right when their own personal world is threatened by other men—it was the natural predisposition to ferocious hatred that dwells within the heart of every man when he must share what is his, what he has exhaustively built up in his own miserable little life, brick after brick, through pain and tragedy, with unrelenting willpower, with—more often—fortune and misfortune; that sense of wretchedness so strong that one's own little things, material or immaterial, just cannot be shared with or offered to another person; they must in fact be defended at the cost of bloodshed, because altruism leads to violence, to the unacceptability of the other's existence. The other is the enemy.

Marco sensed this and realized that Lotfi would never accept the outcome of the lottery. They had done the same draw the first time and Nicola had pulled the shortest straw. Nicola had to leave the greenhouse and look for an exit, for help. The very same gleam had flashed through Nicola's eyes too, but Marco and Lotfi would have surely overpowered him.

Now they were one against one and Lotfi was trying to figure out, in those instants, if he could get the better of Marco and if it was worth it. Marco anticipated his move. "We could both go."

Lotfi's gaze concealed what he was about to do. "That's a good idea."

The two men seized the notepad and tore out a page each. They both wrote something—Lotfi in Arabic, Marco in Italian—they folded their respective sheets and pocketed them. They went to one of the two doors. Lotfi opened it. A dark, red hallway awaited them, just like all the others. "And what do we do when we find the old lady?"

Marco took the pen from his Elite Maintenance waistcoat. "I'll stab her in the throat with this."

Lotfi gave him an empty look. "Let's move it," he said.

When Mastorna had met that gruesome end a few hours (or *days?*) ago, they had rushed into the hallway to escape. The old lady was right behind them. She wasn't fast enough, though. Being outside that room, for some sick reason, became an exertion—she could move, but it taxed her. They moved slowly but still managed to distance her; still, they could sense that she was there, always one step behind them, always waiting around the next corner; no matter how far they got away, she was always on their tails. It was a silent escape and ended only when they reached the greenhouse. They locked themselves in, barricading themselves, and tried to talk, to understand. Their memories were hazy but in that patio things cleared up some. Maybe it was the open sky up there. It cleansed them somehow. Even if everything was distorted, even if they felt completely drunk, with the same nauseous feeling, the same reeling gait, the same babbled words of a drunkard, even though their thoughts were convulsive, intertwined, they managed to figure something out. They were imprisoned in that impossible nightmare. And the old lady was its kingpin.

Then someone had knocked on the door. Marco could remember it, as he and Lotfi walked through the house's corridors in Indian file, among antique furniture, the silent but sick witness of their journey. Marco did his best to concentrate, to remain lucid, to remember. Not to forget.

Yes, because that was the problem. The man who had knocked on the door a few hours before was Mastorna. Horribly disfigured and almost lifeless, he had come to them. And he couldn't remember the old lady. Those hallways, those rooms obliterated one's memory. Only in the patio, in the greenhouse, did something come back. But leaving that place meant cleaning the slate, forgetting where they were, and thus forgetting about the danger. Forgetting about the old lady.

Mastorna had died soon after and they had had to toss him out of the door opposite to where he had come from. And they had come up with a plan. They had to get out; they would pull straws and one of them would search for a way out and alert the others. But what if he ran into the old lady? He wouldn't remember who she was—that murdering whore—so they decided that whoever left the greenhouse would carry a sheet of paper with something written on it so as to remember and remain alert.

Nicola had pulled the shortest straw but things hadn't gone according to plan. They had heard his screams. The old lady had caught him, just as she had Mastorna.

And now—and now Marco and Lotfi, oblivious to what had happened, looked at each other dumbfounded, not knowing what to do or where to go, through places like the squares of a sadistic game of snakes and ladders. Marco fished a folded piece of paper out of his pocket and unfolded it. The writing was familiar. His own? It bore the following words, in shivering handwriting:

*THE OLD LADY IS A FUCKING MURDERER!*
*DON'T TRUST HER!*
*KILL HER BEFORE SHE KILLS YOU!*

As he read and wondered who he was, what he was doing there with that delirious piece of paper; the man there with him, a man with olive skin and north-African features, stopped him and pointed to a fork in the hallway. To one side, a dead end. To the other, a door, a white door with ground-glass windows.

In a daze, the men drew closer and noticed some blood on the carpet, on the walls, and frantic handprints. Someone had been dragged into the room. Someone, still alive and clawing at the door with blood-soaked hands, but his resistance had been in vain. And right outside the door, a dirty crumpled piece of paper. The dark-skinned man took it and spread it out. Marco regarded him like an alien. He felt like throwing up. He craned his neck and read, feeling far, far away from everything, feeling lost in a nightmare. He was dreaming. Yes, it had to be that—it was a dream, a nightmare, albeit real, tangible.

The sheet bore these blood-smeared words:

*WATCH OUT!*
*THE OLD LADY'S HIDING IN THIS ROOM!*

And just below, underlined over and over again:

*KEEP OUT!*

The two men stared at each other. Marco gestured to keep quiet (Did he know him? He thought he did, but who the *hell* was he?) and pointed toward the room. The man understood and gestured to wait. He hunkered down to peek through the keyhole and see what was hidden on the other side. Marco found this quite smart, despite the hallucinating context.

"See anything?" Marco whispered. "Let me see, too!"

The man gestured to him to wait. "Hang on!" he whispered. "I can't…"

Lotfi! His name was Lotfi! He knew him. Of course he knew him. He was a maintenance team colleague who…

Lotfi let out a bestial cry—a cry that shattered the unnatural silence of that nightmare labyrinth—and flew back as if he was being pulled by invisible strings. His hands were over his face. He appeared in front of Marco, who barely managed to scream.

From his right eye—the one at the keyhole—there protruded a long, slim, shiny knitting needle; only half of it visible, because the other half stuck in his face, piercing his brain like a skewer.

The old lady had jabbed her knitting needle through the key-hole and right into his eye. Lotfi cried out, writhing on the carpet that lined the floor, and Marco, who could barely remember his name, tried to help him. The wooden door behind him creaked. Just over Marco's shoulder he saw the small silhouette of the old house-owner.

"Poor dear, is he hurt?" she asked lovingly as she pointed at Lotfi, who had stopped screaming and crouched in a corner, groaning, his head turned to the wall, his legs twitching.

Marco stumbled over the body and broke into a run along the hallway without ever turning back but knowing, knowing all too well that a dark and evasive form hunted him down, just beyond the barely visible corner, and he ran and ran not even remembering his own surname, not even knowing what he was doing in that sick dream. Each time he tried to turn he saw that little silhouette moving quickly, popping up from around the corner; he could just catch a small detail—an old lady's smile, a cotton wisp of white hair, a surgical boot; it was the old lady, the old lady who was always right behind him, always

*Godless dog, forsworn sodomite, that's what you are.*

right behind him.

At the last turn—and he turned back to look at the ump-teenth hallway after the umpteenth turn—he crashed into a wooden door, knocking it down with a resounding bang. He landed on the other side like a human avalanche and he was in a new room. He knew who he was. His name was Marco, he was a plumbing technician, he was twenty-eight years old, he had a life, a girlfriend, friends, and he didn't want to die like all the others, no way. He glanced around the room. He grabbed hold of a cupboard and tugged until it blocked the doorway. He gave one last look and he saw that dark silhouette bending around the corner and in an instant it was the old house-owner, wearing a grey, worn -out overcoat, her hands crossed in front of her, walking toward him with her little surgical boots, and she smiled at him, she smiled and maybe she would treat him to a cup of black tea and some butter cookies (remember what they're made with) and he'd forget everything and he'd follow her, and then what would happen? Marco didn't even want to think about it.

He turned around. The room was long and narrow and there was a small window at eye-level. He ran toward it and looked outside. His spirits fell; the lattice was thick and it was impossible to get out, but someone was passing by out there. Cyclists. Damn cyclists.

"Hello! Help! Hey!" He banged his fists against the glass. He looked around, seized a piece of wood from the broken door and struck the glass. It didn't break. Marco was shattered. Devastated by anguish, he slumped down on the dusty floor, thinking it was over. He wanted to let go, to lie down and wait for the old lady to come in.

*Here I come, you stale little sperm.*

"Come with me!" yelled a voice. A man called from the opposite end of the narrow room. He wore a dark coat and had a long beard and moustache. His hair was black and also very long. "Come. She won't stay out there forever. She'll figure out a way in. She always does."

"What...what..."

"Come on, man. If you want to live."

Marco got up and, in a fever, followed the man to the other exit, the other wooden door. He didn't understand why but he knew he had to do it. "Who are you?" he asked as they moved through new, old shadowy hallways, over dark carpets, drenched with a stench of sour soup. Wood and chalk frames gave a nice touch to that nightmarish place.

"Can you hear her? She's above us now," he said, ignoring him. Marco looked up and heard a slight creak from the floorboards above. "She always knows where I am but she can't get at me everywhere. I know the way. I know how to move around without being caught. At first she always found me. She found me and tried to bite me."

"Who? Who the fuck are you talking about?"

"The old lady. The house-owner. The one that killed your friends. I know the way. I know how to get to the places she can't get into. There are rules. I don't know who made them, man, but there are rules. There's the greenhouse and then there's the bedroom. There it is," he said and they went around a corner, reaching a dark door. The man went in and showed Marco the small, cramped room, a cubicle full of tiny, dark, and lugubrious pieces of furniture, a sofa with a floral pattern in one corner, and a round window.

"Can we get out? Can we get out from there?" yelled Marco, running to that slit that looked out onto the outside world. Dark stains of dampness ate away at the ceiling. Desperation reigned in that place.

The man guffawed. "Don't you see? There is no way out of this place. I spent the first months banging on the windows. They won't break and nobody out there can hear you. Cyclists pass by during the day and gypsies during the night but nobody can hear your cries. Sometimes some kids play soccer in that field over there, but in here we're alone. We're on our own with her."

Marco held his head. "No, no no…" he said, dismayed. He slumped onto the sofa, mumbling incoherently.

"I sleep there. On that sofa. It's not so bad. I mean, you get used to it."

"How long…how long have you…"

"No idea. *Years*, I'd reckon."

"And how…how did you survive so…"

The long-haired, long-bearded man banged his fist against the wall. Marco started. As if to reply through mimicry, the man looked at where his fist had landed—he had just squished a huge spider with extraordinarily long legs. He took its body between two fingers and popped it into his mouth. He swallowed it in one gulp. Marco stared at him, mouth agape. He was so disgusted that he felt like throwing up.

"You get used to everything. If you want to live, that is." The man leaned against the wall and slipped down on the floor into a sitting position.

"Who is she?" Marco asked his new, unexpected companion.

The man shrugged. "Who knows. Sometimes, even at night, even though day and night are the same thing, I can hear her walking upstairs, I can feel her *sniffing me out*, because she wants me, she wants to catch me, but she can't..." he explained, his eyes wild, red all around, as he stared at the black stain on the wall where he had squished the spider. "...so I cling to that sofa, that sofa that reeks of death, I clench my eyes and I imagine that she's just an animal, a very hungry animal. That's all," he said and turned to look at the round window and its lattice, beyond which flowed life and the Martesana. Exhausted, Marco looked toward the round window, too, and saw a group of cyclists passing by. He didn't even have the strength to cry out.

"Someone's going to come looking for us eventually." The man stared blankly at the round window. Marco couldn't even answer as he focused on the cyclists passing just a few feet from them. He simply opened his mouth and moved his lips, soundlessly. They wouldn't have heard him anyway.

From above them came a furtive shuffle. It was the old lady. She *could* smell them.

She couldn't get to them, but she could wait.

# Tiger Baby

## JY Yang

*JY Yang is Singaporean author whose short stories have been published in* Clarkesworld, Strange Horizons, Apex Magazine, *and many others.*

FELICITY WAKES FROM a dream of hunting. She moves her hands, sleep-heavy, and is surprised to find them human-shaped, with hairless fingers that curl and end in flat, dirty nails. Sheets tangle around her legs, clinging damply to fleshy thighs, knotting around an inert lump she comes to realize is her body.

Sometimes, not always, she forgets she is human. Especially on mornings like this, with her mind's eye still burning bright, breathing forests of the night. The taste of her true form lingers: not this body with its rock of pain nestling in between neck and shoulder and the blood pounding in the head and the rancid feel of its dry mouth. Feli closes her eyes, hoping to slip back into the wonderful light darkness, into her true flesh, dread hands dread feet running across warm concrete, searching, singing, wind sluicing through striped fur as she streaks through the neighbourhood.

The door makes a loud noise and she startles into wakefulness, craning her head to look. Her mother stands in the doorway, knuckles flush to wood. "You don't need to work today? You'll be late."

Resentment surges up like a storm wave, like a predator springing from the grass. Her mother does not understand, will never understand, standing in the doorway with her faded shirt and heavy pear-hips and shiny face beginning its irreversible droop. She sees her grandmother reflected in there, worn away by time until the eyes hold only emptiness. Wherever her wild streak comes from, it is not here. Feli drops a hand to the bedspread. "I'm awake."

She can't remember when it started. Which came first, the dreams or the realization of what she was meant to be? How many youthful hours did she spend in corners, softly reciting Blake and feeling a weighty truth?

Her earliest memory is of tigers, swimming in a moat. How she watched one, on the rock above, pace back and forth in the enclosure, while her father shouted warnings about staying put and her infant sister cried to no one in particular. She is too young to know the word *majestic*, but from that moment she compares everything to the effortless rippling of muscle under skin, and finds it inadequate.

She was born in 1986, the Year of the Tiger, the Fire Tiger. These things happen for a reason.

The knowledge of her true form has been with Feli so long, she's stopped noticing how it flavours her life. In the shower, glass walls thick with fog, she imagines the water streaming down fur instead of pale, spotty skin. Breakfast—eggs and kaya toast—tastes like cardboard, like tree bark: she wants fresh meat, she wants heft she can tear into, she wants to drink lightly salted blood and not kopi, scalding and bitter. Walking to the train station, the cadence of her arms and legs falls into a feline rhythm, propelling her past the other commuters. Phantom muscles move under her skin, unhobble her from the limitations humanity picked up when it split from its mammalian ancestors. She read that on the internet.

Robert from IT talks to her at work. He always talks to her at work. A Chinese man with a soft belly and a hairline wearing thin in the middle, he somehow manages to find time in his morning to hover over the semi-partitions of her cubicle, stringing together words that she makes monosyllabic replies to. In her first weeks on the job one of the ladies, a generic over-powdered law clerk who had moved on a few months later, had told her: "He only talks to you because you're single." That had been five years ago, when she'd still had her toes dipped in her twenties. Five years later, nothing much has changed, except the size of her trousers and Robert's bald patch. It's not that she finds him unpleasant. But Robert is like a wolf to her, strange and canine: she has no use for his loping gait and pricked ears and readily wagging tail.

He tries to ask her if she's doing anything tonight, without actually ever asking. She gives noncommittal replies without ever saying no. Her voice rumbles low as she says, "Robert, you know month-ends are very busy for Accounting," and her throat tickles, as if there's something stuck in it, like the flexible hyoid bone of big cats that allows them to roar where domestic cats cannot. The sound she wants to unleash would send this entire open-concept office scampering. Scaring Robert isn't worth that.

At night she brings the bag of feed down to the void deck. As she spills it on a spread of newsprint, the neighbourhood cats come up and rub against her legs, one after another, like subjects paying respects to their queen. She beckons to their de facto leader, the green-eyed orange moggie, who leaps into her lap and stretches. These times, with the weight of a cat in her lap and the smell of fur against her skin, are the realest parts of her day. She purrs and growls as they swarm around her, their eyes glittering sparks. They will eat only after she leaves.

Her friends ask her sometimes why she doesn't keep a cat, doesn't invite one of the strays she loves so much into her home. But she looks at the eyes burning in the dusk and she knows that she could never inflict that on them.

The moggie in her lap rumbles, the closest it can manage to a roar. "One day," she says. "One day they'll stop asking."

It's funny how time slips past, in between the chunks of work and sleep and feeding the cats, and days roll into weeks roll into months and years. Feli continues the motions of getting up every morning and eating her cardboard breakfast and compressing herself on the way to work and back. The surface of calm she presents to the world hides the fearful symmetry she keeps in the roiling deep.

The Lunar New Year comes around in an explosion of reds and golds, showers of drums and cymbals and recordings of the sound of firecrackers. Smiling relatives hide pot bellies in starched shirts and wrinkles in extra layers of makeup, passing around sweet, sour, salty, deep-fried excuses for affection in little plastic bottles with red screw-on lids. Years of going through these obligations have dulled the stabs of pain in Feli's neck and shoulders that these reunions cause. She has learned to suppress her flight instincts, to put on a sickle-cell smile when asked the tickbox questions she gets every year.

But this year the aunts and uncles leave her alone for the star of the exhibit, swarming around the younger sister who ripens like a fruit, peppering her with questions. About the new house, how big, the due date, did they know the sex? Her sister, with big veiny feet and hair swept into a loose homely bun, entertains them with toothy laughs and fluid sweeps of her straight white arms.

Feli feels pity for her and the comfort she feels. It's the same pity she feels when she looks at the dull faces of the office workers who surround her on morning commutes. Her sister will never know what it's like to be free, will never know the sensation of running in the night, will never know the pleasure of growling low and feeling it deep in the lungs.

Feli wonders about the child growing in her sister's belly. It, too, will be born in the Year of the Tiger. Will it be like its Auntie Feli? Impossible. And *Auntie Feli*. What an ugly collection of syllables.

Her mother stands with her sister, glowing, looking younger than her sixty years. Afterwards, after the yu sheng has been tossed, her father speaks to her on the sidelines, as the bulk of the family gather around the television with disposable plates of the mess. Tells her how they are thinking of selling the flat, her mother and he, downgrading to one of those three-room flats. She's turning 36 and now she's finally eligible to buy government flats as a singleton, and there were a few public launches coming up with studio apartments, weren't there?

Cornered, she can only nod mutely, her hands flexing and unflexing. She can't imagine a house, its confines suffocating her, weighing her down like a brick. She looks out of the window. Leaping away would be easier. Vanish into the night.

Her parents are bothered because she hardly goes out anymore. She comes home right after work on weekdays (to feed the cats) and stays in most weekends (because she feels too lazy to go out cycling anymore and the board gaming sessions have become tedious).

They invite her to their movie nights, try to get her interested in whatever's on the television, as if that would settle the wild bones rattling inside her.

She talks to Andy. "It's that Blake poem," she says, "I keep seeing and hearing it everywhere. Sometimes at work, I'll see the words on my spreadsheet instead of numbers."

Andy was the only one who hadn't laughed when Feli had told her the truth back in school. The sunlight catches in her hair as she leans back into the grass of the Botanic Gardens. "Is it just the poem bothering you?"

"Everything is bothering me. I have dreams every night now. I feel like, I don't know, something's about to burst out of me. Like it's getting harder to hold it back."

"You're just getting more in sync with your true self. Becoming one with the tiger." Andy's fingers flutter. She likes animals, draws pictures of half-human creatures with animal heads, and talks about herself as though she were a lynx. Sometimes, listening to Andy babble on like a shopping mall water feature, she thinks they could have taken their friendship to a different level if she hadn't ignored Andy's advances. But Andy peppers their text conversations with nuggets like *flattens ears* and *offers sympathy paw*, and each one grates under the skin like badly fitting joints. Such things should be kept private; broadcasting them to the world is crass. Shameless.

No, Andy understands, but she doesn't understand. Feli smiles and stretches beside her, focusing on the smell of the grass, the sunlight warming her belly. The turmoil she has to keep inside herself. It's like smothering a forest fire with a second-hand blanket.

She knows something is wrong even before she pads into the senior partner's cubicle. It's the small hushes that have been descending in pockets of the office, the subtle shunting of emails and duties in the weeks before, the pow-wows that see upper management cloistered in one of their mahogany-lined rooms. Even Robert hadn't come by that morning.

The firm is run by two men, an older and a younger partner. She can talk to the older one, Yong Chew, a grandfatherly figure who sees reason and could be persuaded. But it is Walter, the younger partner, who wants to see her. He has a face like a marble sculpture, blank alien eyes. Her hands curve as she sits down, a curling motion playing at her lips.

"There's no good way to say this," Walter begins.

"Am I being fired?"

A soft huff comes out of Walter as he leans back in his chair. "Well, if we're going to be so direct."

Rushing heat spreads from her stomach to her fingertips, crackling softly. "I am being fired."

Walter sighs. Feli's predator gaze focuses on the lines under his eyes, and the grey in his hair that hadn't been there when she had started in the job. She feels sorry for him then, sorry for a life that is hollowing him out from the inside. "You know we've been trying to cut costs in the last few months. Times are tough. We need to downsize, it's the only way." Walter clears his throat. "It was a difficult decision, but the accounting department was one of the areas we identified. And we, uh, we made a decision."

"I understand." If they had to pick one person to keep, it would not be her. It would never be her, this ill-fitting, elusive thing.

He leans forward, his face and demeanour telegraphing sorrow. "Nobody wants this, Felicia."

"Felicity."

Walter's eyes flicker downwards. She rises to her feet, hands crouched on the table for support. "I'll pack my things."

The house is dark. Feli sits on the edge of the bed, soaked in sweat, imagining a stone sinking to the bottom of the ocean, the glow of its burn fading as it descends into a watery grave. She is afraid to sleep, afraid that when she closes her eyes she will be irreversibly pulled into a chasm at the bottom of the ocean, filled with the sideways glances of her colleagues and Robert's wilting look, and her parents' concerned eyes.

So she stares straight ahead. Down, down, down she sinks.

Felicity, the girl, is burning away, sloughing off in ashy bits that fall away into the water. There wasn't much left of her to begin with, she thinks, from a distance. She feels her human body get up and move toward the door, and she realizes this is instinct: like a caterpillar knowing when it's time to find a branch and become the butterfly it's meant to be. Her strides are long and lazy as she slips out of the front door, naked as the day she was born, feet padding across bare concrete and warm, unwashed lift landing tiles.

It is time.

Soon, she will be walking these grounds in a new body, four hundred pounds of flesh and power, great heart beating, fearsome mind burning with the fire of a hundred furnaces. She will cover a thousand paces in one bound, nobody to stop her or tell her where to go. It will be deadly. It will be terrible.

Downstairs she goes, into the deserted void deck, hair spilling over shoulders, hands held out. The lights flicker and extinguish with a hissing sound as she passes them by, plunging the space into sequential darkness. In the inkiness pairs of eyes glint, reflecting moonlight, pupils blown. Her flock has come to her, mouths open and mewing. The orange moggie pushes to the forefront, eyes expectant.

It is time.

She gets down on her hands and knees. "I'm here," she whispers. But the sound comes out as a long, high noise. The topography of her throat is changing, the genetic material fluttering and resettling into another pattern. As a child she had watched the National Day Parade, how groups of dancers would change one picture into another by flipping coloured boards, exposing the underside, exposing the other nature. The boards of her physical self are changing. Her bones are compressing. Her skin is changing. She crouches on the ground as the wave of boards sweeps over her.

It is time.

The gathered cats fall silent and still.

Claws click on the ground. No more tangly fingers. She stretches and a tail flicks behind her, a strange and new sensation. A pleasing one.

Yet something seems wrong. The feel of her muscles is nothing like in her dreams.

She opens her eyes, her freshly shaped eyes, and everything is crisper, more alive—and looming. Walls tower above her. The green plastic dustbin in the corner looks like the Incredible Hulk, an impossible mass she will never be able to jump on top of, much less knock over. She stretches forward, and delicate, sienna paws come into view, striped gently with white.

The orange moggie looks at her, pleased.

She opens her mouth, pushes air through her larynx, tiny chest constricting—instead of a roar, there is a meow. The lump in her throat, the hyoid bone, is small and stiff and makes little noises. Meow. Meow. In the glittering eyes of the orange moggie with its tail-flicks she sees a lifetime of stalking through gutters, fighting with rats, and finding quiet spots under stairs to nap.

This is it. This is who she is. Not a dread terror of the night, but a small supple being that slips through the cracks like water. She jumps on the spot, once, twice experimentally: her back arches and her feet have a wondrous spring to them. How light and free she is, with her new sight and ears sharp as bowls.

The cats around her meow their welcome.

The orange moggie comes close and brushes slightly past her. No more ear-rubs; they are equals, now. She purrs briefly, then springs away. She understands their new code, the code of the cat, where boundaries are both protection and respect.

The gathered felines spring away into the night, dispersing in a thousand directions like a firework. She joins them. Behind her, the lights of the void deck flutter back to life, casting their mottled shadows over the blank space where the girl used to be. She doesn't look back.

# Jinki and the Paradox

## Sathya Stone

*Sri Lankan author Sathya Stone's stories have appeared in* Strange Horizons *and* Every Day Fiction, *among others.*

MR. QUEST MADE people out of cards. He took a deck of cards, hearts and spades and diamonds and clubs, and he gave them little heads and little arms and skinny legs to stand on. The kings and queens had little crowns, and the knaves had little hats. All the other cards were soldiers.

Mr. Quest said that he got the idea from a book called *Alice in Wonderland*. Mostly they just ran into each other. They were kind of stupid, Jinki thought, but it was a marvelous gift, even so. Jinki wasn't allowed a lot of toys, and anyhow, the adults were always too busy to make *frivolous* things for him. Jinki had learned to say *frivolous* from Mother.

Mother said the word with a sort of sneer, as if it was…not a bad word, exactly, but a word that didn't make her happy. Some words she said with bright seriousness. Mother was nicest when she was saying words like *sub-committee* and *utilitarian viewpoint*. Jinki thought they were nice words, too, they sounded like you were beating out a rhythm with a spoon on a saucepan.

Mother said Mr. Quest was a very *frivolous* man. Jinki thought that was true, but he also knew that Mr. Quest was in a lot of sub-committees. Mr. Quest was on more sub-committees than anyone ever, so it was all right for Jinki to spend time with him.

The other interesting thing Mr. Quest had, other than *Alice in Wonderland*, was a garden. No, well, everybody had a garden, but Mr. Quest had a *frivolous* garden. Mother hadn't actually said so, but Jinki knew frivolous when he saw it. Mr. Quest had the most interesting pots, delicate and melon-shaped and a color he said was called jade. They were really old and priceless pots, and they were made to put tea and things in, a long time ago, back when there were kings outside a card pack, and even emperors. But Mr. Quest thought that the pots had retired now, being so old. When you retire, Mr. Quest said, you should make it your business to do lovely and pointless things. So he grew flowers in the ancient pots.

Jinki liked big, colorful flowers, though, with lots of petals. The flowers in Mr. Quest's garden weren't that interesting. They were small and only had about five petals and they were boring colors like white and pale blue and yellow.

"Ain't no rocks in the plains, ain't no rocks in the sea, ain't no rocks but the rocks that come when the gods in the sky do a wee." Jinki laughed so much he was almost sick. He'd heard of falling stars, of course, and he'd even seen a few, but he'd never been told that they were the gods' wee. It was the best story he had ever heard.

"You can wish on them," said Mr. Quest.

"I know," said Jinki. "But that's only pretend."

"You'd be surprised," said Mr. Quest. "Interesting stuff, rocks, anyhow. Full of stories."

"Really?" said Jinki.

"It's difficult to find rocks on this part of the planet, of course, else I'd show you. Aye." Mr. Quest liked to say 'aye'. It meant *yes*. "Years of erosion, that means the wind and water broke bits off the mountain along that way." He pointed east. "And brought them down here, to be dust."

"What mountains?"

"They're gone now," said Mr. Quest. "Eroded. You can see them if you look through Time."

"I'm not allowed," said Jinki. "Mother says it'll cause a pa-ra-dox." He savored the word. "Mr. Quest?"

"Aye, lad?"

"Why are you in so many sub-committees?"

"When you're older and sadder you'll understand better, or worse, or the same," said Mr. Quest. When he said things you heard a second voice echoing the final words, like a chant or a song, softly, like you were hearing it with your mind rather than with your ears. "Tricksters need a place, a still point in the chaos potential (*chaos potential*). Like the middle of a see-saw, lad. I shall have to get about making you one of those, one of these days (*one of these days*). But—ah—also a place from which the chaos extends, trickles out, and gets bigger and bigger (*and bigger and bigger and bigger*), but not so powerful a place that the chaos destroys (*destroys*). *I wouldn't want to be president, no, no (no no no no no).*"

"I'd like to be president," said Jinki. "I'd like to see a rock, Mr. Quest."

He said it because you just had to say things to Mr. Quest, and then they happened.

"Well, that's easy, lad. It's as easy as anything, if you think a little with your great big head."

"Mother," said Jinki, as she was getting ready to tuck him into the mirror that night. "What's a Trickster?"

"It's a random error," said Mother. "It's an engineered random error, Jinki. Mr. Quest is a Trickster."

"What does that mean?" said Jinki, brightening up now that she was answering. Mother didn't always answer questions.

"You know the Rathki, dear?"

"Yeah?" He knew a lot about the Rathki, though he'd never met one. He'd read that they were the Mathematicians of the Universe, which was a bit annoying, because Jinki was made to learn math for hours and hours and hours and no one ever called him a Mathematician of the Universe. The Rathki were cool looking though, because they had crystalline brains and bodies. Miss Pillow said that they were made of Carbon, which humans like Mother were also made of, but Carbon came in different disguises. Mr. Quest said that Carbon was the Trickster of the Universe.

Jinki didn't know exactly what he was made of, because Miss Pillow hadn't got to the 'corporeal bodies' the humans made for the Kai people yet. He did know what corporeal meant, it meant solid. Mother said that there was plenty of time to learn, but Jinki thought that was only because Mother didn't like to think about Jinki being adopted. Mother wanted to think that she'd given birth to Jinki herself.

"Well," said Mother, radiating disapproval. "The Rathki believe that civilization rises only because of the random error, events no one can predict. If you have the usual probability math governing events, then you'll only ever get unicellular organisms, or maybe just no life at all, because life is a random error."

"But doesn't math say nothing is random?" said Jinki, hesitantly. He was good at math, but what he'd meant to say was that, actually, *Alice in Wonderland* said nothing was random even if it appeared to be so, and he knew *Alice in Wonderland* was math in disguise, sort of.

"Very good," said Mother, and smiled. She was beautiful when she smiled, her brain glowed a wonderful orange color. "That's the problem of course. It's a load of nonsense. Things arise from other things, even if we can't predict it." She sighed. "There are different schools of thought, Jinki. The Rathki think that if they have Mr. Quest be random and do random things long enough, they'll learn something important about the Universe. They think the Universe is designed to even out the random errors in the space-time fabric." She rolled her eyes, and Jinki could tell that this was the stupidest thing she'd ever heard in her life. "Our homeworld gets so much help from the Rathki, we've gone and taken up all their silly ideas." She gestured to say preparation was done, and he went into the mirror. She kissed it. "Now go to sleep, Jinbaby."

"Mr. Quest?" said Jinki, one cold evening. "Why aren't there other children in the colony?"

It was one of those questions that just didn't occur to you until you eavesdropped on someone talking about it. Mr. Quest was unusually serious.

"Because even if the colony dies Jinki, you can't (*you can't*). Light doesn't die, you could hide in the fragments of mirrors and speckles of glass (*speckles of glass*) until the rescue mission got in with a new body for you. Human babies would die in the toxic world (*toxic world*) if the colony failed."

"That's sad," said Jinki. "Did the government say you can't bring human children, Mr. Quest?"

"Aye, they did, Jinki. But we needed a child, we did. I asked. My Trickster brain said to me, ask for a child. They can't say no (*can't say no*), when the Trickster asks (*Trickster asks*). That would defeat the whole experiment."

"What experiment?" said Jinki, interested. He loved experiments. Instead of Miss Pillow droning on and on, her brain the color of wet sand, sometimes they did experiments in his special classes, which were fun, and Miss Pillow's brain went a pretty, pretty blue color. And sometimes, on experiment days, the other grown-ups helped set things up. That was fun, because Father said that in real human School Cities, you had lots of students and lots of teachers. But Jinki didn't want to go to one of those, of course. Then he wouldn't see Mother every day.

Mr. Quest laughed. It wasn't a very nice laugh. "It's sad and you don't need to be sad yet, because sadness is a thing of great proportions that won't fit in your little head. That's why it's so uncomfortable to be sad, Jinki, (*Jinki*), because it's too big to fit inside you."

That evening Jinki put all the card-people inside the anti-gravity ball and watched them all scream as they tumbled and crashed into each other. It was a cruel thing to do, but they weren't real people. They were just robots. He would never be mean to real people.

"Guinea pigs," said Mother, bitterly. "Lab rats. To test their stupid theories."

"Flirting with death," said Father, who, Jinki knew, was a *frivolous* man. "Makes you feel alive, honey. Makes your blood pound like the drums in a rock song, honey. My honey. Come and dance."

"What ridiculous nonsense," said Mother, but Jinki could just make out that her brain had gone the nice red color it did when Father made her happy and not angry. "We have our child to think of."

"It is a glorious, glorious feeling," said Father. "To have a child that cannot die."

"The odd thing is that they're so stupid," said someone, and Jinki thought that was *such* a mean thing to say. "You'd assume that a species made out of *light* would think faster than any other sentient creature."

"That's uninformed garbage," said Mother's voice. "They *are* faster, for your information," she added, in that imperious voice that Jinki loved when it wasn't directed at him. Mother was badass in committee meetings. She was probably sneering, too. "But they have to learn to exist inside Time, in order to interact with us, and live inside synthetic bodies with the conventional senses, it *zaps* them. It's difficult in ways we can't imagine, to be trapped in a meatsuit." What Mother meant was that the other lady couldn't imagine it, because she was stupid. Mother was clever. "They have to get used to it, Kendra, and that takes hundreds of years. Jinki isn't allowed to look outside Time just for that purpose. If he knew the feeling, he would do it constantly." There was a pause. "And some say it'll be a paradox, because he's entwined with a human timeline, since we can't just ignore Time like the Kai do. Load of nonsense, I suspect, but it scares him enough so that he doesn't do it."

"He can't even sleep until we put him inside the mirror," Father added. "It's damned difficult to coax him out after the minute is up, he says it's so much nicer in there, poor little thing."

It *was* nicer inside the mirror, but Jinki liked having a body. You could touch things and go where you wanted, not just bounce everywhere because you didn't have a choice.

"It's a blessing he's such an obedient child," said another voice that Jinki felt like he ought to recognize. In a few years, Mother said, he'd be able to identify voices much better. Jinki had to learn to maneuver the senses like the human children did, naturally.

"He's very well behaved," said Mother, proudly.

"They gave me a Kai child and ancient pots and *Alice in Wonderland*," said Mr. Quest, sadly. "They gave me madness inside my robot skull (*robot skull*) and a place in all the sub-committees to my heart's desire (*desire desire desire*). They gave me all of you and all of your lives. You must rise against them and destroy them all! (*all! all! all!*)"

"He's a *robot?*" screeched Jinki.

"Destroy the *Rathki?*" yelled everybody else.

Mr. Quest shrugged. "Random event generator, remember, it is my job to voice the ridiculous."

Mother sighed. "A tempting suggestion, Mr. Quest, if not a practical one."

The experiment, Mother explained when Jinki wouldn't stop asking, went like this:

You had three colonies on the planet. One had a Trickster, that one was theirs; they didn't necessarily have to listen to the Trickster, he just had to be there. One had no Trickster and all decisions were made by a coin-toss; the colony could not disobey the coin, if they did, the experiment terminated for them and they were released to go home. The third was a conventional colony of the sort Earthmen had favored for centuries that was the control. Rescue teams were constantly on standby in case anything went wrong.

Then the Rathki just waited to see what would happen.

It had been three years now. The coin-toss colony was shut down after a week into the experiment. The other two colonies were neither thriving nor deteriorating (which was a *really* good word, so Jinki memorized it). The Rathki provided all resources and technology, and humans had always wanted to colonize this particular planet because of the plutonium reserves, Mother said. After the experiment concluded, the Rathki had arranged for the world to become Earth territory. It wasn't a bad exchange in turn for humoring a bit of Rathki frivolousness.

"Well," said Father to Mother., "they said symbolic algebra was stupid, too, honey."

"What difference has having a Trickster made?" said Mother. "Whenever he suggests something too stupid we just ignore him. He's a constrained random error. It's nonsense. The Rathki are just messing with us."

"Why on earth would an advanced race like theirs want to play cheap tricks on the likes of us?"

"They would rather we own this planet than one of their enemies. *They* certainly can't claim it without causing a furor." Jinki could imagine Mother's lips going thin, and her eyes going narrow and a bit scary. But Father was brave. "Terrans have good relations with everyone, Dabir, and if the Rathki say they're giving it to us, they can just about get away with it!"

"For plutonium?" said Father, with a derisive laugh. "They wouldn't go to that kind of trouble for plutonium."

"Something else then, something we don't know about," said Mother. "Come on, we all know this experiment is ridiculous to a degree that-"

"Conspiracy theorist," said Father, and then they had an argument.

Well, it was obvious, really. In a dumb way. Jinki had never seen a rock, at least not within the time his meatsuit memory banks recorded. So he sat in the observatory and watched and waited, until it finally came, shining across the sky like a trail of wee after you'd drunk something really bad, like something radioactive maybe.

Jinki tried to think up the right sort of words.

"I wish that the falling star I'm wishing on will fall where I can gather it," he said aloud and winced at how stupid it sounded. "Come and be mine," he added, brightly, which sounded much nicer. "Come and be mine, falling star!"

"Can't be done," said Mr. Quest, coming out of nowhere. "Breaks the fundamental law of wishing on things. You can't wish on the thing for itself, you can't ask a genie to be yours. It's like saying 'I wish I had a wish'."

"But why?" said Jinki.

"Ah," said the Trickster, and capered on the spot for a moment, in his chrome suit that seemed to have a diamond pattern, just for a second, before the play of light and dark shifted. "And there it is, at long last. The first random error."

The small asteroid fell a few meters away, raising a fountain of dark dust. Jinki gasped. "You said-"

"Sometimes they have a bit of quartz in them, a bit of raw glass," said Mr. Quest. "That a baby made of light might hide in." Jinki noticed that the echo was gone from his voice. "There's many a reason a light baby mustn't walk through Time. You shouldn't, Jinki, because you're tied with the human timeline, you'd cause a thing, a great big knot of a thing like a briar-rose patch, called a paradox. A pa-ra-dox! As you Mother says—ah. You could never go live in the still eye of the storm of Time like your people do, not anymore, not anymore. Time shut its tiny door on you the moment your Mother took you to her bosom. Little Jinki, neither here nor there. You'd break down the Rathki mathematics like you were a great whale in space if you were to treat Old Time like your people do, like He didn't exist."

"Space whale," said Jinki, uncertain. "There are space whales?"

The Trickster grinned.

So some people in space suits went out and gathered up the asteroid and put it in a sealed container. They laid it on a table, where it cooled rapidly. Father said space rocks weren't even hot when they landed, because they'd been in the vacuum so long, a bit of burning atmosphere didn't heat them up much. Father said it like a bit of burning atmosphere deserved everyone's contempt.

Only Jinki could touch it with his skin, said Mr. Quest, because if anyone else did, all the energy from violating the fundamental law of wishing on things would eat them. Mother muttered about it being nonsense, and who knew what was on that thing, and no child of hers was touching it, and many other things, and so they went and informed the Rathki Overlords, as Mother called them, and they came and took the asteroid away.

"It's me, isn't it, Mr. Quest?" said Jinki, a week later, playing with the flowers in the pots. "It's me that's in the asteroid, hiding in the quartz. I could feel me in there, I was old and sad. I was playing in the stars, long, long ago in the future, and then I came back in Time and hid in an asteroid because I wanted to give myself my own wish. That's nice of me, isn't it? So I didn't break the fundamental law of wishing on things. Because I granted my own wish." He felt like he should say 'ha!' or something like that, but it was too sad.

He wasn't allowed to go through Time yet, of course, he'd have to wait until he was older.

"And now you must remember to do it, Jinki," Mr. Quest said, with great gravity. "You must do it no matter what, because if you don't, you'll break the stable Time loop and then who knows what will happen (*what will happen, what will happen*)." He laughed, and laughed, and laughed. "Ah, you will see when you are old and sad. They've got what they've always wanted, the Rathki with their mathematics. That's all they ever want (*want want want*). They've got themselves a paradox. Plutonium, pah!" Mr. Quest paused, delighted at having said pah! with such panache. "What do they care for stuff, Jinki? They're the Mathematicians of the Universe."

"What will they do to me in the asteroid, Mr. Quest?"

"Nothing worse than math, Jinki, nothing worse than math (*math, math*)."

"Will it hurt?" said Jinki.

"Jinki," said the Trickster, very gently, "you should know by now. Math always hurts."

# Colour Me Grey

## Swabir Silavi

*Swabir Silayi is a Kenyan writer and occasional poet.
He draws from his travels, trains as a physicist, and
studies in post-modern and African literature for his
fiction.*

THEY CAME FOR him in the night. It was a cool night, the
moonlight reflecting off the droplets that told of a just
ended drizzle, giving everything a surreal sparkle that livened up
the dominant grey of the walls and everything else. They came
with their boots stomping into the concrete streets, doors crashing, shouting orders with everybody else and everything else silent. Even Mother made no sound. Him, he sat in his chair, not
even turning his head as the hinges buckled and the locks broke.

This was the year of the Mango in the time after the end of
Modernity. Not that anybody knew what a mango was. But the
BigBelleChiefMan had declared it. He made a lot of declarations.
Like the time he decreed the Funny-Funny day to be celebrated
once every new-moon-rise with a statement he issued. He called
them 'jokes'.

> Joke number 1—What did the bean say to the
> bean? He said, 'How you been?'

These are strange times, Grandmother used to say. She said there
used to be color. But how was that possible? Everything was grey, it
has been since I could remember. And all other colors were banned,
as the BigBelleChiefMan had decreed. She said that once upon a
time, you could spend even up to ten minutes just getting to find

out how people were doing, no matter if you had been with them two days ago. Scandalous! Had not the BigBelleChiefMan declared that no one was to shake another one's hand more than once? Grip hands, up, down, release? Had he not declared that in our own best interest if any man or woman should interact with another man or woman for the purposes of greeting they had no more than forty-five seconds to get it over with, with an additional thirty seconds for those that had not seen each other for a period no less than three moon-rises? Ten minutes, eat my hat! I thought about how many people I could greet in that amount of time.

How things hardly ever change, Grandmother used to say. I would laugh because she also said these were strange times. But was that not contradictory? Did not logic as it was approved by the BigBelleChiefMan state that the truth is singular? That things cannot be one and another? So how could the times be strange and yet hardly ever change? If it never changed, would it not cease to be strange? Silly Grandmother. She had such fantastically incredulous stories. But I had always preferred the stories in the BigBelleChiefMan approved course book for the stories-of-the-past-days of the Newafrik. Before, there used to be too much color. And too much sun, and too much time. But then the seas rose, and the skies darkened, and there was lightning and thunder and strong winds that uprooted even the baobabs. And when it was all done, it was time for these new times. These grey times.

There had been a ChiefMan before this BigBelleChiefMan. And there had been another before that, but he had been known simply as the Man. In the final days of too much sun and too much time, when there was too much color and too much chaos, the Man had appeared. And he preached. He enlightened us on the causes of all our problems. The rising seas? That was our enemies out to drown us obviously. Were we not the most worthy of the land and were they not very envious of our worthiness? The Man spoke the truth. The proliferation of time? Were we so blind to the machinations of the enemies of our people? They gave us so much time that we thought we had all the time. But they made the sun shine too beautifully and there was too much color and all that beauty distracted us from our worthiness. And thus we wasted too much time not thinking of how worthy we were and instead admiring the color and the beauty of everything else. By the time they were done, we would be finished! "They are out to finish us, my people!" the Man declared and all hailed the Man.

And so our people built the walls to shield them from the dangers of the others. And the Man, he had a tall tower built from which only he could look out and warn us of what they were planning against us. All the extra time that we had had no use for was given to him. And we blacked out the sun because it distracted in its brilliance, and everything was made grey. And the days passed.

Then came the ChiefMan, for who better to keep protecting us than the son of the Man? And he built the tower higher and made everything moregrey. And when he was done, came the BigBelleChiefMan, the son of the ChiefMan who was the son of the Man. And he gave us 'jokes'.

> Joke number 2—Papa Tomato, Mama Tomato, and Baby Tomato are walking. Baby Tomato is moving too slowly and the others are pulling ahead so Papa Tomato goes back, squashes him, and says, "Catch up!"

The wisdom of the Man, the order of the grey, the comfort of the tower that was built ever higher for the BigBelleChiefMan to see farther—these were the things that made life what it was and kept everything as it had to be. I did not understand the Malcontents and their agitation for color. What was color if not the very antithesis of grey? Why would anybody want to allow back those death rays of sunlight that carried poisonous color and would re-intoxicate us with the chaos the Man had sacrificed so much to eliminate? Truly, they must have been infected by the lingering radiation of color. It said in the books that we would never truly be free of it.

I saw my father shake another man's hand twice. Twice. When they met. And again when they parted. Twice. I saw my father stand under the illuminating post letting the glow wash over him as he did nothing, like he had some extra time. On some days, there were others that came into our house to talk and, as far as I could tell, they had no agenda for discussion. In fact, sometimes, some of them came after the others had already started to talk!

I was confused.

I had grown up in the grey. I had been inspired by the stories of sacrifices the Man had made. I had devoured the escapades of the ChiefMan as he tangled with and dispatched our enemies from within, those agents of color, while always keeping an eye out from the tower for any threats from the outsiders. As the Big-BelleChiefMan decreed, I was always ten minutes early for my rendezvous, and was fastidious in my greetings- shaking once and keeping it under forty-five seconds. I kept everything grey as it was supposed to be. In the grey, there was order and balance that allowed us to achieve great things. We could never have built the tower so high in the chaos of color.

I was unable to understand the actions of my father. And the stories of my grandmother caused even more consternation. In her fantastical stories she had sometimes crooned these spontaneous arrangements that went against everything grey. Had not the ChiefMan declared and the BigBelleChiefMan affirmed that every composition must be deliberate and conform to the preapproved musical format? Grandmother was old. She must have been forgetful of the official standards. Which was probably why they finally took her away. But my father? Perhaps he had been infected by the color radiation.

Perhaps I too had been exposed. I said to the watcher of the desk of the Department of Color Radiation Extermination that I might be suffering from the early effects of exposure. I said to him that my father had probably been exposed because he was acting very un-grey. I said perhaps they should aid us in the extermination of these early signs before we were completely taken over by color. They said they would come.

That was the first time they came for him. For me, they brought a letter.

The letter said, 'In recognition of your model us-ness, and your complete devotion to our cause of preservation against those others that would seek nothing less than to see us finished and bring back color and the chaos that comes with it, I, the BigBelleChiefMan, the son of the ChiefMan who was the son of the Man, the watcher in the tower and the greyer of the walls and the keeper of the extra time, do here invite you to a supper-just-as-the -moon-sets in the tower. Keep on keeping it grey. TBBCM'

Such an honor was usually reserved only for a precious few that caught the eye of the watchers in the tower who sent their names up to the apex where the BigBelleChiefMan stood guarding against threats to the grey. None ever came back down but with an even greater grasp of what it meant to keep things grey. It was time to be colored completely grey.

I was there right on time, ten minutes before the appointment time. And I was careful in my greetings, firm grip and just one shake, making sure to keep within the time limit of forty-five seconds. I was ushered into the elevator that would take me up to the top of the tower where I was supposed to meet the BigBelleChiefMan himself, and he would show me the world over the walls and the chaos that he protected us from. It was said you could see the sun from the tower, that source of color and chaos. I was looking forward to finally getting to curse it for all the trouble it had caused. I was looking forward to meeting the BigBelleChiefMan, who kept us true to the ways of the Man.

I stepped out of the elevator into a room such as I had never before in my life imagined. The light was different, I could not see grey. Instead, my senses were overpowered by an infusion that felt like something in the grey had been let loose and was wreaking havoc on my optical receptors. It amplified a thousand fold in me the stirrings I had felt listening to my grandmother's stories. I remembered her descriptions of what color would look like and I realized that this must be white. These feelings I was having, was this what the chaos felt like?

As my senses settled, I saw that in front of me were windows in the white walls and they let in rays of light much like the light from the moon but more brilliant. I put my hand out in their path and I felt a warmth in them that was a contrast to the coolness of the moonlight. Curious, I moved closer to the window to look out of the tower and what I saw so shocked me my knees buckled. It could have been nothing else. Color! The rush of color! The expanse! The brilliant hue of the sea that spread out in front of me as far as the eyes could see. The lush hills that rolled out under me in a shade of color that made you want to stare forever. And the sky that was not grey, like the sea had been overturned and made weightless, and the sun, the sun! Was that the sun? Was this really chaos that I felt? I felt the tears on my face before I realized they had escaped my eyes. There, on my knees at the window on top of the tower, I was moved.

Chaos was so beautiful. So completely beautiful. And engulfed in its chaotic beauty, I experienced a moment of terror when I longed for the order of greyness.

'And now you understand.' The voice said into my ear. Half my mind registered that it was the BigBelleChiefMan speaking to me, but I was transfixed by the scene before me. I could not move, I could not speak, completely overwhelmed.

'And now you understand why we need the grey.' The voice kept on. 'Can you imagine if everything was as you see still, and everyone was so overwhelmed as you are right now? It would be the end of us all. There would be no order, and we would be distracted from what we need to do to protect ourselves from being finished. From building our walls higher and our tower taller. From progress. Can you feel the chaos infecting you? This is why grey is good.'

Then everything was grey. Then black. A complete absence of color.

I don't remember how I got back down and out of the tower. I don't remember how it is that I was standing now under the street lamp taking comfort in the cold light of the moon that was so invitingly familiar. But I could not shake the sun and the colors and their chaos. For many nights and many days I thought and thought. I thought of contradictions, things being one and at the same time another. How I had feared chaos and yet loved it. How in the moment of loving and fearing I had longed for grey yet felt trapped in its confines. For the first time, I doubted the Man.

Joke number 3—on me. On us.

I realized, the truth can be contradictory.

My father was an agent of color. A proponent of chaos. A distributer of propaganda that aimed at finishing us. He dilly dallied, he told stories of times when things were more than grey, he doubted the grey truth as had been declared by the Man. Those were the accusations that they made against him as he stood in the judgment circle. Looking into my mother's eyes, he had repented and avowed all that. He had promised to no longer go against the teachings of the Man as they were enforced by the son of the ChiefMan, the BigBelleChiefMan. They let him go. But then they came for him in the night. They said he had been infected by color. His chaos was a permanent affliction.

I am my father's son. I have stood at the top of the tower and had my blood infected by the warmth of the sun and my eyes made impure by the colors of the world beyond the walls of grey. I am afflicted by chaos. Now the grey seems so dull not even the moon light adds any shine to it. Now the walls seem so stifling. I am questioning the ideas of the Man. Were there really others who were out to finish us using colors and chaos? Would it be so bad to live under chaos and color?

The other day, I arrived right on time for a meeting. I extended my greeting for an extra five seconds, refusing to let go of the other man's hand even as the seconds counted on. From Grandmother's old things, I found a scarf that was a different shade of grey and I wrapped it around my neck. I found the contrast with my coat delicious. Soon, they will come for me, as they came for my father, as they came for Grandmother. I have become an agent of color.

Joke number 4—Things hardly ever change.
These are strange times.

I had even made up my own 'joke'.

# Like a Coin Entrusted in Faith

## Shimon Adaf

### Translated by the author

*Shimon Adaf was born in Israel to parents of Moroccan origin. He has published three collections of poetry and eight novels. Amongst his numerous awards are Israel's Sapir Prize for his novel* Mox Nox *and the Yehuda Amichai Poetry Award.*

## 1

THEY WAKE UP Sultana the midwife at the dead of night. Poundings on the door, which she disguises in her sleep. Hides them within the symbolism of the dreams. But her consciousness arises at last. She identifies the knocking, the intervals between knockings. And she is alarmed. The alarm is not shaped yet. She covers herself quickly. Out of habit. Ties her headdress and goes out. In spite of the urgency of the knocks, the man is standing with his back to her hut. Almost indifferent, his small cart, tied to a grey ass, in the starlight of the beginning of autumn in Morocco, is also cut from the landscape.

Afterwards she remembers the light gallop of the ass and the cart on the slope, the rustle of the world she senses whenever she leaves the hamlet, out of the protective imagination of its inhabitants. The wind is warm still, unexpected warmness, and the lucidity of the air. She smells the sea in it, Essaouira's daily commotion caught in it even at midnight. But they circumvent the city. She already recognised the driver, Shlomo Benbenishti. It's been years since she's last seen him. He hurries the ass. He tells it, run like the storm, my beauty, and laughs. She does not understand the laughter. A shred of shyness is apparent in it. Maybe nervousness.

The road becomes steep. The ass brays, even neighs. Shlomo turns to her. He says, do not eat or drink anything in the house at which we are about to arrive. Had dar hadi fiah Jnoon.[1] The Moroccan is light on his tongue, and his Hebrew heavier, the heritage of the synagogue. He knows that she understands Hebrew, though she's a woman. She nods. Now she grasps the nature of her alarm. The moon is a thin etch in the thickening darkness, thickening more and more as they near their destination. The moon still breathes his first breaths of the month. That is the alarm. Why was she summoned now? The time is the ten days of repentance.

## 2

The mother died with a scream. Her face was veiled and the scream was almost silenced. Sometimes they are marked; the demon leaves his marks on their cheeks. A scar of a bite. Every now and then, when Sultana hands them their baby, they remove the veil and she sees. But the woman died while delivering. She twisted and turned with spasms when Sultana came in. Sultana imagined her nails burrowing into the flesh of the hand. A small lamp threw light on her round belly, about to burst. Shlomo stayed outside. Inside, close to one of the dark hut's clay walls stood a man she couldn't make out clearly. She said she didn't want to deliver the baby, that they shouldn't have called her during the ten days of repentance between Rosh Hashanah and Yom Kippur. The man insisted. He switched to Hebrew, he said, what is forbidden within the boundaries of the land of Israel, isn't forbidden in foreign lands. *Is he Jewish?* she thought to herself. The accent was strange, but his voice, she knew the voice, where from?

The mother shuddered at her touch. Her cries begun. The newborn fought, Sultana could tell. She lifted the woman's dress. She saw the little egg-shaped skull, through the widened lips of the vagina, smeared with blood and liquids of the womb. She pressed on the belly. He was blue, the baby, his skin, his hair, his eyes when

---

[1] There are demons in this house (Jewish Moroccan)

opened shortly. The irises filled the sockets. She couldn't figure out if he was blind. A spark of intelligence burned in his eyes, curiosity almost. She shook. When she severed the umbilical cord the newborn shook, too, and went still.

The man told her to put the dead baby alongside his mother's corpse. I told you, she said. Her voice broke a little. He didn't react. Shlomo's head peered from the entrance and he called her name delicately. She followed him. Anger grew in her during the journey back. When he stopped near her hut, she said, why are you working for them, why? He asked her, with his former softness, why they sent for you, you tell me.

**3**

From: Tiberia Assido
To: Doron Aflalo
RE: Rose of Judea

Say, what is this nonsense you've been sending me? You promised to report what you've been discovering about Rabbi SBRJ. Instead you're telling me some made-up tale about the days Rabbi Shlomo was young? I realize that stories about demon births were widespread in the villages in Morocco. My mother told Akko and me a similar tale once. Akko couldn't sleep that night. But what has that to do with the Rose of Judea? If I recall, you claimed that evil spirits are nothing but a story intended to cover up the involvement of Externals in Jewish history. You also claimed that they aren't born, but are some kind of Jews who've been mutated in a distant future, didn't you?

Akko is advancing with the development of "Solium Salomonis", at least with parts I'm exposed to. He makes me talk daily with the software. A little scary. When we started the output was confused (look at me, writing as if I had the first clue about computing), without any relevance to the sentences I typed. Now, half of the time she answers my questions.

BTW, it's beautiful here in Massachusetts. Thanks for asking. And I enjoy being around Akko, even though he kept all his annoying habits from when we were children. He still won't talk to me about his sexuality. It's beneath him to show any interest in such an inferior human activity. He also forgets to eat. Anyway, he needs as detailed information as possible, not stories.

What about you? Haven't gone crazy yet from staying at your parents' place in Mevoe-Yam?

T.

## 4

But certain stories are sometimes the only way to give someone a key. The stories of my father were left hidden. My mother forgot. Only Miriam, once, told me a real horror story. The birds' song, she said, is full of razors. When she's passing by, they sing about it to her. Not the content of the song, but the song itself, the way it slashes through the air and reaches her ears. That's the razor. It cuts reality. In the following days I ceased listening. Like I turned toward other voices. The world called my name.

Years went by before I figured out that it's not what we fear that frightens us. What frightens us lurks at the edges, behind the gates of cognition. The fear we know is nothing but a defense mechanism against this, the thing. How to explain? Maybe that I understood that Tel Aviv fell on New Year's Eve of the year 5767 to creation. Suddenly I saw only parts of the reality of the city. On the stairs leading to the university, on Jaffa pier, on Allenby. They peered through the shroud of the city. What is reality if not the memory of others leaping from you when you look? Their life, their bodies that created in their movement the space you occupy, gave it meaning. Yet, woven in this weave of remembrance, you are left to your own devices; you have a resting place, a place of becoming. And the city was lost, as Miriam was lost, washed into the abyss from which only a choked, undecipherable sound is coming back. And the stupid dreams of the Tel Aviv dwellers preserved the city, a dull copy under the sun of Israel.

## 5

Sultana remembered Shlomo. She remembered him when she lay awake on her bed, and she remembered him afterwards, when she slouched to the cave at the break of dawn. He was a Yeshiva student, who came from a community in Istanbul with a recommendation letter from the community's rabbi. She was about to get married and didn't pay him much attention, even though her father, the rabbi of the newly formed community in Essaouira, whose members retired from one of the communities in Fez, took him in.

For a while he was her father's protégé. He was rumored to be extremely gifted. He knew many tractates from the Babylonian and the Jerusalem Talmud by heart, and was versed in the writings of the Geniuses and Maimonides; he even read the prohibited book. He was exchanging epistles with an Israeli sage, Rabbi Yosef Karo, and her father let his pride be known at Sabbath meals, when she and her husband came to visit, and she was carrying a child in her womb. But something changed. She was only able to get some parts of the story. The young lad Benbenishti and her father were becoming estranged. She couldn't attend to it; her husband fell ill and she was about to give birth. When she returned to her parents' home, after her husband's death, her father wouldn't hear about Shlomo Benbenishti. He wasn't welcomed anymore.

## 6

Her mother told her, when Shlomo appeared one day famished at the kitchen entrance of their house. Her mother fed him somewhat fearfully, as if he were a leper, and made Sultana stand watch at the doorway to the house, to warn her if her father or one of her younger brothers was approaching. Shlomo couldn't make a living. No member of the community would hire him. Occasionally he would work for Arabs, to drive a cart, to run errands, to sell in the market, to whitewash houses.

Shlomo would pursue issues best left alone. He asked about corpses coming back to life: are they still infused with the profanity of the dead, can they be cleansed by bathing in a mikveh? Is the tent in which a body is vitalized clear of its impurity, the tent and every object within its space? What was the status of the children revived by Elijah and Elisha? Were they still in need of redcow ashes? What was the meaning of the Jerusalem Talmud argument that the dead live among the dew? And so on, and so forth. Her father, who detested any discussion of the sort, was convinced he was possessed, God forbid, La Yister.[2]

The memory flooded her—no, slashed her. That day, when the males of the family went to pray mincha, the afternoon prayer, and the soft light anticipated the coming of the evening.

---

[2] May God protect us (Jewish Moroccan)

Shlomo sat in front of her mother and her in the kitchen, munching leftovers of couscous and meat, his eyes darkly sleep-deprived, haunted.

## 7

From: Tiberia Assido
To: Doron Aflalo
RE: Rose of Judea

Doron,

I'm a murderess, murderess. I know the term is a bit melodramatic, but it describes well my shock. I've killed Akko's software. I've already named it in my mind: Malka. You know how you'll ascribe human features to everything that shows a will or imitates life, like pets or toys, when you're child? When I was eight, one of the girls in the neighborhood got a talking doll. Akko coveted it so much that I helped him steal it. It made me feel sick when he took it apart to see its inner workings. I heard her crying in my head, begging me to stop the torture. Now, thinking back, I think the doll's owner was Malka. Or maybe I'm rewriting the recollection to make it meaningful.

I wasn't doing it on purpose. I just held my daily conversation with her. And I couldn't resist. I quoted, half joking, the dubious exegesis my father taught Akko, about King Solomon's throne (solium salomonis) and the kings of Edom and the Externals fighting over it, and I asked Malka her thoughts on the matter (I was tired and bored). She crashed. Akko claims that restarting her won't do us any good, that the backups won't help, because she'll only crash again. He says I need to start training a blank module anew, and that he hasn't much time to deal with it at the moment.

Poor Malka, I've destroyed her. How can I raise another module, to see it grow, develop a consciousness?

And Akko won't tell me why he's so adamant about me being the one who raises it. True, it's crucial to him that the software language be Hebrew. He has this hypothesis that Hebrew is prevalent all over the Worlds, that it's the Ur-language. No, that in each and every one of the Worlds, a version of Hebrew came to be out of a family of languages similar to it. That's why Hebrew is the closest to the Ursprechen. But why the hell me? He can hire an Israeli student. They are fucking everywhere nowadays.

So you have time to get serious with your investigation. Yet, why is your story so indirect? Why do you suspend the information? What's your point, really?

T.

# 8

Sultana remembered. She stood in the cave, in whose depths her son was kept, and he failed to appear, even when she called out his name. Hosea.

# 9

When your son shows signs of a mysterious illness, which brought down his father, an illness gnawing his organs while the spirit stays sane, trapped in the cage of flesh, it is easy to prevent his death. All you need is a device to stop time.

But there's a setback; there's always a setback. Time-halting objects aren't as widespread as they used to be. Let's say Moses' wand. Or Joshua's Shofar.

# 10

And there's always a price, evidently.

# 11

She'd been told there was an Arab who lived on a mountain. He was a master of the dying. She walked many miles. Wore out two pairs of shoes. Her son was with her, riding a donkey, his life force leaking.

The Arab gave her a ring made of a bone of the upupa epops that was passed down from King Solomon's hand to the hands of the Kahlif Harun El Rashid, and lastly came to his possession. The ring radiated decay and corruption and gangrene. He commanded her to change her name, to leave her parents' house without speaking to them. He told her to dwell in a certain hamlet, outside of Essaouira, and study how to serve as a midwife. He said that she would be called for, that he for long has waited for a Jewish woman to come his way.

# 12

1. All conscious creatures are sentenced to die.

1.1 But not all of them are sentenced to perish.

1.1.1 The consciousness may linger after the death of the body; parts of it may. A knot of memories and sentiments. The ghost is best suited to depict this sort of lingering.

1.1.2 The body, a complex system of appetites and cravings, may survive alone, without the bridles of consciousness. The vampire, one can argue, is the representation of this sort of lingering.

1.1.3 What is the third variation of outliving death that's illustrated by the zombie? In contrast to the other two, the zombie is devoid of memory, identity, passion. The living entity was erased. Only a blind instinct is left, the will of another that possesses it whole. It has been devoured.

1.2 The livings are constantly thrown into mourning.

1.2.1 Which means the complete collapse of the means of expression.

1.2.2 Nevertheless, every culture aspires to endow loss with meaning, to tame it through rituals.

1.2.3 All of human experience is characterized by the tension between the urgent need to be expressed and the failure of language to fully express it.

1.2.4 The greatest and most unbearable tension is to be found in grief. And in the mystical experience. That's why those two are the ones driving humans to the highest degree of creativity, to a multitude of forms of expression.

1.2.5 For a while, therefore, there's an identity between the two.

2. A categorical border divides the living from the dead.

2.1 The ability to experience the border from both sides is the mystical ability in itself.

## 13

From: Tiberia Assido
To: Doron Aflalo
RE: Rose of Judea

You ask what I did with Malka before I quoted her the exegesis. (Malka! Suddenly I get that Malka, queen, is the Hebrew word Sultana. What was her name before she changed it? Please don't tell me it was Malka. What is it, one of your exaggerated poetical devices? But you couldn't have known it's the name I chose for the module. Are all coincidences this dreary?)

Akko has also asked me.

I quoted her some of my poems. Not *The Artificial Child* that refers to Akko and solium salomonis. It was the first time Malka was exposed to the term. Do you think the system in the whole became intelligent enough that, through the quote, she realised she was made-up, might have understood her raison d'etre: to uncover the Ursprechen in which the Name-givers hold the Worlds? That she understood it is the task of (the) Rose of Judea? It seems far-fetched.

I told Akko my suspicions. I don't know how the other modules of the project function. He said he couldn't be bothered. An Israeli writer wrote him to inquire about the part of exegesis I mention in *The Artificial Child*. It's funny someone still reads that magazine we published.

(Do you still write poetry? I have to ask, even if you'd give the same answer all over again, that poetry per se isn't enough for you.)

Anyhow, Akko did say he was bothered by the timing. Do you get it? He is bothered by the timing and not by months of work gone down the drain for no apparent reason. I never am going to get this kid.

I know he's already a man, but for me he's the kid with the grumpy manners, who closed himself in the garage with his computers. The same kid who became hard all of a sudden, distant. The kid I'm the only human he can show emotions toward.

My heart goes out to him, as if he were twelve.

It's stupid.

But maybe I'm overflowed with feelings because I haven't yet overcome Malka's passing. Parts of me were imbedded in her. Is this clinging narcissistic? Because in every loss we lose the parts of us that were immersed in others who left us? Do we mourn ourselves really?

I refuse to believe that.

Write me back soon,

T.

## 14

I refuse to believe it either. If love may save us for a moment from our perpetual egoism, then losing it is losing a possibility of salvation. Another way out that has been blocked for us, that keeps us so much in here.

## 15

Sultana was very stingy with the time left for her son. The ring suspended his life. She put him in the cave, near the hamlet she was told to live in, and she waited. They called for her. Always around midnight. She watched demon offspring, with crooked organs and features, being delivered from human females wombs, and every time refused the food and drinks she was offered. And there was always someone who came and took the hybrids. She didn't see the takers' faces, didn't recognized them. And every morning following the birth, she went to the cave, where she undid the time paralysis she had casted upon her son, and he was beautiful and spoke to her. And she remembered why she was willing to assist the strange births. Why she continued to live in the shadow of the Sitra Ahara.

But this morning Hosea wasn't there. And she thought, Shlomo, for no reason she could fathom, just out of basic fright. It's Shlomo's doing.

## 16

*Externals: in Jewish folklore the expression serves as a substitute term for the Sitra Ahara, the more common Aramaic name for the powers of evil, whose meaning is literally 'The Other Side'.

The disciples of the order of the Rose of Judea believe that the Externals are a group of shape-shifting entities whose influence can be traced throughout Jewish history, and that they are the servants of the kings of Edom, a nation whose home world was destroyed and who now roam the other worlds in order to find the keys to the destruction of the Chain of Worlds. These keys, as the Rosaic tradition goes, are implanted in the Namegivers' consciousness.

Their belief is based on the interpretation of a series of Jewish exegesis from the second half of the third millennium to creation, and is related to the sage Ben-Zoma and his acolytes. These exegeses are not part of the holy canon of mainstream Judaism today.

One of the important exegeses is as follow:
The Rabbi's mind was not set as to Solomon's throne till

Ben-Zoma explained—

It's written, It is an abomination to kings to commit wicked-ness, for the throne is established by righteousness, for the de-scendants of heavens and the offspring of Edom were fighting over its construction, this one says it is my craft and the other says it is my hand making, and it stood between the sky and the earth until the sun retreated.

An extreme interpretation, which isn't considered valid, claims that the Externals are not connected to the kings of Edom, but are mutant Jews from the future who travel in time and memory, and whose goal is to collect every piece of information relevant to the Rose of Judea and manipulate it for their own ends.

# 17

Shlomo looks at her bewildered. He doesn't understand what she's talking about. He repeats her words, a cave, a ring, a son. Sultana stops midway through the blame and starts anew. Slowly she realizes that he doesn't have a clue. That's the first time he's been hired for a job like this. That he was paid handsomely for it. He's able to deduce much from what she's been saying. He is sharp. He has an ear for nuances. The story is clear to him in its fullest extent. Until now he stood in front of her; she sat at the table in the centre of her hut. He sits down heavily. His eyes are ablaze with thoughts. A pretty man, she notices, a soft darkness floats in the irises, and the cloud of thoughts enhances his beauty. Suddenly she's aware of her appearance. She tightens the cover over her hair, glides a hand down her face, as if she could smooth the skin. She's four or five years older than he is, but he seems younger to her, a lad.

Shlomo asks if she knows if in this village, outside the bor-ders of Essaouira, demonic forces are more active there. She says she doesn't know, that she delivers a hybrid once a month at least. But never during the ten days of repentance.

The holiness of the days, Shlomo says, and nods. He asks about Hosea, how the black ring is able to time-freeze him. She looks at the ring for the first time since she left the cave earlier that morning. Shlomo is right. The green and ivory shades faded. It's totally black.

He inquires about her recollection of the Arab warlock. She

says she doesn't remember a thing. Did he wear the ring? She says that he didn't. He pronounced a few words and then some windows were torn in the air. They moved very slowly, the windows. The Arab reached into one of them and pulled out the ring.

Windows, Shlomo muses: a similar account is to be found in the stories of Raba bar bar Hana in Baba Batra.

In the Talmud? she asks.

Yes, Shlomo says and adds that bar bar Hana tells about a meeting with an Arab who showed him windows in heaven, where the sky and the earth kiss, and the sky turns as a wheel. The stories were always dismissed as fiction, but he believes they have some kernel of truth in them.

And the home owner, he asks, did she know him?

She says his voice was familiar, but she couldn't exactly tell where from.

Shlomo suggests they return to that hut: maybe they'll find a lead.

On the way there he turns his head. The small ass is walking at a moderate pace. He says it amuses him that the daughter of Rabbi Aflalo found a way to cheat death. She asks for the reason. He says Rabbi Aflalo expelled him from the yeshiva because he argued that underneath the Talmud sages' discussions about necromancy and seers lurks a knowledge they wished to discard. Rabbi Aflalo accused him of idolatry.

## 18

From: Tiberia Assido
To: Doron Aflalo
RE: Rose of Judea

You're right. I wasn't very sensitive in my last mail. I didn't take into account what you're going through. But you are also to blame. Whenever we talked about Miriam and what she'd done, you insisted you moved on, that you can't dwell in sorrow, in guilt. Tell me more about the book you're writing. In what way does it deal with the impossible language of loss? Once you wrote in a poem, "There comes a moment / you know / your hymn from down under / no soul could speak." What happened to that moment? Why does it flicker?

Yesterday we held a ceremony. Akko said it would help me

let go of Malka. He didn't say, "Help you let go of Malka," he said, "Maybe you'd stop nagging." Midway he cried. Of course, it wasn't Malka he was missing. He has several servers he calls the Cemetery Cloud. He stores his dead software there. The little conniving bastard. Not once did he mention that it wasn't the first time a module of solium salomonis has crashed beyond repair. He doesn't say « store », btw. He says « lay to rest ».

T.

## 19

From: Tiberia Assido
To: Doron Aflalo
RE: Rose of Judea

I almost forgot. You ask what I mean by "died"?

You push the module icon and the software doesn't run. Akko said he ran Malka's code through a debugger (tell you anything?) and he ran diagnostics on the databases built by her. Everything seems to be fine. No reason why she wouldn't work. Yet she doesn't, like a body whose life spark's been extinguished.

T.

## 20

Out of the urban mischief, out of the wreckage, my sister Miriam rose. Still 17 and not ceasing to rise. And Tel Aviv already fell. In aimless roaming I was nearly run down by bike riders. Sons of bitches. Lately they multiply. The year 5767 and the city is lost. Their eyes hollow, their mouths gaping with a groan. Among the dust-ridden trees, in the delayed autumn. New Year's Eve at my back, and they're around me, circling, copies of what they were once, blind urges in flesh golems of streets and traffic lights. Trampling. I have to get out of here. I have to go back to Mevo-Yam.

## 21

The recently deceased mother's hut is empty. It's almost evening. Sultana and Shlomo stand inside and inspect it for traces. The ring on Sultana's finger is black as a scorched bone. There's no cradle. No bed for a child. The kitchen is infested with shadows.

Shlomo asks her what else she knows. All of a sudden she's

indignant. It's not his business. It's not your business, she says. He lifts the lamp he brought with him and lights it. It's requied. The night fell quickly, unnoticeable. His expression is a mix of curiosity and alarm. A rage builds inside Sultana. She says, Hosea, and begins singing, a song her mother sung, when she cradled her son who wasn't named yet, in his firsts days on this land—

Stahit ana me'a momo lilah fi lilah
Wal'am he'tata yiduz geer fehal ha lilah
Lochan ma tenzar shams, ma tedwi gemara
Geer didlma fi kulal rachan
Wunbit ana wu-momo, geer sehara fi laman...[3]

She sings, hums to herself. Shlomo lowers his head. In the lamp light his hair is anointed with glamour. Someone is knocking on the door, beating with urgency.

## 22

From: Tiberia Assido
To: Doron Aflalo
RE: Rose of Judea

We're having a little crisis here. It has nothing to do with the Israeli writer inquest. Akko resolved that matter. Something else. I started working with the new linguistic module yesterday. This time I was cautious about getting attached. I typed simple indicative sentences. Something happened at night. It's not clear what. In the morning I sat in front of the screen. Ozymandias (yeah, maybe such a ridiculous name will prevent me from developing feelings) didn't react at first to the sentences I fed it. After several minutes words appeared on the screen: ARRGGG, GRRRR, ARRGGGG…

Funny, right?

But then the computer started emitting sounds. The other computers in the lab present similar symptoms. Akko lost his temper. At last he was able to show rage. There's a good side to it,

---

[4] I wished to spend with the baby night after night
To be with him a full 12 months like this night
And the sun might not rise, the moon won't shine
Only darkness all around
And the baby and I would sleep like a coin entrusted in faith. (Jewish Moroccan)

to see him in a human moment.

I'm scared.

T.

## 23

The door fell.

In spite of the lamp in Shlomo's hand, the outside seemed more lit.

The glee of autumn stars in Morocco's sky, apparently.

The shining heaven above Essaouira.

Against the glare of the busted door a small figure shows.

Its stride slow.

The organs rigid, mechanical.

And still its face is unseen yet.

Shlomo takes out a small chain from his galabia's pocket.

It shimmers. It has a certain glow.

He throws it. It wraps around the figure's neck.

Shlomo cries: Shma De-Marach Alech![4] Shma De-Marach Alech!

The figure continues to advance, oblivious to Shlomo's cries.

Shlomo retreats.

He puts the lamp on the floor and takes a stool from next to the wall.

He raises it.

His silence releases Sultana from her short paralysis.

She bends to have a better look.

Now she screams.

## 24

From: Tiberia Assido
To: Doron Aflalo
RE: Rose of Judea

I left Akko alone with his codes in the lab for several days and went on walks in the institute's grounds. Akko suggested I take the laptop he prepared for me, with all the insane amount of security he put on it. Before I left he asked if the laptop was con-

---

[4] The name of your master binds you (Aramaic)

nected to the lab's intranet. I haven't turned it on since he gave it to me. There was enough computing for me with the computer that ran Malka's module, may she rest in peace, and Ozymandias's module, curse it.

Akko also said, strangely, that the programs' codes in the cemetery cloud were corrupted. That they're full of inexplicable characters. He said, « As if they've rotted somehow. »

I was hoping to have my spirit lifted by the gnaw marks autumn left on the trees, the seasonal decline in temperature, the pressure of coolness against the skin, and the architecture, by which I was enthralled when I first got here. Instead, I think of Israel, on my tongue the syllables of the month Tishrey are rolling. Before Rosh Hashanah we called our mother to congratulate her for the New Year. Akko was choked with excitement. He was stricken by longing. Then we called our father. I mean, I called. Akko still refuses to speak with him. Who would have thought we'll all be here, in 2011, some years after the fall of Tel Aviv.

Well, the architecture is still lovely. The state centre's game of perspectives are wonderful, I'll give you that. The placement of futuristic buildings in the gloomy surroundings of New England as well.

I wonder if they burned witches here.

I think about your Sultana.

Where is the story going? I wait for the part in which young Shlomo is entering the Pardes and gets the knowledge of the Chain of Worlds, and becomes Rabbi SBRJ. That's your intention, right? To illustrate the revelation of the Rose of Judea.

But why tell the story from Sultana's point of view? Shlomo is the interesting character.

I don't want to push you. I know you too well for that. But what happens here seems to stem from our efforts to find the Ursprechen of the Worlds. It seems we reached some forbidden zone. Years ago Akko told me that this knowledge has the price tag of loss, of guilt, and you said—bad luck.

Well, Doron, bad luck has caught up with us. And I'm scared.

I sit at a café in Cambridge, MA, and I write to you.

I need desperately to understand something. But what is it? This is the awful thing here, isn't it? That we can't identify the real mystery. Help me, Doron.

T.

## 25

*Pardes (Orchard). Entering the Pardes: more than a few visitations of humans to the realms of angles in heaven are accounted for in the Jewish esoteric literature from the second half of the third millennium to creation. The literature of Hechalot (Palaces), for instance, is a detailed one. Yet the term Entering the Pardes is ascribed to one mystical experience only, the experience of four sages of the Mishna around the year 3890. The chronicles of the Entering are mainly reported in the tractate Hagiga in the Babylonian and Jerusalem versions of the Talmud.

No doubt an elementary form of experience is outlined in the exegeses. It's possible that the four sages represent four different attitudes toward the place of mysticism in Jewish life: Akiva ben Yosef, who goes through the experience unharmed, is its exemplar. According to his method, Judaism is hiding the magical thinking at its base and sanctifies practices of study and memorizing instead. Shimon ben Azay died while entering the Pardes and left no evidence for his method. Elisha ben Avoya turned to heresy, id est, cancelled the validity of Judaism as a worthy practice for gaining wisdom. Of Shimon ben Zoma, it was said that he peered and was harmed or, in the common interpretation, lost his sanity. His experience is the most curious, for what is insanity in the context of mysticism?

The devotees of the Rose of Judea believe that the knowledge ben Zoma unveiled contains a different description of the structure of reality.

## 26

When the features of the small figure are clear to Sultana, her scream dwindles and she gazes. Parts of the child's body—it's a child after all—are blue. An arm and half of the face. The expression is empty. The skin at the other part is sallow, pale, oozes viscous miasma. The right eye is buried in its socket, and worms twist in it. The bare teeth are spreading a sickly glow. And he, the child, doesn't smile, but his lips are stretched in a spasm.

He advances slowly, jerking. His arms are reaching for her. She's unable to move. Even the stench and the whiteness of the worms turning in the right eye can't force her nerves to shock her into motion. The child emits guttural syllables, indecipherable.

He's almost upon her; his nails are ready to cut her flesh.

And Shlomo pushes her aside and hits the creature with the stool. The blow is muted, not even the sound of a crushing bone, just a heavy note, the note of an object sinking in soft mud, in clay. The neck is crooked, the head lies on the left shoulder. His stretched lips stay the same and he keeps on moving forward in a rigid, stubborn walk.

Shlomo stands between her and the creature, blocks her view, but she knows nothing will stop it, that what drives it is beyond the decaying flesh, that the flesh is but a realization of a will. She knows that as well as she knows the origin of the organs that have been made into this shape, Hosea, and the baby she helped deliver just a while ago. Shlomo hits it again. Something like a fart escapes its body. The stench grows. The child-thing starts to shrill, a high pitched, ear-shattering shrill, like the cry of a prisoner being tortured in a concealed, underground cell. And Shlomo hits it again and calls to her. He says, get out of here Sultana, run.

## 27

From: Tiberia Assido
To: Doron Aflalo
RE: Rose of Judea

It's awful, Doron. I'm here, in the storage room of the lab, with all the pieces of useless equipment.

I've just arrived at the lab. Akko was crouched over his keyboard, motionless. I didn't understand what he was waiting for. I haven't seen him for a couple of days and he didn't even turn his head to look at me. Then I realized the screens were all displaying the same words ARRGG, GRRR, ARRGGG, GRRRR, GRRR and some animation of a viscous liquid, a green-yellow jelly, shaking, oozing down the screen, the inside of the screen.

I approached Akko and touched his shoulder. His small body was rigid. His head moved, turned, like it was revolving on the spine. His eyes were opaque, and the skin bloodless, the face without expression. The smile, it had nothing to do with the facial muscles. It terrified me. He didn't say anything.

I retreated, stupid me, to the first door in my sight. The storage room.

It's terrible. But the panic I felt before, when I walked around the institute, weakened. I've already dreamed this scene. I've seen it to its last detail, and I know the blows on the door are coming next.

In spite of Akko's warnings, I connected ARRGGG the laptop to the lab's intranet. So my GRRRR time is short. The ruined computers here start to hum*%*$#_)++

I'm thinking hard—Rose of Judea, the revelation of Ben-Zoma, the retrieval of the knowledge in Rabbi Shlomo Benbenishi's era, in the 16th century. I've always been bad at pattern&$&$*%( recognition. There must be something ARGGRRR you can tell, some detail you observed, in the story GRRRRG that escaped me.

&what is in our investigation that raise the dead&
&and how to put them back to the dust&
&even the digital ones&
He###########lp me, Do***************ron.

Don't leave me ARRGGG alone again, in half-light, as you did ARGGGRRR years ago.

Please, DoARRGGG GRRR ARRRRG ARRRG
GRRRRRRRRRRRRRRRRRRRRRRRRRRRRRRRR

# 28

[Clear sky, in which huge stars are buried. The moon is like a Chinese brush stroke. Dark trees. A wind is passing through them. Light rustle, like a buzz. Sultana is running out of a hut. She's terrified. She stops. A Man comes out from the shadow of trees.]

Sultana: Halt, you stranger, tell me who you are.
A Man: I am who I am. Though not whom you assume.
Sultana: And yet, someone you are, whoever that be.
    Tell me who.
A Man: The shape, the speech
    Are nothing but skin.
Sultana: Now I know, now
    Sevenfold my fear grows. You are deceased.
A Man: I told you, body, looks, are but a skin
    Which entities would wear to come here.
Sultana: Here. Where is here?
A Man: The Humilitas.

Sultana: My beloved's flesh you wear, and he is not you.
    Who you are, you stranger, tell me.
A Man: Centuries will pass before I'm born and for millennia
    I've lived, I walked this world, the Humilitas.
    Its paths of time are clear to me, I am at home
    But this is not my home. The chains of human voices
    Of human cries, I left behind, and even then
    I'm forced to cloak myself with them
    If my will is to find my kind's place within the Worlds.
Sultana: Your kind? Who are they? Who are you? The man
    Who spoke from shadows in this house? What
    Was the faith of the dead infant?
    Why was my boy snatched from me, and you show
    Yourself in semblance of his dead dad?
A Man: Faith, Conspiracy, simple and transparent, but
    as for you—
Sultana: It's wrapped in mystery. I do not wish to hear.
    What do you strive for, devil?
A Man (laughs): Devil I'm not.
Sultana (aside): Nor man he is. Oh Lord
    Who tortures us, who draws a line
    Between the living and the dead which we
    Crave to transgress.
A Man: Hush. Soon you'll see.
Sultana: But Hosea, my son, and the unnamed child
    You control them, the boy whose organs
    You assembled and your will drives.
    For what end?
A Man: I roamed Humilitas
    In the third millennium I wore the body of
    A Jewish sage, Rabba bar bar Hanna, I
    Spoke through his lips, I fought warlocks
    And magicians, I weaved my nets in silence
    Now comes an hour I put to test
    Will he transfer the knowledge destined
    To give us life, if we chose wisely—
    A child who was prevented from
    The realms of death and a child dead
    From womb.

Sultana: Not a child was he
  But demon.
A Man: There are no demons. Just folktales
  Claiming them to be. No plan is fertile
  Without misguiding and mischiefs, tricks
  As old as humanity.
Sultana: Nonsense. Insanity.
A Man: My part I've done, woman, and so did you
  It is my time to go back to my shelter in the shadows.


[Man exits. Sultana falls to her knees with a howl.]

# 29

Sultana's face is streaked with dust when she looks up. Shlomo is coming toward her. His face bears an expression of elation. His arms are stretched and the sleeves of his galabia are torn. The arms are covered in bite marks, small circles, tiny imprints of teeth, and shiny beads of blood. His hands are cupped, as if he is carrying a precious gem, but to Sultana the hands look empty. He gazes from the invisible content of his hands to Sultana and back. His features are washed with glamour. He says, Rose of Judea. He repeats the enigmatic phrase, Rose of Judea, Rose of Judea, till Sultana is back on her feet and puts her hand on his mouth.

# 30

I would have helped you, Tiberia. I would have left everything and rushed to you. But Miriam is filling my dreams, and my mother walks the house. I'm sure she put a tap on my heart beats.

But what it is I wish to say and can't convey any other way, is that the words in Hebrew, they had been through fire and water, they were killed by the sword and by strangulation. And we salvaged them from their grave.

They carry knowledge from beyond death, Tiberia, maybe the knowledge we need to retrieve Ben-Zoma's method. But in what form they are coming back and what they ask of the living, this we will have to find out the hard way.

# Single Entry

## Celeste Rita Baker

*Celeste Rita Baker is a Virgin Islander who lives in New York and has moved between the two places for the last fifty years. Her short stories have appeared in* The Caribbean Writer, Calabash, Scarab, Moko, *and elsewhere. Her short story collection,* Back, Belly, and Side *was published in 2015.*

CARNIVAL TIME COME, and I a single entry. I not in any troup or nothing. I just parading in me costume, all by meself. Everybody asking me what song dat is and where me music coming from. I tell dem I write de song, which is true and it coming from an iPod and dese little speakers ringing me North and South Poles, which not true. I projecting de song from me core, but dey ain't need to know dat.

De sun hot, just like I like it and no clouds dressing de sky. De crowds of people is like from before, when people didn't used ta be fraid of crowds. All de children dem being told ta keep still, but dey can't, from de excitement in de air. Grown folks drinking all kinda rum and eating with dey fingers. Water and ice giving way for free ta keep people from passing out in de heat. De music blasting, bumping, blaring so as ta make de ground shake. Heart and hips can't help but keep de beat, de groove growing to encompass all a dem like wet cover water.

It start ta happen when I finish in Post Office Square. Dat's de big demonstration place. You balance you high wid you sober and do you best dance dere. Try ta remember you routine if you have one. Impress de judges and give people a good show. Make de camera dem like you so de people at home could feel like dey dere bamboushaying wid you.

Before Post Office Square is de start of Main Street where it have de old warehouses which make inta expensive stores lining both sides of de narrow street. It hard for some of de bands and costumes to pass through cause it so narrow. But I like it cause it intensifies de sounds and all de colors feel like hot pepper in you eye, so bright. But den when you pass out inta de Square de vibes change, because it so big, like swimming from a river inta de clean blue sea. I blow up me presence ta fill de whole Square.

Single entry me 'rass. I was everybody and everything. I was de whole friggin' planet. De globe I telling you, de world dancing on two feet. Course you couldn't self see me feet. And I no touch de ground.

On Main Street de people push back, push back ta make me pass. Everyone grinding pon one anodda. Is smiles, cheers, and waves. De children hush quiet wid awe, de grown folks rushing me, trying ta touch, ta see if me water wet. Try find de string between de sun and me. De moon and me. Try see how a cloud what seem ta be above Cruz could have de frangipani trees dem dripping in old Tutu. How I bright where de sun reach and dark when I turn 'round. You like it, eh?

When I reach de Square is blow I blow up. Before I was round twenty five feet at my equator, but I was fifty by de time I reach de Judges Stand. Ole Lady Stinking Toe petals drippin from me steada sweat. Jasmine petals drifting in me breeze scenting the whole Square. I have volcanos erupting on de bass and trade winds blowing loud like horns. Earthquakes trembling de drums. Is de earth song, you see. I's de earth. And dey loving me.

De crowd gone wild. Dey never see nothing so. De ocean sloshing and Rock City really rocking. Cameramen zooming in, capturing a single live guana sunning on Coral Bay. Let 'em look dey look. We all here, Everytreerockstoneandflea.

I could dance, too, you know. And not only spin, neida, though me bounce ain't so high and does take quite a while. Every now and again I does let off some sparks in de air. Stars burning bright.

Dey loving me and I loving dem, too. Feeling all de little souls tickling me, tickling me and I glad.

When time ta move on I shrink down ta fit again. Less people here and dey more watching each odda dan me. I feeling little pains, like a drilling and a cutting and a breaking up. Shrinking faster dan I want and I can't stop atall. Time I pass Joe's Bar I hardly de size of a big car. By Senior Citizen's Viewing Stand I coulda fit inta a black plastic garbage bag. On de way ta de Field de people dem clap and smile but I could tell dey seen too much ta pay special mind ta me. Is de crowd energy dat let me blow up so. Make all me beautiful intricacies flow just so. Now only a few people studying me and I dripping and losing form. Mud sliding and whales beaching. I turnoff and head back ta de parking lot ta go have a drink in de Village.

Wellsir, I can't self see de counter. I smaller dan a greedy-man's dream and can't make no arms again neida.

People tripping over me, cussing, and is smaller and smaller I getting. Little boy try ta pick me up like I was a toy throw way in a gutter. I make thunder, he ain't hear. De most I could do is get up some lightening and he drop me. I roll under a table and hunch up next to a leg.

Parade done. Sun gone down. People streaming inta de Village for Last Lap. Last drink, last dance, last chance ta have big fun. Everybody in a frenzy ta get and ta have. Nobody ain't see me. I hear dem talking bout me, dat single entry. So pretty. So magical. So sure ta win. And I deydey, kick under de bar. Huddling in de dark, rum and hot grease dripping down through me mountains.

# The Good Matter

## Nene Ormes

### Translated by the author and Lisa J Isaksson

*Nene Ormes has a past as an archaeologist and as a tour guide in Egypt and now lives in Malmö, Sweden. Her debut novel,* Udda verklighet *(Touched), is the first in a series of urban fantasies set in her home town. The second novel,* Särskild *(Dreamer) won her a culture award. "The Good Matter" takes place in the same world as the novels.*

YOU SEE," GUSTAV said to the woman in the armchair, "relics are hard to come by these days, so many turn out to be forgeries or distortions rather than the real thing. And it's not as if there are that many new saints to collect from." He poured the tea for himself and his guest, the thin bone china making discreet tinkling noises as he set each cup and saucer down on the table. "You might say that goodness has fallen out of fashion."

They sat in armchairs angled toward each other with a small table filling the space between them. The room was illuminated by candles on side tables and the soft backlight from the wall mounted glass display cases containing his prized possessions.

The woman in the other armchair - she had only given her first name, Eve - reached for her cup with a gloved hand and sipped her tea. "I wouldn't say that goodness has ever been in fashion," she said, "but that does make it even more unique when it appears, wouldn't you say?"

She briefly looked Gustav straight in the eye before turning her attention to the room itself.

It was a room worthy of study, if he said so himself, hidden at the back of the antique store and filled with things of great variation, but at this moment the one feature of the room that interested him was his guest and what she'd brought.

Eve was impeccably dressed, her shoes beautifully uncomfortable and the stockings opaque. She had let him take her coat but had kept her gloves and scarf on and they complimented her suit nicely. A single strand of pearls lay on her collarbone and moved when she swallowed. It was a serious mode of dress, for a serious transaction.

Keeping her gloves and scarf on could be a display of her ability, or it could be a courtesy, to keep him from accidentally touching her.

No matter her attire or the intriguing question of her abilities, Gustav felt his eyes return to the briefcase at her feet and he trembled. The mere thought of the contents of that case and the possibility inside made his mouth dry and sucked at his attention.

But this moment had to be savoured. The possible end of a quest, the treasure-hunter's excitement before opening the vault and catching the first glitter of treasure.

Or of dust.

There really was no telling which it would be until he had his ungloved hands on it.

Her legs, next to the case, uncrossed, stretched, and crossed again, the movement pulling him out of his reverie. With effort he lifted his eyes to hers again. She was watching him, one well-painted eyebrow cocked.

Eve did not tremble. A smile formed on her lips, the first since entering the antique shop, and he was sure she had watched him as he gazed at the case.

He couldn't help but blush and hope against hope that she hadn't noticed. Like a young, eager lover, he thought, amused and embarrassed at himself.

"You could have a closer look at my collection if you want to." Gustav nodded toward the glass displays set into the walls. "I think I may have a couple of artefacts that could be of interest to you, or your client, even if most of them are of a more personal value."

She rose in one fluid movement, her poise pure elegance, like a ballet dancer. Her bearing made Gustav straighten in his chair.

She made a circuit of the room. Each case got a fair glance, and some made her tilt her head a bit, but she didn't ask about any of them. Not about the broken fan, open to show its fractured ribs, not the child-sized dinner set in pale blue, not the bell on its stand even though that case was open. No, it was obvious after a moment that she gravitated toward the last glass case, her face turned so that she missed seeing the glass orb and the verdigrised bronze belt buckle. She stopped in front of the obsidian dagger.

"I assume it's authentic." It wasn't a question, but Gustav nodded anyway, not that she looked at him. "May I open it?" she asked.

He murmured a consent and held his breath when she moved the door to one side. The knife was displayed on a pink silk cushion and the greenish-black glass had an inviting shine, in stark contrast to the jagged saw teeth punched into the blade.

The hair on his arms stood on end. Gustav had only touched the thing once, to verify its age and value, and would never do so again.

She placed her gloved hand on the blade, exhaled, and withdrew it. With languid movements she took off her glove, one finger at a time. Very slowly, she touched the edge of the blade with her index finger.

From the armchair, Gustav could see waves of shivers run through her body, her cheeks flushed, and her back arched slightly. She pulled away, reluctantly, he thought, and turned her back to him. A few moments passed. Gustav tried not to show any reaction to her heavy breathing and the struggle to regain control over it, and pretended not to notice how she twisted the glove between her hands, over and over again. He knew something of how it felt and would've liked privacy himself.

"I dare say that you have at least one item that my client might be interested in." Eve's voice, less calm than before, reminded him of a smoky whisky, rough but still warm.

He cleared his throat. "Would you like some more tea?"

"Please. Or if you have something stronger."

Gustav opened a bottle of cognac and poured the amber liquid into two perfect nineteenth century crystal glasses. He handed her one of them.

"Now, I can't promise that this is the very cognac that they drank at court in the day, but it is possible. The glasses come from the very table of Emperor Napoleon. They came to Sweden by way of his steward and ended up with me as part of a gambling debt. Together, they make for the most delightful experience."

He watched her expectantly. Would he be right? Was she like him? Would she feel the passing of the decades back to the engraver who had patiently and proudly worked each glass by hand? Or would she feel something else?

After what seemed like an eternity she reached toward the glass and grabbed it by its foot. She held it in three fingertips, her hand unsteady as she lifted the glass to her lips.

Gustav felt a knot in his gut and could not take his eyes off her. The cognac passed the rim of the glass and she swallowed, looking beyond the confines of his room.

If he had been less focused on her, he would never have noticed her body going limp, her arm losing strength and almost dropping the glass. He quickly stretched over the table, grabbed her by the elbow and placed his other hand under the glass. Without touching her skin.

"You didn't get these thanks to a gambling debt," Eve said. "The financial dilemma was caused by other vices."

"But…"

"Trust me, knowing people's darkest secrets is my…specialty."

"Oh, I am so sorry!" Gustav felt rather slow. He really should've guessed, after the knife. "I didn't mean for you to go through something like that without due warning…"

She smiled at him again, warmly. "Don't worry. My 'gift' doesn't trouble me. I just thought that you ought to know."

Without withdrawing her arm from Gustav's firm grip, she twisted her wrist to move the glass to her lips again and touched the rim with her tongue. It was soft, pink, and moist from the cognac. He swallowed hard.

"He was quite a character, your nobleman." Her voice had a dreamy quality. "Deviant, depraved, and ruthless. Most delightful."

As she set down the glass, she let her hand travel along his sleeve to the cuff, where she rested it and looked at him.

"Would you be willing to negotiate the knife for what I have brought? Or should we leave it for another time?"

"Ah…yes. I mean, let's have a look at the item before we

discuss that, shall we?"

Gustav cursed his trembling voice and the dryness of his throat as she placed the briefcase on the table and opened it. Set into the middle of the padding was a small box. She took it out, closed the briefcase, and placed the box on the table before taking a small key from her jacket pocket and unlocking it.

"Now, I would like to see the payment before proceeding."

Gustav retrieved a large carton box from the sideboard, and opened the lid. With two sets of tweezers he peeled back the tissue paper inside to reveal a faded, embroidered waistcoat.

"One piece of clothing, worn by Marquis de Sade." He couldn't control the wave of shivers going up his arm.

"Excellent." Eve opened the box. "Mother Teresa's head-cloth. Guaranteed authenticity."

Gustav could barely think straight. His ears were buzzing and his fingertips itched. Would he finally experience true goodness? Unaware of his movements, he reached for the box and was surprised when she grabbed him by the arm.

"I would prefer that we finalised this transaction first. We don't want to risk damaging any future dealings between us, do we?"

He, reluctantly and with some difficulty, tore his attention from the tempting glimpse of white. It was no more than a piece of fabric, but it had been part of something bigger. A wholeness. A life.

"Of course."

"You contacted my client, through an agent, and made an agreement regarding Mother Teresa's head-cloth, in part or whole, in exchange for clothing worn by Marquis de Sade, of which you have given previous proof of authenticity." She placed a small stack of documents on the table. "As per the agreement, these documents give a detailed account of all locations that the head-cloth has passed through since Mother Teresa last took it off. The people who have handled it have been kept anonymous for…business purposes. That, too, is in accordance with the agreement."

Gustav scanned the documents, not really caring, and nodded, looking up at her. "Everything seems to be in order."

"Good." She slid the box over to him and, for a brief moment, her fingers touched the back of his hand. Gustav caught a short glimpse of an obsidian blade caressing a woman's leg, over a stocking and naked skin before cutting a garter in one swift motion.

When the vision had faded, he found her sitting with her legs primly crossed and her gaze fixed on the knife display.

"Ah, yes, about the knife… Perhaps we could reach an agreement?"

"Perhaps." She smiled warmly at him as she pulled her glove back on, wrapped up the large box, and stood up. "But I can see that your mind is elsewhere, and that knife deserves complete attention, wouldn't you say?"

Since Gustav could not let the glimpse of white out of his mind, he had nothing to say, but her comment still made his mouth go dry. As she stood, Gustav rose immediately, got her coat and held it out for her.

"It has been a pleasure doing business with you. I do hope to see you again soon."

That was a weak version of what he would've liked to say, but he stumbled over even that.

He knew that she had seen his desire at the same time as he had seen the vision of hers. So, he made an effort to quiet his mind and think of nothing but the woman in front of him. Of her ability, of the knife, of everything that two people with such similar, but still opposite, gifts could have to offer one another. She stood very still as he put the coat over her shoulders, and with her subtle scent in his nostrils he caressed the skin right above her pearls with the tips of his fingers. She gasped and stepped away.

"I believe we will meet again," her voice rough around the edges, "soon."

Without a second glance she took the large parcel and walked out of his sanctuary. He heard the chiming doorbell over the front door as she left the shop.

Gustav sat down again, reached for the box, and set it on his lap. The wood was cool and smooth. He made himself sit with it just so, closed, for a little while. If this was to be the end of his quest, he wanted to treasure this moment of anticipation. And if not?

Well, there was only one way to know.

With trembling fingers he opened the lid, gripped the delicate fabric, and lost himself. The world fell away and turned into minute details: vegetable fibres, processing, weaving, sewing, then the daily use, the gentle touch of hands shrivelled with age. Snapshots of prayers, wishes and pleas for mercy flickered by. Desperation, rapture, deep love. Worship. Kindness. Mild and tired. It filled him to the brim and he flowed over.

But it was not what he had been looking for.

Not a pure, unadulterated feeling of goodness.

Gustav wiped his cheeks with the backs of his hands, stroking away the tears that kept rolling, before he carefully put the fabric back in its box and locked it.

Better luck next time, he thought, draining the last drops of cognac from Eve's glass.

# Pepe

## Tang Fei

### Translated by John Chu

*Tang Fei is a speculative fiction writer whose fiction has been featured (under various pen names) in magazines in China such as* Science Fiction World, Jiuzhou Fantasy, *and* Fantasy Old and New. *She is also a genre critic, and her critical essays have been published in* The Economic Observer. *Her stories have been published in* Apex Magazine, Clarkesworld, *and in* The Year's Best Science Fiction & Fantasy 2014.

L ET'S GO TO the amusement park." As Pepe speaks, a ray of red light scratches her face. Her face looks wounded then healed, welcoming some other color of light.

"But we're already here." I look silly holding the cigarette, but I'm holding it anyway.

We stand in the shadow of the Ferris wheel. Pepe's white, silk skirt billows in the wind. Her long, slender legs never seem to touch the ground. I have to keep hold of her. This makes me look stupid, so it makes me angry.

Even more annoying, when she hits me with her lollipop, I can't hit back.

"Hey, idiot, let's go to the amusement park."

"But we're already here."

Her eyes grow wide. She grabs my cigarette, take a deep drag, then realizes I've only been pretending.

"Pepe." I want her to look at me.

But her scarlet lips pout, then she blows a smoke ring at the sky. The way she looks at the sky always make me nervous. Our creator put a tightly wound spring into our bodies. But, in the end, even he forgot where each spring's key went to. By the time he died, rust covered our springs like lichen on his tombstone. Because we'll never have tombstones, our creator gave us springs.

He was fair. I tell myself that a lot. I know that was me telling a lie, but who cares. I only lie when I'm telling stories and, whenever I speak, I can only tell stories.

We were created to tell stories. On a good day, a person can tell so many, many stories. They ought to have some principles in them—storytelling principles. But we don't know any. We're driven by tightly wound springs. Once they start turning, stories spin out of our bodies. We scatter them like seeds wherever we run to. When we tell stories, our lips wriggle as fast as flight. The people listening to us get dizzy. It's better when they close their eyes as they listen. When they close their eyes, they can understand better the stories we tell. However, they can never fully understand.

This is how our creator first designed us. People called him a drunk. One day, after he poured his thirteenth shot of tequila (he'd downed only twelve shots at most before), suddenly, he smacked his head, then rushed home. Black and white blocks of ideas collided in a great dark and bright river inside his body. Pain shook his hands, twisted his back, and made him howl. The night our creator downed his thirteenth shot of tequila, he went home, then he created us.

He said we were salt. The salt of his palm. The salt of the earth.

When he finished speaking, he drove us all away.

The scene was so chaotic. So small a house. So many people. Everyone craned their necks. So crowded. Bodies squeezed against bodies. All of them alike.

The hot air was insufferable. My skin hurt. My nose hurt. The pain in my throat rushed down into my heart. We exhaled the burning air then inhaled again. Everyone hurt but no one left. We were waiting for our creator to speak again but he didn't. He rose brandishing his fist to drive us all out of the house. Everyone ran, pushing and squeezing their way to the door, the extremely narrow door. Random shadows and screams rose from inside the room. Rocking and swaying, we collided onto the street.

The outside was so cool. The wind poured into my head through my ears. It blew away the screams but our shadows continued to scramble up the walls. My head opened like a gate and let the wind scream into an empty darkness just like how the room I'd just left was now.

Without a thought, I ran and ran and ran.

Before I realized what had happened, it had happened. Pepe's hand was in mine. Her hair and skirt fluttered backward in the wind like outstretched wings. We ran hand in hand into the darkness.

This is exactly how it happened.

I was wearing khaki shorts. Pepe was wearing her white skirt. We ran hand in hand into the darkness.

We are story-telling machine kids. We'll never grow up. Forever wearing khaki shorts. Forever wearing a white skirt. Forever, except for telling stories, unable to speak.


The crowd waiting to ride the pirate ship parts in two. The people in front scatter to make room for us. Adults, children, even infants all look at us with friendly expressions. I've told them Pepe is my kid sister, that she has a serious illness and that she doesn't have many days left to live. Pepe is thrilled because she doesn't need to wait in line to ride the pirate ship. She runs dragging me to the front. I hear some people sigh. Pepe definitely doesn't look normal. This makes them believe my story even more. In the story I told these kind-hearted people, she'll die soon. So no matter what she does, it will be forgiven. So long as she doesn't say anything.

"Before this world could yet have been considered a world, thirteen witches passed through here. As a result, they chose here to settle down. As a result, they became this world's first witches. They predate this world."

I cover Pepe's mouth and drag her away from the woman taking tickets. Pepe's white skirt rustles as it grazes the woman's red skirt. The ticket woman is still thinking about what Pepe said. When people speak, it must be for some practical reason. She can't understand what Pepe's words mean.

"Your tickets?" Her gaze lingers on me.

I hand over the tickets. At the same time, I compliment her eyes. "Once, I met a girl. Her eyes were extremely beautiful. Just like yours."

She smiles a little. She can understand my words. Or so she thinks.

Pepe and I sit at the prow of the pirate ship. Soon, the entire ship has filled up. People next to Pepe and me look at our legs, which shake up and down as though we had leg cramps. They treat us like misbehaving children. If they knew who we were, they'd call the police to arrest us, or wait until the pirate ship swung into mid-air, then toss us out.

However, that era has long passed. That's what their grandparents had done. Back then, they weren't that old yet and they were stronger than us. Their bloodshot eyes, flaring nostrils, angry slogans, and the loss of life. The fanaticism that fermented during day, the fanaticism that fermented during the deep purple night. I remember all those things.

Those people were all drunk. In throngs, they searched every corner. They wanted to expose us, separate us from the other children wearing full, white skirts and khaki shorts. It always goes like this: They chase us, they block us, they surround us, they ask us questions. All the kids who can't answer are grabbed by the ankle, lifted into the air, then shaken like empty pockets back and forth against walls, against utility poles, against the ground, against railings. Our bodies are so light. That's how our creator designed us. Even if they smash us to pieces, we won't leak tears.

We also don't have blood.

People walked over the tumbling bits of us that now covered the ground. They never wanted to know that originally we had hearts, too. They just wanted us to die. We shouldn't have been discovered. This world doesn't need any stories because stories are wrong. They are dangerous and despicable. Desires meet and shine a light on the secrets of the heart. After the first time someone discovered his secret in a story, after that secret spread, people gradually fell out of love with listening to our nonsense. In it, they heard their own past, what they didn't want other people to know. They shut our mouths. It's always like that. This was just one battle.

They wanted to kill us then throw us away. So, they first let themselves think we were harmful beings to be feared. If they didn't prevent it, one day in the future, we'd become so powerful and destructive, nothing could compare to us. After they convinced themselves, they started to tell others. At last, the most eloquent of them was selected to be their leader. When they assembled, he stood on a great, big platform and roared into the microphone. The dark, dense, and turbulent crowd below, like the sea echoing the wind, roared in response.

At last, they waged war. They won.

Many years later, the people who waged and fought the war were placed into Intensive Care Units, slow catheters inserted into their bodies. They were old now, settled down, near to death. The deathly pale hospital light shrouded their dull, ashen skin like a layer of dirty snow on the road. They'd finally calmed down. And I still have Pepe, sitting next to the children of their children riding the pirate ship together.

The pirate ship starts to move. Pepe squirms, tugging at my sleeve. She's afraid of being rocked back and forth. The big machine starts to buzz. The first downswing is just a gentle sway. Pepe looks like she wanted to cry. She won't stop beating her temples with her fists. I grab her wrists, but the disaster is about to start. Her tongue is moving, continuing the story she just started:

"The witches loved to sing. They sang of the earth and there was the earth. They sang of the sky and there was the sky. They kept singing and this world changed into what it is now. At last, one day, the witches didn't think this was fun anymore. They had nothing left to sing about.

'I don't think we're needed any more,' the best tempered witch said.

'Then let's change the game we play,' the smartest witch said.

'Are you suggesting subtraction?' the witch who understood people the best guessed as she cocked her head.

'Right. Play a punishment game,' the most brutal witch yelled, waving her arms.

The rest of the witches agreed, one after another. Just like that, the witches agreed to play the subtraction game."

I hug Pepe. No one listens to her story. Light and lively music starts to play. The pirate ship flies into the air. Everyone screams. Now the ship stops at the peak of its swing to the right for a couple seconds or maybe an hour. We're at the bottom of the ship looking at the people at the top bowing their heads and staring at us. Their mouths stretch into large, black holes, exposing their throats. Only Pepe doesn't scream. Her soft red lips change shape. She continues to tell her story. No one listens.

I practically clamp her under my arms. Stay still, Pepe.

Pepe lets me. Her head droops. Just like before, she doesn't move, not even one bit, her arms wrapped around my waist. I let go a little. Suddenly, the pirate ship falls. It swoops down from its peak on the right and inertia pushes it up to the left. I scream, pushing myself away from Pepe. She throws herself on me, choking me. Her fingernails have grown long again. I always remember to cut her fingernails. Every time, I cut down to nothing and, by the time we fight, I'm still scratched by them just the same. Her fingernails grow so fast. Pepe is just that kind of kid. Her hair and fingernails grow and grow like mad. Like the weeds in a wasteland, they never stop. When she goes crazy, she doesn't care who she hurts or what she destroys.

I cave under her attack. She definitely hates me to death, brandishing her arms, wanting to rip me to pieces. My hairband breaks. Black hair scatters, fluttering like snakes in the air. Far away, the sky and earth quiver and sway. The music and shouting mix in the wind. The pirate ship stops. We're at the very top, nearly parallel to the ground, our whole body weight straining against the seatbelts. You're OK as long as you hold onto the armrest. However, I have to hold onto Pepe's wrists. Loosen my grip even a little and she'll start beating me again. Next time, she might use her teeth. Pepe, stay still, stay still. I face her and gaze into her eyes. That way, she'll stay still. However, she hides her eyes behind her hair.

"The witches want to play the subtraction game," she says.

Pepe opens her mouth. A moist, warm breath rushes out. She cries. I stare at her, wordlessly. I want to save my strength.

The pirate ship drops to the ground. The moment of weightlessness is like leaving our bodies. I begin to laugh.

Our arms untangle. She immediately curls into a ball.

Pepe must hate me to death. I've never told her stories. When she told stories, I never listened. Finally, I didn't even let her tell stories. She knew why. However, she still has never paid any attention to me.

So, she became the way she is now. The stories that sprawled like weeds in her head filled her. Her eyes grew blacker by the day.

Later, her fingernails grew black, too. Finally, even her lips grew black. I had to take her to the doctor. (Our heads are the same as human's. Even doctors can't tell the difference.) The X-ray was completely black. I knew why. It was because of all the untold stories, but I couldn't tell the doctors that. I couldn't even tell Pepe. The doctors met for a few days and still didn't know what to do. At last, I suggested plastic surgery, at least to change her lips back. Pepe constantly biting me had given her a chocolate smile.

The surgery was a huge success. They gave her strawberry red lips. Everyone was thrilled. Pepe thought she'd been completely cured. That day, she was truly happy, but she still bit my ear lobes. Finally, I realized that, by then, Pepe was already wrong in the head. Her eyes seemed just like black pools, almost without whites. Not long after, Pepe became truly crazy.

Her eyes seem just like black pools, shining with a fuliginous light.

As long as I listen to her stories, everything's fine. This way, she won't get frenzied. I can also tell her my stories. This way, we'll both be a little more comfortable. However, I don't want to. I'm fed up. I hate Pepe.

Even though I can pretend what I do is for her own good, and she's definitely getting better by the day, even though I can pretend I don't know I'm hurting her, I know she's not happy. She's crazy now. What I'm doing I do on purpose. I hate her and her stories.

Come on, Pepe. Use your fingernails to rip open my chest. I want to tear off your scalp.

Things are always like this. We wrestle, claw, and hate each other to death. But neither one of us ever leaves the other.

Maybe I'm also going crazy. Maybe I'm already crazy.

I never let Pepe know about going crazy. On the other hand, I still wanted to work hard to pretend we were normal kids. No, we weren't kids who told stories. No, we didn't tell stories at all. People believed us. They knew our creator didn't give us programs for telling intentional lies. Our creator created us only to tell stories. Except for stories, we couldn't say anything. This was how people recognized us.

They asked us questions.

They killed those who couldn't speak.

They killed those who told stories.

Those kids were exactly like us. They were shaken back and forth like empty flour sacks, just like us right now.

When the massacre started, Pepe and I saw them die with our own eyes. We didn't grieve. We didn't get angry. After all, death is death. Death is also nothing. Death is slight, just like an empty flour sack.

I didn't want to die, not one bit. When they ripped me away from the rest of the kids, I held onto Pepe's hand and never let go. A lot of people tried to pry our hands apart, but they were wasting their strength. A fool carrying a knife threatened to cut off our hands if we didn't let go. Pepe and I set our throats free. We began crying. Immediately, all the other kids began crying too. The adults panicked. At last, the adult who started this let us answer their questions together. "Either they both are or they both aren't. Answering together might save some time." So they asked their questions.

I opened my mouth. I made sounds. I spoke. I didn't tell stories. As a result, we survived.

They gave us yellow, five-pointed stars. We stuck them on our chests as we walked into another group of kids. They wore khaki pants or full, white skirts. They all had yellow, five-pointed stars fastened on their chests. The kids who didn't have yellow, five-pointed stars were on the other side. Among them, so many looked at me, astounded. Their pale faces shone with the blackness of night. They looked at me with amazement, to the point that they forgot that they were about to die.

This was not part of our creator's original plan. We were created following the same steps for the same purpose. Finally, for the same reason, we ought to be killed in the same way. I shouldn't leave them because we're the same kind of kids. They knew that but had no way to say it.

Perhaps they could have told stories, told treasonous and false stories. If the adults were smart, perhaps they could have figure out that I was actually telling a story, one that didn't believe that it was story. However, the kids didn't have time. They'd be dead soon. After they died, they'd be like empty flour sacks. They'd be nothing.

Nothing I did could seem out of the ordinary. When they asked me questions, I was certainly telling them stories. I treated everything that happened as a story to tell. You see, survival was just that simple. None of this is the truth. All of this is a story. As long as you think this, you can recount events in the way humans speak because you're telling a story. This isn't anything unusual. Those who are like us are unusual. I, myself, am also a little unusual.

Only Pepe doesn't seem unusual. Maybe she knew long ago that I'd act like this. Because she was also not unusual, we could survive. Even though the rest of the kids who told stories were all unusual, they wanted to survive. From among those kids, I saved only Pepe. This was inevitable after we'd rushed out of that black room together. I thought, for kids who told stories, Pepe and I had brains that were atypical.

We were atypical from the start. This notion stops my hand. A few hits later, Pepe also calms down. Her black eyes gaze at me, her long hair draped over her shoulders. The world is no longer in upheaval. The pirate ship has stopped.

People disembark from the pirate ship. A girl with blond hair tied with a pink butterfly bow walks ahead of us. Her skirt is also pink, highly creased and topped with lace. Very pretty, but not as pretty as the graceful arc of her calves. I can't see her face.

"The tortoise and the hare raced. The tortoise was always behind. He wanted to see the hare's face. That way, he could find out the color of her eyes."

That is Pepe telling her shortest story.

I laugh. Pepe doesn't know that the tortoise also longed for the hare's lips. She's still too young, so she doesn't understand desire. But I have desire. I want to know. Kids who tell stories are kids who have no needs. We eat. We sleep. We tell stories, but not from need. But on that day, when I came to treat this world as a story, I suddenly developed desire. At that moment, I understood this world even better. I understood even better the stories we told and spread.

"Let's ride the carousel, OK?" I said to Pepe.

She lowers her head, staring at her rounded leather shoes. Pink Butterfly Bow has just entered a gold pumpkin carriage.

"Come." I drag Pepe, rushing to the ticket taker before the carriage starts to move. Very few people are riding the carousel. I pick a red horse for Pepe, then climb onto the wooden horse closest to the gold pumpkin carriage. The carousel starts to move.

Odd music begins to play. We ride up and down among the colored lights. Butterfly Bow is really happy. She smiles, waving her hands at her side. I see her eyes, a charming emerald green. In stories, men call girls whose eyes are this shade of green sirens. The men bring those girls home, fondle them, then let them cry. I start to get excited. The horse under my body chases the carriage ahead of it with all its power.

Butterfly Bow looks as though her heart has opened with joy. She probably feels like she must be a real princess. I hope that she'll also wave at me and smile and she does. Her smile brushes past us and I feel so lucky. She's really beautiful. I'll remember her the way she is right now, forever.

I love her. I always fall rashly in love with these sorts of girls. When they're young, I meet them by chance then I fall in love with them. It's a harmless love. Nothing ever comes of it.

I can put my love for them into the drawer of my heart. Pepe isn't there. She's not like those girls.

Because she is my drawer. Pepe knows I've never put her into the drawer of my heart. But she doesn't know she is my drawer. This point is very important, and also very unimportant. In any case, we hate each other to death.

I hate Pepe, hate her telling her never ending stories. Even without having her spring wound, those stories—so annoying they should just die—gush non-stop out of her body. Yet, pushing words out of me is gradually getting harder and harder. I've no strength left. I haven't been speaking as much lately. I'll speak even less until my mouth shuts up, forever.

Once, I searched all over without finding a trace of the key. I've already become a very person-like thing. I just need the key and I'll be a person. No key and I will be dead. I'm almost dead now. Pepe is still telling stories non-stop.

The carousel keeps spinning round and round. We surround a large post, revolving around it. I'm behind Butterfly Bow, Butterfly Bow is behind Pepe, and Pepe is behind me. No, Pepe, you're in front of me. The carousel keeps spinning round and round. We surround a large post, revolving around it. I can't see Pepe. However, Pepe, you must be there. Pepe, my Pepe.

I can just make out someone speaking. It's Pepe. She's telling stories again. The sound of her voice is odd, as though it's being stretched and stretched by something. Drunks croon like this but, Pepe, why are you? This is not good.

It's awkward and dangerous. I must have forgotten something important. As I was telling you the story, I must have left out something really important. I should have realized sooner. Every good storyteller ought to have mastered this sort of narration technique. I should have realized sooner. Because when we escaped from the house, I was the one who held Pepe's hand tight. Out of so many people, I held her hand tight and have never ever let go.

I don't realize this is a problem until we reach the Ferris wheel. Now, it's too late. You can't blame me for this. Pepe keeps telling stories. That story about witches wanting to play the subtraction game she's told over a thousand times, but she's never finished it even once. She is already mad. She glares at the sky, waiting, waiting, waiting, for the story to continue. Because she doesn't continue the story herself, she grabs and scratches me like mad. A sharp, fearful sound erupts from her body. What is it, what is it, what is it? Blue-green fish swim across the black pools on her face. That sound still rings, piercing my ears.

Pepe's an idiot. All she knows is to tell these stories she doesn't understand over and over again. She doesn't understand anything, but she wants to speak anyway. That's simply how our creator designed us. The spring keeps unwinding. Stories are told. But after so many years have passed, no one remembers where, whatever weird place, those keys have been kept. At first, no one worried about this problem. Maybe because we can't even find our own springs? Besides, that was a problem for years in the future. Many years have now passed, we've gone mad and the other kids have died. No one cares about those keys. No one worries about something that won't matter yet for years. There's just no story, that's all.

It'll be OK. It'll be OK.

Bright light fills the amusement park. The smell of popcorn lingers in the air. The flavor of sweat, engine oil, and sausages stick to the light bulbs. Lamps light the Ferris wheel, making it seem like a giant pinwheel spinning slowly in the transparent wind. The places where Pepe grabbed me begin to itch. One by one, I scratch each itch. From all the rubbing, my body smells rotten. If not for wounds, kids who tell stories would never rot.

Underneath my khaki pants, my legs are filled with scars of wounds unable to heal.

Pepe is looking at me. She sits across from me, so peaceful. When she can't go on with a story, she turns her face out the window. The sky is purple. The window faintly reflects us sitting together side by side. The Ferris wheel slowly rises. The people below us shrink. Pepe stands from her seat. She tugs a little at her full, white skirt.

"Let's go to the amusement park," she says as she leans out of the window, facing distant lights.

I stared closely at her. "This isn't a story, Pepe. You can just speak now."

Pepe's head turns around. Laughter rushes at me. She hasn't laughed like this in a long time.

I hold on to the railing as I fasten the catch. The wind's blocked out. We've ridden in Ferris wheel compartment to its highest point and soon it'll slowly descend. On the ground, one by one, a crowd gathers facing something small and white. It's so small that it's more like a white speck.

Pepe, why are they talking about you? From up here, I can't see clearly what you look like now. The Ferris wheel has already reached its highest point. The carriage will stop here for a moment, hanging by itself in mid-air. Then, it'll descend, descend to the earth. I'll visit your body then leave. In my heart, I play over and over everything that will happen. It's so chaotic below. They won't pay any attention to me. I'll show some sorrow and confusion. This way, they'll believe you and I have nothing to do with each other, then they'll release me. Maybe they already know you're a kid who tells stories. They'll still guess you either jumped or were pushed from the top of the Ferris wheel. So I still have to play innocent for a while.

As far as I'm concerned, this isn't hard. You know that I can lie. I think of what happens to me as a story. In a loud voice, I'll recite the story version of me like an actor's lines. As a result, they'll think I'm a normal kid. What I'll say are all things a normal kid says. They can't see my spring unwind. It unwinds and unwinds, pushing hard against this scary world, turning what happened into a story. In my mind, I tell myself none of this is real.

This is a story. A story, so a lie is no longer a lie. I've merely changed the way that I tell stories. Yes, Pepe, you knew. That's why you laughed.

You kept laughing because you knew—the story of this amusement park was your final story.

I think maybe I'm wrong, perhaps I haven't changed the way I tell stories, rather, I'm just living in a story. No, you'll never understand these two aren't the same. We'll never understand.

But this doesn't matter. You lie on the ground, peaceful, broken, accepting the crowd's chatter. I'll pass by your body then innocently leave.

That there's no key isn't my fault. Soon, I'll become utterly silent yet alive forever. Killing you also isn't my fault. I'll live forever, and be utterly silent.

"Excuse me, you dropped something." As I'm leaving the crowd, a woman calls to me. She sneaks me something. It's ice cold and I almost shake it off my hand. I gaze at it. It's a smashed up heart-shaped key. Your name is carved on it, Pepe. I know that this must be your heart. I know that this must be my key. I know.

But, Pepe, you know, I can no longer find my spring.

I lost it long ago.

We all lost our springs long ago.

# Six Things We Found During the Autopsy

## Kuzhali Manickavel

*Indian writer Kuzhali Manickavel's short fiction collections are* Things We Found During the Autopsy *and* Insects Are Just Like You and Me Except Some of Them Have Wings, *and echapbook* Eating Sugar, Telling Lies. *Her work has also appeared in* Granta, Agni, Subtropics, *and elsewhere.*

### 1. PLAYBOY

A PLAYBOY WAS hidden behind her jaw, rolled and bent like she had stashed it there in a hurry. Black and white alarm clocks were pasted over the women's breasts and the words !wUt aLarming bOobeez! were scrawled across the stomach. It was hard to tell if she had done this herself or if someone else had done it for her.

We could not find any incisions so we decided she must have rammed the Playboy into her ear and hoped for the best. We thought this made her stoic, medically marvelous, and gay. We wondered if she had a secret crush on one of us and while we unanimously agreed that this was possible, we knew in our hearts that it was not.

### 2. BLACK ANTS

The ants were an ongoing observation, like watching fish. They floated up gently through her skin, broke the surface, and lay there like the journey had made them tired and they just needed to lie down for a while. We discovered that there were no ants near her elbows but could not come to a consensus as to how this was significant. We thought we saw something that resembled an abnormally thick spiderweb under her pancreas and decided not to pursue that line of inquiry because it obviously had nothing to do with the ants.

We wondered if she had let the ants in or if they had smashed their way through her, vandalizing her body with starred and spangled railroads, towers, and pornography. Now that she was dead, the ants probably had no reason to stay. We thought this was heartbreaking but also the best option for everyone involved.

### 3. ANGELS

The angels were clustered and nested behind her heart and lungs. They had to be pulled out with tweezers, which was not easy because they kept hanging onto her esophagus with their angry fingers and teeth. They had no nipples, bellybuttons, or genitalia, which made them like dolls but we did not feel like combing their hair. Their feet looked like hands and they dug their heels into our faces as a sign of protest. They caterwauled. They sounded like prehistoric birds that were heartbroken because they were going to die in the evening.

We thought she must have been a closeted Catholic. We thought she had probably been more into the angels than she was into Jesus, which is why she had allowed them to stay in such a communally sensitive area. We thought it was racist to assume that only Catholics had an affinity for angels.

### 4. ST. SEBASTIAN

St. Sebastian was tied to her spinal column, eyes looking heavenward, an arrow running into his chin and out of his forehead. His body was peppered with arrows but it was the one through his forehead that made us untie him. We thought that untying him would make him feel better. We didn't touch the arrow because we thought it would make his head fall off.

We thought the angels and St. Sebastian were probably good friends. We imagined them hanging out in the late afternoon, folding discarded angel wings into boats and sailing them on her bloodstream, hoping they would return filled with things that were sweet and useful.

### 5. TYPHOID

It was only later, when we were delirious, sour-mouthed and tired, that we realized we all had typhoid. While we waited for it to go away, we cleverly and calculatingly deduced where we got it from. The typhoid was a shiny black slab that was stuck to the back of her liver. It came apart in layers but could not be removed completely.

We thought she was a typhoid carrier. We thought she had probably infected all of us and the typhoid was sticking to our livers, too. We decided that we were angry at the world and this was what people with cancer felt like. We thought it must be a neat thing to be a typhoid carrier.

## 6. PLAYGIRL

The Playgirl was spread across her ribcage like a placemat. Hairless, half-aroused men stared sexily into our faces and we looked at their half-arousal and sighed. We pasted the heads of Siberian Huskies onto their faces and decided this made them more regal and less attainable. We also decided that if we ever created a pantheon of gods, there would be a set of twins who would be barechested and Siberian Husky-headed.

We knew she was the only one who could have made it with a hairless, half-aroused Playgirl man with a Siberian Husky head. We imagined it happening in a series of well-lit photographs where she and the Playgirl man were naked and open-mouthed but not sweating. We contrasted the open Playgirl with the rolled and bent Playboy and decided that she had been conflicted about her sexuality. We thought we could have been the awesome friends who held her hand while we dragged her out of the closet. We thought we could have convinced her it was okay to like girls even if she didn't like any of us.

# The Symphony of Ice and Dust

## Julie Novakova

*Julie Novakova was born in Prague, the Czech Republic. She is a writer, evolutionary biologist, and occasional translator who has published seven novels, one anthology, and more than thirty short stories in Czech. Some of her English stories have been published in* Clarkesworld, Perihelion SF, *and* Fantasy Scroll.

I T'S GOING TO be the greatest symphony anyone has ever composed," said Jurriaan. "Our best work. Something we'll be remembered for in the next millennia. A frail melody comprised of ice and dust, of distance and cold. It will be our masterpiece."

Chiara listened absently and closed her eyes. Jurriaan had never touched ice, seen dust, been able to imagine real-world distances, or experienced cold. Everything he had was his music. And he *was* one of the best; at least among organic minds.

Sometimes she felt sorry for him.

And sometimes she envied him.

She imagined the world waiting for them, strange, freezing, lonely, and beautiful, and a moment came when she could not envy Jurriaan his gift—or his curse—at all. She checked with *Orpheus* how long the rest of the journey would last. The answer was prompt.

*In three days, we will approach Sedna.*

Chiara decided to dream for the rest of the voyage.

Her dreams were filled with images, sounds, tastes, smells, and emotions. Especially emotions. She *felt* the inner Oort cloud before she had even stepped outside the ship. *Orpheus* slowly fed her with some of the gathered data and her unique brain made a fantastical dream of nearly all of it.

When Chiara woke up, she knew that they were orbiting Sedna and sending down probes. *Orpheus* had taken care of it, partly from the ship's own initiative, partly because of Manuel. The Thinker of their mission was still unconscious, but actively communicating with *Orpheus* through his interface.

She connected to the data stream from the first probe which had already landed and recorded everything. *Sedna... We are the first here at least since the last perihelion more than eleven thousand years ago. It feels like an overwhelming gap—and yet so close!*

It almost filled her eyes with tears. Chiara was the Aesthete of their group by the Jovian Consortium standards. Feeling, sensing, and imagining things was her job—as well as it was Manuel's job to primarily go through hard data, connect the dots, think everything through, even the compositions, the results of their combined effort—and Jurriaan's job to focus on nothing but the music.

She sent a mental note to Manuel. *When can we go to the surface?*

The response was immediate. *When I conclude it's safe.*

*Safe is bad. It's stripped of fear, awe, even of most of the curiosity! I need them to work properly, they're essential. Let me go there first.*

*All right*, he replied.

Chiara smiled a little. She learned to use logic to persuade Manuel long ago—and most of the time she was successful.

As she was dressing in the protective suit, a memory of a similar moment some years ago came to her and sent a shiver through her body. It was on Io and she stayed on the surface far too long even for her highly augmented body to withstand. When it became clear that she'd need a new one because of the amount of received radiation, she decided to give that one at least an interesting death—and she let it boil and melt near one of the volcanoes. Although her new brain was a slightly inadequate copy of the last one, thanks to the implants she remembered the pain—and then nothing, just a curious observation of the suit and her body slowly disintegrating—as if it happened to this very body.

She didn't intend to do anything like that here. No; here she perceived a cold and fragile beauty. There should be no pain associated to it, no horror. Fear, maybe. Awe, definitely yes. Standing there on the icy surface, the Sun a mere bright star, darkness everywhere—she ought to feel awe.

Chiara felt she had a good chance of being the first human being who ever stood on Sedna. The dwarf planet was nearing its perihelion now, still almost a hundred astronomical units from the Sun, and there were no reports of any expeditions before them during the recent period.

When the lander touched the surface of Sedna, she stayed inside for a little while, getting used to the alien landscape around her. It had a strange sense of tranquility to it. Chiara was used to the icy moons of the Jovian system which she called home, but this landscape was far smoother than what she knew from there. It was also darker—and an odd shade of brown-red.

She turned off the lander's lights and stepped outside through the airlock, into the darkness.

It wasn't a complete darkness. But the sun was not currently visible from this side of the dwarf planet and it felt like being lonelier, further away than ever before. She was able to see the disc of the galaxy clearer than from anywhere else she had been to.

She knelt and slowly touched the surface with one of her suit's haptic gloves.

*We've found something, Chiara,* suddenly Manuel's voice resonated in her head. *See for yourself.*

He sent her a mental image of a couple of objects not deep beneath the icy surface found by one of the numerous little probes. The biggest one resembled a ship. A small, stumpy, ancient-looking ship, unmistakably of a human origin. They were not the first.

But these must have come here a *very* long time ago.

And a few miles further and far beneath it, another shape was discovered by their sensors. A bigger, stranger shape.

Probably from much, much longer ago than the first one...

It took less than an hour to drill through the ice to the first ship. Getting inside it then was a matter of minutes.

Chiara saw the two bodies as the probes approached them. Both dead—but almost intact. One male, one female. The probes suggested the small chambers they found them inside were probably designed for cryosleep. They must have been prepared for the procedure or already frozen when they died.

The ship was long dead, too but that didn't constitute much of a problem for the probes. They quickly repaired the computers and what was left of the data.

They found the ship's logs and sent it to the crew of *Orpheus* even before others had time to drill deep enough to reach the other object.

Chiara was back aboard at the time they opened the file and heard the voice of the long gone woman.

▼

*I think I don't have much time left. I have no means of getting from here in time. But I know that there will be others who come here to explore. I hope you find this. I'm telling our story for you.*

*Ten days ago, I discovered something...—wait, let me start from the beginning.*

"How is it going, love?"

Theodora smiled while unscrewing another panel on the probe. "Good. Suppose we could use this one tomorrow on the last picked site. I've got just one more bug to repair."

She was wearing a thin suit, protecting her in the vacuum and cold of the storage chamber, very flexible and quite comfortable compared to EVA suits. Despite that, she'd prefer to be outside the ship, walking on the surface of Triton which *Kittiwake* was orbiting for more than two years now.

*Kittiwake* was a small ship, but sufficient for sustaining two people aboard even for a couple of decades if necessary. Provided with enough hydrogen, easily extractable practically everywhere, its bimodal MITEE could function for half a century without any serious problems. If one element failed, it still had many others and could push the ship forward with a good specific impulse and a decent thrust while also providing the electrical energy needed by the ship.

Now the mission on Triton was nearing its end. Theodora didn't know whether to be happy and relieved that she and her husband would finally return to Earth after so many years of isolation, or sad that she wouldn't ever see this remarkable place again.

When she was done with the ice-drilling probe, she went through several airlocks to the habitation deck. It was tiny, but sufficient enough for hers and Dimitri's needs.

"It seems we have a word from the outside world," her husband smiled as she entered the cabin. "*Kittiwake* just picked it up."

After checking the signal for malware, the ship automatically showed them the recording. The face of their superior, OSS Mission Supervisor Ronald Blythe, appeared on the screen. He congratulated them for their results on Triton and mentioned that a window for another long-term scientific expedition was opening. Theodora's stomach rocked. She was eager to find out. But still... a new expedition would mean yet more years away from the rest of humanity. The company picked her and Dimitri because they were a stable, non-conflict couple with steady personalities and a lot of technical and scientific experience. They were *supposed* to be able to spend years without any other human contact in a tiny space of their ship, exploring the outer solar system, without a chance for a vacation, without feeling the Earth's gravity, smells, wind... *However, we had a contract for eight years. The time's almost up. Are they proposing to prolong it? And what for?* thought Theodora.

"Last week, we received a signal from Nerivik 2."

"Isn't that the probe sent to Sedna in the eighties that stopped transmitting before it reached an orbit?" murmured Theodora.

It was. Blythe went on explaining how they lost contact with the probe for more than ten years and suddenly, out of thin air, it sent out a signal five days ago. Scientists at the FAST observatory who picked up the signal by accident were a bit surprised, to put it mildly. They began analyzing it immediately—and fortunately didn't keep intercepting the transmission for themselves.

"And the findings were...weird. It became clear that the probe lost its orbit, crashed, but probably regained control of its thrusters shortly before the crash and tried to change the collision into a landing. It was just damaged. It's possible that it kept transmitting most of the time, but without aiming the signal, the probability of reaching any receivers in the system was very low. However, it probably had time to send down its two landers before the crash. They kept measuring all they were supposed to record— and among other tasks, they tried mapping the ice layer. That's where it became really strange."

Theodora listened avidly as Blythe started explaining. Her interest grew every second.

The ultrasonic pulses showed an intriguing structure some two hundred meters below surface. It could not be told how large it was, but it had at least one hundred meters in diameter; maybe a lot more. The signature seemed like metal.

Blythe included the data in the transmission so that Theodora was able to look at it while he was speaking. It really was strange. It could have been a part of a metal-rich rock layer. But what would it be doing on Sedna? The dwarf planet was supposed to have a thick, largely icy layer composed mostly of methane, nitrogen, ethane, methanol, tholins, and water ice. Nothing even remotely like *this*. Maybe a big metal-rich meteorite buried in the ice crust after an impact then?

"We don't know what it is, or even if the measurement was correct. But it surely is interesting. It would be desirable to send a manned mission there. This looks like a situation that needs more resourcefulness and improvisations than robots can do," continued Blythe.

And for this, they needed someone with an expertise of frozen bodies of the outer solar system; someone stable, resourceful, and determined; and of course, preferably someone whom the journey would take around five instead of ten years. Sedna was still quite near its perihelion, but growing away slowly every year. In short: They needed someone like two experienced workers closing their successful mission on Neptune's icy moon Triton.

"...of course, I cannot force you into this. But with prolonging the contract, you'll receive extra money for such a long stay on your own and all the associated risks. I attach the new version of your contract to this message. I expect your answer in three days."

Theodora didn't have to look at the document to know the bonuses would be large; almost unimaginably large. There were medical risks associated with long-term radiation exposure, dangerous activities, immense psychical pressure, staying in micronavigation, and, above all, the cryosleep necessary to travel so far away without losing many years just by the voyage itself.

But it wasn't the money that primarily tempted her to accept the contract.

Theodora and Dimitri looked at each other expectantly. "Well," she broke the silence first, "looks like we're gonna take a rather long nap; do you agree?"

Theodora shivered. At the first moment, she felt exposed and frightened without any obvious reason, which was even worse. Then she remembered; she was in the cryosleep chamber and slowly awakening. They must be near Sedna now.

"Dimi?" she croaked. There was no reply, although the ship was supposed to transmit every conversation to the other chamber—which meant that Dimitri hadn't achieved consciousness yet.

It took Theodora another hour before she could gather her thoughts well enough to start going through the data. When she was in the middle of checking their velocity and trajectory, the speaker in the chamber came alive: "Darling? Are you awake?"

"Yes, how are you?"

"Well, nothing's better than a good long sleep!"

Theodora laughed. Her throat burned and she still felt a bit stiff, but she couldn't stop. They actually were there; further than any human beings ever before!

In the next couple of days, Dimitri and Theodora had little time to rest although they didn't do anything physically demanding and were still recovering from the cryosleep. First they searched for and found the Nerivik 2 crash site and the two nearby stationed landers. The ice in the area seemed different from other sites, as if it had been gradually modified by inner volcanic activity. That explained why Nerivik 2 sent both its landers there in the first place. *Kittiwake* sent down a probe, continued mapping the surface, and after that sent a few other probes on different locations. It was a standard procedure, but it needed a lot of time.

When the first results from the probe near Nerivik 2 arrived, Dimitri sat still for a moment and then found his voice and called: "Dora! You must come see this."

The readings were peculiar. The object buried almost two hundred meters below the surface seemed a bit like an asteroid now, more than a hundred meters in diameter in one direction and over five hundred in the other. According to the ultrasonic pulses data, its shape seemed conical and the layer reflecting the pulses quite smooth. A very unusual asteroid indeed.

"What do you think it is?"

Theodora shrugged. "Don't know—and can't very well imagine, to be precise. Until it's proven otherwise, I'm betting on an asteroid, albeit a weird one. But let's find out soon."

"I'll send down the drilling machinery, shall I? Or do you propose to wait for even more readings?"

"Send it."

*Kittiwake* had two major drilling devices—three before Triton—and one backup machine. Theodora and Dimitri decided to send two at once. It was riskier, but they wanted to compare the data from an area with the anomaly and from another place chosen because of its similar surface structures. The equipment was old but reliable and lived through many more or less improvisational repairs.

At the end of the first day of drilling, they reached almost thirty meters below surface. On day three, they were about one hundred meters deep. On day four, the probe got through almost one hundred and fifty meters of ice and stopped.

Theodora had the uncomfortable feeling of vertigo every time she performed telemetric control. She guided the repair drone carefully to the drilling probe's main panel. She felt strangely dissociated with her body when the robot picked the cover and she felt as if it were her arms raising it and putting it aside. There she was. "Oh, not this," she sighed.

No wonder Dimitri had no success trying to get the probe running again from here. It was no software bug, temporary failure, or anything the self-repair systems could handle. Most of the processors were fried and needed replacing. The repair drone didn't have all of the components. They could send them down during some of the next orbit. But—

She lost her connection to the drone, as *Kittiwake* disappeared over the horizon from the drone's perspective, before she could end it herself. She gasped. It felt as if her limb had been cut off. She gulped and tried to concentrate again.

Yes, they could send the parts down. But Theodora feared that although the drone itself had more than sufficient AI for common repairs and had all the blueprints in its memory, it might overlook something else, something an AI would not notice and that might cause future trouble. She'd not be happy if they had to replace the processors again, like it happened once on Triton. She could control the drone from distance again, but there was no chance she could achieve that much precision and look everywhere through telemetry.

Well, they wanted to initiate manned exploration anyway. It would just have to be sooner than expected.

Dimitri watched Theodora's descent. He knew that she performed similar procedures many times before—but that never prevented him from worrying.

The view distorted as *Kittiwake* started losing connection. In another thirty minutes or so, it would rise up the horizon again. But Dimitri had considered changing their orbit to stationary and decided to do so. They didn't need to monitor so much of the surface anymore with the ship. He finally got two satellites to work and deployed them on an equatorial and a polar orbit. He could make them relay stations so that *Kittiwake* wouldn't need to change its orbit, but he liked the possibility to communicate directly with Theodora, her landing module, her rover, and the drilling probe. Less things could go wrong. And after years spent so far from Earth, they knew that things often *went* wrong.

He gave the engine command for more thrust and checked on the planned stationary transfer orbit. Everything seemed fine for a while.

Until a red light flashed next to the screen and a warning presented itself.

Theodora was descending through the tunnel in the ice. It was dark except for the light from the LEDs on her suit and the reflectors from the top of the shaft. Her rope was winding down gradually. She could see the drilling device below now.

The light above seemed faint when she reached the probe. It took her only an hour to get it operational again. She smiled and let the winch pull her up again.

Just as she neared the surface, she heard a noise in the speakers of her suit. "Dimitri?" she spoke. "What is it?"

"Have to…come down…"

She barely understood him through the static.

"Dimitri!"

For a while, she heard nothing. Then the static returned—and after that, Dimitri's distorted voice. "…have to land." Cracking and humming. Theodora tried to amplify the sound frantically. "…send you the coordinates…hope it works out…"

A file found its way through the transmission. It was a technical report generated by *Kittiwake*. Theodora opened it and glimpsed through it quickly.

"Oh no," she whispered.

Dimitri was doing his best to lead the remains of the ship on a trajectory ending with something that would approximate a landing more than a crash.

It was less than twenty minutes from the moment he accelerated *Kittiwake* to reach the transfer orbit but it seemed like an eternity. During that time, a warning indicated that the main turbine in the ship's power station was not working properly. He ran a more detailed scan and a moment later, everything was flashing with error reports.

The turbine in the power cycle broke down. It was tested for signs of wearing down regularly, but a hairline crack might have been overlooked in the control. The ship was moving with inertia most of the journey, the crack could have expanded during the deceleration phase and ruptured now, when the engine was working a little more again.

Things could go wrong. And they went wrong. Worse even, one of the blades pierced the coating of the reactor and the heated helium-xenon gas started leaking rapidly. The damage was too much for the automated repair systems. It was still leaking into the space between the coatings.

And the reactor itself was overheating quickly. Once the turbine stopped working, the gas still trapped in the cycle kept getting more and more heat from the MITEE—but couldn't continue through the cycle and cool down.

It was not critical yet, but would be in another couple of minutes. Dimitri sent all the repair drones to help the built-in repair and emergency systems but could see that it was not enough. He had also shut down the MITEE and all the rods were now safely turned to stop the reaction. It still wasn't enough. The overheating continued and could lead to an explosion. It could happen in a few minutes if not cooled down quickly.

It was just the way life went. Nothing serious happened in years and suddenly he's got *minutes*.

He knew there was only one thing to do. So he gave a command for the valves in the outer reactor coating to open. Then all the gas would leak outside. The ship would be useless without it, but it was the better one of two bad scenarios.

So far, only a minute had elapsed from the breakdown.

In the next few seconds, things went from bad to worse.

"Shit," exhaled Dimitri as he felt how the *Kittiwake* started spinning. One of the valves must have been stuck, so that the gas started leaking outside in just one direction and it quickly sent the ship into rotation.

Dimitri tried to compensate it with thrusters on both RCSs, but then *Kittiwake* shook hideously and then many of the screens went down. He realized what happened.

The rotation was too much. The ship was never constructed for this. There was too much tension in the wrong direction… She tore apart.

Still coping with the rotation, he checked the systems. He was right. The engine section was gone. He was lucky that the habitation section was still operating almost normally. There was his chance.

This section's reaction control system was apparently still working. The RCS's thrusters were small, but it was all he had.

He tested them with a short blast. Actually working; good. He used them to provide a little more distance from the other remains of the ship and then reviewed his situation calmer. He had to land if he wanted to live; and he needed to do it quickly, otherwise he'd drift into space with no means of correcting his trajectory.

He smiled rather sadly.

About twenty minutes after the turbine breakdown, Dimitri was now leading the rest of the ship down on Sedna and praying he could actually land instead of crashing.

"Dora?" he called. He hoped she'd pick up the transmission. "Dora, can you hear me? The reactor had a breakdown and the ship tore apart! I'm left with our section's remains. I have to come down…"

Theodora was driving her rover frantically to the landing site. She could not contact Dimitri, but that didn't mean anything; the antenna could have been damaged, while most of the ship could be perfectly fine. *It's all right. He is fine.*

She wished she could go faster, but as on most ice-rocky bodies, Sedna's surface could be treacherous. It had far less cracks or ridges than Europa or Ganymede and was actually very smooth compared to them, but it was still an alien landscape, not resembling anything on Earth at all. Himalaya's glaciers were children's toys compared to Sedna. The perspective was wrong, the measures were wrong, the shadows were wrong; it wasn't a land fit for human eyes and spatial recognition.

Finally, she approached the site. Her heart skipped a beat when she saw the habitation section in the lights of the rover. It seemed almost intact.

She ran to the nearest reachable airlock. It was still functioning; she could get inside.

It didn't look as if the ship had been through a bad accident. The corridor looked nearly normal. Everything was strapped or permanently fixed anyway, so a sight of total chaos wasn't to be expected. However, most of the systems were disabled, as she found out by logging into the network.

The door of the control room opened in front of her, a little damaged, but working.

"Dimitri!"

He found time to get in an emergency suit and was safely strapped in his chair. *Good.* Theodora leaned over him. He looked unconscious. She logged in to his suit and read the data quickly.

*Time of death… Suit's healthcare mechanisms could not help…*

"Oh, Dimitri," she croaked. Her throat was dry and she felt tears coming to her eyes. She forced them down. No time for this. Not now. She must do what he'd do in her place.

She moved his body in the suit to the cryosleep chamber. Once she managed it there, she ran a similar procedure as they had gone through many times before. Only this time it was slightly different, designed to keep a dead brain as little damaged as possible, in a state usable for later scanning of the neural network. Theodora knew that her Dimitri was gone; but they could use this data, complete it by every tiny bit of information available about his life, and create a virtual personality approximating Dimitri. He wouldn't be gone so…completely.

After that, she checked on the ship's systems again. No change whatsoever. Nothing needed her immediate attention now, at least for a short while.

She leaned on a wall and finally let the tears come.

*This is a part of an older log, but I don't want to repeat all that happened to me… I must go to sleep soon.*

Kittiwake *is dead now, as is Dimitri. I could do nothing in either case. I've got only one option, a quite desperate one. I have to equip my landing module in a way that it could carry me home. We went through this possibility in several emergency scenarios; I know what to do and that I* can *do it.*

*Of course, I'll have to spend the journey awake. The module hasn't got any cryosleep chamber and the one from the ship cannot be moved. But if the recycling systems work well, I can do it. I've got enough rations for about five years if I save the food a little. It doesn't get me anywhere near Earth, but I looked through the possible trajectories into the inner solar system and it could get me near Saturn if I leave here in three weeks, before this window closes. If I don't make it in this time, I'm as well as dead. But let's suppose I make it, I must… During the journey, I can contact Earth and another ship, even if only an automatic one with more supplies and equipment, could meet me on the way. I'll get home eventually.*

*If I succeed in rebuilding the landing module for an interplanetary journey. No one actually expected this to happen, but here I am. I must try.*

The next few days were busy. Theodora kept salvaging things from *Kittiwake* and carefully enhancing the module's systems. In most cases, enhancement was all she needed. Then she had to get rid of some parts needed only for the purposes of landing and surface operations—and finally attach the emergency fuel tanks and generate the fuel.

The module had a classical internal combustion engine. High thrust, but despairingly high need of fuel.

Fortunately, she was surrounded by methane and water ice—and purified liquid methane and oxygen were just the two things she needed. Once she got the separation and purification cycle running, the tanks were slowly being refilled. At least this was working as it should.

She'd very much like to let Earth know about the accident, but she couldn't. Most of the relay stations were behind the sun from her perspective now and the rest were unreachable by a weak antenna on the module; the one on the ship was too badly damaged. The Earth would know nothing about this until she was on her way back.

The plan seemed more and more feasible each day. She clung to it like to what it really was—her only chance of surviving.

When a message that the drilling probe had reached its target depth and stopped drilling appeared on the screen of her helmet, Theodora was confused for a couple of seconds before she realized what it was about. It seemed like a whole different world—mapping the surface from above, sending probes… In the last three days, she had little sleep and focused on her works on the module only. She had completely forgotten about the probe.

Well, after she checks the fuel generators again, she should have some time to look at it, she was well ahead of the schedule. After all, true explorers didn't abandon their aims even in times of great distress.

> *I'm glad I decided to have a look at it. Otherwise I'd die desperate and hopeless. Now, I'm strangely calm. It's just what a discovery like this does with you. It makes you feel small. The amazement and awe…*

Theodora couldn't believe the results until she personally got down the shaft into a small space the probe had made around a part of the thing.

She stood in the small ice cave, looking at it full of wonder. She dared not touch it yet.

The surface was dark and smooth. Just about two square meters of it were uncovered; the rest was still surrounded by ice. According to the measurements, the thing was at least five hundred meters long and had a conic shape. There was no doubt that she discovered...a ship.

*You cannot possibly imagine the feeling until you're right there. And I wasn't even expecting it. It was... I cannot really describe it. Unearthly. Wonderful. Amazing. Terrifying. All that and much more, mixed together.*

*I gave the alien ship every single moment I could spare. My module needed less and less tending to and I had almost two weeks until the flight window would close.*

*I named her* Peregrine. *It seemed appropriate to me. This wasn't a small interplanetary ship like* Kittiwake; *this bird could fly a lot faster. But still...she seemed too small to be an interstellar vessel, even if this was only a habitation section and the engines were gone.*

*It was probably the greatest discovery in all of human history yet. Just too bad I didn't have a chance to tell anyone. I really hope someone's listening.*

Theodora directed all the resources she didn't vitally need for her module to *Peregrine*. Only a day after her initial discovery, the probes picked up another strange shape buried in the ice not far from the ship.

When they also reached it, Theodora was struck with wonder. It was clearly an *engine* section!

While she worked on her module, she kept receiving new data about it and everything suggested that *Peregrine* used some kind of fusion drive; at this first glance not far more advanced than human engine systems. It seemed to her even more intriguing than if she had found something completely unknown.

*I was eventually able to run a radiometric dating of the ice surrounding the ship. The results suggest that she landed here some two-hundred and fifty million years ago. The ice preserved it well. But I must wonder…what were they doing here? Why have they come to our solar system—and why just this once? Although I don't understand a lot of what I see, the ship doesn't seem that much sophisticated to me. Maybe it's even something we could manage to make. But why use something like this for interstellar travel? With too little velocity, they'd never make it here in fewer than hundreds of years even if they came from the Alpha Centauri system!*

*Unless…the distance was smaller. We still don't know the history of the solar system in much detail. It's supposed that Sedna's orbit was disturbed by the passing of another star from an open cluster, where the Sun probably originated, about eight hundred astronomical units away not long after the formation of our system.*

*But what if an event like this occurred more times? Could it possibly have also been a quarter of a billion years ago? Just about any star on an adequate trajectory could have interfered with the solar system. In some million and half years, Gliese 710 should pass through the Oort cloud. We wouldn't have much evidence if an event like this happened in a distant past—only some perturbed orbits and more comet and asteroid bombardment of the planets later.*

*Hundreds AU is still a great distance, but surely not impossible. Hell, I'm almost one hundred AU from the sun now, although I haven't traveled the whole distance at one time. If we used a gravity assist from the sun, we could overcome even the distance of a thousand AU within a decade only! They could have done it, too, maybe hoping to reach the inner part of the system, but something had prevented them. And possibly the very first object they encountered, quite near their own star at the time, was a frozen dwarf planet from about a hundred to almost a thousand AU far from the sun, sent on its eccentric orbit by an earlier passing star and now disturbed again. They must have been lucky that Sedna wasn't captured by their star at the time. Or could it have been that theirs was the original star that deviated Sedna's orbit that much? Anyway, they'd have had to cross hundreds AU, but that's doable. If we had a sufficient motivation, we could manage a lot more.*

*Let's assume for a moment that my crazy hypothesis is right…*

*Then, I wonder what kind of motivation they had.*

It happened three days before her planned departure.

She was at the surface at the time, which might have saved her life—or rather prolonged it.

The quakes came without any warning. She was getting a little sleep in her rover when it woke her up. Four, maybe five points on the Richter scale, Theodora guessed. Her throat was suddenly very, very dry.

*The fuel generators…*

After the quake stopped, she went to check on them. Overcoming the little distance between her and them seemed to take an eternity; new cracks formed in the ice.

When she saw them, Theodora knew she ought to feel anger, panic, or desperation. But she just felt impossibly tired.

Two of the tanks were completely destroyed and the generators were damaged. She performed a more detailed control anyway but the result did not surprise her.

They couldn't be repaired; not in time. Maybe in months… but she'd be too late in less than a *week*.

She sat back in the rover, exhausted but suddenly very, very calm. What was a threat a while ago was a certainty now. She wasn't going to make it and she knew it.

The best that she could do was to use her remaining time as effectively as she was able to.

*When I'm done here, I'll freeze myself. But this time I'll set the...*final *cryogenic procedure.*

*If you found us and it's not too late... Well, we might talk again.*

The original shaft was destroyed by the quake, but she used the remaining probe, continued drilling with a maximum achievable speed, and kept measuring the ice layer via the ultrasonics. While these processes were running, Theodora tried to find out more about *Peregrine*. She was able to get spectroscopic readings which suggested that its surface consisted mainly of titanium; however, she couldn't read all the spectral characteristics; the alloy seemed to have too many components.

She also obtained more results on the thickness of the ice crust. The probe got almost two kilometers deep. Its results suggested that a liquid ocean beneath the layer might be possible—maybe fifteen, maybe twenty kilometers deeper than she was now. Theodora knew she'd never live to see a definitive answer; but these measurements might still be useful for someone else. If they could intercept her message.

She tried several times to send the data back to Earth, but she knew the chances too well to be even a little optimistic, although she salvaged a bigger antenna from Nerivik 2. But the transmitter was still rather weak and the aim far too inadequate. Without reaching relay stations, her message would become a cosmic noise, nothing more. The most reliable way to let the humanity see the data some-day was to store them here in as many copies as she could and hope it would suffice. She didn't have much of an option.

She kept thinking about the alien ship. If her dating was correct and it landed here a quarter of a billion years ago, it would vaguely coincide with the Great Permian-Triassic Extinction Event. It was usually attributed mostly to geological factors, but there was a possibility of a contribution of other effects—a disturbance of the Oort cloud and more comets sent to the inner solar system afterward would do. She was recently able to measure how long *Peregrine* had been exposed to cosmic radiation and it seemed to be just several hundred years unless there was a mistake or some factor she didn't know about. There was no chance any ship like this could have come here from another star system in such extremely short time—unless the star was really close at the time. It started to make more and more sense to Theodora, although all she had was still just a speculation.

"And it will remain a speculation until someone else finds us," she said aloud, glancing at *Peregrine*. "But they will. You'll see."

However, she wasn't so sure. Would the company send a new expedition after they realize that Theodora and Dimitri were not going to ever call back? It depended mostly on the budget; she was rather pessimistic. And about other companies or countries, she couldn't even guess. But Sedna's distance would grow each year. Before another mission could be sufficiently prepared and launched, years would probably pass. And other years during its voyage. Then even more years on the way back.

She had to admit to herself the possibility that no one was going to discover them soon—maybe not until the next perihelion. So far away in the future she couldn't even imagine it.

She looked at the other ship and touched the dark metal surface. *But still closer than how long you had to wait...*

"You were shipwrecked here, too, am I right?" Theodora managed a little smile. "Pity that we cannot talk about what happened to us. I'd really like to hear your story. And it looks like we're gonna be stuck here together for a while." Her smile grew wider yet more sorrowful at the same time. "Probably for a long while."

> *I hope you found us and heard our story, whoever you are. I really wish you did.*

▲

"Very interesting," said Manuel. "We must report these findings to the Consortium immediately."

Without waiting for an approval from Chiara or Jurriaan, he started mentally assembling a compact data transmission with the help of *Orpheus*. In a few minutes, they were prepared to send it.

Nor Chiara, nor Jurriaan objected.

When he was done, Manuel sent them a mental note of what he intended to do next.

"No!" burst out Chiara. "You cannot! They don't deserve this kind of treatment. They died far too long ago for this procedure to be a success. You won't revive them; you'll get pathetic fragments if anything at all! They were heroes. They *died* heroes. You cannot do this to them."

"It has a considerable scientific value. These bodies were preserved in an almost intact ice, sufficiently deep for shielding most of the radiation. We have never tried to revive bodies this old—and in such a good condition. We must do it."

"He's right," interjected Jurriaan. Chiara looked at him in surprise. It was probably the first thing he had said on this voyage that didn't involve his music.

She was outvoted. Even *Orpheus* expressed a support for Manuel's proposal, although the Consortium didn't give AIs full voting rights.

She left the cabin silently.

It took Manuel several days of an unceasing effort just to prepare the bodies. He filled them with nanobots and went through the results. He kept them under constant temperature and atmosphere. He retrieved what he could from the long dead ship about their medical records.

And then he began performing the procedure. He carefully opened the skulls, exposed the brains, and started *repairing* them. There wasn't much useful material left after eleven thousand years. But with the help of cutting edge designed bacteria and the nans, there was still a chance of doing a decent scan.

After another week, he started with that.

Chiara finally felt at peace. From their rendezvous with Sedna, she felt more filled with various emotions every day and finally she thought she couldn't bear it anymore. As she stepped inside *Orpheus* after the last scheduled visit of the surface of Sedna, she knew it was time.

Inside her cabin, she lay down calmly and let *Orpheus* pump a precisely mixed cocktail of modulators into her brain. Then Chiara entered her Dreamland.

She designed this environment herself some decades ago in order to facilitate the process of creating new musical themes and ideas from her emotions and memories as effectively as she could. And Chiara felt that the story of the ancient alien ship, Theodora, Dimitri, and Sedna would make wonderful musical variations. Then it will be primarily Jurriaan's task to assemble hers and Manuel's pieces, often dramatically different, into a symphony such as the world has never heard. Such that will make them famous even beyond the Jovian Consortium, possibly both among the Traditionalists and the Transitioned. They will all remember them.

Chiara smiled and drifted away from a normal consciousness.

During her stay in the Dreamland, *Orpheus* slowly abandoned the orbit of Sedna and set on a trajectory leading back to the territory of the Jovian Consortium. Another expedition, triggered by their reports back, was already on their way to Sedna, eager to find out more, especially about the alien ship and to drill through the ice crust into the possible inner ocean.

Chiara, Manuel, and Jurriaan had little equipment to explore the ship safely—but they didn't regret it. They had everything they needed. Now was the time to start assembling it all together carefully, piece by piece, like putting back a shattered antique vase.

Even Manuel didn't regret going away from this discovery. He had the bodies—and trying to revive their personalities now kept most of his attention. A few days after their departure from Sedna, he finished the procedure.

Chiara was awake again at the time, the burden of new feelings longing to be transformed into music gone. She didn't mind now what Manuel had done; it would be pointless to feel anything about it after she had already created her part of the masterpiece.

Manuel first activated the simulation of Dimitri's personality.

"*Where am I? Dora...Dora...Dora,*" it repeated like a stuck gramophone record.

"His brain suffered more damage than hers after he died," Manuel admitted. "She had time to go through a fairly common cryopreservation procedure. However..."

"*I'm stuck here. Our reactor broke down and the ship tore apart. There is too much damage. My husband is dead... But we found something, I have to pass this message on... But I feel disoriented, what have I finished? Where am I? What's happening?*" After a while, the female voice started again: "*Have I said this already? I don't know. I'm stuck here. Our reactor broke down...*"

"They are both mere fragments, a little memories from before death, a few emotions, and almost no useful cognitive capacity. I couldn't have retrieved more. Nevertheless, this is still a giant leap forward. Theoretically, we shouldn't have been able to retrieve this much after more than eleven thousand years."

Chiara listened to the feeble voices of the dead and was suddenly overwhelmed with sorrow. It chimed every piece of her body and her mind was full of it. It was almost unbearable. And it was also beautiful.

"It is great indeed," she whispered.

She didn't have to say more. Jurriaan learned her thoughts through the open channel. She knew he was thinking the same. He listened all the time. In his mind and with help of *Orpheus*, he kept listening to the recordings obtained by Manuel, shifting them, changing frequencies, changing them...making them into a melody.

"Keep a few of their words in it, will you?" Chiara spoke softly. "Please."

*I will. They'll make a great introduction. They will give the listeners a sense of the ages long gone and of personalities of former humans.* And he immersed into his composition once again. She knew better than to interrupt him now. In a few days or weeks, he will be done; he'll have gone through all her and Manuel's musical suggestions and come up with a draft of the symphony. Then it will take feedback from her and Manuel to complete it. But Jurriaan will have the final say in it. He is, after all, the Composer.

And after that, they should come up with a proper name. A Symphony of Ice and Dust, perhaps? And maybe they should add a subtitle. Ghosts of Theodora and Dimitri Live On Forever? No, certainly not; far too pompous and unsuitable for a largely classical piece. Voices of the Dead? A Song of the Shipwrecked?

Or simply: A Tribute.

# The Lady of the Soler Colony

## Rocío Rincón

Translated by James & Marian Womack

*Rocío Rincón Fernández is a writer and reviewer who lives in Barcelona.* Her work has been published *in* Timey Wimeys, The Best of Spanish Steampunk, Brujas: IV Antología de Relatos Fantásticos, *and elsewhere.*

HIS TIN FINGERS against my bedstead, metal against metal, like rain on the pipes. That was how my brother woke me every morning for the seven years we worked at the Soler textile colony.

This was also how he woke me the day that the colony collapsed like an old empire, sunk in water, rubble and thick *lludllitz*, ridiculous under the implacable eyes of The Lady.

Guillem seemed to start each day with his body perfectly prepared for work, while I rubbed my eyes in front of the day's gruel, sometimes served with butter and sometimes with honey. Leaving the street where the workers' houses were, everyone stood in line for the communal bathroom in the corridor, then stood in line to get into the factory, then stood in line for the foreman to make a note of us as we came in. Most people's faces showed sleepiness and resignation, but not my brother's. For those seven years, Guillem always went ahead, pulling on my hand as we went to the factory, his eyes bright and a smile on his face because he was going to see The Lady.

Although they were all around twenty metres tall, and their

sarcophagi were made from the same darkened, slightly iridescent metal, each one of the Ladies of the nine Catalan colonies was unique. The Lady of the Saltmartí Colony was like a Roman statue, with wide inexpressive pupil-less eyes. She stood high over her factory in a regal pose, wearing a pleated tunic from which sprang thick stems and thorns, like those of a rose bush. The Lady of the Espader Colony, nicknamed La Teresina, had her eyes closed and her mouth open, as if she was singing, and from her tunic came many long arms, with hands to help and bless all those who looked upon her.

Our Lady, The Lady, was a little different: younger, curvier, with an insolent expression, and curls that snaked around her face in the shape of a heart. Perhaps because of this, because she was so pretty, Mossèn Francesc didn't make us sing all that many hymns to her, nor did he allow us to swap cards with her picture at the gate to the church. The poor Mossèn, the colony's priest, reminded us regularly that The Lady's official name was Carmen, named after the patron saint of seafarers, but The Lady did not seem like someone to whom one should pray. She stood like a fisherwoman, with one hand on her waist and the other held out, beckoning. She shrugged the shoulder that lifted up out of her swooping shirt, raised an eyebrow like a star, and her close-lipped smile twisted one side of her mouth. She wore a bell skirt over her wide hips, and tentacles and seaweed grew from her belly, then changed into tubes which carried the steam into the factory's workings. Complicated and crude workings that in no way resembled the delicate shape of The Lady.

*It is not good, a cult based round a machine*, the Mossèn had said to Senör Roval, the teacher, on the morning when the roof of the factory exploded in a rain of glass and broken ceramic. When the Mossèn had taken the last of the workers from the colony to Olistany station, the teacher had sunk under the weight of so much worship, so much machinery, so much *lludllitz*.

For all that the Mossèn didn't like it, hymns were sung to The Lady in the workers' accommodation, round the stove, far from mass. Her picture was pinned at the head of all our beds. Families recalled, in whispers, the first time they had heard her soft moaning, in the first days of the colony, when we didn't even have a bakery. Back then we didn't have a night watchman, and the first foreman, a man with a sarcastic smile, had attempted to force himself on a girl. That night, The Lady's singing had woken the neighbours. The Lady sang most often on rainy nights, when the water came in through the little skylight and poured over her curls, her cheeks, down her breast. Her voice, that warm reverberation that sometimes was a ditty and sometimes was a sob, sounded to us like justice.

Only once had The Lady sung while the sun was out, the day my brother lost his hand, when the factory had been operating for scarcely three months. Guillem, who couldn't have been more than eight years old, was watching the thread on the shuttles, to know when he should put in more. I remember that with the noise of the machines and the shouts of the workers nobody heard my brother screaming until an urgent noise came from the body of the Lady herself. Mother was the first to see my brother's bloodied fingers, staining everything they touched, ruining the cloth. When they finally got my brother out from under the loom, separating threads of cotton, flesh, and metal, the Lady's voice died away with the sound of a fading bell. A few minutes more and Guillem would have lost his arm.

The Guillem of those days, the one I remember with affection, rarely frowned. The Guillem of today never smiles, except to himself or at clients. He is not sweet now, but affectionate, and everything that he seems to find important is too far away, or else hurts Mother.

After the surgery, Guillem had to spend several months in bed, as no one knew if his body would accept the metal prosthesis. However, he would spend the afternoons out with Señora Soler's little metal horse, and she would position him on its back with an almost maternal air. Back then the owners had not yet returned to Barcelona, and Señora Soler, the young señora, would walk through the colony with her flounced white dress and her blonde chignon and ringlets. Señora Soler was pregnant and said that coaches and trains made her dizzy and that she was too tired to walk. That was why they had brought one of those fashionable horses over from Africa, with its large metallic hindquarters, long pastel-coloured mane, and golden eyelashes. It seemed like a gigantic toy, which rather than trotting moved with erratic and tentative paces, halfway between a mad dance and a dressage leap. It was such an advanced model that its tin heart even beat, although it did occasionally bolt for no reason. There was a stable boy whose only job was to spend hours winding it up, just in case Señora Soler wanted to go out riding at dawn, or at teatime, or before going to bed. On horseback she would ride every Sunday between the church and Olistany, the nearest village. She was like a little girl, too delicate for the colony and for that belly, much younger than the workers who were bent over with age. She had no calluses on her hands and nothing to worry about.

She was one of those delicate spirits, the kind that rich people can allow themselves to be. She would have cried to see that candyfloss-coloured mane dyed with a strong-smelling black liquid. She would have cried more than for Señor Roval, I believe, to have seen her horse fall to the ground, with its once-powerful hooves moving clumsily. Mother saw the horse on the day we left as well, its belly cut open revealing the bright coggy metal guts. She did not say anything at the time, but I know that she held tighter onto Guillem's good hand.

One time Señora Soler came to our house to speak with Mother, after one of her rides with Guillem. We children had to go outside to play, and when I came back I saw Mother crying discreetly, with dignity, as she packed the bags for us to leave. When we reached Señor Soler's house, the one who was crying was the owner's wife. We stayed in the colony, as if nothing had happened, but Mother spent weeks sunk into a stubborn silence, her jaw tense. Señora Soler now only took the horse out once a week to ride to Olistany, and after she had given birth she went back to Barcelona.

When Guillem went back to work at the factory he no longer had to keep an eye on the shuttles, he had been set to work at one of the looms. My brother had changed, he went to work every morning with a new determination. He rested his new hand on The Lady's skirt, on that metal which seemed as warm as human skin. When the factory was running at full speed and the operator who ran The Lady went in through the little side door to see that everything was running well beneath her skirts, steam would come out of the irises of The Lady's eyes, through holes little larger than a penny. Guillem always saw when this happened and frowned, as if he were seeing an animal that was being made to work too hard. I had joined the mechanics at that time and I also noticed The Lady more, as she was the only machine in the whole colony that I was not allowed anywhere near.

Of course, Guillem had not been born when The Ladies of The Factories came to Barcelona, in boats that were so large that they seemed to be islands docking. He did not remember that the workers tried to boycott them in the beginning, that lots of people disappeared during the protests. For the first years, people saw The Ladies and remembered the pale sunken faces of those who had come back from the expedition into Russian waters.

When The Ladies came, Father was still alive. I remember this because it was a Saturday afternoon, when mother was working in the sweetshop. We went to the port to greet the brave adventurers, back from the Antarctic after months of work. We saw The Ladies approaching as if they themselves were floating, gigantic bodies that became even more impressive when they reached the land, bearing with them their terrible dignity. The tubes that came from their bellies fell heavily onto the decks of the boats, with nothing to connect them to. The sailors got them unloaded and then headed for home or the nearest tavern, but they argued first with the owner of the boats who spat on the ground and then disappeared into the dazzled crowd. People were scared and surprised, like a little child who hears a creaking door in the dark, at Christmastime.

I know that Guillem always thought that it was Señor Soler's fault, when he decided to build a huge waterwheel that, he assured us, would double the colony's productivity. They had to cut down the little wood that grew up round the main factory building and divert the course of the Velet River. No one was really happy with the plans because who knew if they could adapt themselves to the new rhythm? No one ever mentioned hiring new people, just effort and enthusiasm.

As a mechanic, I was there throughout the whole installation process. I remember the hours of frustration when the plans did not fit with the result we had hoped, the nights of sitting up worried because the parts that we needed to fulfil Señor Soler's deadline had not arrived. We mechanics had spent days drinking milk of magnesia to calm our stomachs. And I remember the day before the inauguration when our tests made The Lady sing. A thick steam came out of her eyes and you could hear rhythmic thumps coming from her chest, getting ever faster.

At the inauguration, on a fine morning, Señor Soler gave a speech accompanied by a few of his investors and the mayor of Olistany. The children were in their Sunday best and the adults all looked serious. When the speeches were over, they all went home to change and then go to work, more rapidly than usual. The teacher and the Mossèn stood on either side of Señor Soler, who made grandiloquent gestures with his arms and hands. The river flowed over new ground and the magpies settled on the factory roof. My brother closed his eyes, insisting that he would not participate in this. I remember this as a scene from a mural, static and brightly lit. Ephemeral.

The survivors insist that it was the moment when the holy water hit the river that it started. When the Mossèn blessed the waterwheel the air started to taste of salt and a scream that would have bloodied any human throat came from the factory. It was not the singing voice we remembered, but a complaint, the denunciation of an abuse. The heavy sound of falling machinery accompanied the groaning noise. We were all still and a girl at my side vomited the castor oil they had made her take that morning.

As soon as he was able to react, Guillem ran toward the factory with my mother behind him. I followed them, covering my face, with my back soaked in a cold sweat, while the glass fell and the people screamed. I got there just in time to see The Lady's coffin opening slowly, surrounded by warm salt steam.

I still do not know what it was that kept us still, while a huge creature, the size of Our Lady, squirmed elastically amid the wreckage of the building where we had worked for seven years and which now collapsed as she passed over it as if it were a sandcastle. Perhaps it was the kind of fear that takes charge of a nocturnal beast when the lights are suddenly turned on, the white terror that paralyses all your limbs. Perhaps it was the sight of that oily mass, like the sea during a storm, a bluish black with green and purplish tints that took up the space that The Lady had previously occupied. The creature was howling, deafeningly so, with a mouth that at times was as tiny as the eye of a needle and sometimes so large that its deformed head seemed to lack both nose and eyes. The creature stood like The Lady had stood, but the hand on its hip had fused with its waist and its shirt. It seemed to be forgetting, moment by moment, the shape of its sarcophagus, and it rapidly transformed itself. The seaweed and tentacles in her belly seemed to have taken on a life of their own and set off from the body, touching the walls, touching the ceiling and the floor quickly, as if palpating them, leaving a blackish sticky residue behind them.

'Lady, go back!' Guillem shouted as he ran after her, a child once again under her imposing form, trying to catch hold of her skirt with his metal hand, but unable to find anything to hold on to. The monster to whom we had prayed so much, our kind and bountiful Lady, turned her head at an unnatural angle and looked at him with an intensity that was almost curious. After a few terrifying seconds, she turned her head back and carried on walking. As she moved, the metal slowly fell away. Some debris reached my face, and though I remember that the blow hurt less than it should have, we still had no option other than to run.

Standing by the river, the people saw a kind of thick liquid building up in the back wall of the factory, crossing through the porous material of the façade. When The Lady came through the wall, Señor Soler had his back broken by a falling column. As the creature crossed through it, the river rose up and swept away the people who were closest to the shore. The creature walked straight across and then started to head downhill.

The Mossèn was the first to react, coolly and with common sense enough to save many lives. The sad-faced man whose boring sermons had made all of us youngsters laugh in secret got the survivors to the train station with short and direct orders. We followed him, trying not to look back, not to see where the creature was headed. Nothing we did seemed to matter in the slightest to The Lady, who carried on straight toward Barcelona.

Among all the confusion, no one realised that my brother's metal fingers had stayed on the floor of the factory, in a shining pool that looked like mercury. The old reddened stump with its dry skin was now a young hand once again, well-shaped and complete. Luckily enough no one noticed, because the change had taken place when he had sunk his fingers into the gelatinous skirts of the creature, the same creature that had drowned our master and crumbled our home to the ground. My brother looked at The Lady without blinking, with his eyes open and with the same expression of adoration as always. Looking at him, as hot blood slipped from my hurt lip down my chin, I stopped feeling scared for us, and started to feel scared for him.

In Olistany station, our muscles aching from the tension, we took one last look at the hill where the remains of the colony stood. Inside the skeleton of the factory, with the machines half melted like ice under the sun, The Lady's sarcophagus stood wide open. There was no kind of mechanism inside; all we could see was an empty carcass.

We shivered in a heap on the train when the sky suddenly filled with the shouts and songs of the other Ladies, like the calls of exotic birds, or the wind blowing through a badly-closed window. Apparently they were responding to Our Lady's calls, and they moved with the same trembling step, their bodies, made of the same strange material losing their original shape with each step. Those of us who were by the windows saw them leave. Like eroded walking mountains, they walked down into the sea and carried on walking until they were lost from sight.

There was no damage caused to the city, they left no remains as they had done in the various colonies. The people who saw them said that they slipped between the buildings, barely touching them, like benign tornadoes, like the smoke from a fire, flexible and discreet, but dark and fearful as well. When the seven Ladies went into the water, the sea-level rose so much that boats ended up being lifted onto the pier.

No one could return to the colonies, which had been filled with this highly toxic material that was inflammable and destroyed any metal with which it came into contact. Soon woods grew up where our streets had been and life prospered without us.

The Russians, fast and clever, christened these remnants that covered our colonies Лед слизь, which we turned into *lludllitz*. There were some people who thought of it as a kind of Luddite action, flesh against machinery, as if the whole atrocity had been planned as some kind of social protest. It was a feeble attempt to try to get back a degree of the control we had lost when these beings looked at us and decided to turn their backs on us forever.

For my mother, *lludllitz* was something absolute, a moment from which there was now no return, a sign of the need to abandon physical objects, to move forward or to drown.

We knew that the metal that made the bodies of The Ladies

had been drawn from Lake Vostok. The sarcophagi had been based on a popular actress, something that was painfully obvious once we were told. What we never knew was whether they returned to their distant lake, perhaps because that is what the international investors had decided, who left Barcelona along with their money and their promises, to see if the Italians had better transport systems or a better workforce. No one blamed them; they did not have the strength left to do so.

Mother went back to work at the pastry-stall on the market and a few months later married her boss, a well-mannered but shy man, a widower, who treated us with a respect to which we were not accustomed. We went to live in a little house with draughty walls, cold in the winter and warm in summer, but much better than the charity wards where a lot of the former workers at the Soler colony were living.

I found work in the fisherman's guild, working from the Barceloneta, and I am still there, soldering, repairing. I lost my colony girl accent and now speak like one of the workers, many of whom are from Andalucia. Although the pay is not very good, it is enough to live on. When I could save up a bit of money, I built one of those metal warehouse boys to help in the pastry stall. Although it looks a little rudimentary, it can use its hooks to pick up and unload packages and save my mother's bent back. We take it once a week to the public charging point in the middle of the market. Guillem never comes to the steam generator, neither does he use the warehouse boy. He has become sensitive now, surrounded by technology, as if he had forgotten his mechanical hand. Or as if he still remembered it.

For me, the *lludllitz* is the chance to come back to the surface after having touched rock-bottom, having lost a great deal. I don't know if I'm happier in the city than in the colony, but this life is enough for me. My brother no longer wakes me up, and he looks at my tools with mistrust.

Guillem is the only one who has not mentally overcome the collapse of the Colony. He walks through the world like a visionary: slowly, touching everything gently, his eyebrows bent in an eternal question. His hand never hurts, not even in bad weather. When he says he wants to go to Antarctica to study *lludllitz* and the sarcophagi that are still there, my mother argues with him for hours. He pronounces the word like the Russian scientists do and has scratched it in Cyrillic all over the house.

What he finds in *lludllitz* are truths that are whispered to him in the dark, like prayers, about regimes that fall, about ethics, charity, pain. For Guillem, *lludllitz* is more to do with Señora Soler and her little metal horse than with our family.

Occasionally, but less and less often, my brother brings a girl home with him when he comes for Sunday lunch. Sometimes, more and more often, the girl has wavy hair and a twisted smile. We are all quiet, and if we are lucky, the noise of rain on the pipes fills the silence.

# The Four Generations of Chang E

## Zen Cho

*Zen Cho was born and raised in Malaysia and currently lives in London. She is the author of the Crawford Award-winning short story collection* Spirits Abroad, *and is the editor of the anthology* Cyberpunk: Malaysia. *Her debut novel,* Sorcerer to the Crown, *was published in 2015.*

### The First Generation

IN THE FINAL days of Earth as we knew it, Chang E won the moon lottery.

For Earthlings who were neither rich nor well-connected, the lottery was the only way to get on the Lunar Habitation Programme. (This was the Earthlings' name for it. The moon people said: "those fucking immigrants".)

Chang E sold everything she had: the car, the family heirloom enamel hairpin collection, her external brain. Humans were so much less intelligent than Moonites anyway. The extra brain would have made little difference.

She was entitled to the hairpins. Her grandmother had pressed them into Chang E's hands herself, her soft old hands folding over Chang E's.

"In the future it will be dangerous to be a woman," her grandmother had said. "Maybe even more dangerous than when my grandmother was a girl. You look after yourself, OK?"

It was not as if anyone else would. There was a row over the hairpins. Her parents had been saving them to pay for Elder Brother's education.

Hah! Education! Who had time for education in days like

these? In these times you mated young before you died young, you plucked your roses before you came down with some hideous mutation or discovered one in your child, or else you did something crazy—like go to the moon. Like survive.

Chang E could see the signs. Her parents' eyes had started following her around hungrily, as if they were Bugs Bunny and she was a giant carrot. One night Chang E would wake up to find herself trussed up on the altar they had erected to Elder Brother.

Since the change, Elder Brother had spent most of his time in his room, slumbering Kraken-like in the gloomful depths of his bed. But by the pricking of their thumbs, by the lengthening of his teeth, Mother and Father trusted that he was their way out of the last war, their guard against assault and cannibalism.

Offerings of oranges, watermelons, and pink steamed rice cakes piled up around his bed. One day Chang E would join them. Everyone knew the new gods liked the taste of the flesh of women best.

So Chang E sold her last keepsake of her grandmother and pulled on her moon boots without regret.

On the moon Chang E floated free, untrammelled by the Earth's ponderous gravity, untroubled by that sticky thing called family. In the curious glances of the moon people, in their condescension ("your Lunarish is very good!") she was reinvented.

Away from home, you could be anything. Nobody knew who you'd been. Nobody cared.

She lived in one of the human ghettos, learnt to walk without needing the boots to tether her to the ground, married a human who chopped wood unceasingly to displace his intolerable homesickness.

One night she woke up and saw the light lying at the foot of her bed like snow on the grass. Lifting her head, she saw the weeping blue eye of home. The thought, exultant, thrilled through her: *I'm free! I'm free!*

## The Second Generation

Her mother had had a pet moon rabbit. This was before we found out they were sentient. She'd always treated it well, said Chang E. That was the irony: how well we had treated the rabbits! How little some of them deserved it!

Though if any rabbit had ever deserved good treatment, it

was her mother's pet rabbit. When Chang E was little, it had made herbal tea for her when she was ill and sung her nursery rhymes in its native moon rabbit tongue—little songs, simple and savage, but rather sweet. Of course Chang E wouldn't have been able to sing them to you now. She'd forgotten.

But she was grateful to that rabbit. It had been like a second mother to her, said Chang E.

What Chang E didn't like was the rabbit claiming to be intelligent. It's one thing to cradle babies to your breast and sing them songs, stroking your silken paw across their foreheads. It's another to want the vote, demand entrance to schools, move in to the best part of town and start building warrens.

When Chang E went to university there was a rabbit living in her student hall. Imagine that. A rabbit sharing their kitchen, using their plates, filling the pantry with its food.

Chang E kept her chopsticks and bowls in her bedroom, bringing them back from the kitchen every time she finished a meal. She was polite, in memory of her nanny, but it wasn't pleasant. The entire hall smelled of rabbit food. You worried other people would smell it on you.

Chang E was tired of smelling funny. She was tired of being ugly. She was tired of not fitting in. She'd learnt Lunarish from her immigrant mother, who'd made it sound like a song in a foreign language.

Her first day at school Chang E had sat on the floor, one of three humans among twenty children learning to add and subtract. When her teacher had asked what one and two made, her hand shot up.

"Tree!" she said.

Her teacher had smiled. She'd called up a tree on the holographic display.

"This is a tree." She called up the image of the number three. "Now, this is three."

She made the high-pitched clicking sound in the throat which is so difficult for humans to reproduce.

"Which is it, Changey?"

"Tree," Chang E had said stupidly. "Tree. Tree." Like a broken down robot.

In a month her Lunarish was perfect, accentless, and she

rolled her eyes at her mother's singsong, "Chang E, you got listen or not?"

Chang E would have liked to be motherless, pastless, selfless. Why was her skin so yellow, her eyes so small, when she felt so green inside?

After she turned 16, Chang E begged the money off her dad, who was conveniently indulgent since the divorce, and went in secret for the surgery.

When she saw herself in the mirror for the first time after the operation she gasped.

Long ovoid eyes, the last word in Lunar beauty, all iris, no ugly inconvenient whites or dark browns to spoil that perfect reflective surface. The eyes took up half her face. They were like black eggs, like jewels.

Her mother screamed when she saw Chang E. Then she cried.

It was strange. Chang E had wanted this surgery with every fiber of her being—her nose hairs swooning with longing, her liver contracting with want.

Yet she would have cried, too, seeing her mother so upset if her new eyes had let her. But Moonite eyes didn't have tear ducts. No eyelids to cradle tears, no eyelashes to sweep them away. She stared unblinking and felt sorry for her mother, who was still alive, but locked in an inaccessible past.

## The Third Generation

Chang E met H'yi in the lab, on her first day at work. He was the only rabbit there and he had the wary, closed-off look so many rabbits had.

At Chang E's school the rabbit students had kept themselves to themselves. They had their own associations—Rabbit Moonball Club, the Lapin Lacemaking Society—and sat in quiet groups at their own tables in the cafeteria.

Chang E had sat with her Moonite friends.

"There's only so much you can do," they'd said. "If they're not making any effort to integrate…"

But Chang E had wondered secretly if the rabbits had the right idea. When she met other Earthlings, each one alone in a group of Moonites, they'd exchange brief embarrassed glances before subsiding back into invisibility. The basic wrongness of being an Earthling was intensified in the presence of other Earthlings. When you were with normal people you could almost forget.

Around humans Chang E could feel her face become used to smiling and frowning, every emotion transmitted to her face with that flexibility of expression that was so distasteful to Moonites. As a child this had pained her, and she'd avoided it as much as possible—better the smoothness of the surface that came to her when she was hidden among Moonites.

At 24, Chang E was coming to understand that this was no way to live. But it was a difficult business, this easing into being. She and H'yi did not speak to each other at first, though they were the only non-Moonites in the lab.

The first time she brought human food to work, filling the place with strange warm smells, she kept her head down over her lunch, shrinking from the Moonites' glances. H'yi looked over at her.

"Smells good," he said. "I love noodles."

"Have you had this before?" said Chang E. H'yi's ears twitched. His face didn't change, but somehow Chang E knew he was laughing.

"I haven't spent my *entire* life in a warren," he said. "We do get out once in a while."

The first time Chang E slept over at his, she felt like she was coming home. The close dark warren was just big enough for her. It smelt of moon dust.

In H'yi's arms, her face buried in his fur, she felt as if the planet itself had caught her up in its embrace. She felt the wall vibrate: next door H'yi's mother was humming to her new litter. It was the moon's own lullaby.

Chang E's mother stopped speaking to her when she got married. It was rebellion, Ma said, but did she have to take it so far?

"I should have known when you changed your name," Ma wept. "After all the effort I went to, giving you a Moonite name. Having the throat operation so I could pronounce it. Sending you to all the best schools and making sure we lived in the right neighbourhoods. When will you grow up?"

Growing up meant wanting to be Moonite. Ma had always been disappointed by how bad Chang E was at this.

They only reconciled after Chang E had the baby. Her

mother came to visit, sitting stiffly on the sofa. H'yi made himself invisible in the kitchen.

The carpet on the floor between Chang E and her mother may as well have been a maria. But the baby stirred and yawned in Chang E's arms—and stolen glance by jealous, stolen glance, her mother fell in love.

One day Chang E came home from the lab and heard her mother singing to the baby. She stopped outside the nursery and listened, her heart still.

Her mother was singing a rabbit song.

Creaky and true, the voice of an old peasant rabbit unwound from her mouth. The accent was flawless. Her face was innocent, wiped clean of murky passions, as if she'd gone back in time to a self that had not yet discovered its capacity for cruelty.

## The Fourth Generation

When Chang E was 16, her mother died. The next year Chang E left school and went to Earth, taking her mother's ashes with her in a brown ceramic urn.

The place her mother had chosen was on an island just above the equator, where, Ma had said, their Earthling ancestors had been buried. When Chang E came out of the environment-controlled port building, the air wrapped around her, sticky and close. It was like stepping into a god's mouth and being enclosed by his warm humid breath.

Even on Earth most people travelled by hovercraft, but on this remote outpost wheeled vehicles were still in use. The journey was bumpy—the wheels rendered them victim to every stray imperfection in the road. Chang E hugged the urn to her and stared out the window, trying to ignore her nausea.

It was strange to see so many humans around, and only humans. In the capital city you'd see plenty of Moonites, expats, and tourists, but not in a small town like this.

Here, thought Chang E, was what her mother had dreamt of. Earthlings would not be like moon humans, always looking anxiously over their shoulder for the next way in which they would be found wanting.

And yet her mother had not chosen to come here in life. Only in death. Where would Chang E find the answer to that riddle?

Not in the graveyard. This was on an orange hill, studded

with white and grey tombstones, the vermillion earth furred in places with scrubby grass.

The sun bore close to the Earth here. The sunshine was almost a tangible thing, the heat a repeated hammer's blow against the temple. The only shade was from the trees, starred with yellow-hearted white flowers. They smelled sweet when Chang E picked them. She put one in her pocket.

The illness had been sudden, but they'd expected the death. Chang E's mother had arranged everything in advance, so that once Chang E arrived she did not have to do or understand anything. The nuns took over.

Following them, listening with only half her attention on their droning chant in a language she did not know to a god she did not recognise, she looked down on the town below. The air was thick with light over the stubby low buildings, crowded close together the way human habitations tended to be.

How godlike the Moonites must have felt when they entered these skies and saw such towns from above. To love a new world, you had to get close to the ground and listen.

You were not allowed to watch them lower the urn into the ground and cover it with soil. Chang E looked up obediently.

In the blue sky there was a dragon.

She blinked. It was a flock of birds, forming a long line against the sky. A cluster of birds at one end made it look like the dragon had turned its head. The sunlight glinting off their white bodies made it seem that the dragon looked straight at her with luminous eyes.

She stood and watched the sky, her hand shading her eyes, long after the dragon had left, until the urn was buried and her mother was back in the Earth.

What was the point of this funeral so far from home, a sky's worth of stars lying between Chang E's mother and everyone she had ever known? Had her mother wanted Chang E to stay? Had she hoped Chang E would fall in love with the home of her ancestors, find a human to marry, and by so doing somehow return them all to a place where they were known?

Chang E put her hand in her pocket and found the flower. The petals were waxen, the texture oddly plastic between her fingertips. They had none of the fragility she'd been taught to associate with flowers.

Here is a secret Chang E knew, though her mother didn't.

Past a certain point, you stop being able to go home. At this point, when you have gotten this far from where you were from, the thread snaps. The narrative breaks. And you are forced, past-less, motherless, selfless, to invent yourself anew.

At a certain point, this stops being sad—but who knows if any human has ever reached that point?

Chang E wiped her eyes and her streaming forehead, followed the nuns back to the temple, and knelt to pray to her nameless forebears.

She was at the exit when she remembered the flower. The Lunar Border Agency got funny if you tried to bring Earth vegetation in. She left the flower on the steps to the temple.

Then Chang E flew back to the moon.

# Pockets Full of Stones

## Vajra Chandrasekera

*Vajra Chandrasekera lives in Colombo, Sri Lanka, and his short stories have appeared in* Clarkesworld, Lightspeed, *and* Black Static, *among others.*

THE GHOST OF my grandfather Rais flickered when he talked about first contact. He was a decade younger than me now, unwrinkled and black-haired, far from grandfatherly.

Beside me, Hadil gestured for a pause. My grandfather's ghost stopped talking, his features losing expression. The rich brown of his skin faded, became ghostlier, as the imago switched over to standby mode.

"Dike," Hadil said, nudging me unnecessarily. "You notice the flicker?"

"Probably lost some frames in the cooker," I said. Error-correction was tricky with neutrino-based communications over the light-years. The original Rais, very much alive, was extremely far away and travelling fast. "Did he say first contact?"

"He did," Hadil said. He took off his augmented-reality glasses to rub his temples. Without them, his eyes looked too big, the red veins standing out. Too much time behind the glasses. "But I think that's all the time he's going to spend on it, no matter how important it might be. He just wants to talk to you."

I would have argued, except it was true.

*Picked up a neutrino transmission*, the ghost of Rais had said tiredly. *Could be pulsar activity. Some talk of first contact. See attached update for details.* As if that closed the matter. Then he had changed the subject to his obsession: the petition to open up a bandwidth allocation for family members of his twenty thousand fellow colonists on the *Cây Cúc*. The right to talk to the Earth they'd left behind.

"Let me take a look at the attachment before Da Nang comes up," Hadil said. On Makemake Station, we lived in epicycles. The station's magnetic transmission horns tracked Earth in her orbit, waiting every day for the planet to spin Da Nang Mission Control into our line of sight so we could report home. There were a few hours left to go today.

"Do you mind if—" I nodded at the silent ghost. Without his glasses on Hadil couldn't see the imago, but it hadn't moved since he paused it.

"Go ahead," Hadil said, getting up. "It's *your* Grandpa. He probably spends the next twenty minutes crying about bandwidth and your Grandma, anyway."

I scowled at his back as he walked to the other side of the workroom, walking through all the phantom displays he couldn't see without his glasses on: bright screens and blinking glyphs, the scale model of Makemake Station in the corner, the wall of clocks hovering in mid-air, my silent flickering grandfather, and my favorite Gauguin, *D'où Venons Nous / Que Sommes Nous / Où Allons Nous*. Hadil had once complained it gave him nightmares, but I found it both soothing and ironically appropriate.

I had pulled rank and kept it at full size, four meters wide in our shared virtual space. Hadil always sat facing away from it.

As the relay station, the only link between Earth and her first colony ship, we could read the Updates from the *Cây Cúc* but they weren't meant for us. Once we transmitted it back to Earth, it would be unpacked and pored over by analysts at Da Nang. This Update would have details about the mystery transmission, phrased carefully so that Da Nang wouldn't think that the crew of the *Cây Cúc* was having a collective psychotic break. But there wouldn't be much in the way of analysis from the *Cây Cúc*, just raw data. The time dilation meant they had no time to sit on information.

And neither did I. Hadil could satisfy his curiosity, but I had laws to break and no time for hypothetical aliens.

*It couldn't possibly be real aliens. They've probably discovered a new kind of pulsar.*

"You want coffee?" Hadil said.

"No, thanks."

The slightly acrid smell of instant coffee filled the room. You couldn't virtualize a kettle, Hadil always said. "Do we have any fresh fruit left?" I asked, not turning around.

The fridge door opened and closed behind me. "Nope. Three days to the next supply drop."

When he first got here, Hadil had been a little shocked to discover what I was doing. Makemake Station was a two-person miniature civilization at the outer edge of the solar system. There could be no secrets here, so I had just told him: I was dipping into that precious bandwidth to talk to my grandfather on the *Cây Cúc*. A strange crime, I'd admitted, but a crime nevertheless. He could have reported me, had me shipped off back home, banned from space.

But Da Nang was very political, even so many years after the troubles. He would be tainted by association, I had told him. I didn't say that I would make sure of it. He wasn't stupid. After a few months, he had relaxed. After his first year, we had become friends.

Given enough time, all problems are solvable.

"Oh, crap. Look at this," Hadil said. He pushed an array of screens across the room in my direction, displacing my own virtual workspace. Process listings and system status monitors, bars in the green flickering up to angry reds.

I rubbed my hands over my close-shaven scalp. "What did you do now?"

"There was an executable binary in the Update," Hadil moaned. "It was part of the signal they said they picked up."

"You opened an attachment...from space?"

"No! I swear," Hadil said. He sounded guilty. "Only in a sandbox. I was curious. I'm rebooting."

I waved at the illegal ghost of my grandfather to continue. Color bled back into the imago's skin and light into his eyes.

*Dear Dikeledi*, Rais said. *Granddaughter.* He kept looking down at the photo in his hands. I'd walked over and looked at it once, but it cycled through so many pictures of my grandmother and Mom as a baby that it came across blurry and indistinct in the imago. *Please let me know about the petition. Has Da Nang given an answer?* His voice was warm, a little too loud. Little puffs of air from the tiny speakers in my glasses, as if my too-young grandfather had his lips pressed to the soft skin behind my ear.

If things had been different, I would have been one of the twenty thousand colonists. No, that wasn't right—I wouldn't even be born yet. If Rais had been allowed to take his wife, Abena, and their infant daughter along with him, my grandmother would be a young woman, my mother still a baby. I wouldn't be born for another four hundred years.

But he hadn't been allowed to take them with him. Something happened, eighty years ago, while the family was preparing for departure. My grandmother wouldn't speak of it except elliptically, to say that Rais made an enemy of someone powerful, someone in the junta, someone with control over the colonization project's approvals board. I didn't know exactly what it was that Rais had done to deserve this—Grandma Abena wouldn't speak of it, and Mom didn't know. It had been serious enough that after Rais left, Grandma Abena had changed her name and gone into hiding for a while. But by the time Mom was grown up, the urgency and the terror had faded. By the time I was born, it was only history.

I could even appreciate the clever cruelty of it: to give him the choice of being part of the colony, but only if he went alone.

*A forced decision, made in haste.* I distrusted haste. Decisions needed planning, strategy, not a wild leap into a dilemma constructed by somebody else. And it was still so recent for him, just a year and a half at relativistic speeds. A year and a half of recent memories and regrets, against eighty years of half-forgotten family history for me.

There had been no contact for all of that time, until he got that first message from me. An older woman who called him "grandfather" and told him that his wife and daughter had grown old and died, that I was his only family.

*I look forward very much to your next message*, Rais said. *Your last before you leave Makemake. Perhaps the petition will move faster when you are back in Da Nang.*

Rais kept pausing, as if expecting an answer. He wasn't used to one-way messages yet, having only been doing them for a few weeks. His messages were full of awkward pauses and non sequiturs. Or perhaps the error correction at this range was poorer than I'd accounted for and parts were being lost. There was no way to tell.

Family, under time dilation: he'd append a personal message to the *Cây Cúc*'s daily update; I'd get it every two months. I'd add a small personal message to the annual update from Makemake; he'd get one of those every week.

When it ended, he would have spent a month talking to me. I would have spent five years, the full term of my contract on Makemake Station. It was almost done.

I nudged Hadil. "Your spikes are on the host network now." I'd just noticed the angry red spikes indicating increased activity on Makemake Station's computers both physical and virtual.

"Everything's showing spikes," Hadil said. "Except ops and life support."

"Those are physically separate networks," I said, absently. The CPU temperature graph was climbing steadily. I'd missed something Rais said. I'd have to rewind him later.

"Will you please switch off your Grandpa and check the logs?" I could hear the glare in Hadil's voice. He was right, but I was reluctant to stop listening.

I'd been ten years younger than Rais was now, when the plan occurred to me. I was still at Nha Trang University, working through the qualifying courses to apply for extraplanetary duty. Plan—more of an intention, then, an understanding that I *wanted* to do this, that maybe I could, that maybe I should. I'd grown up hearing about Rais from Grandma and dreaming of space, which may have had something to do with my choice of career. But that was the year I put the plan together. The time dilation, Makemake Station, my career, the time and training I'd need to get there. I could talk to Rais himself; I could close the loop, answer the nagging little questions.

Now at forty-two I was as old as Mom when she had me. Ten years older than Rais, who had aged less than a year in my two decades of putting all the pieces together. I'd thought I knew him from Grandma Abena's stories, from the things Mom didn't say. Rais had grown bigger in the tellings, his absence having density and mass.

In person, he was too small, too young.

My grandfather's ghost was flickering again, almost strobing.

Hadil and I both looked at it.

"Did your Grandpa break the imago?" Hadil said.

"Shut up," I said. "I'm pretty sure this is all your fault." I grinned at him to take the sting out of it a little, while swiping rapidly through the last hour of logs. Makemake generated a lot of logs even when not doing anything in particular. Anything of note should have been flagged. There was nothing.

*I really miss Abena*, Rais said. He said this every time. He had never known her as a grandmother, with the wrinkles and the white hair that I kept expecting him to have. He wouldn't talk about Mom at all.

I'd told him in my second message that Mom had lived into her eighties and taught art history. She specialized in Lý dynasty ceramics. But he didn't acknowledge what I said—or he did and it was lost in the sea, neutrinos that didn't ping. To him she was still a baby, or should have been.

When I made my plans I had intended to ask him questions. *Why leave? Why not stay? Did they force you? Did you choose?*

But well-made plans adapt to changing circumstances. I realized when I first saw his imago that closing the loop wasn't about getting answers to those questions. It was about resetting our time-twisted family's history back into a single story. It was the open-endedness that nagged at me, the sense that Rais had vanished into some other world—the future, perhaps, or the past—which was forever cut off.

*I hope you plan to have kids*, Rais whispered.

Rais believed that the petition would allow him to talk to any descendants I left behind, after I died. He didn't put it like that, but we were all mayflies to him now. Four centuries would elapse on Earth by the time he set foot on his colony world in a few years. At least a dozen generations. Would my descendants even want to talk to him? I didn't know, but it felt distant and irrelevant to me.

I didn't know if I wanted children. I'd had my eggs stored before I left Earth, left myself options. But I didn't want to pass Rais down like a demented heirloom. I'd made up the story about the petition to get him to stop talking like I was a candle about to be blown out, and now he was obsessed with it.

There was no petition, of course. I wasn't stupid. That would just attract the wrong sort of attention in Da Nang. People would figure out what I'd been doing here. At the very least, I'd never work in space again.

"Hey, Dike," Hadil said. "Is *everything* flickering for you?" He had taken his glasses off and was rubbing his eyes. "It's giving me a migraine."

"Mine seems fine, except for Grandpa," I said, looking around. "Here, use these. I need a break anyway." I walked over to him and handed him my glasses.

With my eyes bared, the room was empty and silent. The walls were a neutral grey, designed to be unseen to operators who would cover them with virtual displays. I looked for the spot where the imago had stood, but of course there was nothing there.

I stretched, relaxing my eyes, rolling my neck. On Earth, at least there was a world for the glasses to augment. The sky might be covered in advertising, but you could take the glasses off to see it be blue. Here, it felt like being in an abandoned house. Everything gone but for these ratty old chairs, a couple of desks, the kettle and the fridge in the corner. No color to any of it. I already missed the bright yellows and haunted blues of the Gauguin.

Hadil was waving his arms in the air as if conducting an invisible orchestra.

When they built this habitat and set it spinning eighty years ago, they had ensured that operators would experience standard Earth gravity, for health and sanity. So just sitting, standing, drinking water from a cup, were all reminders that we lived in a tin can on a string.

The status glyph in one corner of the workroom—invisible to me now without my glasses, but after five years as familiar as the furniture—only drove that home. Makemake Station, rendered as a football-sized globe. The muon storage rings were just faint lines describing great circles on the sphere's surface; the fusion reactor a tiny, indistinct blob; the magnetic horns of our transmitter, too small to be seen and represented only by an icon. The habitat we lived in was just a dot on a near-invisible tether, sweeping around that giant sphere like the hand of a clock, doing a circuit every half hour.

Almost all of Makemake Station by volume was accounted for by the millions of cubic kilometers of heavy water inside the sphere. Neutrinos were ghost particles, easy to lose if you didn't have a whole sea to listen with. Hadil claimed he could hear it sloshing, for all that it was kilometers away and separated from us by vacuum; I dreamed about it sometimes, swimming in a pitch darkness broken only by tiny flashes like fireflies.

"Dike," Hadil said.

"Yes?"

He looked at me with both eyebrows raised. Sweat was beading on his temples. "I think I've figured it out."

"Really?" I walked over to him and tried to grab the glasses off his face. "Show me!"

"Wait, wait, wait," Hadil said, fending me off. "Or try mine, maybe they'll work for you." His old pair was still sitting on the shelf, next to his gently steaming coffee.

"No thanks, I'd rather not borrow your headache," I said. "Just tell me."

"This signal the *Cây Cúc* picked up," Hadil said, speaking so fast he was almost breathless. "It's like a virus but more so. Like artificial life. It can rewrite itself to adapt to new architectures."

"It evolves?" I leaned against the back of his chair.

"I suppose," Hadil said. He wiped the sweat from his forehead. "Our hardware's a lot faster than what they've got on the *Cây Cúc*. So it's cycling faster. We've got an infection."

"Start shutting everything down," I said. My head felt a little light. "Shut down everything that's already infected or connected to anything that's infected. We'll restore from a clean backup." At least life support wasn't threatened.

Hadil pulled the glasses off abruptly and threw them down. I jumped aside as broken glass and tiny electronics littered the room.

"Hadil, what's wrong?"

"Flicker," Hadil said, thickly. His scalp was shiny through his close-cropped hair. "I can't feel my legs." His voice sounded both slurred and very small, as if not quite certain what he was saying.

"You can't—" I grabbed him by the shoulders, too hard. "Okay, okay. Let me get you to your bunk." I reached for the other pair of glasses to put them on, run a medical diagnostic, but Hadil stopped me, clutching at my wrist.

"Don't," he said. He was trembling.

I tucked them into the collar of my shirt instead. "Okay. Let's get you lying down and then you can talk me through why not."

Helping him into his bunk was difficult. His legs dangled, dead weight. He drank the water I gave him, though I had to help him sit up. Lying down again, he seemed to recover a little. He seemed even younger than he was.

"Your Grandpa's talking again," he said.

I fished the glasses from my collar, but Hadil stopped me again.

"I'll have to eventually," I said, as gently as I could. Without the glasses, I had no way to interact with Makemake Station. No computation, no communications, no medical telemetry, no helpful wiki. "Is it the flicker?"

He stared at me, unblinking, sweating freely. "My head hurts."

Strobe lights at some frequencies could induce seizures—or I thought so, at least, without the wiki I couldn't be sure. I suggested this theory to Hadil but he shook his head, and then winced.

"I feel drunk," he said. He was speaking with exaggerated care now, slow and deliberate. "Your Grandpa's still talking," he said, then pointed at his head. No glasses, no little speakers tucked behind the ear.

"What's he saying?" Stupid question. Was I feeding a delusion? I was really starting to miss the wiki.

"Gibberish," Hadil said. He closed his eyes.

"Just get some rest," I babbled. My basic medical training

hadn't covered anything like this. It didn't need to: Earth could provide emergency support within a day. "I'll call Da Nang, we'll get help."

"They figured it out," Hadil muttered too quickly as if he was trying to get the words out. "Figured us out."

"Who?"

"The aliens, Dike," Hadil said. His eyes were still closed, as if unwilling to face his own words.

"The aliens who sent the signal?"

"They *are* the signal." Hadil said. "The human brain is a computational substrate. They've adapted to our architecture."

"That's ridiculous," I said, automatically, then winced. "How would they even—"

"Listen," Hadil said. He opened his eyes. His pupils were very wide, frightened. I realized I was holding his hand. "They hacked me. I can feel it. It's jumbling up my—"

He paused for a moment, as if expecting me to interrupt again, but I didn't. When I touched his temple he didn't react. The vein was pulsing violently.

"Don't look into the glasses," Hadil said, finally. "They must hack the brain through the eye. The visual cortex. It's transmitting some sort of compressed signal, that's got to be why the displays are flickering."

"Without the glasses, I can't call for medical assistance," I said. I tried to put motherly reassurance in my voice, tried to remember what Mom had sounded like when I was young and broke my arm falling out of a tree. *Make a plan.* "I need to be able to run the diagnostics on you, I need to update Da Nang that something weird is going on—at least that we may have been infected with a virus from the *Cây Cúc*—"

"It's not a virus," Hadil said. He sounded very tired. "Not infection. Invasion." I squeezed his hand and listened to him breathe, but he didn't say anything more.

When he died it was sudden. He wheezed twice, horribly, and then he was gone. I closed his eyes, my hands trembling and cold.

My head was too full of ghosts.

When I was an undergrad at Nha Trang, before I came up with the plan, I'd drive down to Ba Ho once every few weeks.

Early in the morning before the tourists came, I'd climb the rocks beside the waterfall and then leap off with my eyes closed, nothing but the wind in my face and the hammering of my heart. Blind, terrified, exhilarated. I felt like that now.

*Don't put on the glasses*, Hadil said.

I didn't want to look at his body. I went back to the workroom and sat in his chair instead of mine. Glass crunched under my shoes.

The other pair of glasses still sat on the shelf. If I put them on, I would see all the screens and displays that filled this empty room. The ghost of my grandfather, standing in the corner, perhaps still talking about the wife and child he left behind.

The telemetry would tell me that one of Makemake's operators was dead. There would be data on his death. I could find out what had really happened. Explain his hallucinations, if that's what they were. A stroke? A seizure?

There would be a clock to tell me how much time was left until I could send a message back to Da Nang Mission Control. It would take five hours for my message to reach them, and Earth would spin Da Nang into line of sight within—how long? An hour? Two? The Update from the *Cây Cúc* would be already queued for automatic forwarding. I could hold that back and send a call for help instead.

Unless Hadil was right, and then if I put the glasses on, I would die like he did.

Was Rais still undead and unaging? Were they all dead on the *Cây Cúc*? If the aliens could infect the human brain—many of the colonists could have been wearing a slightly older version of the augmented reality glasses. If the vulnerability was in the visual cortex then any kind of display might do. Any screen, physical or virtual. A book, a phone, a photo. Like the one that Rais always had in his hand.

But Rais was still alive when he sent the message, and many people would have been exposed by then, but there was no indication anyone had died. Maybe their hardware was just too slow. Despite us sending them tech schematics every year and them using the ship's fabricators, they couldn't keep up with time-dilated technological change. A lot of the hardware on the ship was eighty years out of date.

*Your Grandma hated him for leaving*, Mom said. *But we don't need fathers, you and me.*

Rais would send another message tomorrow, but that wouldn't arrive at Makemake Station for a couple of months.

*I hope you have kids someday*, Rais said.

"Yes, yes," I said. My own voice was shockingly loud in the silence.

Hadil said it wasn't a virus. More than a virus. Something smart, something that could explore and experiment. Find new territories, expand into them, adjust the terrain to their liking.

Informational life. Ghosts. Like infectious ideas that echoed in our heads until we could not think of anything else, until we forgot how to move, how to beat our hearts, how to breathe. Did they know they were killing us? Did they even know we existed? That there was a whole plane of physical reality that lay beneath theirs?

*Rais could have stayed behind*, said Grandma Abena. *He could have turned down the adventure. He was selfish.*

*They must have made him go*, said Mom. *Maybe they threatened to kill us if he stayed.*

"You're both dead, give it a rest," I said. "He was barely a grown man. He ran, that was all." Just leaped into the unknown, eyes closed and heart hammering.

Was that what it was like to be a ghost? Jumping off the ledge, not knowing if it was water or rock at the bottom, terrified and laughing? Were they conscious? They could only be conscious when they had something to haunt. Crossing light-years as signals, riding pulsars across the galaxy—

There couldn't be more than an hour left before Makemake Station automatically forwarded the last Update to Earth. I needed to switch that off.

*I don't want you to tell me about him*, Mom said. *I don't need to know.*

Mom had insisted on that, when I finally told her my plan for contacting Rais. I waited until the last moment to tell her, just before I left for Makemake Station. That was only a year before she died. "It was Grandma who would have really wanted to know," I said.

*You don't know what I wanted*, said Grandma Abena. *You were just a child.*

*When I got your first message*, Rais said, *I knew it couldn't be, but I thought you were Abena. You look just like her. Only older.*

Maybe the ghosts were mayflies. Maybe generations passed in the twenty minutes it took them to kill Hadil. His coffee wasn't even cold yet.

"I know you're in me already," I said. "My ghosts aren't usually this literal."

I put the glasses on. *Decisions made in haste. Look, grandfather, we have something in common after all.*

*We were going to the colony as a family*, Rais said. *That was the plan. I'm so sorry it didn't work out that way.*

I didn't notice the flickering anymore, or perhaps it had stopped. My head was pounding.

*He was afraid*, Grandma Abena said. *The stars are wonderful, but if you lower your eyes to ground level you'll see the men with guns in the night.*

The clock said I had ten minutes left to the automated Update to Earth. Less than I had thought.

*After I grew up*, Mom said, *I didn't waste any more time thinking about that man. I got on with my life, and so should you.*

I disabled the scheduled transmission, reoriented the magnetic horns away from Earth, told them to always point out into empty space. To stop tracking their targets, to forget. Such a simple thing, but my hands were slick with sweat and trembling when I was done.

Could the ghosts reset this? Could they manipulate the system, move the horns back? They could, but why would they understand the universe of ships and stations and worlds? Could they even find Earth again? I invoked superuser access, deleted the memory of Earth's path from Makemake Station. Would it be enough?

Maybe they wouldn't care. Maybe even if they managed to get the transmissions working again, they would be happy to spill out endlessly into the dark, neutrinos passing intangibly through rock and vacuum alike. Maybe that was how they got into the signal that the *Cây Cúc* picked up in the first place. Someone else, somewhere, impotent and desperate as me.

I couldn't feel my legs anymore.

My arms shook as I lowered myself to the floor. Something cut my hand painfully when I rested my weight on it. A shard from Hadil's broken glasses. I wanted to go sit with Hadil in his room, but I didn't think I could get that far. My chest felt hollow.

*One more thing*, Hadil reminded.

With Makemake silent, Da Nang would send a team within a day. As soon as they entered the station, their glasses or helmets would connect with Makemake's network and open themselves to invasion. They'd probably re-establish communications with Earth before they realized something was wrong.

I started an imago recording of myself, looping it to display everywhere in the station. I'd have to keep it short. It was getting hard to breathe, and the first responders would not have much time before they died.

*It's just like the waterfall, but with your pockets full of stones when you jump.*

"If you're seeing this, you're already dead," I began, and made myself a ghost.

# The Corpse

## Sese Yane

*Sese Yane was born in Kenya, has also lived in Uganda, and currently practices law in Nairobi. This short story was his first published work when it appeared in* Terra Incognita.

## I

THE CORONER, a pitiful recluse, once found himself burdened with a so-called occurrence at the morgue that he could not retell to his wife, but could not keep from her either, it seemed to him. He lay next to his wife that night, listening to his silence and how it was being shattered in a manner that amused him. His silence, it occurred to him, was persisting throughout his speech, and therefore, in a way, he was never robbed of it; that overwhelming will to silence, that is—that fundamental part of his being. Naturally, as long as he avoided talking about this so-called occurrence, he was not saying anything at all, and that's how we can only assume it seemed to him.

One warm Tuesday afternoon, a middle-aged man snaked his way onto the bus, where he sat by the window and waited. His window was slightly open and he thought he might close it later when the bus got into motion and the wind became too much for his face.

The middle-aged man, it's important to say, had sideburns that sloped sharply along his cheekbones to join his moustache. Naturally, this gave him a wolfish appearance.

A young man occupied the seat next to him, but the middle-aged man, a very private man, despite being the proud owner of very public sideburns, did not notice this young man. He only concerned himself with the general happenings inside and outside the bus, without focusing on anything in particular. Therefore it's true to say that he indeed noticed the general fact that a young man had taken up the seat next to him but beyond that general activity of this sitting down by a young man, he noticed nothing about the particulars of the person doing the sitting. This was because, naturally, he was not interested, for sitting down has always been a mundane activity to some people. This folding up of one's body, halving of oneself, so to say, has, for some curious reason, never interested many people in the world.

When the bus left the station, the middle-aged man kept himself occupied with the illusory movement of buildings and trees along the way. This illusory movement had always fascinated him since childhood. He'd kept his eyes so focused on things rushing by that by the time he got to the country, his head was pounding with a headache. But now, as a grownup, he knew how to regulate his observation. He did not, so he thought of his art, have to pour himself out of his eyes, because, so he said to himself, his eyes were narrow, far too small for the act of seeing, and to see, he thought, one had to be artful.

He would focus on something definite that was far away and watch how it slowly changed position almost anonymously, until it slid out of the window of perception again, almost anonymously. And so in this art of his, he followed a house perched like an old bird at the top of a distant hill, its red tiles fascinating him, its hedge of evenly spaced trees that had arrow-tipped crowns... He followed a purple-crowned tree by the ravine, and for the next few kilometres found himself counting every purple-crowned tree that appeared, without keeping up with the number—counting by beginning over and over, but counting every purple-crowned tree nonetheless.

On this day, he was greatly pleased, because he didn't have to close his window. Its angle of opening and his angle of sitting allowed just enough wind without irritating his ears or his face, and just enough wind to allow him to keep his coat on, for, out of lethargy, he didn't want to remove his heavy coat. Besides, it would have meant extra luggage for his hands, which were already busy drumming the briefcase on his lap.

The road that cut through the township was damaged from a poor drainage system that flooded the asphalt surface, and here the bus had to slow down. At this point, there were more passengers alighting than those who were boarding. The middle-aged man had about three kilometres to go, he thought. As the bus slowed down once again to negotiate a puddle that might or might not have been concealing a pothole, the middle-aged man saw the rotting remains of a dog on the shoulder of the road. The smell of death hit his nose from the open window before he immediately decided to hold his breath. It was quicker than closing the window.

But as the bus tore its way farther and farther away from the black dead dog, the middle-aged man could still see behind his eyelids the sardonic smile of the black dead dog, that disturbing smile we see on naked skulls and rotting carcasses. The middle-aged man continued holding his breath out of disgust. Minutes rushed past his open window and they dragged with them trees and houses and people, and still the middle-aged man held his breath, amazed that he could do this. His eyes actually lit up as eyes do when they're threatening to smile…way past a minute, past two minutes, past three minutes, passengers alighting, someone excusing themselves for stepping on another's shoes, a hearty laugh somewhere at the front, perhaps the driver's, or the conductor's, still holding his breath out of fascination of his ability to do so.

But past ten minutes, and fifteen, he was no longer amazed but afraid that he could do such a thing. He decided, against this childish merriment, to get his lungs back to their use. Something was terribly amiss. No matter how hard he tried, he couldn't suck in air from the outside world. His lungs impenetrable, his nose a pair of blocked tunnels, he seemed not to remember how to breathe in.

He dropped his briefcase to the floor.

*Why won't they fix this road anyway*, he thought.

The young man who had sat next to the middle-aged man had already alighted from the bus, the man now noticed.

*God! I have overshot my destination…*

When the bus conductor found the middle-aged man, sprawled out, half on the seat and half on the floor, it was the hideous sideburns that struck him first. He prodded the body with the tip of his boot, and once he was sure, took the seat directly on the other side of the aisle and stared at the corpse for a while before calling out to the driver.

## II

*Death by asphyxia*, the coroner wrote in his report then quickly moved the body to a small moveable freezer, covered it with rags and a broken squeegee, and pushed the small freezer into the store. For a moment, he could not decide what corridor to follow, and made his way for the toilet, but changed his mind halfway. He returned to the store and reset the squeegee, nervously patted the rag, then hurriedly walked all the way past the lockers until he came to the fire exit. He ran down the stairs all the way to a dead end in what looked like it used to be a vestibule but was littered with all manner of equipment.

The effect it had on him was sudden. Entrapment. He forgot he had come down on a stairwell. Lost in this sea of broken chairs, broken lamps, broken trolleys, and bed-stretchers, old buckets, old stained books, and strewn papers, as three fluorescent tubes widely spaced above him illuminated this dusty sea of broken things. Under a sustained hum, he remembered, almost with what can be said to be an exaggerated childlike triumph, where he had run up the stairwell again, until he came to the correct corridor and made for the glass doors, heaving past the human-traffic, trolleys, stretchers, breathing hard but breathless nonetheless.

"No one saw me," he said to himself, almost too loudly. *What a moustache! But of course no one will suspect me*, the coroner thought at the gardens. He didn't notice the bench until he had sat on it. *It is not unusual for the morgue to lose a body. They lose bodies all the time, all the time, certainly, and people pick up wrong bodies all the time. In any case, I won't be here. I should call in sick tomorrow just in case. A headache, yes a headache, I have a headache, after all. It won't be lying…*

He fumbled a cigarette from his breast pocket and stared at it thoughtfully. What he felt was fear, not that he was afraid of being found out. After all, he wouldn't be caned if he were to be found out. He was too old for the cane, it now occurred to him; he was afraid entirely for something else—the unnameable fear of being a source, or perhaps being at the source, of some vague disorder in the world.

The coroner lay next to his wife that night and thought of the moustachioed corpse, now lying in an old, unused water tank in his garden shed.

After several attempts at words, just as someone might wait impatiently for the mocking swash of a wave to lick their foot, he spoke, "This corpse, Honey, beautiful moustache, you see. That's the first thing that tells you that he's different, but that's a disguise too...I'm standing there, I'm thinking...I have done this over a hundred times, right, but for some reason, and I don't know how, I must say, one usually gets the feeling that something is about to happen before it happens...I may say I don't believe what I finally see, but at the same time it's as if I'm opening him up with the specific intention of seeing what I'm now seeing," the coroner said and went quiet for a while, for it now occurred to him that he could not retell his story with the accuracy of how it had unfolded itself to him; the suspense and alarm of it all was now, to his frustration, being lost in his narration.

"Anyway, I write *asphyxia* in my report," said the coroner, "because it's asphyxia, too... But I believe, strongly believe, the reverse is what happened. Not the reverse as we might know it but the reverse as we might speculate a new kind of reverse no one has ever experienced before. Well, until this man.

"The man had no lungs," said the coroner.

"Born without lungs, can you believe it? Ah, but that's a ridiculous story. It's unscientific." The coroner laughed a silent laughter of embarrassment.

The coroner had not intended to disclose the incident of the strange corpse to anyone, or at least not yet. As he lay next to his wife, he thought how curious it was that his intern, this day of all days, had not shown up to work. She had offered the most ridiculous of excuses for her absence. "It's as if the universe knew," said the coroner to himself. *I should not have known what to do in such event...*

### III

"Well, I guess, in a way, someone can," said the coroner to his wife, absentmindedly, pulling the bed sheet to his side. There's always an excuse, wouldn't you say, one way or the other. I think people are naturally lazy. A word here to replace an activity there;

you don't have to show up if you can explain your absence. The grand miracle of words, so to speak, but don't get me wrong. There's a good reason for laziness, certainly. There's always a good reason for everything, otherwise there would be nothing."

The coroner was trying to avoid thinking about the corpse; trying to conceal his enthusiasm from himself. He was half tempted to jump out of bed and run to the garden shed to be with his corpse, but was held back by the even greater beauty of pro-crastinating and having something interesting to look forward to in the morning.

But he also wanted to talk about the corpse.

He sighed against his wife's neck, ecstatic with this beautiful dilemma, and searched for her hand under the sheets until he found the small hand and clasped it tightly over her warm thigh. He closed his eyes and smiled to himself, snuggled closer to her so that he felt his skin being warmed up by her nightshirt as his body pressed hard against her behind. The coroner again sighed that sigh of defeat, and watched the back of his wife's head. She had been quiet all the while and was looking away from him.

The coroner had never talked so much to his wife, he now thought. If he had to keep talking, he would have to explain his years of silence, too—a silence that had always seemed to him to be executed by malicious will. Unless he was giving his report, and in a mathematical language, the coroner found it unbearable to talk to people. At home, he usually stayed in the library, dissolving himself in the dark timber shelving, and in the panelling, or turn-ing the pages of one of his numerous books…or looking outside the window, at the twittering long-tailed birds jumping from tree to tree in the garden, now at the changing blue of the sky, now at the different shades of green on the foliage—basically hiding from his wife but trying not to think of it as such…

When his daughter stood at the door, watching him, (if he called her, she would hide behind the door, but if he decided not to notice her, she would keep coming piecemeal until she reached his leg) he would sit her down by his side and passion-ately instruct her from one of his books, or from a train ticket for a journey he once took to Tbilisi from Batumi, or from a receipt for a latte in Turin, from anything, really. All this was to avoid or to atone for this avoidance, or even to punish himself for this avoidance, of talking to his wife, who might be in the kitchen or somewhere in the house.

You see, even after eight years of marriage, he still dreaded running into her in the corridors of their house. He got into bed with the airs of one too tired for a conversation; his consciousness of the exaggeration of conversation crippled his relationship with everyone. But this particular night, certainly because of the strange corpse, he had already said too much, and now he kept talking because he thought stopping abruptly would interfere with the equilibrium of a room he had already filled with his sound. In his estimation, he should perhaps keep talking until his words died naturally and proportionately to the falling volume of his sound.

"This intern," said the coroner, "apparently I'm too old-school. I know and yet…makes you think, though, so much has happened around you. Where were you, all this time…Christ! There's nothing left for me to do. I've done everything. I've got everything. I don't want anything. What am I going to do now? That's exactly what I was thinking, standing there…before her frog-like eyes, big, beautiful," said the coroner to annoy his wife.

"I've never been so scared in my life, I'll tell you that. Have you ever lost something that never existed? That's the greatest loss…and yet how careless of us? I mean the garret. I was thinking about the garret. It's been years…all these years, so many years…

"Why was I still holding onto all these inaccurate tales? I'm thinking, it all comes back to me, flood-like, but I can't discern a thing. Mr Monkey, that's all I have on my mind, this vague memory, a silly sock monkey. I didn't lose Mr Monkey. I threw him in the garret, and I lied because I love Father. Father thought I was afraid of him. I could see through him clear like glass. I am the one who made him," said the coroner…

"*Bring a cane!* he would pretend to shout to me after being given the report of one thing or the other I had done during the day, *a good cane!* But I was never afraid of him. I pitied him instead. Brought him the best cane. I was very confident that he wouldn't, but I wanted him to cane me, too, badly…but, by my foolishness, I had already manipulated him by bringing him the best cane. Naturally he couldn't cane me. The cane was too perfect," said the coroner, "simply too perfect… Had I brought him a bad cane, a poor cane, so to say, there's no doubt he should have gotten angry and used it. But the perfect cane incapacitated him, always…

"I used to wait for him at the gate every day as he came home from work. I don't know, perhaps a little afraid that he wouldn't come. And when I saw his figure in front of the sunset, like an apparition, as if he were walking from inside the sunset itself, I ran to my room and hid. In my childish soul I thought he was overburdened by his own presence. In a way, that's why I believed I had lost Mr Monkey, for Father's sake. I could never lie to him. I had to believe that I had lost the toy and not thrown it away, naturally for Father's sake. I never attempted to fool Mother, though, never pitied her that way. We were equals in pitying Father, I thought," said the coroner, "but I've always pitied her in her own way, and I've always pitied everyone else in their own way, too…

"But it was those frog-like eyes of hers that reminded me of the long-forgotten, inaccurate tale I had made up for myself to protect Father from a lie. She's *young*," said the coroner, hoping this would enrage his wife, excited by the thought of the corpse in his garden shed. "Timid, like a sweet little kitten, domineering when talking to those corpses. In fact, she's more eloquent when talking to them than when she's talking to the living. She's got a natural stammer, but very comprehensible when talking to a corpse, can you believe that? When I ask her a question, for instance, because she's *somehow* comfortable in my presence, because apparently I'm too 'old-school', as she puts it, she answers me by way of telling the corpse and so I have to listen to what she's telling the corpse because that's meant for me.

"But she can't do this when talking to the other staffers. For some reason, she chooses the option of stammering. I guess you can say I'm special in that regard," said the coroner hoping to irritate his wife… "And so, for a laugh, because, naturally, that's what she wants, you see, I will sometimes talk to her through all these things in the morgue. For instance I'll ask the fluorescent tube to tell her to hand me a scalpel, the window to tell her that I need some cotton wool, etc, etc, and how she laughs when I do that."

The coroner was overwhelmed with excitement just thinking of the strange corpse in his garden shed.

## IV

*Oh, how right I was to be brave enough to move the corpse from the hospital's storeroom this evening instead of waiting to come up with a better plan,* thought the coroner.

There was no better plan, and it now indeed surprised him that he had gone along with what now looked like the worst plan. He could obviously not have gone through with such a poor plan the following day, he thought as he started talking about the lung-less man to his wife, again—talking of the lung-less man as if he were not real but a story he was inventing for the sole purposes of annoying her. Indeed, he talked about the corpse with the intention of annoying his wife; he described the corpse in flowery language, because poetry can never be believed, and is proof of madness. Similarly, according to him, verbosity was proof of deceit, for he had already talked too much. To justify this unnatural occurrence, the coroner was trying to convince his wife, but also more himself, that he had lost his mind.

He squeezed his wife's small hand again, put his lips to her neck, and, with that little touch, his mind dissolved into vertigo. He thought he heard the distant howling of dogs, the whistling of trees. Oh how beautiful life is, especially whenever his wife wore a pinafore dress, how beads of rain trickled down the windowpane, how nothing seemed to exist when you pulled away from the eyepiece of the microscope... How small and ridiculous and yet amazing everything seemed to be, especially because it was small and ridiculous. His eyes misted. To disclose by concealing, or to conceal by disclosing. This sharing with his wife was a truth he could not tell anyone else, not even her, and it gave him a thrill this making of himself unbelievable...and he, for his own amusement, and also to his utter disbelief, which was also part of his own amusement, was at this time convinced that he was making up the story about the corpse.

At that very moment, after his unprecedented monologue, loneliness finally crept in to claim what had always belonged to it, just what the coroner, unbeknown to him, had been desperately waiting for. He turned onto his side and slept.

# Sarama

## Deepak Unnikrishnan

*Deepak Unnikrishnan is a writer from Abu Dhabi, who currently lives in Chicago. His fiction and essays have appeared in* Guernica, Himal, Drunken Boat, *and others. He is the recipient of the 2014 Gwendolyn Brooks Open Mic Award.*

IT'S QUITE SIMPLE really; my family owes its existence to the forest demon, Surpanakha.

My maternal great grandmother, Parvathy Amma, was born in a village near Talikulam, Kerala.

The word for great grandmother in Malayalam is Muthassi. She was the first woman to hold me, to bathe me, my first loved one to die. She decided on my name, Bhagyanathan. She would call me nothing else, she hated nicknames. "Bhagyanathan!" she would yell. When she called my name, she said it like one would address a king. When she said Bhagyanathan, you would almost expect to hear the sound of chariots, the neighing of horses, the sound of footmen. I was her king.

Muthassi was a renowned storyteller in my village and in her younger days used to be invited to participate in festivals all over Kerala. Her specialty was stories from The Ramayana.

Some people have a voice made for stories, their vocal chords fashioned by Brahma himself. Muthassi's voice was like that. Her pitch, unusual for a woman, very low, a rumble, like the purr of a cat. Age added to its mystique. Her voice grabbed you, didn't let you go; the stories poured into your veins and intoxicated your brain. You listened until she finished; you didn't have a choice.

But she was also a treasure trove of other tales, much darker ones, which she was always happy to share with me. Popping balls of rice into my mouth, she often warned me to be aware of the snakes in our garden: "They transform into human form at night, eager to snatch game they slink into the netherworld."

I was around four years old when she started telling me stories from The Ramayana. She recited the epic to me out of sequence, concentrating more on the characters than the story itself. "Everybody," she liked to say, "has a past that ought to be heard. The present is paralyzed without a past."

The scriptures I know come from her. I preferred listening to reading. I think she innately understood that.

The night she decided I needed to know the story I am about to share, four crows cawed outside our house at twilight for over an hour. I had just turned ten. It was monsoon season but the rains still hadn't come. I was listening to the radio when the power went out. As usual she called out to me. She needed someone to talk to in the dark. My parents were to be back the following morning. I had been left in charge, the man of the house.

I was still a small boy and struggling with the kerosene lamp, its heat kissing my thighs, when I walked into her room and asked if she needed anything.

"Close the door, my dear," she said slowly.

"Blow out your lamp."

I did.

The room smelled strongly of the after breath of smoke and kerosene.

"Give me your right arm," she said.

I did, and she began rubbing my fingers one by one.

When I was still a child, people noticed quickly that my palms and feet were frog-like, too big for the rest of my body. Some kids in the village hopped like frogs, pretended to be toads, or stuck their tongues out like lizards when they wanted to make it clear I couldn't play with them. It didn't bother me. I was built to be alone.

Muthassi tugged my fingers, at weird angles, bending them in degrees I didn't think possible. When she snapped my index finger off, breaking it like a twig, I stared. There was no pain. I was more alarmed than frightened, worried about Amma's reaction when she noticed. Muthassi smiled kindly.

"Don't worry, little one, I will put it back, I wanted to check, that's all," she said.

And before I knew it, she stuck my index finger back on. I stared at it, wiggled it a little bit to make sure it still did what it used to do.

"Don't be afraid now," is what she told me gently before she calmly unscrewed her head, twisting it off like a bottle cap and placing it on her lap.

"I would like to go outside, Bhagyanathan," she decided all of a sudden, "it's too hot here; let's go by the pond, it's cooler there, carry Muthassi out."

I held Muthassi's head carefully and walked out of the house toward the pond, a place I was forbidden to venture to by myself, especially at night.

I placed Muthashi's head on the flat stones where Amma did our washing, facing the black and slimy water, which would turn green again at dawn. In the darkness, the pond looked like cobra skin.

"Water is significant to us," she began, eyes drifting toward the pond. "One of our ancestors, The Male, crossed into Lanka over water."

"This creature, a monkey, we are almost certain," Muthassi said, "was a soldier in the Monkey King Sugriva's army, first working under the supervision of Nala and Neel, famed builders without whom the construction of The Floating Bridge would have been impossible. He, our ancestor, along with others, slaved night and day on this massive undertaking until his muscles hurt, until his body refused to cooperate."

At night, he tended to blisters swollen with pus. It was tough work.

A significant number of monkeys and bears from the kingdom of Kishkindha died building the bridge. Many collapsed out of exhaustion, some forgetting to eat or drink, perishing on the job. They were driven hard, not allowed to venture home, forced to sleep near the construction site.

Sugriva was a hard taskmaster. Yet in his eagerness to repay the debt he owed Rama, Sugriva often forgot his soldiers were mortal. Some of them didn't appreciate the treatment and began to bitch and gossip. The situation took a serious turn when rumors started circulating about Sugriva's chicanery in getting rid of Vali, his elder brother. Without Ram, Sugriva would still be on the run from Vali, the grapevine opined—an honorable warrior wouldn't have resorted to treachery in battle; only an honorable warrior deserved a seat on the throne, deserved to bed Queen Tara. The following day, the parties who started the rumor were executed.

I picture this creature often, The Male, marching with other beasts, forced to deal with the drudgeries of war, crossing into an alien land to do battle for the prince of Ayodhya, a prince he possibly did not speak to, and I begin to wonder whether the air started to smell of war as soon as he walked over the bridge with other comrades in arms, whether giant vultures circled in the foreground, waiting to feast, and whether my ancestor felt fear.

But the story of my family's lineage does not begin with Rama looking out to sea, imagining the tip of the land that held his young bride captive, as monkeys and bears busied themselves hauling stones to get the bridge built quickly. It doesn't even begin when The Male, a biped like I, marched onwards to Lanka. Our history begins with the humiliation of Surpanakha.

The women in our family, Muthassi shared, could be traced back to a long line of demons. These were women granted numerous boons by the lords of the netherworld and the gods in heaven, rakshashis with power, who were feared, who made mortals realize they were mortal, women who were shape shifters, unafraid of the sound of forests and of being alone with spirits who refused to be born again after their bodies were fire-lit on pyres.

In my great grandmother's words, "The Female of our race was one-legged, two-legged, three-legged, many-headed, short, fat, squat, tall, alive, hideous, glorious—so alive! We were so swollen with life, with glut, that we frightened those who barely lived."

"The word demon is tainted," Muthassi lamented, "riddled with hyperbole, caked in fear. Demon only implies evil beings from the netherworld. Rakshashis may only be beasts. It is a simplification, alluding that those who navigate the netherworld can only possess organs dark as soot. The truth, my child, is our ancestors were women who did what they wanted, for whom dharma meant accepting their urges, following them to their very ends, not belittling or suppressing them. Our women tested the gods, made them wish they were half-god, half-demon, down to our level, one foot knee-deep in vice and pleasure, the other foot still tentatively holding on to Mount Meru."

Muthassi's head pivoted to face me, moving like a little clay bowl on the flat stones where Amma smashed wet clothes. Her hair, a mop of dirty white curls the color of gnawed bone, danced in the breeze. She stared at me for a long time, as Amma's great grandmother may have done when she told this very tale.

"Bhagyanathan," she finally said, "our women folk made mistakes. But sometimes we wanted to make them. We learned by being!"

She calmed down after that outburst, her head rocking a little from side to side from all the fuss.

It was then she spoke her name. When Muthassi said "The womb of Sarama, The Old One, is where we believe our line begins," it was the first time I had heard of the name. She had never mentioned her before.

Among the rakshashis entrusted to guard Sita at the palace groves, Sarama was as old as the trees themselves, Muthassi said. She was from a time when our women folk were constantly abused by the mortals, hunted like vermin, pinned to trees, and sacrificed at will and without warning. It was why they turned to the gods, performing penance, sacrificing. The gods, pleased, granted them many boons. But over time, even the gods grew envious of their power, of their grasp on the underworld, and started scheming and turning against them, wary of the consequences if the rakshashas decided to invade Mt. Meru.

"This war between the netherworld and the heavens lasted eons," Muthassi said. "It has not ended."

Sarama, our ancestor, was old enough to remember Tataka, Surpanakha's grandmother. She remembered Tataka's beauty. And she remembered the monster she mutated into, taller than a mountain, tusks sprouting out her nose like daggers, wearing the skulls of the ones she killed, a body of pure hate.

"Agastya turned her into the beast she became," Muthassi said, "he killed her husband; in turn, she tried to kill Agastya. Only the forests could home that rage. It was her turf."

In Surpanakha, Tataka's beloved granddaughter, whom Sarama had seen since she was a baby, could clearly see glimpses of her grandmother. A beautiful child, like Tataka, Surpanakha's spirit belonged in the forest, where she was most free, becoming one with the land, living, sleeping, hunting, mating. It was her home as much as it had been her grandmother's.

Many years later, after the war, The Old One still shuddered when she recalled the state of Surpanakha's mutilation. What Lakshmana's blade had done! Oh, what it had done!

"There are texts that write lies about her form," Muthassi seethed. "It is as though the scribes are afraid to be truthful. They write her skin is polluted, calling it foul, bloating her physique, making her out to be a monster so vile she putrefied anything she touched. They lie!"

"She was beautiful," Muthassi said, "a beauty that could drive men and women mad."

"She knew fully well every inch of her body; her form evoked desire, possibly frightening the young god-king and his brother equally. Frightening scribes to have their quills lie so boldly."

"Surpanakha was not Sita," Muthassi admitted, "but Sita could never have been Surpanakha."

"They write that she was brutal," Muthassi said, giving me a wry smile. "Her brutality lay only in the manner she acknowledged and chased her desire."

"She refused to suppress her wants," Muthassi concluded.

She paid for such audacity, marching through Ravana's palace doors with sliced breasts, no ears, and a disfigured nose. Ravana's guards, men used to the bedlam of war, stood by, stunned into silence, letting her pass. She would not crouch, she did not whimper, she was defiant, walking bare-bosomed into Ravana's court; she met everyone's eye. When she spoke, the courtiers and the ministers turned their faces away, unable to look. She was visibly in pain. But they heard her; they heard the screams, of rage, of hurt, of vengeance. And when the king himself jumped from his throne to comfort his mutilated sister, the siblings, reunited for the first time since the troubling circumstances of her husband Dushtabuddhi's death, embraced in anguish. And wept.

The ten-headed Ravana, weeping tears of fury, caressed his sister's hair, held her body like she was little again, running after her older brothers in the forests, watched by Tataka who doted on her grandchildren. He did this openly, in front of his courtiers and guards. But she would have none of it, composing herself quickly.

Pity wasn't what Surpanakha had come for. She refused to let Ravana drape her body with cloth. The pain would pass; her wounds would remain bare and unclothed until she had her revenge.

Our ancestor Sarama awoke from her slumber to the sound of a ten-headed scream that filled the air with dread, a scream Muthassi mimicked, her mouth opening as wide as the hole that swallowed Sita, so wide that her head became all mouth. It was a terrible scream.

In the village, those who heard that guttural cry that night woke and began to pray; animals whimpered; woodland spirits stopped moving. The gloom was exactly as it had been when the leaves of Lanka turned grey, birds falling from the sky refusing to fly, and the trees beginning to bleed.

Ravana had made up his mind, Muthassi said; he would avenge Surpanakha's humiliation. His prize would be Sita. There would be war. There would be war. There would be war.

Sarama found Sita a silly creature to fight a war over. She was beautiful certainly, but Sarama had seen different kinds of beauty in her time, beauty that possessed you, turned you inside-out, forced you to be impatient. Sita's beauty almost made her untouchable, too pure, too good, too right. Sarama spurned such beauty, it made her uneasy. Maybe that is why Ravana desired Sita, she felt. He wanted to pollute her, to consume her, to make her more real.

Still, as The Old One, our ancestor, helped keep watch over the young princess of Ayodhya, the would-be girl-queen began to intrigue her.

She paid close attention as Sita fought Ravana practically every day, refusing to be intimidated by his advances. Even when the rakshashis tried to scare her into relenting, shaking the earth, turning the sky foul and ominous, threatening to eat her alive, theatrics that made most mortals quiver and piss, she held firm. Sarama smelled fear in the young Sita, but she also admired her audacity, her will. Sarama could tell Sita would never submit to Ravana's lust. If he tried to touch her, Sarama knew, Sita, the daughter of Janaka, would rage against her tormentor, scratch him, maim him, pull out tufts of hair from any of his ten heads, until her body no longer pulsed. Sarama respected that rage, a rage she didn't believe Sita, a would-be girl queen, possessed at first, the sort of rage that only became evident when Rama refused to take her back when the war had ended. Because she respected such rage, when Ravana threw Rama's decapitated head near Sita's feet, Sarama told the would-be girl that it was an illusion, that Rama was still safe, and that his forces were crossing into Lanka.

Muthassi pivoted her head toward the pond again, staring at the water, taking some time before moving on to the next phase in the tale. It was important to her that everything be clear.

The evening before the great battle between the two armies, one bestial, the other demonic, Sarama found Surpanakha sitting by the gardens where Ravana held Sita captive. Surpanakha avoided the forlorn-looking Sita, preferring to sit by herself. They would meet later, after the war, after Rama's death. For now, they both stared silently into the open, deep in thought.

The other rakshashis had been afraid to approach Surpanakha. They left her alone, to stew in her rage. But Sarama was braver. She was also concerned, inching her way to the mutilated lady, where she watched a grieving Surpanakha gently touching what was left of her nose, her ears, her butchered breast.

Surpanakha felt the rawness of the wounds, imagining the sight she had become. She wouldn't look into a mirror just yet. She couldn't. She had almost caught a glimpse of her new state when she drank water from a stream. She would wait until the war was over, the mortals who did this to her slain. Then she would take the corpse of Rama, fling it at his young widow and dance pitilessly and mercilessly over the dead man, like Kali. She would delight in watching Sita as she did this. Then, in quiet, she would sneak Rama's remains away, cremating his body, extinguishing it in fire, as Yama, The Lord of Death, would wait patiently on his buffalo, his giant club resting on the ungulate's belly.

Sita's plight would be different. Surpanakha would scheme to keep the princess alive for thousands of years, refusing to let her die, breaking her heart as many times as it could be broken.

Lakhsmana's bones and entrails, she would wear, his flesh fed as carrion.

When Sarama The Old One, our ancestor, finally reached Surpanakha, she was holding her bloodied breasts, trembling. There were tears. Sarama also realized flies had laid eggs in her open wounds, and the larvae would soon hatch. Samara reached out to touch her. Gently. Surpanakha seized the gnarled hand, ready to tear it off the person who dared disturb her. When she saw who it was, she calmed down a little, but still spitting in Sarama's face, screamed "Not pity, old hag, not pity!"

Sarama, understanding, knelt low, pressed her palms to Surpanakha's feet and whispered, "It isn't pity, child, your wounds must be tended to. Let me. Let the old one through. I knew Tataka, I knew Tataka."

At the mention of her grandmother's name, Surpanakha relented, allowing herself to be touched and held. And there they sat, the two of them, Sarama tenderly washing Surpanakha's wounds and picking out larvae, as Surpanakha, tired and overwhelmed, fell asleep. The following morning, when the two armies rode out to battle, the beginning of war, Sarama searched for Surpanakha. She had slipped away. The two would never meet again.

When Ravana was finally slain, the war over, our ancestor Sarama stepped out of the palace grounds and walked toward the battlefield, followed by concerned wives and children, family of the missing soldiers in Ravana's army.

The battlefield reeked of the dead, stinking of dried blood, piss, shit, men, demons, monkeys, bears, pachyderms, horses, and giant birds. The wounded lay everywhere, waiting to die or be rescued—rakshashas called out for help, dying monkeys and bears pleaded for water, while other beasts of war, elephants with no trunks and crushed legs, the horses with broken backs, the raptors with torn beaks and burnt wings, squirmed, struggling to breathe. And amidst the wreckage were anxious wives and children, picking through the rubble, calling out and hunting for loved ones, frantic to find bodies to burn or salvage, as the four-eyed dogs of Yama prowled the dead zone with ease.

Into this mayhem walked victorious Rama, followed by his brother Lakshmana, the new king of Lanka, Vibhishana, the Monkey King Sugriva, and Hanuman, whose tail lit Lanka for days.

Grateful for their support and relieved with victory, a visibly tired Rama, close to tears, invited the bears and giant vultures who participated in battle to feast on the carrion, their deserved spoils of war.

"As the soldiers celebrated," said Muthassi, "Rama and the others started making their way to the palace gates. For Sita."

"But all is never as it seems," warned Muthassi. "Behind the scenes lived the uglier underbelly of war, unscrupulous soldiers from Rama's army who scoured the conquered land like parasites, interested in loot and women, the dirtier spoils of war."

But virtuous warriors also fought on Rama's side. Many, although injured themselves, offered to help set pyres for the dead, finding sages and priests to perform the last rites quickly. Some opted to sit with the children of dead rakshashas, while their mothers searched for their fathers. Others, they didn't care, they pillaged, raped.

Even Sarama became prey to such wanton feasting, grabbed by a soldier from Sugriva's camp, bent with rage, The Male, our ancestor, ferociously and brutally violating her on the very battlefield where moments ago, Ravana's ten heads scanned for Rama, his heart still healthy with life and blood.

Sarama watched the creature forcing himself on her, dirtied from war, raging because of it. She paid attention to his hands, callused from bridge building, tired of killing, tired from killing. She felt pity. And then she remembered the war, of Surpanakha's mutilation, of Ravana's insistence on punishing the brothers by punishing the young princess instead, of how after the loss of so much life, one hoped the war was won by a just lord, his virtuous army. And right there, as the creature shuddered inside her, spilling his seed into her old womb, she howled with rage, screaming with such force that she tore a hole in the monkey's chest, exposing his heart. Sarama reached in, and held his beating red organ in the palm of her hand as it continued to pump blood. The monkey, The Male, our ancestor, alarmed, looked at Sarama, his body still trembling.

Looking him in the eye, Sarama slowly crushed his heart.

In the celebratory din, no one noticed. Nearby, giant vultures tore through an elephant as it waited to die.

She picked herself up quickly, forgetting in her haste to wipe the mud, spittle, and blood off her body. She would deal with the shock later. For now, she headed for the palace gates. She needed to be there. In the garden. When Rama received Sita. She needed to see the end to all this madness.

Sarama felt a sense of dread when Rama didn't meet Sita immediately. Even Vibhishana seemed embarrassed when he greeted the lady on Rama's behalf, requesting her to bathe and be bedecked in her finery. Her lord would see her then.

And when they walked her out, and Rama stood in front of his wife like a guest, a stranger, Sarama sighed. Surpanakha's revenge was complete. Rama had shunned Sita publicly. Neither would fully recover from the hurt. Ayodhya would never let them forget it.

Sarama understood quite well why Rama did what he did. As she waited for Sita to appear in public, even she heard and recoiled from the spite with which soldiers from Rama's own army, men, monkeys, bears, and other half-beasts he had commanded only a few hours ago, discussed the young princess' lost virtue. When a group of them were shushed, the gossiping would stop, only for the cackling to resume soon after. In Ayodhya, too, it would be the same. Yet when Sita stepped into the lit pyre, not a sound was made. You could only hear burning. The crackle of embers. The burning of virtue and the fury it brings.

And as Sarama stared at Sita, she spied tears of rage through the flames, fire which refused to touch the sullied princess of Ayodhya, as though afraid. She, Sita, burnt harder than fire, swallowing fire itself, her rage burning through fire, scorching even Agni, who pleaded with Rama to accept his virtuous queen, whose purity, if questioned further, would burn every living thing into oblivion.

When Rama was appeased, and the test, the public trial, over, the fire extinguished, the young couple faced each other once more, as husband and wife, Crown Prince and Princess of Ayodhya. Sarama did not wait to see Rama walk toward his absolved wife.

Sarama, our ancestor, didn't wait at all. She started to walk. Even as shouts of Long Live! burst across Lanka, as garlands rained down from the gods.

She walked, disgusted, walking away from Lanka, refusing to

stop. She could have used her powers to transport herself elsewhere. She could still fly. But she decided against it. She wanted to walk, inhaling the mayhem, recalling the egos that helped mutilate two women and burn Lanka.

She stopped only when she started approaching the bridge the creature who raped her helped build, The Male, our ancestor, the father of the child she would conceive. She stared long and hard at the beach.

The water was calm but red, the shore quiet, yet stinking of decomposing flesh. Seagulls circled the shoreline, rats started to surface. Sarama stepped forward, didn't look back. Not even once. The war was over, but she believed little that was worthwhile had been salvaged. She began to walk across the bridge. The salty wind would ravage her face but she didn't care. The sound of the sea kept her company until she reached the end.

"And when she reached the other side," Muthassi ended, "Sarama, our ancestor, her belly was swollen."

# A Cup of Salt Tears

## Isabel Yap

*Isabel Yap was born and raised in Manila, and has since lived in California and London. Her stories have been published in* The Year's Best Weird Fiction Volume 2, Tor.com, Interfictions Online, Shimmer, *and elsewhere.*

S OMEONE ONCE TOLD Makino that women in grief are more beautiful. *So I must be the most beautiful woman in the world right now*, she thinks, as she shucks off her boots and leaves them by the door. The warm air of the onsen's changing room makes her skin tingle. She slips off her stockings, skirt, and blouse; folds her underwear and tucks her glasses into her clean clothes; picks up her bucket of toiletries, and enters the washing area. The thick, hot air is difficult to breathe. She lifts a stool from the stack by the door, walks to her favorite spot, and squats down, resting for a few beats.

Kappa kapparatta.

Kappa rappa kapparatta.

She holds the shower nozzle and douses herself in warm water, trying to get the smell of sickness off her skin.

Tottechitteta.

She soaps and shampoos with great deliberation, repeating the rhyme in her head: *kappa snatched; kappa snatched a trumpet. The trumpet blares.* It is welcomed nonsense, an empty refrain to keep her mind clear. She rinses off, running her fingers through her sopping hair, before standing and padding over to the edge of the hot bath. It is a blessing this onsen keeps late hours; she can only come once she knows Tetsuya's doctors won't call her. She tests the water with one foot, shuddering at the heat, then slips in completely.

No one else ever comes to witness her grief, her pale lips and sallow skin. Once upon a time, looking at her might have been a privilege; she spent some years smiling within the pages of *Cancam* and *Vivi*, touting crystal-encrusted fingernails and perfectly glossed lips. She never graced a cover, but she did spend a few weeks on the posters for *Liz Lisa* in Shibuya 109. It was different after she got married and left Tokyo, of course. She and Tetsuya decided to move back to her hometown. Rent was cheaper, and there were good jobs for doctors like him. She quickly found work at the bakery, selling melon pan and croissants. Occasionally they visited her mother, who, wanting little else from life, had grown sweet and mellow with age. Makino thought she understood that well; she had been quite content, until Tetsuya fell ill.

She wades to her favorite corner of the bath and sinks down until only her head is above the water. She squeezes her eyes shut. *How long will he live*, she thinks, *how long will we live together?*

She hears a soft splash and opens her eyes. Someone has entered the tub, and seems to be approaching her. She sinks deeper, letting the water cover her upper lip. As the figure nears, she sees its features through the mist: the green flesh, the webbed hands, the sara—the little bowl that forms the top of its head—filled with water that wobbles as it moves. It does not smell of rotting fish at all. Instead, it smells like a river, wet and earthy. Alive. Some things are different: it is more man-sized than child-sized, it has flesh over its ribs; but otherwise it looks just as she always imagined.

"Good evening," the kappa says. The words spill out of its beak, smoothly liquid.

Makino does not scream. She does not move. Instead she looks at the closest edge of the bath, measuring how long her backside will be exposed if she runs. She won't make it. She presses against the cold tile and thinks, *Tetsuya needs me*, thinks, *no, that's a lie, I can't even help him.* Her fear dissipates, replaced by helplessness, a brittle calm.

"This is the women's bath," she says. "The men's bath is on the other side."

"Am I a man?"

She hears the ripples of laughter in its voice, and feels indignant, feels ashamed.

"No. Are you going to eat me?"

"Why should I eat you, when you are dear to me?" Its round black eyes glimmer at her in earnest.

The water seems to turn from hot to scalding, and she stands upright, flushed and dizzy. "I don't know who you are!" she shouts. "Go away!"

"But you do know me. You fell into the river and I buoyed you to safety. You fell into the river and I kissed your hair."

"That wasn't you," she says, but she never did find out who it was. She thinks about certain death; thinks, *is it any different from how I live now?* It can't possibly know this about her, can't see the holes that Tetsuya's illness has pierced through her; but then, what *does* it know?

"I would not lie to you," it says, shaking its head. The water in its sara sloshes gently. "Don't be afraid. I won't touch you if you don't wish me to."

"And why not?" She lifts her chin.

"Because I love you, Makino."

She reads to Tetsuya from the book on her lap, even when she knows he isn't listening. He stares out the window with glassy eyes, tracing the movements of invisible birds. The falling snow is delicate, not white so much as the ghost of white, the color of his skin. Tetsuya never liked fairytales much, but she indulges herself, because the days are long, and she hates hospitals. The only things she can bear to read are the stories of her childhood, walls of words that keep back the tide of desperation when Tetsuya turns to her and says, "Excuse me, but I would like to rest now."

It's still better than the times when he jerks and lifts his head, eyes crowding with tears, and says, "I'm so sorry, Makino." Then he attempts to stand, to raise himself from the bed, but of course he can't, and she must rush over and put her hand on his knee to keep him from moving, she must kiss his forehead and each of his wet eyes and tell him, "No, it's all right, it's all right." There is a cadence to the words that makes her almost believe them.

Tetsuya is twelve years her senior. They met just before she started her modeling career. He was not handsome. There was something monkeylike about his features, and his upper lip formed a strange peak over his lower lip. But he was gentle, careful; a doctor-in-training with the longest, most beautiful fingers she had ever seen. He was a guest at the home of her tea ceremony sensei. When she handed the cup to him, he cradled her fingers in his for a moment, so that her skin was trapped between his hands and the hot ceramic. When he raised the drink to his lips, his eyes kept darting to her face, though she pretended not to notice by busying herself with the next cup.

He thanked her then as he does now, shyly, one stranger to another.

She has barely settled in the bath when it appears.

"You've come back," it says.

She shrugs. Her shoulders bob out of the water. As a girl Makino was often chided for her precociousness by all except her mother, who held her own odd beliefs. Whenever they visited a temple, Makino would whisper to the statues, hoping they would give her some sign they existed—a wink, maybe, or a small utterance. Some kind of blessing. She did this even in Tokyo Disney-Sea, to the statue of Rajah the Tiger, the pet of her beloved Princess Jasmine. There was a period in her life when she wanted nothing more than to be a Disney Princess.

It figures, of course, that the only yōkai that ever speaks to her is a kappa. The tips of its dark hair trail in the water, and its beaklike mouth is half-open in an expression she cannot name. The ceiling lights float gently in the water of its sara.

She does not speak, but it does not go away. It seems content to watch her. *Can't you leave me here, with my grief?*

"Why do you love me?" she asks at last.

It blinks slowly at her, pale green lids sliding over its eyes. She tries not to shudder, and fails.

"Your hips are pale like the moon, yet move like the curves of ink on parchment. Your eyes are broken and delicate and your hands are empty." It drifts closer. "Your hair is hair I've kissed before; I do not forget the hair of women I love."

*I am an ugly woman now*, she thinks, but looking at its gaze, she doesn't believe that. Instead she says, "Kappa don't save people. They drown them."

"Not I," it says.

Makino does not remember drowning in the river. She does not remember any of those days spent in bed. Her mother told her afterward that a policeman saved her, or it might have been the grocer's son, or a teacher from the nearby elementary school. It was a different story each time. It was only after she was rescued that they finally patched the broken portion of the bridge. But that was so many years ago, a legend of her childhood that was smeared clear by time, whitewashed by age. She told Tetsuya about it once, arms wrapped around his back, one leg between his thighs. He kissed her knuckles and told her she was lucky, it was a good thing she didn't die then, so that he could meet her and marry her and make love to her, the most beautiful girl in the world.

She blinks back tears and holds her tongue.

"I will tell you a fairytale," the kappa says, "Because I know you love fairytales. A girl falls into a river—"

"Stop," she says, "I don't want to hear it." She holds out her hands, to keep it from moving closer. "My husband is dying."

Tetsuya is asleep during her next visit. She cradles his hand in hers, running her thumb over his bony fingers—so wizened now, unable to heal anyone. She recalls the first time she noticed her love for him. She was making koicha, tea to be shared among close companions, under her teacher's watchful gaze. Tetsuya wasn't even present, but she found herself thinking of his teeth, his strange nervous laughter, the last time he took her out for dinner. The rainbow lights of Roppongi made zebra stripes across his skin, but he never dared kiss her, not even when she turned as the train was coming, looking at him expectantly. He never dared look her in the eye, not until she told him she would like to see him again, fingers resting on his sleeve.

She looked down at the tea she was whisking and thought, *this tastes like earth, like the bone marrow of beautiful spirits, like the first love I've yet to have. It is green like the color of spring leaves and my mother's favorite skirt and the skin of a kappa. I'm in love with him.* She whisked the tea too forcefully, some of it splashing over the edge of the cup.

"Makino!" her sensei cried.

She stood, heart drumming in her chest, bowed, apologized, bowed again. The tea had formed a butterfly-shaped splotch on the tatami mats.

Tetsuya's sudden moan jolts her from her thoughts—a broken sound that sets her heart beating as it did that moment, long ago. She spreads her palm over his brow.

*Does a kappa grant wishes? Is it a water god? Will it grant my wish if I let it touch me? Will I let it touch me?*

She gives Tetusya's forehead a kiss. "Don't leave me before the New Year," she says. She really means *don't leave me.*

This time, it appears while she's soaping her body.

It asks if it can wash her hair.

She remains crouched on her stool. The suggestion of touch makes her tremble, but she keeps her voice even. "Why should I let you?"

"Because you are dear to me."

"That isn't true," she says. "I do know about you. You rape women and eat organs and trick people to get their shirikodama, and I'm not giving you that, I'm not going to let you stick your hand up my ass. I don't want to die. And Tetsuya needs me."

"What if I tell you I need you? What if I could give you what you want? What if I…" it looks down at the water, and for a moment, in the rising mist, it looks like Tetsuya, when she first met him. Hesitant and wondering and clearly thinking of her. Monkey-like, but somehow pleasing to her eyes. "What if I could love you like him?"

"You're not him," she says. Yet when it reaches out to touch her, she does not flinch. Its fingers in her hair are long and slim and make her stomach curl, and she only stops holding her breath when it pulls away.

The grocery is full of winter specials: Christmas cakes, discounted vegetables for nabe hotpot, imported hot chocolate mixes. After Christmas is over, these shelves will be rapidly cleared and filled with New Year specials instead, different foods for osechi-ryori. Her mother was always meticulous about a good New Year's meal: herring roe for prosperity, sweet potatoes for wealth, black soybeans for health, giant shrimp for longevity. They're only food, however; not spells, not magic. She ignores the bright display and walks to the fresh vegetables, looking for things to add to her curry.

She's almost finished when she sees the pile of cucumbers, and ghostlike, over it, the kitchen of her childhood. Mother stands next to her, back curved in concentration. She is carving Makino's name into a cucumber's skin with a toothpick. "We'll throw this in the river," Mother says, "so that the kappa won't eat you."

"Does the kappa only appear in the river, mother? And why would the kappa want to eat me?"

"Because it likes the flesh of young children, it likes the flesh of beautiful girls. You must do this every year, and every time you move. And don't let them touch you, darling. I am telling you this for you are often silly, and they are cruel; do not let them touch you."

"But what if it does touch me, Mother?"

"Then you are a foolish girl, and you cannot blame me if it eats up everything inside you."

Young Makino rubs the end of the cucumber.

*Is there no way to befriend them, Mother?* But she doesn't say those words, she merely thinks them, as her mother digs out the last stroke, the tail end of *no* in *Ma-ki-no.*

She frowns at the display, or perhaps at the memory. *If I throw a cucumber in the hot spring it will merely be cooked*, she thinks. She buys a few anyway. At home, she hesitates, and then picks one up and scratches in Tetsuya's name with a knife. She drops it into the river while biking to work the following morning. The rest of them she slices and eats with chilled yogurt.

When it appears next it is close enough that if it reached out, it could touch her, but it stays in place.

"Shall I recite some poetry for you?"

She shakes her head. She thinks, *the skins we inhabit and the things we long to do inside them, why are they so different?*

"I don't even know your name," she says.

The way its beak cracks open looks almost like a smile. "I have many. Which would please you?"

"The true one."

It is quiet for a moment, then it says, "I will give you the name I gave the rice farmer's wife, and the shogun's daughter, and the lady that died on the eve of the firebombs."

"Women you have loved?" Her own voice irritates her, thin and breathless in the steam-filled air.

"Women who have called me Kawataro," it says. "Women who would have drowned, had I not saved them and brought them back to life."

"Kawataro," she says, tears prickling at the corner of her eyes. "Kawataro, why did you save me?"

"Kindness is always worth saving."

"Why do you say I am kind?"

It tips its head, the water inside sloshing precariously. It seems to be saying, will you prove me wrong?

She swallows, lightheaded, full of nothing. Her pulse simmers in her ears. She crosses the distance between them and presses herself against its hard body, kisses its hard little mouth. Its hands, when they come up to stroke her back, are like ice in the boiling water.

Kawataro does not appear in the onsen the next time she visits. There are two foreigners sitting in the bath, smiling at her nervously, aware of their own intrusion. The blonde woman, who is quite lovely, chats with Makino in halting Japanese about how cold it is in winter, how there is nothing more delightful than a warm soak, or at least that's what Makino thinks she is saying. Makino smiles back politely, and does not think about the feeling rising in her stomach—a strange hunger, a low ache, a sharp and painful relief.

This is not a fairytale, Makino knows, and she is no princess, and the moon hanging in the sky is only a moon, not a jewel hanging on a queen's neck, not the spun silk on a weaver's loom. The man she loves is dying, snowfall is filling her ears, and she is going to come apart unless somebody saves him.

The bakery closes for the winter holiday, the last set of customers buying all the cakes on Christmas Eve. Rui comes over as Makino is removing her apron. "Mizuki-san. Thank you for working hard today." She bows. "I'll be leaving now."

"Thank you for working hard today," Makino echoes. She's not the owner, but she is the eldest of the staff, the one who looks least attractive in their puffy, fluffy uniforms. Rui and Ayaka are college students; Yurina and Kaori are young wives, working while they decide whether they want children. Makino gets along with them well enough, but recently their nubile bodies make her tired and restless.

She never had her own children—a fact that Tetsuya mourned, then forgave, because he had a kind heart, because he knew her own was broken. She used to console herself by thinking it was a blessing, that she could keep her slim figure, but even that turned out to be a lie.

Rui twists her fingers in her pleated skirt, hesitating. Makino braces herself for the question, but it never comes, because the bell over the door rings and a skinny, well-dressed boy steps in. Rui's face breaks into a smile, the smile of someone deeply in love. "Just a minute," she calls to the boy. He nods and brings out his phone, tapping away. She turns back to Makino, and dips her head again.

"Enjoy yourself," Makino says with a smile.

"Thank you very much. Merry Christmas," Rui answers. Makino envies her; hates her, briefly, without any real heat. Rui whips off her apron, picks up her bag, and runs to the boy. They stride together into the snowy evening.

That night, the foreigners are gone, and Kawataro is back. It tells her about the shogun's daughter. How she would stand in the river and wait for him, her robes gathered around one fist. How her child, when it was born, was green, and how she drowned it in the river, sobbing, before anyone else could find it. How Kawataro had stroked her hair and kissed her cheeks and—Makino doesn't believe this part—how it had grieved for its child, their child, floating down the river.

"And what happened?" Makino says, trailing one finger idly along Kawataro's shoulders. They are sitting together on the edge of the tub, their knees barely visible in the water.

Kawataro's tongue darts over its beak. Makino thinks about having that tongue in her mouth, tasting the minerals of the bathwater in her throat. She thinks about what it means to be held in a monster's arms, what it means to hold a monster. Kappa nappa katta, kappa nappa ippa katta.

*Am I the leaf he has bought with sweet words, one leaf of many?*

Kawataro turns to her, face solemn as it says, "She drowned herself."

It could not save her, perhaps; or didn't care to by then? Makino thinks about the shogun's daughter: her bloated body sailing through the water, her face blank in the moonlight, the edges of her skin torn by river dwellers. She thinks of Kawataro watching her float away, head bent, the water in its sara shimmering under the stars.

Katte kitte kutta.

*Will I be bought, cut, consumed?*

She presses her damp forehead against Kawataro's sleek green shoulder. *Have I already been?*

"How will this story end?" she asks.

It squeezes her knee with its webbed hand, then slips off the ledge into the water, waiting for her to follow. She does.

She spends Christmas Day in the hospital, alternately napping, reading to Tetsuya, and exchanging pleasantries with the doctors and nurses who come to visit. She leans as close as she can to him, as if proximity might leech the pain from his body, everything that makes him ache, makes him forget. It won't work, she knows. She doesn't have that kind of power over him, over anyone. Perhaps the closest she has come to such power is during sex.

The first time she and Tetsuya made love he'd been tender, just as she imagined, his fingers trembling as he undid the hooks of her bra. She cupped his chin and kissed his jaw and ground her hips against his, trying to let him know she wanted this, he didn't need to be afraid. He gripped her hips and she wrapped her legs around him, licking a wet line from his neck to his ear. He carried her to the bed, collapsing so that they landed in a tangled pile, desperately grappling with the remainders of each other's clothing. His breath was ragged as he moved slowly inside her, and she tried not to cry out, afraid of how much she wanted him, how much she wanted him to want her.

On his lips that night her name was a blessing: the chant of monks, the magic spells all fairytales rest on.

Now he stirs, and his eyes open. He says her name with a strange grace, a searching wonder, as if how they came to know each other is a mystery. "Makino?"

"Yes, my darling?"

His breath, rising up to her, is the stale breath of the dying.

"So that's where you are," he says at last. He gropes for her hand and holds it. "You're there, after all. That's good." He pauses, for too long, and when she looks at him she sees he has fallen asleep once more.

The next time they meet, they spend several minutes soaking together in silence.

She breaks it without preamble. "Kawataro, why do you love me?" Her words are spoken without coyness or fear or fury.

"A woman in grief is a beautiful one," it answers.

"That's not enough."

Kawataro's eyes are two black stones in a waterfall of mist. It is a long time before it finally speaks.

"Four girls," it says. "Four girls drowned in three villages, before they fixed the broken parts in the bridges over the river. My river." It extends its hand and touches the space between her breasts, exerting the barest hint of pressure. Her body tenses, but she keeps silent, immobile. "You were the fifth. You were the only one who accepted my hand when I stretched it out. You," it says, "were the only one who let me lay my hands upon you."

The memory breaks over her, unreal, so that she almost feels like Kawataro has cast a spell on her—forged it out of dreams and warped imaginings. The terrible rain. The realization that she couldn't swim. The way the riverbank swelled, impenetrable as death. How she sliced her hand open on a tree root, trying desperately to grab onto something. How she had seen the webbed hand stretched toward her, looked at the gnarled monkey face, sobbed as she clung for her life, river water and tears and rain mingled on her cheeks. How it tipped its head down and let something fall into her gaping, gurgling mouth, to save her.

"I was a stupid little girl," she says. "I could have drowned then, to spare myself this." She laughs, shocking herself; the sound bounces limply against the tiles.

Kawataro looks away.

"You are breaking my heart, Makino."

"You have no heart to break," she says, in order to hurt it; yet she also wants to be near it, wants it to tell her stories, wants its cold body to temper the heat of the water.

It looks to the left, to the right, and it takes a moment for her to realize that it is shaking its head. Then in one swift motion it wraps its arms around her and squeezes, hard, and Makino remembers how kappa like to wrestle, how they can force the life out of horses and cattle by sheer strength. "I could drain you," it says, hissing into her ear. "I could take you apart, if that would help. I could take everything inside you and leave nothing but a hollow shell of your skin. I do not forget kindness, but I will let you forget yours, if it will please you."

*Yes*, she thinks, and in the same heartbeat, *but no, not like this*.

She pushes against it, and it releases her. She takes several steps back and lifts her head, appraising.

"Will you heal my husband?" she asks.

"Will you love me?" it asks.

The first time she fell in love with Tetsuya, she was making tea. The first time she fell in love, she was drowning in a river.

"I already do."

Kawataro looks at her with its eyes narrowed in something like sadness, if a monster's face could be sad. It bows its head slightly, and she sees the water inside it—everything that gives it strength—sparkling, reflecting nothing but the misted air.

"Come here," it says, quiet and tender. "Come, my darling Makino, and let me wash your back."

Tetsuya drinks the water from Kawataro's sara.

Tetsuya lives.

The doctors cannot stop saying what a miracle it is. They spend New Year's Eve together, eating the osechi-ryori Makino prepared. They wear their traditional attire and visit the temple at midnight, and afterward they watch the sunrise, holding each other's cold hands.

It is still winter, but some stores have already cleared space for their special spring bargains. Makino mouths a rhyme as she sets aside ingredients for dinner. Tetsuya passes her and kisses her cheek, thoughtlessly. He is on his way to the park for his afternoon walk.

"I'm leaving now," he says.

"Come back safely," she answers. She feels just as much affection for Tetsuya as she did before, but nothing else. Some days her hollowness frightens her. Most days she has learned to live with it.

When the door shuts behind him, she spends some moments in the kitchen, silently folding one hand over the other. She decides to take a walk. Perhaps after the walk she will visit her mother. She puts a cucumber and a paring knife into her bag and heads out. By now the cold has become bearable, like the empty feeling in her chest. She follows the river toward the bridge where she once nearly lost her life.

In the middle of the bridge she stands and looks down at the water. She has been saved twice now by the same monster. Twice is more than enough. With a delicate hand, she carves the character for love on the cucumber, her eyes blurring, clearing. She leans over the bridge and lets the cucumber fall.

# About the Editors

**MAHVESH MURAD** is a book critic and recovering radio show host. She writes for multiple publications and hosts the Tor.com podcast *Midnight in Karachi*. She was born and raised in Karachi, Pakistan, where she still lives.

**LAVIE TIDHAR** is the author of the Jerwood Fiction Uncovered Prize winning *A Man Lies Dreaming*, the World Fantasy Award winning *Osama*, and of the critically-acclaimed *The Violent Century*. His other works include *The Bookman Histories* trilogy, several novellas, two collections, and a forthcoming comics mini-series, *Adler*. He currently lives in London.

# About the Artist

**SARAH ANNE LANGTON** has worked as an Illustrator for EA Games, Hodder & Stoughton, Forbidden Planet, The Cartoon Network, Sony, Apple, Marvel Comics, and a wide variety of music events. Written and illustrated for Jurassic London, Fox Spirit, NewCon Press, and The Fizzy Pop Vampire series. Hodderscape dodo creator and Kitschies Inky Tentacle judge. Daylights as Web Mistress for the worlds largest sci-fi and fantasy website. Scribbles a lot about the X-Men, shouts at Photoshop, and drinks an awful lot of tea. Responsible for *Zombie Attack Barbie* and *Joss Whedon is Our Leader Now*. Her work has featured on *io9*, *Clutter Magazine*, *Forbidden Planet*, *Laughing Squid*, and *Creative Review*.

# The Apex Book of World SF: Vol 1

S.P. Somtow
Jetse de Vries
Guy Hasson
Han Song
Kaaron Warren
Yang Ping
Dean Francis Alfar
Nir Yaniv
Jamil Nasir
Tunku Halim
Aliette de Bodard
Kristin Mandigma
Aleksandar Žiljak
Anil Menon
Mélanie Fazi
Zoran Živković

## edited by
# Lavie Tidhar

Among the spirits, technology, and deep recesses of the human mind,
stories abound. Kites sail to the stars, technology transcends physics, and
wheels cry out in the night. Memories come and go like fading echoes and
a train carries its passengers through more than simple space and time.
Dark and bright, beautiful and haunting, the stories herein represent
speculative fiction from a sampling of the finest authors from around
the world.

ISBN: 978-1-937009-36-6   ~   ApexBookCompany.com

# The Apex Book of World SF: Vol 2

Rochita Loenen-Ruiz
Ivor W. Hartmann
Daliso Chaponda
Daniel Salvo
Gustavo Bondoni
Chen Quifan
Joyce Chng
Csilla Kleinheincz
Andrew Drilon
Anabel Enríquez Piñeiro
Lauren Beukes
Raúl Flores
Will Elliott
Shweta Narayan
Fábio Fernandes
Tade Thompson
Hannu Rajaniemi
Silvia Moreno-Garcia
Sergey Gerasimov
Tim Jones
Nnedi Okorafor
Gail Hareven
Ekaterina Sedia
Samit Basu
Andrzej Sapkowski
Jacques Barcia

## edited by
## Lavie Tidhar

In The Apex Book of World Sf 2, World Fantasy Award-winning editor Lavie Tidhar brings together a unique collection of stories from around the world: quiet horror from Cuba and Australia, surrealist fantasy from Russia, epic fantasy from Poland, near-future tales from Mexico and Finland, and cyberpunk from South Africa. In this anthology, one gets a glimpse of the complex and fascinating world of genre fiction--from all over the world.

ISBN: 978-1-937009-35-9   ~   ApexBookCompany.com

# The Apex Book of World SF: Vol 3

Benjanun Sriduangkaew
Xia Jia
Fadzilshah Johanabos
Uko Bendi Udo
Ma Boyong
Athena Andreadis
Zulaikha Nurain Mudzor
Amal El-Mohtar
Nelly Geraldine Garcia-Rosas
Biram Mboob
Myra Çakan
Crystal Koo
Ange
Karin Tidbeck
Swapna Kishore
Berit Ellingsen

## edited by
## Lavie Tidhar

In The Apex Book of World Sf 3, World Fantasy Award-winning editor Lavie
Tidhar collects short stories by science fiction and fantasy authors from
Africa, Asia, South America, and Europe.

"The Apex Book of World SF series has proven to be an excellent way to
sample the diversity of world SFF and to broaden our understanding of the
genre's potential." --Ken Liu, winner of the Hugo Award and
author of *The Grace of Kings*

ISBN: 978-1-937009-34-2   ~   ApexBookCompany.com

# APEX PUBLICATIONS NEWSLETTER

*Why sign up?*

Newsletter-only promotions. Book release announcements. Event invitations. And much, much more!

SUBSCRIBE AND RECEIVE A **15%** DISCOUNT CODE FOR YOUR NEXT ORDER FROM APEXBOOKCOMPANY.COM!

If you choose to sign up for the Apex Publications newsletter, we will send you an email confirmation to insure that you in fact requested the newsletter and to avoid unwanted emails. Your email address is always kept confidential, and we will only use it to send you newsletters or special announcements. You may unsubscribe at any time, and details on how to unsubscribe are included in every newsletter email.

VISIT
HTTP://WWW.APEXBOOKCOMPANY.COM/PAGES/NEWSLETTER